The Vision Blogger

K.T. Morrissey

ISBN-13: 978-0-9853068-0-9 (Seraphim Calls)
ISBN-10: 0-9853068-0-7

First Printing: December 2011

Second Printing: March 2012

10 9 8 7 6 5 4 3 2 1

Printed in the United States of America

For Judy, who gave me shelter and love when I was lost

And…

For Tarod, who is my heart…

Prologue

<ins>Entry #11 – Sarah's Vision Blog – May 19 – 7:00 pm</ins>

I remember back when I was just a little girl. There'd been a storm and my Momma and Daddy were driving us somewhere, I don't remember where. I was sitting in the back seat of the car with my two sisters, looking out the window. The storm had just gotten over and the sun was starting to break through the clouds.

I looked out over the slow-rolling hills of the Georgia countryside and saw these rays of sunlight shooting through the clouds down onto the earth. I know now that was what it was and that there was nothing special about plain old sunlight finding its way through small openings in the thick clouds. That's what it does. It's all perfectly logical. I get that. But, for the little girl that I was at that very moment in time, that light spilling down onto the earth from heaven above became the one and only time I've ever felt completely and utterly safe and loved in my entire life.

Those patches of light represented something to me that made sure of that.

What I saw when I looked through my naïve little eyes was God's radiance. I knew without a doubt that He was sitting on top of those clouds, just there, and that He had come down to protect us all from the storm. Now that the storm was over, He was letting us know everything was okay and that He was there, so we didn't have to worry.

I felt completely secure at that moment, completely safe and loved...

Where did that go?

Now, three decades plus later, I still have yet to feel that way again...

I no longer believe in a god or anything. I'm not an atheist. I mean, I believe we go on after we leave here to somewhere else, I just don't know where or why. I guess that qualifies me as an agnostic, right?

I've had ample opportunity to think about these things over the years. I studied world religions in high school and college. This taught me that no one has a clue what actually happened, but that since time immemorial, everybody's either been trying to figure it out or they've just gone along with what they were taught as kids, never questioning anything.

I guess I was born to be one of the former ones because I've been wondering about this stuff since not long after that one rainy day back in the early 70's. Then, after high school, when I fell in with a certain crowd, we talked about these kinds of things sometimes, though not often. We were all so filled with raging hormones and anger by that time, though, that we didn't believe anything any adults ever told us. Of course, we knew more than they did – doesn't every teenager?

I think I felt abandoned. I couldn't find a reason for living; I couldn't understand why I had to endure all the pain and suffering my life had to offer each day. What had I done to deserve this? How could a god do that to anyone, let alone all the horrible things I was seeing happening to people all over the world?

That's when I discovered I no longer believed what I'd been taught when I was little. I still believed in the soul, I still believed in an afterlife. How could a person not? Otherwise, what's the point? Why not just go ahead and end it whenever the fun is over? I mean, if this is all there is and there's no afterward, then the very moment the whole thing goes south, what's the point in sticking around? Right?

Sheesh! Somebody needs to get their head out of their ass, right there!

Anyway, so there I was, looking for some sort of answer as to where we came from, why we were here, where we were going after here, and that's when I realized there was something else going on. All this time, I'd been looking for somebody or something else to blame for everything I saw going on or everything I was going through. That wasn't the answer though. I finally came to understand that each and every single little thing that ever happened to me in this life was because of choices *I'd* made. Sounds simple, right? *Wrong!*

Why would it be any different before I was born or after I was dead? Unless I had come here to escape a horrible existence elsewhere, which I hope is *not* actually what happened; I had to have chosen to come here, right, but, why? How did I get here, even if I chose it? Where did I come from? Would I go back there once I died here? All kinds of people were talking about reincarnation a lot back then, so did that mean I would come back here at some point after I died?

Mind you, I was still only about sixteen years old while all this was going on in my head, so I hadn't lived an awful lot. Since then, time has taken care of making sure I've gotten lots and lots of experiences under my belt, but at that time I hadn't really experienced too much. I hadn't taken too many wrong turns in the road and I still believed in the general goodness of everyone. My involvement with society's cynicism had only just begun then.

That's when I encountered someone, or some*thing*, that again changed my life.

I'd gone to the doctor's office, for a check-up or something inconsequential like that, and was riding up in the elevator to the office. Even before the doors to the elevator opened, I *felt* something. My heart started racing and I got

3

kind of scared. Then, the doors slid open and a blast of... energy, I guess, hit me full on. I looked frantically around the busy reception room as I stepped off the elevator. I noticed every other person in the room was looking in this one direction, so I looked that way, too, and saw the most beautiful man I'd ever seen in my young life.

He was older, maybe in his thirties (pretty old, I know) and had long black hair that hung loose in a thick blanket down his back, but it didn't make him look like a hippy. He simply looked like he'd stepped out of some other century. His eyes were the brightest ice-blue color I'd ever seen and I felt like I was being drawn toward him. I couldn't keep looking at him, though. He almost seemed to glow with energy and I *had* to look away. I noticed nobody else looked away from him, though.

I could feel him so intensely that I quickly hurried from the room to the doctor's office. It was cowardly, I know, but what else could I do? That man may as well have been a god. I was just some fat sixteen year old and he, well, let's just say he belonged on the cover of some poster advertising the latest and greatest Hollywood blockbuster movie.

But, that feeling...

It was then that I realized that feeling was what I'd been searching for my entire life. That was what I wanted and needed more than life itself. That had to be why I had chosen to come here, if that's how it worked. I wanted it so bad that I was willing to go through everything life could throw at me, no matter what. *Was it the same for everyone*, I wondered. Even now, I look around and see all the movies and books written about ever-lasting love. I hear all the love songs singers croon day and night.

Of course it's the same for everyone! What else is there? I mean, we all get caught up in all the things society says we're supposed to be doing and wanting, but what we really need, what we're really looking for, is that one other who can make us feel so completely safe and loved that nothing else matters.

Here we all are, after doing whatever it is we have to do or go through to get here to this dimension or plane, or whatever, just so we can find that one person who makes us feel utterly safe and loved, that one person we connect with completely. That has to be it. There's no god. We're all here because we chose to come here. Wherever we come from, there's something missing from our existence there. We can only get it by coming here, I bet. So, we do whatever it takes to get here to have the chance to find it. If we mess up and then get to come back, then we come back again and again, still looking for the same thing.

Does any of this make any sense? I mean, I've been writing this blog for only a short time, but I've lived so much during the past few years, experienced so many things I never even dreamed I would experience as I rode in the back seat of that car so many years ago. This is what makes sense to me now. I look on the face of my son each day, and the only thing that makes it okay for me to have brought him into this awful world where people do such horrible and atrocious things to each other and to the earth is the idea, or belief really, that like me, he chose to come here to find that one special person who would be able to make him finally feel safe and secure and completely loved. He fought or worked or whatever it is we have to do in order to make it to this level.

Don't I owe it to him and to myself to continue fighting each day until I can find the one I was meant to be with and help my son as best I can to find his special one? I think so.

Maybe, these things I've been blogging about seeing in my dreams mean something's about to happen? Maybe, I'm just going crazy? If it's something bad, then I don't want to know. I just want to be able to find my other half and to help my son find his other half. Then, I figure I'll be just about done and I can go on to wherever it is we go once we find what we're looking for.

I wonder if that's how it works?

Well, I've gotta get the kid to bed, now. I'll write more later...

Chapter 1

Djibril crossed through the rift in the barrier between realms at Mt. Hermon, headed toward the area where the disturbance had been detected. The electrostatic shock of crossing through the rift was as unpleasant as he remembered. It had been a long time since he'd last been required to cross. He'd hoped he wouldn't have to do this again. After all, the promised return date had been so close and their plan had been fool-proof. Or so they'd thought.

Now, it appeared someone was on the brink of ruining all he and his brethren had done so long ago.

Djibril was constantly observing those in this other realm, as was his duty, until the blessed Great Designers returned. Occasionally, he would notice a disturbance, something that didn't flow the same as the rest of the energies from this realm. This usually meant there was someone who had gained level of abilities to the point of having the capability of disrupting the flow from the path Djibril and his brethren were to uphold. The last time something major like this had happened had been several hundred human years ago. She'd been a very young human female in a place called "France." Jehanne had been her name.

She'd been gone for a long time, but Djibril still recalled her radiance as he swiftly made his way toward his destination. She had emitted a beautifully strong tone, and her frequencies had been through the roof. He'd only witnessed her once, since Mikhail and his followers had been the ones chosen to deal with her, but that one time was enough for Djibril to know she could have done great damage to the web-work he and his brethren had so long ago set in place.

Anyone who radiated that kind of energy was too dangerous to be allowed to roam freely without at least some form of guidance. Visitation was the only course of control the Seraphim had set in place to ensure continuation of the precious society that had flourished in this realm since Djibril's beloved Designers had left. Djibril knew, as did his brethren, that upon the Designers' next arrival, they would be expecting to find that society intact and thriving under the guidance of the Seraphim, so this new disturbance must not to be allowed any opportunity to blossom.

Of course, this wasn't the normal type of issue that came up. Normally, only smaller disturbances were detected. Djibril and the other Seraphim weren't the ones who crossed over to deal with such smaller issues. Those issues required but little fixes, just a little influencing from outside. There were others, the lower classes of Angels who followed and worked under the Seraphim on the Great and Lesser Sanhedrin councils who handled them.

And then, of course, there were the outcasts, the Shaitan and Jinn. Cleaning up the debris from whenever any of *their* numbers crossed over the barrier was almost a full-time job these days for the members of both houses of Sanhedrin.

Djibril and his brethren certainly hadn't wasted the millennia lazily awaiting the return of the blessed Great Designers, though. They took the role of overseers of their beloved city and both realms, Seraphim and human alike, very seriously, spending most of their time personally seeing to matters.

The disturbance Djibril had detected this time, however, was more than what any of the lower Angels could deal with. This one, if he was correct, needed a Seraph to cross the barrier in order for the creature to be steered in a more acceptable direction. Mikhail, Azra'il and the others on the Great Sanhedrin had decided Djibril should be the one to make first contact with this one, since he was the one who had first detected the signal, but also because of the nature of the disturbance he'd sensed. It had been an unusually strong energy fluctuation, to say the least, but it was one of great feeling.

If he was being honest with himself, Djibril admitted, this one gave him cause for great concern. The time of the promised return of the blessed Great Designers had recently come and gone, and here, all of a sudden, there was this tremendous disturbance. It was almost too coincidental for Djibril's taste. Some instinct made him especially wary. The thought that something other than nature and simple genetics might be behind it had occurred to every member of the Great Sanhedrin when they'd learned of this disturbance. That was why Mikhail had asked Djibril, and not one of the lesser Angels, to cross the barrier and make first contact. Of course, what Djibril encountered once he finally found the source of the disturbance would ultimately determine how the issue was to be handled.

Djibril was to cross the barrier and find the source of the disturbance and then report back to the Great Sanhedrin. Depending on his report of what he observed on this first visitation, a decision would be made as to who would deal with it and how. Historically, disturbances of this magnitude turned out to be simple, natural mutations in the genetics of a particular familial line of humans that had led to one of their number being born with far too much soul-energy vibrating at too high a pitch in frequency. These humans were sometimes deemed too powerful to be allowed to continue to exist as they had in the world of mankind. There were difficulties when such creatures went unchecked.

Most of the time when a disturbance was felt, it turned out to be from a creature that had just a slightly above average amount of soul-energy. Unfortunately for those humans, they didn't tend to last long and there was no cause for interference from anyone in Djibril's realm. In fact, quite often the poor creatures went mad and either on their own ended the lives with which they had been blessed or other humans would kill them, either out of fear or out of jealousy of that one's abilities.

Every now and then, however, one would be born into their realm emitting such a powerfully strong and high frequency of soul-energy that it had to be carefully watched by the Seraphim. If that human lived long enough to engage in its kind's society, one from the Great Sanhedrin would be sent to perform a visitation with the creature to steer it onto a path that would help it through its life, as best as one could, without allowing the human's actions to disturb the web-work that had previously been laid in preparation for the return of the blessed Great Designers.

If it was discovered that someone from Djibril's realm was involved in this incident, though, Djibril knew there would be great trouble in Seraphim City.

All throughout this past century, practically everyone in Djibril's realm had been giddy with excitement and anticipation of the blessed Great Designers' promised return. There'd been a push to finish massive erections dedicated to their beloved Designers. The buildings and monuments had been designed in the old way and great love and care had been put into them at every step. Just the thought of the monument Djibril had helped design for his favorite of the Designers brought a smile to his face. However, it was nothing compared to the one Mikhail had built for *his* favorite of the Designers.

As he neared the area where the disturbance had been detected, Djibril's thoughts returned to the task at hand and his smile faded. The noise and energy of the great city below him buffeted his body, almost overwhelming his senses and he quickly erected the second of his six shields around himself for protection. It was a sunny day with many humans outside, going about their business in the warmth of the day. They did not notice him observing them.

Djibril lightly set down onto a paved walkway near a clearing surrounded by buildings of glass and concrete. They were not particularly large buildings by his standards, only four or five stories tall. He hitched an eyebrow as he took in the appearance of the one to his immediate right and thought that they weren't very attractive or even imaginative in their design. He found it a bit sad that so much of what had once been had been lost to these creatures.

In the old days, he recalled, they'd taken great care with the buildings they'd designed, dreaming up great structures that were very imaginative. Their constructions then had either encouraged others' admiration with their grandeur and how pleasing they were to the eye or they'd evoked a tremendous fear of the ones who'd ruled and lived in that kingdom with how fierce they'd appeared.

The fact that so many of those structures still stood to this day was little consolation when one was faced with designs like the ones confronting him now, however. The difficulty with losing certain peoples and languages was that the things those people knew were never to be passed down to others as a way to be continued. Traditions and knowledge were simply lost for all time.

Djibril looked around the clearing, allowing his two shields to return to their normal resting place, searching for the source of the disturbance. There were humans crossing from one end of the clearing to another, obviously on errands to some other area of what looked to be a University campus.

Many of them turned to openly gawk at him, though none dared approach him.

There were groups gathered together in threes and fours, some walking together, some standing about just talking, their backpacks slung casually over their arms. Some of them sat alone, occupying benches or simply dotting the little plots of grass surrounding the clearing. Some sat under trees, but most of those sitting did so out in the open, absorbing the sun's energy.

Djibril spotted his quarry across the clearing. It was a female. She was sitting on top of a large boulder in the middle of one of the grassy areas, her legs stretched out before her with a book open on her lap. She looked to be in her mid- to late twenties, but she very obviously wasn't like the others.

First of all, she glowed with a radiance the likes of which Djibril had never seen from such a creature. Secondly, she had an eminence of knowledge shining clearly in her eyes that said she couldn't be as young as he had originally thought. Djibril noticed her watching him immediately, though she looked quickly away. She didn't look directly at him again, but he knew she was still tracking him in her peripheral vision.

The way the sun reflected off her auburn hair and fair skin was pleasing to his eye. She was petite, not much over five feet tall, and healthy-looking, not one of the twigs one so often encountered of the human females of these modern times. This one lived well, but also played well, he believed. The tones coming from the energy radiating off her were high, but not unpleasant.

There was intelligence there, but some other essence he found surprising. She had a tremendous passion coursing through her soul. It was a caring kind of passion, one of infinite patience and wisdom. On top of that, he felt bravery in her beyond any other of her kind in the small clearing, almost as if she was ready to take on anyone or any*thing* that might spring out to cause harm to any in the clearing. She had a love of her people that came through in the tones radiating from within her.

Djibril wondered how she'd gone so long without detection by those in his realm. Wisdom of this magnitude only came with age, so she *must* have been around for longer than he'd originally assumed. Actually, the wisdom evident in her eyes and emanating off her in waves seemed to be beyond even an aged person's years. He narrowed his eyes as he studied her more intently.

The rest of the creatures milling about the clearing steered clear of her, he noticed. She didn't seem to mind, though. Djibril found them as easy to ignore as the insects buzzing about. The little electronic devices they all seemed to have were an annoyance, though. Djibril was constantly reading about the new technologies of this realm. The technological advancements humans were making seemed almost too fast and Djibril believed much of the information was being gained from negligence on the part of those of his realm crossing over into this one. The thought was enough to make one shiver with fear, to be certain. What he'd already witnessed being done with technology in centuries past in this realm was bad enough. They certainly didn't need any further assistance from Djibril's realm.

One of the humans dared to walk a little too close to him and Djibril heard the distinctive popping sound of glass breaking. The human heard it, too, and took out a little hand-held device that had a thin stream of smoke wafting from within it.

"What the fuck!" the creature barked in disbelieving anger as he looked at the small device in his hand. The glass covering was broken.

Djibril's kind emitted such strong frequencies of energy that the primitive electronics of these creatures' society could not withstand them and the devices often either quit working or, in some cases, exploded from such an immediate and intense overflow of energy.

The devices Djibril and his kind utilized had either been given to them by the blessed Great Designers or were improved-upon models from the ones they'd been given and each was well able to withstand the high Seraphim energy frequencies. The blessed Great Designers had instructed many of Djibril's kind on the nature and construction of their own electrical devices and uses for them so that they might be utilized in Djibril's realm. These creatures, however, were not ready for such knowledge.

Djibril knew, as had the blessed Great Designers, that the destructive power of such knowledge would lead to many wars in this realm. Even without it, the humans couldn't seem to stop warring amongst themselves, even after all this time. Granted, Mikhail and his followers had created some of the situations suitable for conflict and had even led many humans into war time and time again. However, it had only ever been done to preserve human society overall.

When a disturbance was detected, it was imperative to take care of the issue before it got out of hand. These rare creatures genetically pre-disposed to utilizing more of the precious soul-energies were too dangerous to both realms. If they were to be allowed to continue along their paths, there would be no telling what state the world would be in when the blessed Great Designers finally returned.

Djibril didn't like to think ill of his beloved Designers, but even he feared what might transpire should they return to a world that wasn't in a state pleasing to them. That's why Djibril and his kind had worked so hard to keep these creatures in line. Mikhail had been the major player in this realm, though.

From aiding Joshua in his campaigns in the Promised Land to helping Daniel to accept the role of Protector of Israel to instructing Moses on Mount Sinai in 1242 BCE (along with Djibril), from assisting Mohammed in his siege of Mecca in 630 AD to the last of his true visitations with Jehanne D'arc up until her death in 1431 AD, Mikhail had only done what he'd needed to do. His task was to ensure those who had been born genetically pre-disposed to utilizing far greater soul-energies than others of their kind went in a path that would only benefit the society as a whole, even if it meant the death of the creature in question.

Each and every time Mikhail or Djibril or any of their kind interfered, it was with the intention of setting a new course for humans, of giving them a new way of life with a new direction. That usually meant coming up with some new belief system for them, as had always been the case when the blessed Great Designers had inhabited the earth. For some reason, humans couldn't seem to exist without such occasional guidance.

Of course, even Djibril's kind had experienced difficulties when it came to the ability to live without the guidance of someone more advanced than they, as had been seen in the growing number of occurrences over the past millennia of the Shaitans and Jinn crossing hidden rifts in the barrier into this realm to stir up trouble. The Shaitans and Jinn didn't believe the truth about the blessed Great Designers, so they didn't agree that this realm should be off limits to their whims.

The Great Sanhedrin had long ago decreed that this realm was off limits to any and all from the Seraphim realm, other than for missions assigned by the council itself. No one was to cross the barrier without the consent of the Great Sanhedrin. Failure to adhere to this rule meant immediate expulsion from Seraphim City where they all lived, which meant one had to live in the Badlands of their realm. The Badlands was a lawless province, wild and unforgiving.

For almost one hundred thousand of the years counted by humans, the Seraphim and their followers had lived in Seraphim City. The Seraphim and the lower Angels had built it to honor the blessed Great Designers. Of course, the blessed Great Designers couldn't cross the barrier by themselves, but Djibril and his brethren were always happy to help them across. Originally, the Shaitans and Jinn had occupied space within the city, as well. They'd even helped build it, for they, too, had initially wanted to please the Designers.

However, not only had the Shaitan and Jinn leaders declared their disbelief in the stories the blessed Great Designers told of how they had created all the creatures on earth, but once the beloved Designers had left, the Shaitans and Jinn returned and declared their desire to have free reign in both realms. The Great Sanhedrin had been shocked by the leaders' blasphemy and had forbidden Shaitan and Jinn access at all to the human dimension. Additionally, they'd declared there was no place for any Shaitan or Jinn in Seraphim City and the Shaitans and Jinn had been banished, once more, to the Badlands where they had, apparently, thrived.

Over the millennia, there were occurrences that had been brought on in this realm by either Jinn or the Shaitans, which indicated they'd found other portals, or rifts in the barrier, to this realm. It was usually nothing more than a slight issue, easily dealt with by one of the members of the Lesser Sanhedrin of Djibril's realm. Even more often, there was no need for any interference, for the issue didn't even garner enough attention for any but those humans closest to the occurrence to notice.

Now, however, as the time for the promised return of the blessed Great Designers had come and gone, there had been more and more occurrences of interaction of Jinn or the Shaitans with the creatures of this realm and some had proved to be not such slight issues. Many were even starting to garner the notice of a great many of the creatures in this realm.

Djibril studied the female sitting across from him in the clearing. Had she encountered the Shaitans or Jinn? There were no residual energies from any of them that he could detect clinging to her form. The radiance coming from her was not normal, though. It was much too great, the frequencies too high and clean, the tones too pure. Djibril must report this to the Great Sanhedrin. Something would definitely have to be done about this one.

He pulled his shields back around himself and concentrated on moving upward and back toward the east, toward the only rift in the barrier he was allowed to use, and the only one of which he was aware, to his own realm. The time for the promised return of the Great Designers had obviously been delayed for some reason, but it was too close for comfort for this creature to be complicating matters now. A slight shiver shook Djibril's frame at the mere thought of the implications of this new development.

As soon as he crossed over the barrier at Mt. Hermon, Djibril headed directly for the city capitol. Upon entering the prime statehouse where the Great Sanhedrin regularly met, he made his way immediately to Azra'il's chamber. Once there, he found Azra'il and Mikhail engaged in a rousing game of Mankala, a game Djibril and his brethren had played for thousands of years. Normally, Djibril liked watching his brothers play Mankala, greatly enjoying their friendly banter throughout their play. Today, however, the pair immediately stopped playing and stood the moment they noticed Djibril enter the chamber.

"May the blessed Designers keep you," Djibril said in greeting to the pair, nodding once.

"You, as well," the pair said in unison, returning the nod.

"Please sit, brother," Azra'il offered, stretching his arm out toward a sofa a few feet away that had a rich, brightly colored tapestry covering. Azra'il sat in a nearby chair. After ringing for a servant, Mikhail came to sit on the sofa with Djibril, turning to face his two brothers. After a servant entered and took the orders of the three council members, the three got on with their meeting.

"What news do you bring us of this disturbance?" asked Mikhail. Mikhail always got straight to the point, for he loved all people, which meant he was always ready for battle to protect them.

"My encounter with the creature was disturbing, indeed," Djibril said, tongue in cheek, though he wasn't meaning to make light of the situation. He sighed heavily and continued, "This creature is unlike any of their kind I have ever before encountered." He described the female he had found and then voiced his opinion as to whether or not this was an act of nature or otherwise. Neither of his brothers immediately responded.

As the three sat deep in thought, the servant brought in a platter of finger foods and drinks. Djibril gladly scooped up a handful of his favorites and sat munching while his brothers thought over the situation. This would take a great deal of thought, he knew, and they would all have to be involved, one way or another.

Azra'il finally broke the silence, declaring, "We shall have to inform the Great Sanhedrin. This will have to be handled delicately, what with the Designers' eminent promised return."

"Are you sure that's the wisest course of action?" Djibril asked cautiously.

Before Djibril had detected this new disturbance in the other realm, he had commissioned a team of members of the Lesser Sanhedrin to investigate certain happenings that had turned out to be caused by the interference of some of the Shaitans and Jinn who had recently crossed a barrier into the human realm. The team's findings had indicated that there may be a member of the Great Sanhedrin leaking information to the Shaitans and Jinn, or at least that one of their number may be aiding them in some way. Djibril had shared this information with his most trusted brethren, Israfil, Mikhail, and Azra'il.

"We cannot allow this incident to disrupt the flow of their society," Mikhail said. Of all the Seraphim, Mikhail loved the blessed Great Designers the most. He was their staunchest defender and would do almost anything to please them. However, he loved the humans a great deal, too. He loved them so much that he was known to them not only as their protector but as a great healer, for the rare occasions when he had interfered with their affairs, he had indeed protected the righteous and healed the sick and wounded.

"I agree," Azra'il said after a time. "However, if what Djibril suspects is true, we need to use this opportunity to expose the traitor among ourselves. We cannot chance the beloved Designers returning before the traitor is found. It would be too dangerous."

"Agreed," Djibril and Mikhail said in unison.

"We will have to think of some way of telling the Great Sanhedrin what's going on without allowing them too much information," Azra'il continued. "If the creature is not being manipulated by one of our realm and this *is* just a trick of genetics, we'll have to be able to move quickly to do something about her. It sounds as if it's too late for a mere series of visitations to steer her in a direction more suitable for their society." Djibril and Mikhail again agreed with Azra'il's assessment of the situation.

It was decided that Israfil would be summoned this night and, after giving him all the facts, the four of them would think of a story to tell the Great Sanhedrin with just enough truth to hopefully allow them to smoke out the traitor in their midst. It was also decided that it would be beneficial for Djibril to cross the barrier once more to "babysit" the human. If she was being manipulated externally, Djibril might be able to stop such manipulation, though it was still too late for the unfortunate creature. She had already been given too much knowledge and had learned to contain and probably to manipulate far too much soul-energy to be allowed to continue living among her own kind.

If Djibril discovered she wasn't being externally manipulated, he'd be able to quickly intercede to bring her out of her current place in society so that she could be dealt with by the Seraphim. The plan for the moment was merely to end her life, if such was the result of Djibril's observations. Mikhail didn't like this part of the plan, but he could offer no alternative suggestions as to how to deal with the poor creature. They couldn't very well allow her to continue on in the human realm and they couldn't exactly bring her to the Seraphim realm to live without causing total chaos. At least, this way, they'd be able to ensure she didn't suffer needlessly. Djibril and his brethren would see to it she had a painless, peaceful passing.

Djibril returned to his home in the city, first to rest and then to prepare to leave again. His house servant, who had lived in his employ for many tens of thousands of years, was confounded by the announcement that Djibril intended to stay only long enough for a hot meal and a good night's sleep.

"You can't go back into their realm, Master," the man declared. "That place is too dangerous."

Djibril smiled at his servant's display of loyalty. Khamet had been with him so long that Djibril felt genuine affection for the servant and it was good to know such affection was mutual. "Don't worry, old friend," he said. "I'll be back before you know it."

Khamet shook his head and made a tsking sound. "I fear those creatures are going to be the death of you someday, Master."

Djibril clapped the shorter man on the shoulder and said, "I shall endeavor to be extra vigilant, then."

Khamet merely shook his head again and turned to clear away the dishes from the meal Djibril had finished.

"Until then," Djibril continued around a yawn, "I'm going to rest for a few hours."

Khamet asked if there was aught else his master needed and then wished him a good sleep before leaving the room with his tray.

Djibril didn't relish the thought of returning to the human realm, he agreed that he really was the only one for the job, although. Israfil hadn't been in so long and had never seen the creature. His duty was to be ever watchful for the promised return of the Great Designers. His leaving this realm would cause too much confusion among the city's inhabitants.

Mikhail was too emotional when it came to the humans. There was no telling what measures he might take in an attempt to save the female's life. The planet might end up engaged in a world-wide war! And then there was Azra'il. Azra'il was never the one sent on these types of missions because his first instinct was to kill and then to ask questions later. It wasn't his fault any more than it was Mikhail's that *his* first inclination bent toward protection and healing. Death was Azra'il's duty, as per the blessed Great Designers.

So, Djibril was the only one of the four who could logically be sent.

He yawned again as he made his way to his bedchamber and undressed. Tomorrow morning was when the Great Sanhedrin would be told of the situation, at least as much as Djibril and his three brothers had decided to tell them. Then, the Designers willing, Djibril would traverse the barrier once more and return to the city where the female human resided. Dallas, it was called. This Dallas would be his home for the foreseeable future.

Although he would never wear such apparel in public in the Seraphim realm, he had acquired a taste for the type of clothing worn by the creatures in the female's part of the world and had over the past few years obtained quite a selection for his personal wardrobe. Now, he was glad of that fact. Packing for the journey wouldn't take long.

As he settled onto his bed and closed his eyes, an image of the female flashed briefly before his mind's eye and Djibril shivered as he wondered what would come of this situation.

The next morning, after the four brothers had met to go over their plan once more, Djibril presented himself before the Great Sanhedrin with as much of the truth of the situation as he was allowed to impart. Mikhail, who was considered the head of the entire council, steered the Great Sanhedrin's decision as to what must be done toward the idea of sending Djibril to watch over the female. As had been hoped, the vote was unanimous and Djibril spent the remainder of the day preparing for his return journey to and extended stay in Dallas, Texas.

This would be the first time he had gotten to spend any measurable length of time in this part of the world in several thousand years and, in a way, Djibril was looking forward to the task. He had studied the area as best he could from books and others' depictions in order to keep track of as many changes as he could to the region since the last time he'd visited. So much had changed during the great floods, though, and so much geographical history had been lost that such a task was nearly impossible.

He still had his memories of how things had been before, with vast cities and enormous populations. The majority of these had been wiped from the earth by the floods at the end of what the humans thought of as the world's last ice age. They knew nothing of the thriving metropolises that had once dotted the shorelines and plains of the continent.

Of course, the majority of that particular land was now deep underwater. The humans had recently found one of the cities deep underwater just off the western coast of a place called Cuba, he'd heard. Djibril wanted to do some exploring of his own to remind himself of the land. However, he was cognizant of his mission and would not fail to keep as close an eye on the creature as possible.

After crossing the dreaded barrier into the creature's realm and traveling to Dallas, the female was easy to find, her frequencies guiding him surer than any map ever could. It was nighttime and she was safely ensconced in a two-story house on the North side of Dallas. The neighborhood was not as crammed as some of the others he'd glimpsed from above, but there were few tall trees for shade and the land was flat. Each house resembled the next, though there were a few slight variations in the designs that showed attempts by the architects to break the monotony.

The house was made mostly of brick, but Djibril could clearly detect the female's radiance even from outside the structure. This one was so much stronger than any the Seraphim had ever encountered. Djibril thought about the fact that he and his brethren would end up having to kill her. It would be a pity, he decided, when they did. He didn't believe any of this to be the fault of the female, whether she was being manipulated or not. She was merely a victim of circumstance and here was he, her messenger of death.

Djibril heaved a sigh and found a spot in the new-fallen snow where he could wait out the evening on what appeared to be a golf course just behind the creature's house. He had several shields up around himself so that none would detect his presence. The night was very cold, but his shields protected him from it. Djibril lifted his gaze to the heavens. Surprisingly, it was a clear night with starlight twinkling as much as it could this close to the city. The weather in this part of the world apparently often turned from warm and sunny to cold and snowy almost overnight during the winter months.

As Djibril took in the beauty of the heavens before him, he wondered where his beloved Designers were and when they would return. He hoped it would be soon. It was already past the time when those of the Seraphim realm had calculated the promised return should have been. However, according to the writings and calculations of those of *this* realm, the promised return was scheduled to happen just a short time from now.

Djibril chuckled ironically. The poor creatures had lost so much of the knowledge left them by the blessed Great Designers that they didn't even know what all those writings and calendars meant. Djibril knew there were wild speculations among humans about the date they'd calculated possibly being a sign of the end of their kind, of the world, of everything. Little did they know, they were soon to get a history lesson that would bring them back in line with a force that simply was not to be denied.

The thought gave Djibril pause and he lowered his gaze from the stars above. He wondered what would happen when his beloved Designers did finally return. Would it be all out war? Would they wipe out the entire race of humans in this realm just to show that their rule was all-encompassing?

Mikhail would be devastated, for he so loved these creatures. Then again, there would be the issue of Baphomet's and Suriyah's reactions, as well.

Djibril pulled the leather jacket he wore closer around himself, a chill suddenly making it seem colder than it had before, even though his shields were up. He didn't want to think of such things. Those two were beyond anyone's reckoning anymore. And, as for the Designers... Who was Djibril to try to figure out the reasoning and intentions of such beings? He was merely a messenger and a guardian. It was what he'd been created to be. His beloved Designers had told him so a hundred thousand years ago.

He would do his duty and not think on things that did not concern him, he determined. He glanced back toward the house in front of him. The creature's radiance was quite clear through the walls of the structure. The frequencies she was emitting had calmed a bit, indicating that she slept. Djibril stretched out on his back on the slight hillside of the golf course, his hands behind his head and his legs crossed at the ankles, and faced the stars once more. This was going to be a long night.

Chapter 2

Entry #711 – Sarah's Vision Blog – February 9 – 9:00 pm

Once again, I write to whomever regarding the demented workings of my mind. I was sitting out in the quad at school a few days ago when, what should appear, but one of the glowing ones. He was almost a foot taller than me, by the looks of him, with long blond hair. The one I'd seen before had had long black hair. The eyes on this one were the same, though. They were a piercing blue and they seemed to flash when his gaze swung my way. I looked away just in time, of course, before he could tell I'd been watching him. Everyone else, I noticed, stared his way, but they weren't turning away like me. They just stared like dumb puppies.

From my periphery, I could see him just standing there, observing us mere mortals. He wore faded blue jeans and an American Joe t-shirt. It was a warm day, so everyone was dressed for summer. His huge biceps strained at the seams of his shirt. The heat radiating off him could've powered a few thousand homes in the Dallas Metroplex, I figured. They never seemed to sweat, though, these glowing ones. I don't know why. I guess my imagination doesn't think sweat is an attractive thing on a guy, or something.

I had half a mind to walk up to him and just start talking. I don't know that I'd ever be able to get that close without fainting dead away, though. That one time I saw one when I'd been a teenager was the closest I've ever gotten to one of them, and I felt like I was going to have a heart attack from the adrenaline rush I got then, and he was all the way across the room from where I stood!

I wouldn't know what to say to one of them anyway, even if he actually turned out to be real. But, I can't believe any of them are real. Who's like that? They're so beautiful and they seem to attract everyone's attention whenever they're around. More than just beautiful people do, I mean.

People avoid them, though. I've never seen anyone approach them or even talk to one of them. I don't know. I mean, people stare at them the same as I do, but there's never any interaction with any of them. I think my sick and demented mind just makes up these beautiful beings simply to give me something to look at so that I don't have to feel so sad and alone.

That's not right. I mean, I'm not sad, per se. I... I just don't know what to think about where I'm going and what's going on and I don't have anyone to talk to. I mean, there's so much strife in the world, so much anger, and so many lonely people who've lost their way. I want to help, but I don't know how. What am I talking about? I'm one of them! Help, please! Somebody! Anybody?

Anyway, I digress.

I had a few questions from some of my readers regarding the last blog in which I talked about the origins and what my recent visions have shown me and I wanted to go ahead and clarify a few things.

As to the question of whether or not the Virgin Mary has appeared to me to show me the things I've written about in this blog, the answer has to be a definite "No!" How do I know this? First off, I'm not Catholic. (Don't you have to be Catholic for the Virgin Mother to show up?) Secondly, I'm not sure anyone in particular has ever showed up in person in any of my visions. I just see things, or rather, I'm just shown things. Maybe, I'm crazy. Your guess is as good as any, right? Who knows? I'm just reporting what I've been shown.

The following are the best descriptions I can think to give of my visions (Who the hell showed them to me is a mystery to me, so you take your best guess, but here you go...):

In a point in space and time, before there was such a thing as time, we were. We were not aware that we were. We just were. We existed in a state of complete darkness and stillness. As far as I could tell from the visions, we were all one stable mass – one single, solid mass of energy.

Then, something happened.

What appeared to be all of a sudden, if one could conceive of such a thing, there was a scattering in all directions and what seemed to be an onset of awareness within us. That's when the first awareness that we were no longer one was felt, but that there was an unfathomable multitude of scatterings of our energies, if that was what we were, throughout the gaping blackness. We were not aware of the blackness, only of our movement throughout it. It was only realized to be a blackness through which we scattered/moved when eventually, after what could have been an eon or not long at all, awareness of lighted objects appeared. These drew our interest and it was observed that some of our numbers would draw closer to these objects.

The means by which movement was accomplished was unclear to me in the visions. We just were and we just moved. Observation of ourselves and other things around us was accomplished by some means unknown to me, as well, for there was no corporealness to any of us of which I was aware in my visions. I was not me, but merely a fraction of the traveling mass.

Next, after some unknown length of time, there came an awareness of separateness and pain because of this separateness. Before, when we had been stable and all together, there had not been separateness. We had been we, not solemn bits of energy. Why we were that no longer was beyond my comprehension.

It was observed eventually that some of our numbers were coming together, joining energies, taking two or more and becoming one whole. That was when an all-consuming loneliness encroached upon those of us who were not paired or part of a group. All still traveled on, though, with very few deviating from the ongoing wave to occasionally draw closer to one of the lighted objects encountered en route to wherever we were headed.

Then, it was observed that there were new objects, previously un-encountered, moving into and among our numbers. These were not like the lighted objects that were occasionally encountered by our numbers. These were altered versions of our own type of energy. Like us, they radiated warmth; but unlike us, they had a solid, separate corporeal form from which a different type of radiance was emitted. These were actual beings that traveled, not like us, but in strange contraptions made of a different, lower class of energy. These beings did not appear to notice us.

After a time, again it could have been an eternity later or not long after at all, some of our numbers took to following these corporeal beings we encountered. Occasionally, these beings would all draw close to one of the lighted objects of which we were encountering more and more frequently. They would draw closer to them than any of our group had ever drawn, would even succumb to the gravitational pull of the object and, indeed, go down to its surface.

Those of our wave who were not following the enclave of the corporeal beings, continued onward and outward.

The awareness of pain and suffering became almost all and the only remedy for this seemed to be in the joining and drawing together of more than one of us into a pairing or group. For some, a simple pairing seemed to suffice. For others, the need for more sharing was observed. This joining together was always between masses that radiated their energies along the same wavelengths and frequencies, though these were felt, rather than measured with any tools, for again we were non-corporeal in nature. The joining together did seem to relieve the pain of the separateness. My own form "felt" so much less pain by the joining, when I finally found another mass that emitted along the same wavelength and frequencies as my own energies.

In that early time (though billions of what we call years here on earth could have passed by this time), there was no awareness of self, still. We were still we, but our numbers were different and we knew there was this separation of all of us. How we knew this, again, I cannot tell you. We simply knew. I just know there was much pain experienced within the visions because of the loss of those who had been part of our group before.

Then, as before, a new type of corporeal entity was encountered. We observed that these new things were again an altered version of our own type of energy, but that they were of such a higher order of energy in that they burned brightly and radiated a warmth and pull toward themselves that seemed almost inescapable. Some of our numbers were frightened of these new things and stayed as far away as possible, even changing trajectory somehow in order to avoid them.

A few of us drew toward these new things, as did the one to which I was paired. I believe there were six pairs of us there with them, at first. These beings seemed to be aware of us in some way, for as we drew closer, they seemed to take over our physical selves and bring us in intentionally, without requiring much effort from us.

That's when it happened...

There appeared one of the low-energy lighted objects and then these new beings changed those of us who'd come in close as pairs, my paired one and I first, separating us and taking one of our numbers from each separation. This was the first time I experienced self in the vision because the one mass of energy I had formed with another was now broken and the part that was splintered off was taken by the new beings and changed into some new thing that was on some other plane of existence. The process seemed to be excruciating, judging from the change in energy radiating from my partner and the other five who had been taken.

As I became aware of my "self," I raced toward the other half of my now broken unit, but found I could not become joined with it again. In fact, it was completely confined within a physical "shell" that seemed to inhibit it from even sensing me and my energy. This greatly distressed me and I hovered as close to my other half as possible.

I hovered there for what seemed a very long time. The glowing, radiating beings who had massacred my little energy unit hovered nearby, as well, though they were concentrating solely on the six forms below. They no longer seemed interested in any of us hovering around near them.

Then, the strange beings left! I and those others who remained who were still aching from having been split apart from our other halves, could only hover and watch. Eventually, the strange beings returned. It was at that time that I noticed other pairings being broken by the beings. The halves they took they transformed into something slightly different from the six they'd originally taken. They looked similar, but there was something not quite as complete about them. They still bore some connection to their former energy units. Those halved bits of energy were left to simply hover as I did, as their other halves were taken and transformed, though they still shared a tenuous connection. It was only a thin, thread-like connection, though.

Had I had a physical form at this time, I know I would have wept, for myself and for the others. We all hovered near the area where the newly-transformed energies were gathered. Then, the beings that had done this horrible thing to us simply up and left... again.

More and more awareness of my own self was being gained throughout this time, though I still did not understand what had happened before. There was still a multitude of others like me occupying the area in which I hovered, or nearby. They had all lost their other halves, too, though again, all but six of us still maintained an energy connection with their other halves. We six, however, were all once again alone. We could watch our other halves down on the lighted object below, but we could not interact with them. They remained completely unaware of us, no matter what we did or tried to do for attention. We were at a loss.

Then, there came a time when those strange new beings returned, though how long they'd been gone was unclear. It was then that my little mass of energy was taken. They pulled all six of the halves that had been stranded the first time they'd been there and did something to us. I was forced to change my shape, though I didn't understand any commands to do so. A portion of my mass was jammed into such a confined space, a space surrounded by a blazing solidity. I pulled back as hard as I could, but some method was being used to keep just a portion of my energy mass firmly ensconced in the solid little ball. It was sheer agony.

There was bright light and more pain than any I had ever conceived...

That's the last of what was seen, at least it was this time around. Will write more later. Until then, keep warm and safe, since we're all stuck in a newly-frozen Dallas!

Sarah signed off, switching off her computer screen as soon as the log off icon appeared on the screen. She was tired. Not that that was anything new. Being a single mom wasn't the easiest of things under the best of circumstances, let alone when one was dead broke, unemployed and living off others' generosity in order to go to school full-time to make a better life for her child and herself.

Where was the honor in that? It was a daily pride swallowing, self-worth-sucking siege through which Sarah suffered because she'd been an idiot in the past.

It was true, she decided with a smirk, that some mistakes cost you years, if not forever, to pay for.

As she straightened from the office chair, she placed a hand at her aching lower back and rubbed hard. It had been a hard week. The kid and she had been forced to stay home yesterday due to the strange weather in Dallas. The roads were slick and there was snow beyond anything they'd ever experienced this time of year. The South just didn't know how to handle such weather and everything had shut down.

Sarah really didn't think she could handle anymore days off of school having to entertain the kid, though. He was a great kid, granted, but a 24-hour menu of kid videos and kid television just didn't sit well with her. That wasn't even including the folks. They were about to drive Sarah nuts!

She crept into her son's room to make sure he was okay. Sleeping soundly, as usual for this time of night. She pulled his covers up and tucked them under his chin before quietly making her way out and silently shutting the door. He was a really good kid. Sometimes, though, she felt really bad about being his mom. She didn't have a clue what she was doing. She had no money, no job, no income, and a future that depended on her earning a degree in a field she'd never had anything to do with.

Sarah had no clue how she'd made it as far as she had in this degree program. She'd been a language major in college before! That was what she called her "former lifetime" because it was pre-kid. What the hell she thought she was going to be able to accomplish with all the science and math courses she was taking now, she didn't know. Add to that the fact that she wasn't exactly your conventional girl/woman in the first place and there was absolutely no way she would ever even get close to being nominated for mom of the year. She didn't know how to be a regular woman and probably wouldn't do it even if she did know how.

The thing was that she had finally realized a couple of years ago that there wasn't going to be a knight in shining armor coming to rescue her son and her. Immediately following that blockbuster came the realization that none of her siblings had any plans, or even the ability, to take care of their parents, should the need ever arise.

What a time to finally grow up, eh?

As Sarah made her way downstairs, she heaved a heavy sigh. This was one of those nights. She made her way to the kitchen and, pulling a stopper from an already open bottle, she poured herself a glass full of a 2002 Shiraz. It wasn't a great one, but she didn't particularly care tonight.

So much had been going on, lately.

The folks were in bed and the dogs were asleep in their kennels in the kitchen. Sarah turned on the television and flipped through a few channels before stopping on one of her favorite movies. Jack Nicholson was extolling the virtues of cheating on one's wife. Was there any wonder Sarah'd never trusted a man enough to accept a marriage proposal?

Who are you kidding? she asked herself. She'd never let anyone get close enough to even get to the point of asking her to marry him. She knew she was worse than the worst male player out there. Men had always been there for her enjoyment and for nothing more. She loved their bodies, loved how strong and powerful they were. She loved how big they were compared with her petite frame. She loved touching them and feeling the hardness of their muscles and then feeling those same muscles tremble at her touch.

The momentary security provided when they held her in their powerful arms was one of the most wonderful feelings in the world. She wanted that and needed that, she always had. There was always something missing, though, something that should have been there that just wasn't. She was always searching for that missing thing, that missing feeling, believing that it was just hidden somewhere inside one of them and all she had to do was to wait for it. Then, the worst would happen.

Just the mere mention of the dreaded four-letter "L" word was a death knell for the relationship. She would always break it off immediately after that. Anyway, how could she let anyone get any closer to her? She was a single mom who lived with her parents. As if that wasn't bad enough, she certainly had a whole boat load of issues, and the main one… What was she supposed to say? "Oh, and by the way, I have visions sometimes. I hope that doesn't freak you out, or anything."

She downed the remaining wine in the glass and debated whether or not to pour herself another.

What the heck, she thought, and went back into the kitchen to pour another glass full. A shot of Morgan Freeman looking out a window at the Himalayas showed on the television screen in front of her as she returned to the living room and settled down onto the couch, wine glass in hand, ready to watch the rest of the movie. As she sank into the comfort of the soft leather furniture in her parents' house, a familiar sense of peace overtook her frame. Everything around her suddenly faded to darkness and her field of vision was filled with a different time and place. The living room in which she sat was forgotten and the movie in her mind started once more, eclipsing all outside awareness, her wineglass held perfectly still, perched on her knee, as she witnessed things from beyond this realm…

When she finally became aware of her surroundings again, Jack Nicholson's character's assistant in the movie was placing a second old-timey tin coffee canister in a box on top of a snowy mountain. It was way past her bed time. She heaved another great sigh. Another round of things that were, she was sure. Who would believe her, though? All she knew was that there was someone somewhere who was showing her things that were really important, things that needed to be told to the world somehow, and she was the one receiving the images.

What could she do?

After dumping out her untouched wine and rinsing out the wineglass in the darkened kitchen, she went back upstairs to the little office her dad had built. After flipping on the light switch, she turned on the computer screen and signed in again. The familiar pages of the blog she'd started almost two and a half years earlier appeared before her eyes and she started typing.

This was her life, lately. What else could she do with the information? If she actually told anyone what was going on with her, they'd think she was crazy. Her folks wouldn't understand. Her mom was Christian and her dad didn't know what he was, he just knew if he couldn't touch it or make sense of it with a mathematical equation, it probably didn't exist.

Her son listened to her when she just couldn't keep things inside anymore, but he wasn't old enough to understand any of it or to give educated answers to any of the questions she had about the visions. Since she'd decided to go back to school, she hadn't had time to hang out with any of her friends, so they'd drifted away and no longer called. She was twice the age of the normal college student and so she hadn't really befriended anyone in her classes, so there'd been no budding friendships there.

The blog was her only release. And so, release she did. She poured everything in her mind into the blog, letting the whole world, or whoever wanted to, know the things she was seeing and experiencing, all in the hopes that someone out there might be experiencing the same things she was. So far, though, there'd been only the usual. Either the crackpots came out of the woodwork wondering if she was an alien being offering information on an invasion that was coming or, as was usually the case, it was just those who were just as lonely and lost as she was and were simply looking for answers.

These were the people she wrote for. She understood their plight. She, too, was a bit lost, without hope and without a clue as to why everyone and everything was. Now, however, since the latest round of visions had started, she understood the answers to some of her questions, to some degree, and she wanted to offer those other people out there hope, in whatever forms the answers took. Her heart bled for those souls and she wanted to give her visions to them, however she could, without bringing harm to her family or herself.

How did one do that in such a mad world, though? It seemed as if the world had gone crazy in the last decade and that anything that wasn't politically correct or non-threatening in any way, shape or form was immediately frowned upon and banned. Cartoonists were being stalked and had death threats being thrown at them by entire cultures. Here she was, on the internet, writing things that might possibly incite riots!

Sarah didn't want to offend anyone. She just wanted to let others know of the visions she'd had. They could choose for themselves to make of the visions whatever they wanted. The visions had given her a measure of hope, so she'd wanted to share them with others in hopes they'd give others a sense of peace of mind.

Was that so bad?

Sarah didn't think so. And, so she wrote. She wrote every detail she could recall from the visions she'd received. She did her best to be objective in her writings. She didn't want to color anything with her own personal beliefs, if possible. What those beliefs were, she wasn't sure. She poured her heart out, though, scrambling as fast as she could before the details disappeared, typing as fast as her fingers could manage.

Around four in the morning, she finally switched off the monitor to the computer and went to bed after checking on her son one more time. At least, it was Saturday and she didn't have school the next day. She would have to catch up on some sleep then, before school started back on Monday. *At least the snow melted for the most part today*, she thought. Her son would probably spend most of Sunday glued to his laptop, so she wouldn't have to worry about entertaining him most of the day.

Sometimes, she really loved technology, as bad as that sounded.

Entry #712 – Sarah's Vision Blog – February 10 – 2:20 am

The process of being born was what was shown to me next. I was actually in a human body, an infant's body, being born.   I was shown this without any form of physical experience being felt in the vision, which leads me to believe what has been said for years about birth being a traumatic experience for the soul of the infant. In fact, there was almost no physical experience associated with the vision until the child's body had matured almost six months, as far as I could tell. Time experience is different when one is just watching as opposed to when one is actively participating in it, though.

The infant's body didn't last very much longer after that. It appeared that some illness was contracted and the body soon stopped functioning. The portion of myself that had been ensconced within the small body quickly vacated it and I experienced such a rush of relief I could have cried. It was as if an unimaginable weight had been lifted and I could suddenly expand to my normal size, however far-reaching that was. I was, once again, non-corporeal. However, I was also still without the energy mass with which I had been coupled prior to the start of all of this business with those strange new beings. The problem, though, was that I no longer knew where my other half's corporeal self resided. I didn't know where to find it and I didn't know where the strange beings were, either. They were all simply gone again.

The form my other half had occupied, I thought, was similar to those that had cared for my infant self on that other plane, so I conceived a plan. I would approach the plane of the physical and attempt to occupy another corporeal body. Surely, if I were there, I would have a greater chance of encountering my other half, of sensing it, than I would by merely remaining where I was, existing as a mere mass of energy on this non-corporeal plane.

Through sheer will alone, I maneuvered as much of my mass close in to the place I had been. I know now this was a planet; Earth, actually. There were those corporeal being types there like those who had taken care of my infant self when I'd been there. I willed myself to draw closer to these beings. They were not as radiant as the other beings, the ones who'd changed everything for my other half and me. They radiated warmth, no doubt, but it was significantly less than those others. The others who'd taken my other half had glowed brightly in their radiance and the frequencies emitted by them were the purest tones I'd ever experienced. Even my other half and I had not radiated frequencies that pure.

These other beings, though, who now occupied the planet, seemed to radiate frequencies very similar to many of the energy masses surrounding the planet with me. As I watched, several of the energy masses hovering nearby approached the planet and then, somehow, each immersed a portion of themselves into separate beings there. I was watching souls going into the wombs of human females as they conceived!

I concentrated all my energy on learning this process. It seemed an easy thing to accomplish, just go on down and hop into an available womb...

Nature, it seems, likes to tease us no matter what stage we're in.

I can't tell you how many times I attempted the trick. I know at one point I had to stop to rest. So much of my energy had been expended on the task I wasn't sure I would ever make it into one of those wombs. Apparently, there were no wombs at the inn. (You know I had to throw that one in there!)

After some indeterminate amount of time, I was able to gather up enough of my energy mass and make a sudden push toward a female human who was copulating, that I finally made it through. I found myself, like before, firmly ensconced within a tight, scalding environment. The heat was searing, but it was a welcome change to the nothingness I usually "felt" as a non-corporeal being. Only a small portion of my entire mass was stuffed inside the body, even as the fetus grew. Because of this, the portion of my mass that was not inside the body was still where I had been before. My energy mass was still one, but it was stretched over a great distance. My non-corporeal portion still hovered where I had been before, while the rest of me resided within the tiny body inside the womb.

There was the birth, again. Like before, the vision was simply a vision with no physical experience being had throughout most of this time. This body turned out to be a male child that lived for some time, around fifteen years, I'd say. I didn't keep track and the people of that time didn't really, either. They seemed to be a nomadic people, constantly traveling. When that body expired, as before, my entire energy mass resumed its hovering just outside the plane of the physical planet. I was exhausted, though. I knew it would take a great deal of time before I would be able to enter another body. So much energy was required just to make the push.

I waited and rested.

Chapter 3

Djibril yawned a couple of days later as he watched the class. *Of course, the creature had to be an early riser*, he thought. He'd been asleep a mere forty minutes on the hillside this morning when he'd felt the female stirring. It wasn't even light out when she got up. He watched as she went about preparing a meal for a young boy, and then prepared another which she put into some sort of container. The entire time, she was flitting from one end of the house to the other and then back again, never sitting down. It was enough to make Djibril tired, just watching her!

Soon after, she and the boy exited the house and climbed into a mechanical device humans called a "car". Djibril took notice of the type of car it was, it's color and any distinguishing features and marks so he would be able to recognize it more easily in the future. He followed the car to a school and watched as the female pressed a kiss to the young boy's cheek before he exited the car with books and the small container of food the female had prepared earlier. Djibril noted the boy seemed embarrassed by the kiss, but he'd allowed it. The female watched the boy until he entered the building, then steered the car into the line of traffic exiting the building's parking lot.

She didn't return to the house. Instead, she drove to the University where Djibril had first encountered her. She parked the car and quickly made her way into one of the ugly campus buildings. He followed her, though none noticed because of his shielding. The room she entered was in the shape of a huge theater, with row upon row of seats and tabletops descending toward a stage area with a podium and some sort of projection device.

The lights near where Djibril positioned himself immediately blew, though the ceiling was high enough in the room to keep them from shattering. Fortunately, none of the creatures in the room came close enough to him that any of their electronic devices could be affected. The female took a position at a seat two rows down from where he stood.

The class turned out to be an Organic Chemistry lecture class. Djibril kept an eye on the female as he listened to the class professor. Everything the man said was kept on a very basic level and Djibril found himself tuning out the droning voice of the man down on the tiny stage. He chose to study the female, instead. The boy she'd dropped off at school this morning had called her "Mom." So, she had a son.

Djibril wondered about the husband who would look after the boy once the female was gone. How was the man able to handle this female? It didn't matter, of course, but it would be interesting if Djibril could study the male creature, as well, in order to discover any anomalies he might possess that enabled him to deal with one such as the female. Most of these creatures wouldn't want to be around someone like her, for they would feel the tremendous energies coming from her on a subconscious level and it would frighten them or, as was normally the case, slightly repulse them.

Djibril didn't really have the time to waste studying the creature's mate, though. The boy would just have to be left with him.

So engrossed in his thoughts Djibril had been that he was startled to realize the class was suddenly over. Students were filing out of the room at several exits and he had to move a couple of times in order to keep the female in sight. As she slowly made her way up the steps with the crowd toward an exit, her eyes suddenly connected directly with his.

He gasped. There was no way she could have seen through his shield. Granted, he only had one of the six up at the time, but she shouldn't have been able to see through it. Djibril quickly put up a second shield and moved, watching to make sure her eyes didn't follow his movement. She appeared to be oblivious to his presence once more and he realized he must have been mistaken. There was no way she could have seen through his first shield. It had to have been mere coincidence that she'd looked directly at him.

He followed her to her next class. It was in a similarly designed room, but on a much smaller scale. It was also packed with students, so Djibril was forced to stand at the very back of the room at the top in a corner. It was as far as he could manage to get from the students while still being able to keep an eye on the female. The light bulbs near him in this classroom did burst and so there was a big hubbub among the students for the first few minutes of class as the ones nearby cleaned as much glass debris off their desks and chairs and out of their hair and clothing as they could.

The female hadn't sat near the corner, but Djibril noticed she kept glancing over toward where he stood throughout most of the class. This class was a cellular neuroscience class, but Djibril paid little attention to the professor. By the time the class ended, he was seriously concerned something was going on. He'd by now erected a third shield, but still she kept swinging glances his way, seemingly looking directly at him, even as she made her way down toward an exit away from where he stood. He needed to find out if she could actually see him or if his imagination was just getting the better of him.

He followed a bit farther behind her than before as she made her way out to her car in the parking lot. As she entered the vehicle, he paused, not wanting to get too close to her. She started the engine, backed up and turned the car toward where he stood. As she approached, her eyes were trained on him. He was dumbfounded to note she was turning her head to stare at him as she passed. A distinct chill shook his frame as he realized she *was* able to see him, indeed. He quickly pulled up all remaining shields and took to the air to follow.

The rest of the day, he stuck to observing her from afar. She went to a food market, a dry-cleaning establishment, a veterinary clinic and back to the house, where she seemed, yet again, to never sit down for a moment. It appeared the foodstuffs had to be put away, and then there was laundry to be done, then dishes. There were two dogs in the house and, when she let them out into the back yard, they went nuts barking at him. By the time the female finally managed to get the two dogs back into the house, Djibril was sure the entire neighborhood could see him.

She returned to the boy's school to pick him up a short time later and then they both returned to the house. At that point, the female busied herself with making a small snack for the boy and helping him with what Djibril figured was homework. Once that was done, the female began preparing the evening meal. Two other adults entered the house not long afterward and, after they all ate, the female finally settled in on a sofa to watch some television with the other three in the house.

Each time the two dogs were let out into the back yard, however, they immediately began barking and wouldn't cease making the infernal noise until forced to return inside the house. Djibril's nerves from dealing with the day's observations were stretched so tight he was infinitely thankful to the blessed Great Designers when the creatures within the house finally settled into their beds for the night.

He returned to the hillside on the golf course behind the house and settled in for the evening, listening to the buzzing sound of technological electricity in use all around him and trying to tune it out. The low, low hum of the biological transmissions was very faint, even with so many houses nearby. The female's tones came through loud and clear, though. That was all he needed.

After tucking her son into bed, Sarah made herself a cup of hot decaffeinated herbal tea and sat down at the computer in the office upstairs to write for a moment or two. She hadn't experienced anymore visions, as yet, but she sure as heck had a subject to blog about! The sight of the glowing man in her O-Chem class this morning had thrown her for a loop. Then, he'd been in her Cellular Neuroscience lecture. He'd even caused a big ruckus when he'd made some light bulbs shatter.

Sarah knew it was he who'd caused the incident because she could feel the energy coming off him. She was shocked the whole campus hadn't experienced a blackout due to overloading of the grid, judging from the waves of pure energy she'd felt from him. She'd sat in that last class, for almost two hours straight, feeling wave after wave of the stuff hit her and never once did it weaken.

How could one man contain so much energy? It made Sarah's skin crawl every time she was around him. It wasn't that he seemed dangerous or anything, it was just that it was so overwhelming that she didn't know if she'd be able to handle being any closer to so much energy. Her heart had raced the entire time he'd been around. The feeling hadn't gone away the rest of the day, either. She knew he'd at least followed her out to the parking lot because she'd seen him as she'd driven away from school after class. She hadn't seen him the rest of the day, but she'd still felt his presence. She even felt his presence, still.

After dinner, she'd sat downstairs with the family watching television. Sarah hadn't seen much of anything on the screen, though. Her mind had been otherwise occupied. The fact that the man had caused the light bulbs to burst in her class meant he was definitely *not* a figment of her imagination. So, what was he? He hadn't seemed as if he'd wanted to hurt anyone or cause malicious mischief or anything. In fact, he'd actually seemed startled by the fact that she could see him. It was almost as if he was trying *not* to be seen.

Sarah wondered if he was a ghost or some other non-corporeal entity that had somehow gotten stuck on this plane. *Great*, she thought, *that's just what I need!* Her life was screwed up enough without some damned poltergeist coming along to mess with it even more. Maybe, he was some sort of demon? But, wouldn't a ghost or a demon or *haint*, as her great-grandmother used to call them, actually *want* to be seen by humans? It didn't make sense. Besides, Sarah didn't even believe in all those things.

Anyway, she decided the best way for her to deal with this for the moment was to just put it all down in her blog. Perhaps, someone out there would read it and be able to make sense of what was going on with her. Perhaps, that someone would write back in response, filling her in and solving all her problems. *Right, and perhaps*, she thought, *he'll be my knight in shining armor and he'll come rescue my son and me from this dreary world by whisking us off to his castle in the sky.* Sarah wasn't going to hold her breath waiting on that one. With a yawn, she signed onto her account and started typing.

Entry #713 – Sarah's Vision Blog – February 10 – 10:15 pm
Today was a bad day. That damned glowing man seems to be popping up everywhere I go! I know he's probably just a figment of my imagination, but dang-it, I wish

he'd just go away. He's been looking at me, but when I look back at him he gets all weirded out, like I'm not supposed to be able to see him or something. It's giving me the creeps and just plain pissing me off! I have half a mind to go punch him in the gut the next time I see him. (I'm so violent, lately! Couldn't be stress or anything, you think?)

School's getting to me. I've been looking for a job, applying for anything and everything I can think of that would work with my schedule, but everybody and their brother are out looking for exactly the same thing at the same time and I'm kind of past my prime, so of course that's just going swell! My kid told me he thinks he's fat, so that means some kids at school have probably been making fun of him and calling him names. He's not fat! He's just getting ready for a growth spurt. He always puts on a little whenever he's about to shoot up another inch or two, or twelve! I've told him this.

On top of all that, my folks just told me I need to be able to house sit/dog sit during the coming week. I tell you, I feel like I'm stretched to the limit and if just one more thing crops up, which it probably will if the past is anything to go by, I'm just gonna pop!

You know, if this guy *isn't* some figment of my imagination, I wish he'd do something to *help* me, instead of just creeping me out by staring at me and being everywhere I go all the frigging time!

I haven't had any visions lately. Sorry. I just needed to vent. I'll write the next time I see anything.

The next morning, Djibril was up and ready before dawn. The female got up at the same time as yesterday. Last evening, Djibril had heard one of the other adults in the house call her Sarah. Sarah meant "princess" or "lady" and Djibril recalled another Sarah who'd been Abraham's wife and Isaac's mother. He liked the name and thought it suited her, for she definitely loved her son. That much was abundantly clear.

Djibril watched her as she completed her morning routine and he followed, though from a much greater distance today, when she went to drop off her son at school. Again, she kissed him goodbye and watched until he was safe inside the building before driving off. Today, however, she didn't go immediately to the University campus. Instead, she visited several businesses in a row.

At each establishment, she would go inside, and then come out very soon after with some sort of paperwork. She'd then sit in her car writing on the paperwork until, at some point, she'd return the paperwork to someone within the establishment. Djibril had no idea what she was doing. It didn't appear to involve any of the Shaitans or Jinn, though, so he just followed along, keeping an eye out for anything out of the ordinary. She repeated this process no less than ten times.

Afterward, she finally headed for the University campus, where she spent the remainder of the day. There was one break in the day when she went to pick up her son from school. Like yesterday, she took him home immediately and got him a snack. However, as soon as that was done, she climbed back into her vehicle and returned to the University.

Djibril didn't follow her into the classroom this time. Instead, he waited outside the building by the entrance she'd used going in. It was getting dark and it was much colder this evening. Djibril pulled his shields more tightly around himself to keep warm as he waited for her to return.

Sarah held onto the railing as she descended the stairs, afraid she might fall from not being able to see where she was stepping. She was crying. She hated that class and wished it wasn't a requirement so she could drop it. It wasn't actually the class she hated so much as the other students in the class. Just because she happened to be interested in the subject matter and asked a lot of questions didn't give them the right to be so mean to her.

Here they were, half her age, *if* that, telling her to shut up and to let the professor just teach! Who the hell did they think they were? And, of course the professor hadn't heard any of it. They'd made sure to say everything just low enough so he wouldn't hear.

What the hell do I care what some punk teenagers think? she wondered. But, it hurt. Sarah had never dealt well with conflict. She liked things pleasant and happy. She cried whenever she got really angry because it just wasn't in her nature to be anything but happy. Of course, whenever she was actually sad, that was the worst. She could boo-hoo with the best of them, though she rarely let her son see her crying. His world was full enough of tough realities. She certainly didn't want him having to deal with the fact that his home life wasn't as perfect as could be with a single mom.

Sarah finally reached the bottom floor of the stairwell and pushed through the large double metal doors. There, directly across from her, stood the glowing man. He was looking directly at her, with that startled "deer-in-the-headlights" look he always wore whenever she saw him. She gasped and he just disappeared into thin air all of a sudden.

"Don't go," Sarah said through her tears. "Please..., don't go... I don't really want to be alone, right now." She sniffled.

After a moment of tense waiting, Sarah had almost given up, figuring he'd gone, when his image suddenly reappeared right where she'd seen him before. Sarah released a quick breath of relief and gave him a watery smile. She sniffled again.

"Thank you," she softly said.

He paused, and then nodded once. His eyes narrowed as he studied her. The glow of the energies radiating from within her was almost startling. *How could this creature contain so much soul-energy,* he wondered.

Sarah turned to step closer to him and he immediately backed off. She halted, hesitating.

"I'm Sarah," she said, cautiously extending her hand toward him.

He looked dubiously at the offered hand but made no move toward her.

After a moment, she nervously lowered it, deciding to slide her hands into the back pockets of her jeans, instead. She hoped that would help him feel more at ease. She glanced around nervously, one side of her lower lip catching between her teeth as she frantically searched for some non-threatening topic of conversation.

She cocked her head to one side and, narrowing her eyes, asked, "Are you a ghost?"

He blinked in surprise and opened his mouth, then closed it. He looked down at his hands, deep in thought, then looked back up at her and moved forward, one arm coming up as he moved. His large hand cupped her cheek and Sarah gasped at how warm it felt. He gasped too, but didn't remove his palm from her pale face. Energy coursed from one to the other, each giving and each receiving.

He marveled at how cool her skin was and how sweet was the tone of the energies coursing through her.

Sarah's heart raced as the energy from him came rushing through her body. It was unlike anything she'd ever experienced.

"Wow!" she exclaimed, stepping back from him, finally breaking the contact.

He took a step back, himself. He still wasn't too sure of himself around her and didn't want to frighten her. He watched her with renewed interest. She was an anomaly, to be certain. He wanted to know more about her, to study her and find out how she came to be the way she was. He wondered if there was some evolutionary link between her and the Jinn or the Shaitans, something that would make her somehow closer to his kind than the other creatures of this realm.

It was suspected the Shaitans and Jinn were constantly slipping in and out of this dimension through rifts in the barrier they'd discovered throughout the Badlands. That made it more likely that she was the result of one of their pairings with one of the creatures here. The energies coursing through her body's channels so closely resembled his own, he was almost sure this was what had occurred, for although the leaders of the Shaitans and the Jinn couldn't conceive, their subjects could, just as could the lesser angels of Seraphim City.

The general population of Shaitans and Jinn no longer physically resembled those in Seraphim City, but Djibril knew they were all still made of pretty much the same cloth. The blessed Great Designers had taught every one of his kind that from the six original creations, the Seraphim, they had made an entire race to serve them. The only reason the Shaitans and Jinn now looked so physically different was because of the hatred coursing through their veins.

This female didn't look so different, though. Her skin was cool to the touch, which had shaken him at his first touch of it, but other than her height, she greatly resembled those of his own realm. The females in his dimension were almost as tall as he, some even taller. This creature was over a foot shorter than he *at least*, he was sure.

As his mind came back to the situation at hand, he realized she was staring at him with almost a sad look on her face.

Curious, he asked, "Is something amiss?"

She cast her eyes downward and swallowed hard. His voice was beautifully deep and he had a strange accent, British but not. When she looked back up, there was a fatalistic dullness to her eyes, tempered with only the barest trace of hope. She cleared her throat and asked, "Am I crazy?"

The question took him by surprise and he chuckled softly, sitting down on a nearby stone retaining wall. "Why would you think you're crazy?" he asked. "You were just given proof that I'm real enough, were you not?" Even seated he was still taller than she by a head.

She approached a section of the wall a couple of feet away from him and sat facing him with one leg bent and lying on top of the wall. After a moment's hesitation, she said, "I guess I was just hoping for crazy."

He frowned at her in confusion.

She gave him a lopsided smile and explained, "Crazy, I could live with. I mean, most of the people who actually know me think I'm crazy anyway. The fact that you're real, though... That doesn't exactly leave me with many options. I mean, if history's any indicator, things don't normally end too well for people like me."

She suddenly threw her head back and heaved a great sigh, her eyes scanning the sky through the nearby barren live oak branches. It was a cool night, but the sky was clear and there weren't too many lights around to block out the view of the brightest stars.

When she looked at him again, she gave him a sad smile, saying, "A minute ago, all I was worried about was why on earth the kids in the class I had tonight thought it was okay to be such jerks to me and how I was just going to have to deal with it for the rest of the semester. Now, now all I can think is that I probably won't even be here at the end of this semester."

He looked away from her. Very intuitive, this one was. Taking a deep breath to steady himself, he glanced up at the stars through the tree's almost leafless canopy and wished for the trillionth time his beloved Designers would return. They always knew what to do. Life had been so simple when they'd been here. They gave an order and he and his brethren carried it out. Simple.

Since the blessed Great Designers had left a little over three thousand years ago, he and his brethren had strived to live as they had before, making every effort to continue with their beloved Designers' traditions. The treachery of the Shaitans and Jinn had been no surprise, as they'd begun their foolish games long before the blessed Great Designers had left. But the creatures of this realm seemed to find every avenue of mischief that could befall a being, stymieing the members of the Great Sanhedrin time and again with their problems.

He and his kind were no gods. How could they be expected to think and reason as gods?

He sighed, closing his eyes. He existed as a guardian of those in this dimension. That was what his beloved Designers expected of him. He knew this creature's fate, as apparently she knew it, too. He didn't particularly relish the thought of killing her needlessly, but he had a job to do.

He opened his eyes and looked over at her. "I need you to come with me," he said softly.

She stared at him a moment, then asked, "Where?"

"To my world," he said.

After a short pause, she asked, "Why me?"

Djibril sought for the right words. "Things will be better for you there," he finally said.

Sara stared at him a moment, then said in a matter-of-fact tone, "I have a son."

"Your son will be fine," he replied.

She shook her head, explaining, "No. You don't understand. What I mean is that I'm not going anywhere without my son."

He'd dealt with this before.

"You don't have to worry about your son. He's going to be just fine." He kept his tone even and soft, full of confidence to reassure her.

She stood and turned toward him, crossing her arms. One eyebrow hitched and she gave him a smirk. "You obviously don't have any children," she said.

He stood, as well, and approached her, trying to block out the pain caused by that particular remark. He placed his hands on her upper arms and rubbed his thumbs across her biceps in a soothing motion, energy zinging through both of them as he smiled at her and assured her, "Everything's going to be all right. Your son and all those you love will go on. They will be fine. You don't need to worry for them."

She narrowed her eyes and clenched her jaws, her voice dripping malice as she said, "I repeat, I'm not going *anywhere* without my son." With that, she turned from his grasp, grabbed her backpack and took off.

As she stalked away from him toward the parking lot, he stood staring at her retreating form, his mouth gaping open. *Maybe she is crazy*, he thought.

He pulled his first shield back around himself and moved into the air to follow her. She had almost reached her car when he suddenly appeared beside the driver's door, blocking her entrance to it. Car alarms of nearby vehicles broke the silence of the night. Sarah gasped and pulled up short, clutching the strap to her backpack with one hand and her keys in the other as she looked wide-eyed up at him. "*You* don't seem to understand," he quietly informed her. "I'm not exactly asking you to come with me. You *will* come and that is that."

Her eyes narrowed to mere slits and she let her backpack fall to the ground beside her. "Is that so?" she asked in a saccharine-sweet voice as she took a step closer to him.

He was on the verge of telling her exactly *how* so that was when all of a sudden, her fisted hand shot up to his neck. She was so small that he didn't even bother to duck or move out of the way at all. After all, she was a weakling compared to him. He realized his mistake the moment he felt the metal of a large key breaking the delicate skin on the side of his neck by his esophagus.

She'd obviously been holding the key so that the pointed end stuck out from between the fingers of her fist. The metal continued on into his neck until he felt the skin of the backs of her fingers, still in its fisted shape. Then, she turned the key, jerked it out and kneed him quickly in the groin. In a flash, she whirled around and slammed her elbow into his eye socket.

A kaleidoscope of colors flashed painfully in his head as he crumpled to the paved ground of the parking lot, moaning and clutching both his neck and his groin. Blood shot out in spurts between the fingers of the hand he held at his neck, his eye and groin throbbing with pain with each spurt of blood.

"I didn't take two semesters of self-defense for nothing, you arrogant jerk! I don't care what you are. You're not taking me without my son!" he heard her shout. With his good eye, he saw her snatch her backpack off the ground and hop into her car. His neck was healing already, but he knew he wouldn't heal fast enough for him to be able to stop her. The sound of her tires pealing out along the pavement sent a fresh form of hell through his brain to add to the wave after wave of pain that was buffeting him from the nearby cars' alarms and he could only thank the beloved Designers for the fact that her car was quickly gone and that at least *that* noise ceased.

This mission was definitely not going as planned.

Chapter 4

Sarah sped out of the parking lot, her heart thumping so hard in her chest she thought it would jump right out. He'd been waiting at her car! *Oh, god,* she thought frantically, *does he know where I live?* If he knew that, he could conceivably already be there at the house waiting for her, or worse. She pushed a little harder down on the accelerator, barely slowing at all on curves and to make turns. Her tires squealed a few times in protest, but Sarah didn't care. She had to get home to her son!

She screeched to a halt in the driveway at her house, uncaring of the black tire marks that would surely be left on the cement. She had the driver's side door open even before she got the engine turned off. Her backpack was forgotten as she rounded the back side of the car to head for the door. After unlocking it, she rushed into the house, barely taking the time to close and lock the door again before racing upstairs to her son's room. She knocked as she opened the door.

"Mom!" her son exclaimed. "I could've been *naked*!"

After taking a quick, deep breath of relief, she said, "Young'un, I've seen and touched every part of your body. Trust me, you don't have anything that would shock me." Normally, she would have laughed at his indignant modesty. Tonight, though, she'd just needed to make sure he was all right, so she'd burst into his room.

She immediately bent and picked up some dirty clothes from the floor in order to cover up for the fact that she was so freaked out. Cleaning had never been high on her son's priority list. "You finish all your homework?" she asked as she continued picking up in the room, her heart rate finally slowing a bit.

"I didn't have any," he said distractedly. His video game held more of his attention than Sarah did.

"Did you practice?" she asked. He'd been taking viola lessons for a couple of years, but it was like pulling teeth to get him to practice.

"Not yet," he said, still concentrating on the video game.

"Well, get to it, Thomas!" she instructed as she stuffed more dirty clothes she'd picked up off the floor into the clothes hamper situated at the bottom of his bed. She knew she was being a bit gruff with him, but she couldn't help it. He was everything to her. Hell, he was her *life* and, somehow, she felt as if she'd come close to losing him tonight.

He griped about having to stop playing his game, but he turned off the console and the television and went to get his instrument from downstairs. As he loped off down the hallway outside his room, Sarah heaved another sigh of relief. She'd been so afraid something would have happened to him before she'd had the chance to get home, illogical as that now seemed to her. It was just the run-in with that damned glowing man! He'd seemed so sure of himself, so certain.

There was something about him, though, that struck a chord of recognition within her.

Whatever, Sarah thought. She didn't care if she'd caught some characteristic in him that had reminded her of someone else! He was still a maniac and she wanted nothing to do with him!

For the remainder of the evening, Sarah stuck like glue to her son. She was still a little afraid he would suddenly disappear, or that she would, and she didn't want to take any chances. Bedtime was almost her undoing. As she stood outside Thomas' bedroom door, after having told him for the go-jillionth time that evening that she loved him, and turned off his light, she realized she was just plain being silly. She and Thomas were perfectly safe in the house. They had the house's alarm system *and* the two dogs downstairs. Even if someone were to get past the alarm system, those dogs heard everything and they were fiercely protective of everyone in the house. No one was gonna get into this place!

Sarah made her way to her computer.

Entry #714 – The Vision Blog – February 11 – 9:21 pm

Just a quick note to describe a horrifying incident today. I had just gotten out of my last class of the evening and was coming out the building exit, when I spotted the glowing man. It had been one of those classes... you know, the kind where it seems like everyone in the friggin' class hates your guts and is out to get you? Well, they'd pushed me *past* my limit tonight and so when I saw him standing outside the building like that, something just seemed to snap inside me.

It was only a flash... I mean, I only caught just the slightest glimpse of him before he vanished into thin air. But, I was feeling so angry and hurt and alone at that moment that I decided, crazy or not, I might as well try to communicate with the thing. I mean, if he really was there, shouldn't I find out more about him and what the hell he is and why the hell he's dogging me each and every day? So, I talked to him.

Guess what? He reappeared!

I couldn't believe it! I mean, there I was crying my eyeballs out trying to figure out what I could do to get out of this class and then he just magically shows up.

I didn't know what to say, so I introduced myself. He seemed almost afraid of me, so I kind of took things slowly. We started talking. Then, at one point, he made physical contact with me and, *whew*, let me tell you... I was blown away!

I've never experienced anything like that. It was kind of like being touched by a cattle prod, but without the pain factor, you know? The energy coming off him was enough to power all of Dallas.

I was all jazzed and getting excited about him being real and all until, all of a sudden, he starts going on about how I had to come with him and I didn't have to worry about my family or loved ones or anything. WTF?!

I got out of there as fast as I could, but he followed. He's fast, too! He even managed to beat me to my car. Yes, I know... The psycho even knew where my car was parked! He's obviously a psychotic stalker-type glowing man.

Gah! That sounds so crazy, doesn't it? Yup, folks... you've got it... this here is the diary of a schizophrenic in the early stages. Pay attention! I'm sure they'll be able to study me for years with all the stuff I'm recording here. I mean, what sane person could even make up anything like this?

Anyway, I finally managed to escape the guy and I made it home okay. I don't know if he knows where I live or not, but I'm kind of freaked out.

I wish I had a friend to talk with about all this stuff. But, I guess I'll have to manage with just recording everything here, hoping someone out there who can help me is actually listening to / reading all of this. I hope they find some way of finding me to help me soon. I feel like I'm about on my last legs, figuratively speaking.

Anyway, I'll write more later.

Sarah signed off the computer and went to bed. There was an aching emptiness in her heart as she lay in bed. The lights were off. The ceiling fan was on. She had plenty of covers on the bed. Everything was as it normally was, but she felt different.

She stared at the ceiling above her bed.

When he'd touched her face, Sarah'd felt some sort of jolt within her brain. It had been like this one time before, when she'd been in high school. She and her classmates had been sitting in French class getting yelled at by the teacher because they'd all failed a particular test he'd given them. The teacher was going over each and every question on the test to explain why the answers were what they were when all of a sudden, Sarah had understood. She'd shouted out loud, "Oh, my god!"

The French teacher had whirled around, panicked, shouting, "What? What's wrong?"

Sarah'd looked at the board, a stunned expression on her face, and said, "I under*stand*."

The French teacher had simply laughed, said, "Well, that's good," and returned to his task of explaining the answer to each question to the rest of the class. What he'd failed to realize at that moment, however, was that he'd just opened a doorway in Sarah's mind that, once opened, would never shut again. From that moment on, Sarah had never had any difficulty learning any language she'd chosen to learn. In fact, she could learn them so quickly and so competently, it stymied her professors.

The older Sarah got, the more she came to realize that she could learn anything quickly, not just foreign languages. In fact, the only thing that had ever stood in her way since that one day in high school was herself. She'd come from a working family, where both parents worked, and there wasn't much time left at the end of the day to spend with the kids. Then, when her older sister had fallen in with the wrong crowd and started doing drugs, Sarah had naturally followed. Fortunately, she'd only ever done the social thing. She'd never smoked pot or anything on her own. Eventually, she'd quit doing all of that and had had the sense to get out of that life before it was too late.

Sarah had tried to start a new life by returning to college in another state. Her folks had helped her move and she'd done okay for a while. The problem was that she was all alone and she'd had no one to talk with regarding how boring her classes were or how she just wanted someone to talk with about anything. In her old life, she'd always had friends to talk with. Sure, they'd always been high or on their way there, but it had been someone she could relate with, someone who was there to listen to her whenever she needed to talk.

But, when she'd moved, she'd made sure to move far enough away that no one knew her. The problem with that was that she didn't know anyone there, either. So, when she'd discovered a friend of hers from her old group of friends had recently moved to the same city, she'd started hanging out with him and his new group of friends and everything had gone to hell again for her.

Sarah had eventually dropped out of school, again, and had moved to another state, again, just to get herself out of the life she'd messed up, again. Once more, her parents were there to help her. They'd moved and had taken her in and given her a place to stay until she was able to get on her feet again.

By this time, Sarah was in her mid-twenties.

She'd found a job in retail and had worked long hours. She got to know some of her co-workers and started hanging out with them. Once more, she'd fallen in with the wrong crowd. In the end, it was a miracle that had saved her.

Unbeknownst to most people, Sarah had been born and raised in a small, one-stop-light town in Georgia. Her biological father had been a strict southern Baptist who'd always wanted to be a minister, but who'd gotten his high school sweetheart pregnant and had had to give up on those dreams even before graduating high school. He and his teenage bride had made the classic mistake of deciding to have another baby, even though they had no money and no future.

Then, a third had appeared out of nowhere and the new American Family had been formed. Husband blamed the wife for all the successes he'd never have. Wife blamed the husband for never seeming able to keep a job because he was always off attempting some new scheme to get rich quick. Kids got to grow up moving from one place to another, never staying in one spot too long, never getting new clothes or healthcare unless someone else paid for it, and that was only under dire circumstances.

But, Sarah *had* been raised with the old-fashioned values one could expect from the Deep South, so when she'd found out she was pregnant, she'd done everything she could to keep it from her family because she'd felt so ashamed. How could she tell them? She was alone, unmarried, still living with her parents, no real job… and pregnant.

That little bundle, when it was finally delivered though, became her saving grace. Oh, she didn't realize it at first, no. But, as the years had gone by, Thomas had turned out to be the one thing in Sarah's life that she knew was right. He loved her unconditionally and she took whatever crappy job she had to in order to make sure he had the best of everything at all times. She made sure he was enrolled in the best schools, that he was able to attend his friends' birthday parties with gifts for them, that he got to participate in extracurricular activities with his friends like sports and orchestra… all the things she'd never gotten to do growing up.

So, because of Thomas, she'd finally grown up. She'd managed to go back to school, to a community college, and had even managed after a year and a half to get into a local university. She was on a degree plan and was doing quite well.

Once again, though, she found herself with no friends. But, she was an adult now. Sarah felt the weight of that thought settle like a ton of bricks onto her shoulders as she lay there. She sighed and closed her eyes.

There was a battle raging all around. Men, dressed in robes and strange leather and metal bindings, traversed the desert in every direction as the war raged. Fallen soldiers littered the sandy floor. Sarah looked around, curious but not afraid. She spotted a familiar face and narrowed her eyes in concentration.

"Brother!" the man cried out to another about ten yards away from where he stood. "We must defeat the heathen Arabs and take the city!"

"Don't worry, Djibril," the other man said. "Mecca will fall to Mohammed and his followers this day, as is the will of the blessed Great Designers."

Sarah couldn't see the face of the man who'd last spoken, but there was something in his voice that sparked her interest. The first man, Djibril, was clearly the glowing man who'd been stalking her recently, his energy brightly flowing in a warm, steady pulse. The other man glowed, as well, though his energy was of a much higher order, it seemed. The heat he gave off pulsed out in great waves that extended far beyond his body.

Sarah wondered what he looked like. As he struggled with a puny human soldier, she could only marvel at how broad and thickly-muscled his body was. He was tall, with long, black hair. He fought well and was soon standing over the prone form of the soldier. As his brother approached him, the man turned and Sarah saw his face.

She gasped aloud, waking herself from the dream. She gulped in great gasps of air. She was hyperventilating. She half-sat up on the bed, grabbing the side of the mattress for stability. As she continued heaving for air, her lungs greatly expanding and then deflating, expanding and deflating, her mind raced. She'd seen him before. Not the one called Djibril, but the other one, the dark-haired one. She remembered him.

Suddenly, she couldn't sit still. She jumped off of bed and turned on the bedside lamp.

Could this be a trick? she wondered. *Could this Djibril have put these images in her mind, somehow?* Her blog was out there for anyone to read and, reality wise, the man did glow and was able to appear and disappear in thin air. Maybe he had psychic powers, too.

But, what if it wasn't a trick? What if what she'd seen had been another vision?

Sarah thought about that as she stood in the middle of her room. She went back over all of it, the visions, the encounters with Djibril. And then she realized, when Djibril had touched her, he seemed to have opened another doorway in her mind, like her French teacher had in high school. He must have done.

Sarah needed to know.

She decided on a course of action. It was dangerous, she acknowledged, but she had to find out if what she'd seen was real or not. She didn't know what she was doing, but if she was right about this, it wouldn't matter what method she used.

It was the middle of the night. Everyone else in the house was asleep. And, here she stood, attempting the craziest thing she'd ever done before. Sarah didn't even hesitate. The excitement and cautious anticipation coursing through her caused her voice to shake a little as she said a single word as clearly as possible, "Djibril."

His form suddenly materialized before her. She gasped, still shaken by the fact that he was able to do such things. The light beside her immediately went out, the light bulb shattering, thin pieces of glass scattering about the table and carpet. He was still clearly visible in the darkness, though, from an innate glow coming from his body.

He held his hands out toward her, palms up, and said in a soft whisper, "Sarah."

Djibril had been stunned when he'd heard her call! She was not a Seraph. How had she known his name? His curiosity over the creature had grown exponentially in the space of that one word, his name, uttered on the lips of this seemingly innocent being. He *had* to get her back to his realm. She was proving daily how much she didn't belong in this dimension. Djibril knew she was much too dangerous to be allowed to continue on here.

He took a step toward her, still holding his hands out in supplication. "You don't belong here, Sarah," he said. "You've never belonged here with them. You know that."

Sarah kept her gaze on him, but her eyes narrowed. "What do you mean?" she asked.

He took another step toward her. "You aren't like them, Sarah. You're nothing like them. They couldn't even begin to understand you. Can't you feel it?" He took another step and lowered his hands. "They go about their simple lives believing whatever they're told and never questioning anything." He stepped to the side and leaned a hip against her small dresser. "You aren't like that, are you, Sarah?"

She turned her head a bit to the side away from him, her eyes still trained on him. She suddenly felt a bit unsure of herself. He was between her and the door, though a little off to the side. As a slight chill raced down her spine, she took a step toward the door. The man didn't move to follow her. She took another step in that direction. He merely turned more fully toward her, ever watchful.

She paused.

"I am not your enemy, Sarah, as I said before," he repeated softly.

A thought suddenly occurred to Sarah and she gathered what courage she could muster. She cautiously took a step toward him, just one, and asked, "Are you from another dimension?"

The man gasped and straightened immediately from his resting position against the dresser. "How did you..." He seemed at a loss for words. He stood staring in disbelief at her.

Sarah stepped a bit closer to him, her fear and anger of earlier disappearing, replaced completely with fascination. He *was* one of the ones from her visions that had been taken initially by those other beings and transformed into something here on Earth. She'd been right. They still existed, just in another dimension!

A wave of excitement rushed through Sarah. All this time, and she'd gotten to re-live much of that time in her visions, and she was suddenly being presented with one of the beings she had been searching for in each and every lifetime she'd spent on this planet. He wasn't the one she sought, she knew, but she also knew he was brother to the one she *did* seek.

He still stared dumbfounded at her, not moving.

"You *are* from another dimension, aren't you?" she asked, a slight smile bowing her lips.

He blinked and nodded his head once. "D-Did the blessed Great Designers send you here?" he asked.

Sarah tilted her head slightly to one side, narrowing her eyes. She'd heard those words in her dream. "Is that what they're called by your kind?" she asked.

His eyes widened. He studied her as if he couldn't believe what he was seeing.

Sarah looked him up and down during his continued silence. She couldn't believe her fortune! All this time, all this wasted, useless time she'd spent being so concerned with trivial things. Who cared about stupid kids in a stupid class? Who cared about what other kids thought about her son? Who cared about anything other than this one creature and the other one like him?

So many times in her life, Sarah had watched other people finding happiness, seeming to have no problems finding someone they connected with on such a deep level that they seemed to be as one. Sarah had never met *anyone* she connected with, not even her son's father. There'd always been something missing.

Now, here with this creature, Sarah knew she was finally getting the chance to find the one that had been taken from her by these so-called designers. All she had to do was to find some way of getting him to take her with him to his dimension so she could search for her other half. Realization dawned a second after this thought. He'd already asked her to come with him! And, what had she done? She'd nearly killed him and run off, that's what.

Well, she was going to fix matters right now. Out of all the lifetimes she'd spent on this miserable planet, always alone, now she was being presented with the perfect opportunity to find what she'd been looking for throughout all of them. She was going to make this work, even if she had to force her way into his dimension.

She took another step toward him and extended her hand. "We haven't been properly introduced. I'm Sarah, as you already know."

He hesitated, then took her hand and shook it. "I am Djibril, as *you* already know, somehow."

"Djibril?" she asked, still holding his hand. "That's an interesting name." It felt so good to have his energies flowing into her hand and arm again.

"You may know me as Gabriel," he said.

Sarah's eyes narrowed. "Like the angel?" she asked.

He smiled and finally broke their physical connection, taking his hand back. "The one and only," he agreed.

"Wow," she remarked, her eyes wide. This was too weird. *So this is what angels are,* she thought. It was no wonder humans worshipped them. One only had to be in the same vicinity as one of them to be able to feel them. Also, the whole glowing thing would seem to fit with everything she'd ever been taught about them, though she certainly was no expert. All she remembered was that they were supposed to have wings and halos and be benevolent and all. But, this Gabriel didn't have wings or a halo. *Strikes one and two for the preacher,* she thought.

Djibril watched her. He was still too floored to react much to anything. *What's going on here,* he wondered incredulously. She knew of the blessed Great Designers! How could that be possible? Yes, she glowed with the radiance of far more soul-energy than any he'd ever encountered in her realm. Yes, she knew of the existence of beings in another dimension. Did that mean the blessed Great Designers had sent her to them to alert Djibril and his brethren of their eminent return? Was she some sort of new messenger they'd created?

Then, another thought occurred to him, an awful, terrible, horrifying thought. What if his beloved Designers had been trying to communicate with him and his brethren all this time by sending this new type of messenger to them? After all, the blessed Great Designers couldn't cross the barrier into the Angelic realm without their assistance, so it would be logical to think any new messengers created would be sent here to this realm to await contact with one of Djibril's kind.

It was already past the time of his beloved Designers' promised return. Had the fact that Djibril and his brethren had never taken the time to get to know one of these creatures, had never brought one of them into their realm for any length of time, made it so that the blessed Great Designers wouldn't or even *couldn't* return?

Djibril couldn't think. This was too much to take in. Surely, he and his brethren couldn't be held responsible by anyone for their lack of vision. After all, the blessed Great Designers had mentioned nothing of this plan when they'd left those thousands of years ago. They'd simply promised to return around three thousand Earth years from the date of their departure.

Djibril swallowed a lump in his throat. Well, he wasn't going to allow anything on his part to keep his beloved designers from returning, if he could help it. He may not have been intelligent enough to reason out their intentions before, but he thought he understood what they meant him to do now and he was going to do everything he could to ensure it was done.

Sarah's thoughts raced. She still wasn't going anywhere without her son, but she had to think of some way to convince this Djibril, or Gabriel, or whatever his name was, to take her *and* Thomas with him back to his dimension. For a second, the realization of just how insane all of this was flashed through her mind and she almost laughed aloud. *Who would believe any of this*, she wondered. All Sarah knew was that, deep down inside, she felt this was the right thing to do.

She took a deep breath and said in a rush, "I wish to go with you, now, but my son has to go with us, too." She waited tensely for his reaction to this announcement. Maybe Gabriel, or whatever his name was, would be able to help her think up something to tell her folks? She hoped so. Her brain was on hyper-drive right now and she still had nothing.

He stared intently at her, considering, then asked, "You'll go with me?"

"As long as my son, Thomas, can go too," she repeated.

He quickly looked her up and down, then nodded once, as was his habit, she noticed.

"He's asleep, right now," she said.

"All the better," he said quietly. "He wouldn't like the journey through the rift in the barrier between realms." He moved toward the door of the room, stopping when he got to it and turning back toward her, waiting.

Sarah didn't know what to do. She'd expected some sort of fight or argument, anything to keep Thomas from being allowed to accompany them on the trip to his dimension. He'd caved almost immediately, though. *What could that mean,* she wondered. But, whatever it meant, she wasn't going to waste time questioning it. She wanted this, no... she needed this.

So, she quickly preceded him through the doorway and led him through the darkened upstairs part of the house to her son's room. He looked almost afraid as he approached the bed where Thomas slept. Sarah wondered why an angel would ever be afraid of a child. But, she didn't say anything about it. She wanted Gabriel to take her and Thomas with him to his dimension and she didn't want to say or do anything that might ruin her chances.

"Gabriel," she whispered, "This is my son, Thomas."

Gabriel looked unbelievably uncomfortable. There was something very strange about the way he almost seemed to cringe back away from the sleeping boy.

"How are we going to do this?" she asked, not sure how they were going to be able to get him out of bed, dressed and into her car without waking him.

Gabriel motioned for her to follow him as he returned to the hallway just outside Thomas' room. Sarah silently followed, quietly closing the door behind her. Gabriel stopped and was silent a moment. Then, he said in a low voice, "I can make sure he stays asleep throughout the entire journey. That way he won't experience anything out of the ordinary and he can just awaken when we reach our destination."

Sarah asked, "Is that one of your talents, as an angel I mean?"

"It's one of the many things I can do, yes," he said with a smile.

"So, you're thinking we should leave tonight?" she asked.

"I was thinking we could leave this very moment, if you don't mind," Gabriel explained.

Sarah hadn't thought of this. It was the middle of the night. What could she tell her parents? They were asleep downstairs. She couldn't just up and leave without giving them some sort of explanation.

She paced a little farther down the hallway, away from Thomas' room, then turned and paced back halfway. She was wracking her brain for some acceptable explanation she could give her folks, but nothing was coming to mind. *Um, Mom and Dad, you won't believe this, but I'm going away with an angel named Gabriel and I'm going to take Thomas with me.* Right! She'd be locked up in some psych ward before she could even blink.

Gabriel was quietly watching her as she paced. When she finally stopped, she was directly in front of him and, when she looked up at him, he raised a single eyebrow in question.

"What about my parents?" she asked. "What can I say to them?"

"Why must you say anything?" Gabriel asked.

"They're my parents," she said, tears clogging her voice. "I can't just go off and leave without telling them *something*, especially not with Thomas!" she exclaimed in a whispered voice. "I have to tell them something or they'll worry themselves to death."

She chewed on her lower lip, a habit Gabriel had noticed she had whenever she was nervous about something. Sarah couldn't just go off and leave with no explanation. She loved her family too much for that. She wasn't going to push things and ask if they could go with her, but she had to think of something.

"Perhaps, I can help?" he suggested.

"How?" she asked doubtfully. She'd happily follow along with any plan he had, but at the moment she couldn't think of a single way out of this.

"I've noticed you have two animals in the house," he said distractedly.

"Yes, our dogs," she answered.

He thought silently for a moment, then said, "I won't be able to go down with you, but I can probably control their minds from here."

Sarah frowned. "The dogs'?" she asked dubiously.

"No, the minds of your parents," he explained.

Sarah cocked an eyebrow. "Then, what?" she asked.

"You go down and take a look at them. I'll stay here and ensure they don't awaken," Gabriel explained.

"Take a look at them?" she exclaimed in a strangled whisper. "I can't wake them up and talk to them?"

"The news of your son and you leaving would be very distressing, yes?" he asked calmly.

"Yes, but...," Sarah blurted.

Gabriel stepped closer and put his hands on her arms, as he had done before, rubbing his thumbs over her biceps, allowing the energy to zing from his body to hers and vice versa. "I'll implant a plausible explanation for your absences from their daily lives which should keep them from worrying," he explained. "Don't worry. This really will be best."

Sarah hesitated, then bowed her head in resignation. She didn't want to leave her parents without so much as waking them to tell them good-bye, but she had to go. She knew this. Her soul, itself, ached for this opportunity.

"Okay," she said at last, breaking the contact with his hands and turning for the stairs. She paused at the top, turning back to him, saying quietly, "I'll be back in a minute. I just want to look in on them before we go."

Gabriel nodded and Sarah turned and made her way down the stairs.

The two dogs met her at the foot of the stairs and, after she'd closed the safety gate there, they followed her into her parents' bedroom. She rubbed each dog's head as she stood staring at her parents' sleeping forms on the king-sized bed in the center of the room. Tears fell from her eyes as she thought of all the times they had rescued her from one disaster or another. How could she now go off and leave them all alone without even telling them good-bye? They would be so upset if they ever found out she'd taken Thomas without saying anything to them.

Sarah cautiously approached the bed, first on one side and then on the other. She bent and kissed the cheek of each one of her parents in turn. She realized she was just going to have to trust Gabriel when he said he would be able to implant an explanation into their minds as to why she and Thomas were no longer around. She gave a last look at the two sleeping people on the bed and then left the room. At the bottom of the stairs, she turned back to the two dogs, who'd followed her back out of her parents' bedroom, and bent to pat each one in turn on the head. "You two look out for them, okay," she said to the two. "Be good boys."

Then she turned, passed through the safety gate, reattached it, and made her way back upstairs to her son's room. Gabriel was waiting for her just outside the door to Thomas' room. His head was bowed and his eyes closed, as if he were praying. After a moment, he took a deep breath and, raising his head, he opened his eyes and looked at her. "All is well," he said with a slight smile.

He seemed to be waiting for something, so Sarah said, "Oh. Good. I mean, I guess we're ready, then."

Gabriel nodded once, then held his hand out toward the door to Thomas' room. Sarah walked past him, opened the door, and preceded him into the room. Gabriel closed the door behind him, then crossed the room over to the bed. He bent and carefully picked up the sleeping boy, then turned and stepped right up next to Sarah.

"Hold on tightly to my arm," he said. Sarah grabbed onto his upper right arm with both hands, her stomach doing little flip-flopping things with nervousness.

Gabriel closed his eyes in concentration.

Chapter 5

Sarah felt, rather than saw, something wrapping around them. It started from their feet, wrapping like broad swaths of leather around their ankles and then upward. It wasn't tight, but it was close enough to plaster their clothes to their bodies. Her hair was soon pressed against her neck and the sides of her face. Once this layer of the invisible blanket of leather-like film had fully encompassed them, Sarah felt another begin its upward journey around them, then another and another until a total of six layers of the invisible stuff surrounded them.

Sarah turned as best she could within their cocoon to look at Gabriel. She wanted to ask what was going on, but she didn't want to break his concentration. Hell, she didn't even know if she could talk while surrounded by the invisible stuff. It felt warm, almost like another layer of skin. It moved and seemed almost to breathe.

Sarah gasped as the three of them suddenly rose as one off the floor of the bedroom and then somehow managed to pass harmlessly through the ceiling of the house and on out into the crisp night air. Their little unit slowly rose a great distance above the house and Sarah watched as the house, their street and then the whole neighborhood got smaller and smaller. Soon, all of Dallas was but a blanket of lights spread on a dark canopy below them. Sarah's breath clouded before her face as they stopped for a moment, but she didn't feel the cold.

"Here we go," Gabriel said and their little unit of three beings immediately shot forward over the land.

They headed westward at an incredible speed. Sarah marveled at the rate at which the American landscape passed below them. They were actually flying, but there was no sound, no machinery she could detect making this possible. Thomas, she noted, slept on as Gabriel cradled him gently in his strong arms. Again, Sarah wanted to ask questions, but again, she kept them to herself.

The Great Rocky Mountains rose before them below and then passed underneath. Soon the California coast came into view. Then, there was just a vast stretch of ocean as far as the eye could see. Hawaii came and went, other island chains as well, then came the eastern coast of Asia with all its island chains. They were chasing the sun and catching up on it very quickly. Sarah wondered where they were headed. Was there some portal to the other dimension in some other country? Was there a spaceship hidden somewhere there? She almost laughed at this thought, but thought better about it and decided to keep quiet.

So many remarkable lands passed beneath them, though only occasionally were there great cities. For the most part now, there was just open land with sparse population. Sarah saw few lights below as she studied the landscape passing by. Occasional mountain ranges would come into view, some much taller than the Rockies. Finally, their progress seemed to slow. She found that they were descending slightly for the first time. There was a mountain top looming in the distance. That seemed to be where they were headed.

"Sarah," Gabriel softly said, catching her attention.

"Yes?" she asked.

He hesitated for a moment, then said, "This next part will not be very pleasant for you. If you'd like, I can induce a sleep state in you in order to spare you."

"You mean you want to put me to sleep like Thomas for the rest of the way?" she asked.

"It would be less painful of an experience for you if I were to do so, yes," he explained.

Sarah thought for a moment. If she were asleep for the remainder of the journey, she would miss everything. He could do whatever he wanted while she slept. She had no idea what that might entail, either. She finally looked up at him and said with firm resolve, "No. I don't want to miss any of it. Please, keep going."

His eyes narrowed slightly, but then he nodded his usual one nod and they moved closer to the mountain top. Suddenly, there was a swirling mass of electricity enveloping them, with little sparks flying and zinging all over the place, rather like a sparkler on the Fourth of July. The little sparks hurt when they hit Sarah's skin, but it was not much worse than an actual sparkler, so she merely brushed them away and rubbed at her skin whenever and wherever they hit her. She took a peek at Thomas to ensure he remained unharmed. He merely slept on.

Sarah was busy watching the swirling bits of electricity and so didn't immediately notice when the landscape below them changed. However, when the outline of an enormous city unlike anything she had ever seen before rose before them on the horizon, she knew without a doubt she was no longer in Kansas, so to speak. The buildings of the city were phenomenally-sized erections, and the architecture. It was indescribable. There was such attention to detail and so much decoration on the buildings and structures that she figured it must have taken millennia to erect such magnificent edifices.

Then, she saw the people...

They were all glowing, like Gabriel glowed, though on a much smaller scale of intensity. Most had long hair in the style he wore, though there were some who sported shorter styles. Their mode of dress was greatly varied and Sarah wondered if some of them had gotten their clothing from the human realm. People were wearing togas, jeans and t-shirts, business suits, etc. Like in any large city, there seemed to be a large population and each person seemed to be rushing from one place to another.

One thing Sarah noticed as being very different was that there were no automobiles on the streets. People moved about in strange-looking round machines that flew silently through the air wherever they were going. Of course, there were plenty of people walking along the streets below.

There was noise filtering up through the air to Sarah as her little trio made its way through the web-work of tall buildings. The buildings were as varied as the glowing people's clothing, with some being made of steel and glass and others of concrete and still others of stone. It was like Egypt meets New York City via Ancient Rome and Greece. The city was magnificent and Sarah's eyes were all agog as the images passed below.

All too soon, her little trio slowed and headed in for a landing at one of the buildings. It was one of the Ancient Greek or Roman buildings made of marble. Five layers of stairs led up to a columned façade. The columns were about three yards in width and ten in height. The doorway was gigantic with massive doors that looked to be made of copper. The doors were standing open with people continuously entering and exiting the building.

Their trio touched down on the top step just before the line of columns and Sarah felt the layers of the invisible warmth that had surrounded them slipping away. It appeared their arrival did not go unnoticed by the other people once the invisible layers were gone, for there were sudden audible gasps and exclamations of surprise and shock emitted by those closest to their little trio. Gabriel took no notice of this as he stalked forward into the great building.

Sarah kept her hands clamped onto his arm. She wasn't so sure she was welcome in this land, judging from some of the looks the other people had been shooting her once the leather-like coverings were gone.

Gabriel walked quickly toward some unknown destination within the building and Sarah nearly had to run in order to keep pace with him. She barely had time to look around, though she did manage to catch glimpses of great tapestries and beautiful paintings adorning the walls of the enormous hallway. There were so many rooms within the building she was sure it would take a lifetime to visit each and every one of them. Some of the rooms' doors were open. Some were closed. There were enormous staircases leading to other floors where she caught glimpses of more rooms with more doors.

Sarah noticed the stares of more and more people as she raced forward with Gabriel. There were gasps whenever she passed and instant conversations started. Gabriel seemed unfazed by the stares and comments. Sarah just hoped they'd get to wherever they were going quickly. She didn't like feeling like this, like she was not welcome. As if he'd read her thoughts, Gabriel finally paused before a closed doorway and knocked. Upon a muffled command from inside, he carefully adjusted his grip on Thomas' still-sleeping form and reached to open the door. He entered half-way, but then turned and waited for Sarah to enter.

She cautiously entered the room, noting there were tall, glass-paned windows that stretched from floor to ceiling along the far side of the room. There, behind a desk just at the center of that particular wall, stood a man with bright red hair and even brighter blue eyes. On the closer side of the desk was another man, this one with light brown hair and light blue eyes. They were both about the same height as Gabriel and glowed just as brightly as he.

Gabriel quietly closed the door and walked over to a sofa near a fireplace Sarah hadn't noticed, where he laid Thomas' sleeping form down. He then turned and approached Sarah.

The man behind the desk barked out something in a language Sarah didn't recognize and Gabriel immediately requested, "Please, speak in English so that everyone may participate."

"What is the meaning of this?" the man behind the desk asked in a gruff voice, presumably reiterating that which he'd already demanded, his eyes narrowed in suspicion. "You were supposed to take her to my home to be dealt with."

Gabriel stepped forward, explaining, "There has been a new development, my brothers. We must call for Mikhail immediately."

The man in front of the desk immediately stepped to the side and tugged on a slender tapestry hanging there with a large tassel at the bottom of it. It was like a bell-pull, Sarah realized. Almost immediately, what Sarah could only assume was a servant stepped into the room. He was given the order to contact the one Gabriel had called Mikhail to request his presence at the meeting immediately. The young man scarce gave any notice to Sarah or Thomas before rushing from the room to complete his task. Sarah was glad. The less people who knew of their presence in the city, the better, she figured.

She wondered what was going to happen to them now. She hadn't really thought about any of this when she'd planned her visit to this new dimension. All she'd thought about was getting the chance to meet the one she believed to be her other half. She'd seen him in her dream vision. Whatever was going to happen, though, was going to happen. She knew she would deal with whatever it was as best she could.

The three males in the room studied her. They were all so tall and forbidding, she almost shrank in fear of them, swallowing a lump in her throat instead as she fought her nerves. It was amazing how beautiful they each were. It didn't matter what color their hair was or that their eyes were all that bright, bright blue color. She could certainly understand why humans had believed them to be angels, though. Their skin was flawless, their teeth white, and their eyes were as bright as could be. And, the constant glow of energy emitting from them made them seem ethereal.

The silence stretched on and Sarah was not dealing well with being the object of such pointed study. She cleared her throat and was on the verge of asking for a glass of water when the door behind her suddenly opened. A whoosh of air was knocked from her lungs by the energy she suddenly felt in the room and she began shaking violently. She dared not turn around. Whatever, or whomever, was behind her was more than she thought she'd be able to deal with. She could feel him. She suddenly knew it was a "him" behind her. She didn't know how she knew, she simply knew.

There was a tense moment of silence, then all was chaos. One moment, Sarah had been standing in the center of the room with the three men in front of her. The next moment, a great arm had banded her waist and dragged her off to the side of the room amid chaotic shouts. Sarah couldn't see much of anything because of the giant man holding her. He was shielding her from the others in the room, his back to her. His right hand was still reaching back to hold her, but he faced the others as he growled something loudly at them in a deep, booming voice.

"Mikhail, wait," Gabriel said, taking a step toward the man and holding out his hand.

Mikhail shouted, "You will not harm her!"

The other three all started shouting at once and Sarah could not make out any individual words, but she didn't care about that. She ran ravenous hands up the spine of the man standing in front of her. Here was the one she'd sought lifetime after lifetime. She could feel it. The realization that there was no more fear inside her, only a serene sense of security and love... and *need*, hit her like a ton of bricks and she reached out to grab onto the one responsible for it. She spread her hands out to cover his shoulder blades, then down the sides of his back and back up. Her mouth hung open as she all but panted with the exuberance of finally knowing that which she'd needed her entire existence, and it *was* a physical need.

Her eyes closed as she leaned forward and sniffed at his back. His scent was divine. Oddly, he smelled of cedar and... sassafras, as if he had recently been outdoors working with those woods. She loved the smell of each. She rubbed her cheek against his back. She heard him gasp as she did this, but it didn't matter. She took another whiff of his scent, feeling her toes curl with delight. She could feel, as well as hear, him growling at the others like some kind of animal. They were all still shouting at each other. He still held her with his hand on her right hip.

Suddenly, she remembered Thomas and she snapped out of her obsession with the feel and smell of her protector. She took his hand and rounded to his side. He immediately stopped growling and looked down at her. She took her first look upon her other half's face full-on from the perspective of this physical realm. It was the same face she'd seen in her dream.

He was beautiful, simply put. He was as tall as the others, well over a foot taller than Sarah, with sun-kissed skin, long black hair that hung in a glossy sheen over one shoulder. His mouth was wide, his nose hawkish, his ice-blue eyes topped by straight slashes of black brows below a broad forehead. His bone structure was perfect, for lack of a better description. Concern for her shone clearly in his eyes and she smiled up at him.

Sarah lifted a hand to touch his cheek, then she looked over to where Thomas lay on the sofa on the other side of the room. Her man, for that was the only way she could think of him now, turned his head to see what had distracted her. He blinked a couple of times, then turned back to her and, taking her other hand from his face, walked with her over to the sleeping boy. Sarah noticed he moved to position himself between her and the others as they crossed the room. She wondered why he would feel a need to protect her from them, especially from Gabriel.

Gabriel took a step toward them, but halted at her man's immediate tension-filled growl. Sarah leaned down to touch Thomas' face. He seemed to be all right, merely asleep. She straightened and sidled up to her man again, grasping his large hand once more with both of hers.

"Mikhail," Gabriel said. He spoke softly, not daring to move. "I will not allow her to be harmed."

"What?" the other two men exclaimed. One had sounded confused, but the red haired one had sounded furious.

"You must hear me out, my brothers," Gabriel continued. "There is much more to this situation than we ever dreamed possible. Now that everyone's here, if we'll all calm down, I'll explain everything."

"You're mad!" was Azra'il's response when Gabriel finally finished speaking.

Gabriel had informed his brothers of his suspicions that Sarah was some sort of link, the latest model to be more precise, meant to be used by the Seraphim to communicate with the blessed Great Designers. He saw this as a sign that their beloved Designers were on their way back and that their return was imminent.

Israfil denied having received any indications the blessed Great Designers were near to returning, saying, "They told us they would contact me to let us know when they were returning. They said there would be a sign and that I would know it when I saw it." He looked over at Sarah, who was now seated beside Mikhail on another sofa. Mikhail's arm was protectively around her shoulders and the two were holding hands. Israfil stared intensely at Sarah, a slight frown marring his beautiful countenance for a moment before some realization dawned on him. "I could be mistaken," Israfil said dubiously, his face once again a mask of boredom. "However, she doesn't look like anything other than a human with too much soul-energy. If she's some sort of sign, I don't get it."

Gabriel sighed in frustration. "She's the conduit," he said, exasperated. "Listen. The blessed Great Designers could not travel into our dimension without our aid when they were here, right?" When the others nodded, he continued, "So, it's conceivable they wouldn't be able to send any sort of signal to us in this dimension. The fact that she was born with so much soul-energy has to be some sort of sign. It has to mean something special, don't you think? We've never encountered one such as she before and the fact that she even knows about the Designers seals it for me." He pointed toward Sarah and solemnly declared, "I believe this creature to be the work of our beloved Designers and I will defend her life to my last breath."

Israfil let out a long, low whistle indicating his surprise at the oath. Azra'il seemed too shocked to speak. Gabriel had defended whole cities before, along with defending certain individuals as well. He was known for standing up for his principles, even before the blessed Great Designers, defying their wishes on numerous occasions when he thought their judgments to be contrary to those lofty principles.

Azra'il knew Gabriel would do as he'd said, that he'd protect this human female to his dying breath. Azra'il also knew, as he threw his gaze over to Mikhail, that there would be no reasoning with either of his Seraphim brethren on this issue.

He pursed his lips as he took a seat behind the desk. He leaned his weight upon his elbows on the desk, steepling his fingers and propping his chin atop them. He regarded Gabriel and asked, "Well, what's to become of her, then? She cannot be allowed to return to her world. If what you've surmised is true, she would make an absolute mess of things in no time at all."

Israfil gruffed, "Huh! Like they're not messed up enough as it is? All I hear about each day at court is how the Shaitans have invaded and influenced this part of the human world or that Jinn are causing chaos in this other part. What harm would it do to send her back?"

"She's not being sent back!" Mikhail nearly shouted as he stood and maneuvered himself to stand protectively before Sarah once more. "She stays with me and I'll kill *anyone* who dares to try and take her from me."

The three other men regarded him in shock. Mikhail was the strongest of all of them. He was the most highly-ranked among the Seraphim and none had ever opposed him. To do so would be tantamount to standing against the blessed Great Designers and none other than Gabriel and Mikhail himself had ever done that.

Gabriel approached him slowly. "My brother," he said calmly. "I promise you, no harm will come to her and no one," he turned his head to glare at Azra'il, "will attempt to take her from you." He turned his gaze back to Mikhail. "I don't believe it would be in our best interests to send her back to her realm," he continued. "I agree that she should stay here. If you wish to house her within your home, I have no problem with that." He turned to his other two brothers and asked, "Is it agreed?"

Israfil studied Mikhail thoughtfully for a moment, a strange expression flitting across his face again, and then shrugged and said, "I don't see why she couldn't stay. If Mikhail wants her, then so be it."

All eyes turned toward Azra'il. He sat as before with his fingers steepled beneath his chin. His eyes locked onto Sarah as she sat on the sofa. He had no love for humans, this was true. It wasn't his purpose. He was here to help guide their souls away from their physical bodies, if they needed it, when their time came. His beloved Designers had decreed this as his duty when they'd first made themselves known to the Seraphim. Azra'il had taken his duty very seriously, no matter how the human world saw him. He knew the creature before him would probably regard him as some kind of monster, not as one of the beautiful creations of the blessed Great Designers. Azra'il didn't care about that, though. What bothered him about the creature was that he couldn't tell when her time was.

When Azra'il looked at a human, he usually saw a lifespan spread before him with each one. There was the pesky string of soul-energy that stretched from the human's body up into some other dimension he couldn't see and he knew that each time when he guided someone's soul from its human life, that soul-energy retreated to that other dimension. Some souls he had sensed on multiple occasions, so Azra'il believed the same souls sometimes returned to the human dimension time and time again, being born and reborn, life after life, their pitiful little human life spans invariably linked with each physical body. Azra'il always knew which to help along the way toward leaving their little shells and which would be around for a while.

But, this human was different. The string of soul-energy stretching from within her human form was only a tenuous thing, barely noticeable to him. She glowed with soul-energy to such a degree that Azra'il would almost swear she was part Seraph, if he didn't know better. Among the Seraphim, he was the only one who could sense these soul-energy strings, so he knew she really was of no relation to the Seraphim, because she did at least have one, tenuous though it may be. This made him wonder.

Why would Mikhail react so violently to protect this female human? He studied his brother and was amazed to realize that Mikhail's soul-energy was now somehow different. Mikhail had always been stronger than any of his brethren, but there was some greater gulf emerging between him and the other three Seraphim in the room that suddenly seemed a dangerous thing. The gulf was widening even as he watched. Azra'il wondered what this could mean.

He didn't know the answer to that question and he would not try to find it at this time. Mikhail was so very obviously not going to be cooperative this night, so Azra'il sat back and cautiously said, "I will agree to your terms, for the now. As long as she is kept out of public view and causes no trouble within Seraphim City, she will be allowed to cohabitate with Mikhail until the Great Sanhedrin can determine what's to become of her."

All eyes turned back to Mikhail, who seemed to visibly relax before them. He gave one quick nod of thanks and turned to retrieve Sarah and the boy from the sofa. He bade the other three men good evening as he made his way out of the room carrying the still-sleeping form of Thomas and waiting as Sarah reached to close the door behind them.

Mikhail stood staring out the window of his study, watching the two humans in the dimly lit secluded gardens of his estate. Mother and son were seated at one of the decorative benches placed by a walkway that wound throughout the gardens. She'd been talking with the boy for a while now, and Mikhail wondered what was taking so long. He didn't like being even this far away from her and he bristled as a wave of what he could only describe as jealousy washed over him. He'd never before experienced this particular emotion, but he'd sensed it in others, in the Shaitans, in Jinn, and in humans.

He reluctantly turned away from the window, returning to the desk in a corner of the room. Gabriel sat on the opposite side of the desk, facing him.

"I don't know," Mikhail said, frustration clearly evident in his tone and a great sigh escaping his lungs. "I just don't know." He sat and covered his face with his hands. After a moment, he plopped his hands down onto his desk and continued, "All I know is I walked into the room, and all of a sudden I simply knew I had to protect her. I knew she was mine, that she was my duty, that everything about her was my duty and that nothing else on this planet mattered anymore. Everything I'd ever thought, ever felt, ever even dreamed no longer existed. There was only her."

Gabriel narrowed his eyes. Mikhail was talking of this human as if she was something he... loved. A quick shiver engulfed Gabriel at the thought. Sacrilege! Such thoughts were forbidden, let alone the actual act of a Seraph *loving* a human. There was a law and it was unbreakable. Another shiver streaked down Gabriel's spine, leaving him shaken and confused.

Mikhail looked beseechingly at his brother. "I know, brother," he said quietly, as if he'd heard Gabriel's frightening thoughts.

Gabriel watched as Mikhail stood and returned to the window to stare out it again.

"I feel as if I'm lost and she's the only beacon of light in a vast blackness," Mikhail said. "I can feel her pulling at me, even now. I feel actual distress at being this far away from her physically." He looked back over to Gabriel, pain clearly etched on his features. After a second, he whispered, "Brother, I'm frightened."

Gabriel was floored!

Mikhail was the strongest of all Seraphim. He was the highest in rank, the most courageous, the most trusted by the blessed Great Designers. And now, this... Gabriel didn't know what to think, what to feel. His brother obviously was in great pain, but Gabriel didn't know how to help.

"Maybe," he began, getting up to pace a bit as he thought, "we can talk with her, get to know her in order to figure out if she really is some sort of link to the beloved Designers?"

Mikhail turned back to the window, his gaze following the two humans as they suddenly stood and started walking back toward the house. His eyes never left his woman. That was how he thought of her now, even though he knew to even think such a thing was blasphemy. He'd defied his beloved Designers before. This time, however, his conviction was even greater than ever before. Forces warred within him as he thought of defying a direct edict of the blessed Great Designers. They had been the only real thing in the entirety of his existence that had kept him going, they and his brothers.

Mikhail loved his Designers. They'd created Seraphim out of the nothingness of space and had given this world to them to maintain. Mikhail didn't remember being created, for there had been no concept of time when the beloved Designers had created Seraphim. Then it had taken a long time before any Seraph had found a rift in the barrier as a way to get to the other dimension where the blessed Great Designers awaited them. Mikhail had been the first.

Because of his bravery at crossing the rift in the barrier at Mt. Hermon, as it was called in the human dimension, and his willingness and ability to learn, his beloved Designers had granted him rule of the Seraphim dimension. Mikhail had learned as much as he could over many millennia from the blessed Great Designers and he'd come to realize that a ruling democracy was the best way to govern an entire race of beings.

He'd created the Great and Lesser Sanhedrin in Seraphim City in honor of his beloved Designers. He'd had colossal structures erected to celebrate each of the beloved Designers whenever they'd come to visit. He'd created schools and houses of worship where his people could go to learn about and to worship their beloved Designers.

The Designers had then instructed Mikhail to protect the humans, as well as his own people. That was two dimensions over which Mikhail was to preside and he took the honor to heart. His existence, such as it was, was owed entirely to his beloved Designers and Mikhail thanked them each and every day of his life. He had his three brothers, his people, and the humans in their realm. There was, of course, the matter of another brother and his sister who had been banished to the Badlands, and the fact that Mikhail and all other Seraphim were ultimately designed to be alone in the universe, but those things were best left alone, as he'd learned over time. His life was full of activity and had been for an eternity, for as long as he could remember.

A frown crept between his brows as the woman on the path below the window disappeared into the house's entrance. Now, everything was different. She was suddenly his entire existence. None of that other stuff mattered anymore. The way he'd felt when he'd entered Azra'il's office at the courthouse, the way everything but her had suddenly been wiped from existence – Mikhail knew there was an irrevocable change that had taken over at that point.

This Sarah was his destiny and she would not be denied. He knew he wouldn't fight it. There was no fighting it. It simply was. Even now, he could feel her energy as she approached his office. He could almost smell the sweet fragrance of her skin, even though the door to his office was still closed. It was a smell resembling magnolia blossoms in the summertime, after a late-afternoon rain on a hot day. Like the heavy humidity of that atmosphere, Mikhail felt her substance surround him and settle onto him like a warm, comforting cloak. After a quick knock, the door to the office opened and she hesitantly poked her head into the room.

"Oh," she quickly said, "I'm sorry. I didn't mean to interrupt."

"Sarah," Gabriel greeted. "Please, come in. You're not interrupting anything." He approached her and took her hand in his, bringing it up to place a quick kiss along her knuckles.

Mikhail's vision blurred with rage and he had to forcibly calm himself. He moved over to his desk and gripped the back of his chair to steady himself. He reminded himself that Gabriel meant no harm, that he was just being polite to Sarah. However, Mikhail knew if Gabriel didn't release her hand quickly, Mikhail was liable to teach him a lesson about taking liberties with his woman.

Thankfully, Sarah took care of matters herself. He relaxed as she withdrew her hand from Gabriel's and rounded the desk to come stand beside Mikhail. He welcomed her into an easy embrace as she sidled up next to him.

Ah, it was like he'd finally found his place in the Universe after an eternity of ignorant wandering.

Gabriel watched the two before him. He felt almost embarrassed to be in the room. What he was seeing was private. It was not for outsiders. It was just for the two participants. *How?* He wondered. *They only just met, not even 12 hours ago.* The strange thing was that the human seemed just as enthralled with Mikhail as Mikhail was with her.

A thought suddenly occurred to Gabriel and he asked, "Sarah, where's Thomas?"

Sarah reluctantly tore her loving gaze from her man's face and turned toward Gabriel, though he noticed she didn't step away from Mikhail. "He's upstairs checking out the house," she said. She turned back to Mikhail and said, "I hope it's okay. I told him he needed to go pick out a room for himself."

"That's fine," Mikhail said, smiling down at her. Frankly, he couldn't care less if the boy claimed the entire upper floor, ground floor, gardens and surrounding countryside as his own, as long as Sarah was happy.

Sarah smiled, then asked, "By the way, I was wondering… where am I supposed to sleep?"

Mikhail's breath caught in his chest. He hadn't thought that far ahead. He'd merely been relieved to have her safely ensconced in his home where he could protect her. He shot a glance over to Gabriel, silently pleading for assistance.

Gabriel cleared his throat and said, "Um, Sarah? We actually have a more pressing issue to deal with at the moment." He approached the desk at her look of confusion. "I need to introduce you to my brother," he said.

Her eyes widened and she turned back to the man at her side. She suddenly laughed, "That's right. We haven't been properly introduced, have we?" Mikhail merely smiled down at her.

"Sarah, this is my brother, Mikhail. You may know him as Michael," Gabriel said.

"Michael," she repeated. "Another angel, hmm? It's nice to finally meet you." After a moment's hesitation, she asked, "Do you prefer Michael or Mikhail?"

As he stared down into her beautiful blue eyes, Mikhail couldn't care less what name she called him, as long as she was his. "Which do you prefer?" he asked her quietly.

"I think I like Mikhail better," she shyly said.

Mikhail reached up with both hands and framed her face. He placed his lips against her forehead and whispered, "Then, Mikhail it is."

Gabriel stood rooted to the spot and shaken to the core. Mikhail was committing a sin right before his very eyes! His beloved brother and leader... Gabriel wanted to run. He wanted to get away as fast has his energies would carry him. He shouldn't be here, he knew. Tragedy had come to Seraphim City and it was in the form of a human female, and Gabriel had been the one to bring it!

The blessed Great Designers would be sure to retaliate, sure to punish those who'd transgressed against the law they'd commanded.

A hollow feeling sprang to life inside him. How could he have brought such ruin to his own people, to his beloved brother? He felt nauseous. He reached behind him for the chair and quietly fell into it, unnoticed by the other two people in the room. They seemed to be in their own world, noticing only each other. Sacrilege!

Gabriel had done this!

When Mikhail finally turned to look at his brother, he was taken aback at the ashen coloring on his kinsman's face. Then, realization dawned on him. He quickly stepped back slightly from Sarah, though he still held her in his arms. He just couldn't bring himself to part from her. This was wrong. He knew it was wrong. As she stared up at him and he stared right back down at her, he also knew it didn't matter. There was no choice here. It wasn't as if there were any options for Sarah and him, he realized.

Then another thought occurred to him, one that made so much sense it was almost insane. He glanced back toward

95

Gabriel, then back to Sarah. After a moment's hesitation, he stepped back from her and said, "Why don't you go upstairs, love, and check on Thomas. I'll have someone sent up to show you to your room and then, we'll have to do something about getting some clothing for the two of you."

Sarah was a bit crestfallen, but quickly hid her feelings of doubt, agreeing, "That would be wonderful." She hesitated for a moment, then said, "Um…, there's one problem. I didn't bring any money with me. I mean, I didn't think about…" She trailed off.

"Don't worry about it," Mikhail quickly reassured her. "There is no currency in Seraphim City. Whatever you need, we'll take care of it." He leaned in to give her another kiss on the forehead and said, "Now, you go on. I have a couple of things to discuss with Djibr…, um, Gabriel."

Gabriel looked up at the mention of his name, his insides still roiling within him at the thought of the disaster he'd condemned his people to endure by bringing Sarah to this dimension.

Sarah smiled a shy, quick smile up at Mikhail, then gave a quick nod to Gabriel before exiting the office, quietly closing the door behind her.

Mikhail calmly rounded his desk chair and took a seat, slowly pulling himself closer to the desk as he regarded his brother. His heart rate was finally calming down. The realization he'd just come to had convinced him that she really was his and that everything was going to be okay. When Gabriel finally returned his gaze, Mikhail had complete confidence in what he was about to say.

"Brother," he began, "Explain to me again, please, your idea that the blessed Great Designers created Sarah as a way of communicating with the Seraphim."

Gabriel's eyes narrowed momentarily. He'd explained all of this twice now to Mikhail, once at the courthouse and again when he'd first arrived at Mikhail's estate this evening.

He couldn't understand why Mikhail required him to explain it all again. Then, realization suddenly dawned. His gaze darted to Mikhail's face. "You think they created her for *you*?" he asked incredulously.

Just hearing it out loud like that, Mikhail realized how crazy it sounded, but he also knew it was correct. "I can taste her frequency," he said. "Her tones slide along my insides like cool silk, coursing through my veins." He closed his eyes and he could feel and hear the sweet, resonant tones floating down from the room upstairs where Sarah sat with her son. Even with the flooring of the house between them, he was still connected to her. He returned his gaze to Gabriel. "She is a part of me, her essence. I feel it more each moment, more intensely than anything I've ever felt before," he declared.

Gabriel regarded him in silence. Could it be? The blessed Great Designers did love their Seraphim, and he knew they loved Mikhail more than any other. Could it truly be that their beloved Designers had finally decided it was time to create a mate for the highest ranking of their beloved Seraphim? Of course, there could be no offspring, but Sarah already had a son. Perhaps, that had been the plan all along? Could that be why the Seraphim had been unable to detect her presence before now?

Mikhail studied Gabriel's face as his brother thought through the possibilities of the idea he'd presented. It was crazy, of course. However, it made just as much sense as the idea that Sarah was some kind of link between the blessed Great Designers and the Seraphim.

Gabriel slammed his palms down onto the arms of the leather chair and shot up to pace excitedly around the room. He finally came to rest behind the chair he'd just occupied and faced his brother. "Yes," he finally said.

Mikhail nodded once.

Gabriel, after another pause, turned and left.

Chapter 6

Mikhail leaned back in his chair, thinking. The pull to go to Sarah was tugging at his mind, but he had a few things to work out first. He knew she was safe upstairs. The problem now would be whether or not he, himself, believed in what he'd just suggested to Gabriel. Once he made a commitment to such a theory, there would be no turning back. The blessed Great Designers would never pardon such an act, if they hadn't sent Sarah to him for such a purpose.

But it didn't make sense otherwise. They had created everything on this planet, even the planet itself. They had to have created her to be the special being she was and that could only mean that she was meant to be with one of the Seraphim. None other would be able to deal with the abundance of soul-energy coursing through her body.

Just the thought of another touching her made Mikhail's blood boil and he quickly stood and left the office to go in search of his woman. He found her sitting in a wing-backed chair watching as her son checked out a control panel on a wall of the sitting room. There was a large flat-screened television mounted onto the wall and a stereo system below it. Speakers were strategically placed throughout the room.

"I don't see any type of on-button on this thing," the boy said. "It's all in some weird language."

"Well, don't fool with it," Sarah instructed. "That thing looks expensive."

"That's an ancient Seraphim language," Mikhail said, as he stepped into the room and closed the door behind him.

Sarah immediately stood and smiled up at him. He stepped over to her and gently took her hand in his.

"Is there a remote?" the boy asked.

"Thomas!" Sarah immediately chided.

Mikhail gave her fingers a little squeeze, saying, "It's okay." He let go of her hand and walked over to a nearby cabinet. Inside was a remote control and he showed Thomas which buttons were for what, then went to sit near where Sarah sat, as she'd returned to the wing backed chair she'd previously vacated.

"Angels have television?" she quietly asked him, keeping her voice low so Thomas wouldn't hear.

"We get the digital feed from the human satellites on this level and are able to monitor everything from here," he explained.

"So, do you get radio and everything else, too?" she asked.

"We have for the past several years, with everything switching to digital," he explained. "The microwaves weren't as reliable and we really didn't bother with them too much because of how bad the reception was. But since most things have switched to digital, some in Seraphim City have found that they enjoy watching and listening to things from your realm." He didn't tell her he was definitely not one of the ones who enjoyed such things. He figured she might not understand his feelings on that subject.

Even in light of his suspicions about the reason for her creation, there was still one issue that rankled. Ever since the Seraphim discovery of the human race, Mikhail had marveled at the idea of being able to reproduce with them. However, when he'd brought up the subject with his most favored of all his beloved Designers, he'd been told summarily to drop it. There'd been no explanation as to why he and his kind were never to be allowed to reproduce. He'd simply been forbidden to speak of it again. Even the lesser Angels among his people could reproduce, so Mikhail just couldn't understand the reasoning behind the blessed Great Designers' thoughts.

That was why Mikhail rarely spent his time concentrating on human matters anymore, that and the fact that humans were just so very *violent*. He had, at one time, thought he wouldn't mind mating with a human to reproduce. After all, if the lesser Angels could do it, why shouldn't he? However, his efforts toward convincing the Designers to that end had failed and now he preferred instead to dwell on the matters of his own people. In truth, it made him sad to think he would never be able to father a child, either with another Angel or with a human.

As he watched Thomas across the room, however, an idea occurred to him.

He turned back to Sarah and quietly asked, "I hope I'm not being rude by asking this, but where is Thomas' father?"

Sarah lowered her gaze for a moment. She'd never been married. She'd had Thomas out of wedlock. And now, here she was, sitting in the home of an Angel, a Seraph no less, and he was asking about her son's dad.

She'd been raised in the Deep South as a Southern Baptist. However, when she'd reached the age of sixteen, she'd discovered she didn't actually believe all the things she'd learned in Sunday school. She'd taken a class on world religions and had decided there wasn't really one out there that seemed to make too much sense to her. That's when she'd decided she would just have to come up with her own system of belief.

Now, though, when faced with one who was mentioned time and again in the Bible, she didn't know what to think. Did this mean there was a God and that everything she'd thought was wrong? If that was the case, what were her visions about?

Sarah decided such thoughts were best left for another time, when she could really take them out and examine them thoroughly. Best policy here, she decided, was to just go ahead and admit the truth and see where things would lead. "I don't know where he is," she said. "We'd already split up when I found out I was pregnant and, even though I told him about the baby, I didn't expect us to get back together or anything."

Mikhail merely turned back to look at Thomas.

Sarah was glad Thomas was so engrossed in the television. She was as nervous as nervous could be and she didn't need to be worrying about him at the moment.

Mikhail reached over to take her hand in his. He smiled at her and said, "I believe I promised we'd go and get some things for you and Thomas." Sarah smiled back at him and nodded. He felt the change of tone in her frequencies. He was glad he'd been able to calm her nerves. He hadn't meant to upset her with his question. He'd merely wanted to make sure the boy's father was not going to be an issue. Mikhail didn't want there to be anything to come between Sarah and him.

A little thrill of excitement rushed through him at the thought of being able to help her raise Thomas. At the same time, however, a spark of uncertainty lanced through his mind. *What if I don't do a good job with the boy?* He wondered. Thomas was already at the age where most human males start puberty. Mikhail didn't really know enough about their society to be able to say he'd be a good father for the boy. After all, he'd never had to raise a human. He'd merely gone to their realm to help them start and win wars against other humans. Sure, he had healed scores of them in times of plague and disease, but what could he offer the boy?

Sarah squeezed his fingers and looked inquiringly up at him from her seat.

Amazing, Mikhail thought as he squeezed back and smiled at her again. *She can sense my emotions.* He knew he'd have to watch that, but it was nice, he realized, having someone else around who actually knew what he was feeling inside.

He stood and, helping Sarah up from her chair, announced that they were all going shopping. Thomas didn't look too thrilled with this announcement, but one sharp look from Sarah had him immediately cooperative. He even politely thanked Mikhail. Mikhail realized he was going to have to do some quick studying in order to keep up with Sarah's strict guidelines. He had no clue how to be a father, but he knew he could learn. And for Sarah, he *would* learn.

After spending the entire evening shopping for many cases worth of clothes for the two of them along with some video games and a gaming system for Thomas for his room, they all headed back to Mikhail's estate. There they indulged in a huge meal consisting of every conceivable meat and pastry, along with many Sarah and Thomas had never even dreamed of. By the time the meal was over, the two of them were so tired they could barely keep their eyes open.

A servant, Narayana was what Mikhail called her, waited patiently while Sarah made sure Thomas was settled in for the evening in the suite of rooms he'd chosen. Then she escorted Sarah to another suite of rooms just down the hallway from Thomas'. Sarah thanked the woman and assured her she was fine for the evening and needed nothing more than a good night's sleep. Narayana left, quietly closing the door behind her, and Sarah headed for the suite's bathroom.

It was huge! The bathroom alone was larger than the bedroom she occupied at her parents' house. Sarah looked longingly at the sunken marble tub and wondered if she dared have a bath tonight. A great yawn escaped her, though, and she decided bathing would have to wait until tomorrow. She quickly changed into one of the gowns Mikhail had gotten for her earlier and made her way to the huge bed at the far part of the suite.

Before she reached the bed, she noticed a door along the far wall. It couldn't lead out to the hallway because it was on the wrong wall. Sarah curiously approached the door and tried the knob. It gave and she opened the door, then gasped. Mikhail stood on the other side of the door, as if he'd been waiting. He had one hand braced on the door frame, his arm stretched straight out.

Sarah blinked up at him. His shirt was unbuttoned all the way down and it just seemed to hang on him. His jeans were still on and fastened, but that broad expanse of tanned skin lightly dusted with black, curly hair was still a dangerous thing, Sarah decided. Her fingers itched to touch him, to feel his skin, to feel his heat. He just stood there, propped against the door frame, watching her.

Sarah blinked again. "I'm sorry," she said. "I didn't know where this door led."

Mikhail studied her face. He'd been standing here for the past five minutes, arguing with himself as to why he should just go to his own bed to sleep and leave her be, but not winning the argument. He looked her up and down, then returned his gaze to her face. She had such beautiful eyes, he decided, and her mouth was sin itself. He reached a hand up to caress the curve of her jaw and allowed the pad of his thumb to gently slide along the ridge of her full lower lip. He heard and felt her sharp intake of breath at his touch and it did strange things to his insides.

Mikhail had never coveted a human female. He'd had his pick of the finest females of the lesser Angels for as long as he could remember. However, not one of them had ever caused his blood to pound through his veins the way this human did. His first instinct was that he was doing something very, very wrong and that he must stop immediately.

But Sarah was different, if what he and Gabriel suspected was true. Mikhail's eyes narrowed as he studied her, trying to find some evidence to prove that it was okay to touch her, to want her, to take her. How could he feel this way if the blessed Great Designers hadn't intended it to be? The fear of disobeying his beloved Designers was immense, but the idea of losing Sarah far outweighed that fear.

Dare I touch her more? He wondered. His need for her was rapidly growing out of control and he wasn't quite sure how to handle that. He stepped even closer to her, pulling away from the door frame. He framed her face with both of his hands, swallowing a great lump in his throat, and held her still as he slowly lowered his lips to hers.

He could feel the energy shooting through her at tremendous speed. The frequencies vibrating through her human form were almost as arousing to him as the tones coming from her. She was still cool to the touch, which lent a queerness to the moment he hadn't expected, but it thrilled him to know it was just another thing that made her unique for him.

As his lips closed over hers, an explosion of light and sound eclipsed his sanity. There was nothing other than his connection with her. The world faded away, everything and everyone. Nothing else mattered except that he stay connected with her. He could feel her energies swamping him, even as his own coursed into her. Everything was so different, so new and intense, that he broke away for a moment, his breathing labored. He held her against him, cradling her head against his chest as he struggled for breath, his eyes closed.

He didn't understand the feelings coursing through him. He couldn't think. He could only feel and, at the moment, there was too much. He felt as if his chest would explode, like it would literally burst open from the tremendous energies compiling within it. *Is it always this way with humans?* he wondered. He could feel how weak she was. He was practically having to hold her up against him. Her breathing was as labored as his. If he didn't do something soon, neither one of them would survive this. And it was just one kiss! His mind boggled at the thought of doing more with her.

Mikhail took a step back from her, opening his eyes to look down upon her face as he held her gently by her upper arms. She was simply the most perfect creature he'd ever beheld. The pure, sweet tone resonating from within her seemed to carry him on a wave of pure bliss. There was no longer anything harsh or sharp in the world. Everything was soft and rounded and pliable and comforting.

She was tired. He felt it, even before a great yawn escaped her petite frame. He brushed away the shy apology she offered and bent to place a kiss on her cool forehead. He quickly straightened away from her, lest he should be drawn in again by her skin's magic. That's what it had to be, he assured himself. Somehow, his beloved Designers had found a way to create in this creature the perfect aphrodisiac for him and him alone. She truly had been created just for him. The doubts he'd had before were completely erased now.

Sarah yawned again and Mikhail chuckled aloud. She apologized again, and he shook his head. He lightly tapped his index finger against the tip of her nose and whispered, "Time for sleep, now, my love. We'll continue this another time."

Sarah gazed intently into his eyes for a moment, though he knew not what she was looking for. Then she lowered her gaze to his chest. Her hands settled there and she rubbed her fingers back and forth the tiniest degree, causing great swaths of heat to sear along the sensitive touch receptors just below the surface of his skin there. She bent and placed an open-mouthed kiss on the center of his chest.

Mikhail sucked in a deep gasp of a breath. Immediately, he was rock hard, wanting her just as intensely as he had just moments before. Of course, she chose that moment to drop her hands and turn away, whispering, "Good-night, Mikhail," as she walked back into her room.

Mikhail fought for control as he watched her get settled onto the bed at the near end of the room. She snuggled beneath the down comforter and reached to turn off the little bedside lamp she guessed Narayana had left on for her. Mikhail stood watching her for a moment, motionless. The light from inside his own bedroom shone into the room and onto her prone form on the bed.

How he wanted to go and join her, to take her, to discover what heights they could reach together. There was still some remaining doubt, he discovered, some niggling nuisance of a doubt that wanted to spoil what Mikhail knew must be. He sighed and quietly closed the door, turning back into his own bedroom. He knew he should take his time with this. Sarah was an unknown entity and he shouldn't rush headlong into a situation like this. After all, he'd only ever copulated with the lesser Angels of his realm. What if things worked differently with a human?

That was ridiculous, he knew. He'd lived long enough to know how things worked in the human realm, pretty much the same way they did in the Angelic realm. But he was so much bigger than she was, he feared he might crush her, or worse, that he might tear her apart.

He sighed again as he finished undressing and climbed into his own massive bed. He turned off the bedside lamp and settled in underneath the covers, punching his pillow to get it to just the correct shape he wanted for sleeping. *Ha!* He thought. *There's no way I'll be sleeping tonight, or any other night for that matter.* Until he could settle the matter of

Sarah and him, he knew sleep would be a virtual stranger. He turned over onto his side and punched his pillow again.

His last thought before he drifted off into a restless sleep was that he wished his beloved Designers would hurry and return so that he would be able to clear up this whole matter. He knew if they didn't return soon, he'd go mad.

Sarah was disoriented. There was a thick fog surrounding her and sounds, though heavily muted, came from all around. She tried to move, but something held her captive within a tightly-confined space. The sounds became more condensed, narrowing down to just two distinctively different tones. It sounded like two different people speaking, though she still couldn't make out any words. The fog surrounding her still managed to keep everything muted and muffled.

One of the tones was much higher than the other. When the other spoke, Sarah felt a rumbling vibration deep within her chest. It was while the higher voice was speaking that the shroud of fog surrounding her suddenly cleared.

Directly before her, what Sarah could only describe as a "blue" man lounged on a round bed covered with plush pillows. He was staring at her, speaking in a high-pitched, whiney voice. Sarah didn't understand a single word he spoke. It was not a language she recognized.

Suddenly, she felt and heard the deeper voice. It was coming from her, or rather it was coming from the body she currently inhabited. She recognized the voice, though she still could not understand the language. It was Mikhail's voice. She tried to look down at her hands, but she couldn't seem to make anything move. She was simply stuck inside his mind, looking through his eyes and feeling everything inside his body.

There was confusion within him. She could feel what he was feeling, every emotion, every breath he took. He was so hot, she felt as if she might burn up. The half-clothed blue man whined again and then made a gesture for Mikhail / Sarah to leave. A burning rage sprang to life within Mikhail's body, but his will was unbelievably strong and Sarah felt him stamp out the anger. Underneath it was confused hurt. Sarah didn't understand why he felt this, she simply knew he felt it. She experienced it with him.

She wanted to hurt the blue man. She wanted to turn Mikhail's body around and go back to kill the blue man for hurting Mikhail. She struggled within her confinement, but it was to no avail. The thick fog was suddenly surrounding her again and she ceased struggling.

The next thing she knew, the fog cleared and she was astounded to find that, although she was still tightly confined, she was in the middle of some sort of raging battle. People were everywhere, fighting and screaming. The flying machines she'd seen in Seraphim City, which Mikhail had explained were called Vimanas, flew all over the place, plasma blasts shooting at this target or another. Human men rushed toward her and as she cowered, she felt Mikhail's strength. She saw his strong arms beat back man after man, attacker after attacker. Some had huge swords, while others wielded wickedly curved blades. Each one fell before Mikhail's strength and skills.

Suddenly, Sarah caught sight of a very large man quickly approaching with some sort of makeshift spear. Mikhail sidestepped at the last moment, grabbed the spear and twisted. The large man swiveled just in time to catch the spearhead entering his viscera. He looked up into Mikhail's face. Mikhail felt a flash of sadness as he felt the life force drain from within the human before him. Sarah felt it, too.

Two men who were fighting nearby bumped into the dead man, knocking him directly onto Mikhail, which made both of them fall to the ground. Sarah felt Mikhail pushing at the body, then kicking it off himself. He stood and looked about at the carnage. Sarah looked down as he did and caught sight of his hands and arms. They were awash with blood. Sadness engulfed Mikhail and Sarah felt overwhelmed by everything. She sobbed within her confinement, struggling to break free. She couldn't move! She was trapped!

Mikhail slowly came out of the dream. He rubbed a hand across his eyes, wondering why he'd dreamed of that particular day. He slowly became aware of a faint sound. He sat up on his bed, looking around in confusion. It sounded like crying.

Realization dawned and he threw back the covers to race from his bed across the room to the connecting door to Sarah's room. Ripping it open, he heard more clearly the sounds of her pitiful sobbing. It was still dark, but he could just make out her huddled form on the bed. She was shaking and crying softly, her body jerking just the tiniest bit every few seconds. Mikhail rushed over and onto the bed, quickly taking her into his arms. In a low, whispering voice, he crooned, "Shh, sweetheart. It's okay."

She was asleep, he realized. "Shh… It's just a dream," he said as he stroked her back. He continued to whisper to her as he held her.

Sarah slowly emerged from the dream to find Mikhail holding her. He was rubbing his hand up and down her back, whispering to her in the most soothing way that everything was okay, that she was just having a bad dream. She took a moment to snuggle closer to him, wrapping her arms tightly around his lower back and pressing herself more intimately against the front of his body. He was so warm and she felt so very cold at the moment.

The sight of all that blood and all those dying men had unnerved her. She'd never experienced anything like that in her life. Sure, she'd seen movies galore that showed all kinds of violence like that. But, that was all make believe. That was what Hollywood gave to the world in exchange for people not having to experience first-hand such violence.

Sarah shivered.

She didn't want to experience anything like that ever again.

"You okay?" Mikhail asked.

Sarah looked up at him and whispered, "The dream. There was so much blood. I didn't know what to do and everyone was dying and I was so afraid." Tears started flowing down her face once more and Mikhail gently cradled her head against his broad chest.

"Shh," he whispered. "You don't have to worry about anything, love. I will never let anything hurt you."

Sarah pulled back from him and looked up into his brilliant blue eyes. "How could you stand it?" she asked pitifully.

Mikhail's eyes narrowed and he went completely still. After a moment, he whispered shakily, "What do you mean?"

"It was you," she explained. "I was seeing things through your eyes as you fought." Sarah explained everything she'd felt and heard and experienced, ending with, "And when you looked down at your hands, I saw all the blood covering you and all the dead and dying men all around you and I just knew something awful was going to happen to you and that I wouldn't be able to do anything to stop it or to help you." She was crying again, near hysteria, and Mikhail embraced her closely once more.

Mikhail was floored. She'd linked with him during their sleep. He'd never heard of such a thing, especially not among Seraphim. For a million years he had walked this planet with his brothers and the lesser Angels. Never had Mikhail encountered any creature other than his one sibling able to breach his psychic defenses. As he held her he wondered if it was because of her special nature, because of the unique qualities his beloved Designers had built within her, that she was able to do this.

After a moment, she was able to talk again and she choked out, "And, what was the deal with that blue guy?"

"What?" Mikhail managed, barely.

"That blue man you were talking to," she explained. "Who, or what, was he?"

Mikhail froze. Why wouldn't she recognize one of the blessed Great Designers? She was of them, created by them, Gabriel had even said she'd spoken of them with him, so why wouldn't she be able to tell when she was faced with one of them? He remembered the time before he'd finally encountered his beloved Designers in the human realm. He'd already lived over five hundred thousand years at that point and he hadn't had any recall of them before he met them in the human realm, so why would she?

Realization dawned on him, suddenly. The blessed Great Designers had been gone for the last three thousand years. Whatever process they used to keep new humans being born was done by remote, so they'd said. Why should she recognize one of their kind? She was new to this planet, barely having stepped foot on it, in terms of the Seraphim. Of course she wouldn't recognize one of the beloved Designers.

Mikhail squeezed her shoulders a little and explained, "That's Ningizzida, the son of one of the blessed Great Designers, love."

She pulled away from him and looked at him with a confused frown upon her face. "No," she said, shaking her head just slightly. "He wasn't one."

A chill washed down Mikhail's spine and he stared at her questioningly.

"He was one of those other things, not one of the creators," she explained.

Mikhail's eyebrows narrowed. He merely stared uncomprehendingly at her. *What is she saying?* He wondered.

Sarah sat Indian-style on the bed facing him. "I've seen the creators. I know what they look like. That man was *not* one of them."

Mikhail continued staring at her, lost in thought. Sarah finally reached out to touch his cheek, but he merely tilted his head slightly and continued regarding her.

"You don't know," she softly said. At his continued stare, Sarah breathed in deeply and looked away. What could she say? She'd blogged about the visions she'd been given, but how did one explain such things to another person... to a Seraph? She had no clue.

Mikhail was suddenly stunned to realize he could actually feel the certainty within her. Here, he'd been wondering how he could tell her that she was wrong, when she actually seemed to know something he didn't about the origins of Seraphim and of humans. He knew she knew it because she believed it completely. He reached out to place his hand against her cheek, turning her face toward him once more.

As she stared up into his eyes, he saw the depth of her sadness for the fact that she had no words with which to explain things to him. Somewhere within her mind, he knew there were answers to a puzzle he hadn't even known he was trying to solve. She wasn't trying to keep the knowledge from him, he could tell it was tearing her up inside not to be able to explain things to him.

Mikhail leaned forward and touched his forehead to hers, his nose alongside hers, their lips a whisper apart. The thrill of touching her had him rock-hard again in an instant. He inhaled deeply, her scent invading him, creating a molten flow within his veins. There was an ocean of sound pounding within his brain and he slid his hands along her shoulders and down the sides of her back. He closed his eyes and allowed his lips to touch hers, just for the briefest of moments. It was barely even a kiss.

Fire and ice exploded within him on contact with her mouth. The breath slammed out of him and he reached more fully for her, crushing her petite frame to his chest. His mouth suddenly ground against hers, accepting nothing less than complete acquiescence.

Sarah didn't resist. She reached her arms around him and held him as tightly as she could manage while he assaulted her mouth. Her eyes drifted closed and she moaned. It felt so good holding onto this heated dynamo, this glowing god, this being who had already afforded her more of a sense of security than she'd ever felt before in her life.

This creature had never once asked her for anything. He'd merely stepped into a room and had immediately come to her as her own personal champion. That, in itself, was something completely unheard of in Sarah's book, but when added to the fact that just being near him sent her senses reeling, the overall effect was to make her madly in love with the man already.

Sarah jerked back suddenly, pulling out of his embrace and breaking the kiss. She stared a bit wildly at him, her eyes darting all over his face, then away, then back again. What was she thinking? She got up off the bed and walked a few paces away from him, her back to him. How could she be in love with this being? He was something completely different. He even lived in another dimension!

Yes, she had the visions and, if they were to be believed, then she had ample evidence that this was her actual, honest-to-goodness soul mate. She knew that. The problem was that she was still simply a human and all this stuff seemed so unbelievable, even to her. She'd also been in relationships before, so she knew how easy it was to be fooled by another person. True, she hadn't ever been in a relationship with an Angel, but he was still a guy. How could she trust him? She turned back to face him once more, though she didn't move back toward the bed.

"Sarah?" He asked as he reached out a hand for her.

She immediately took a step toward him without even thinking. That's when she heard a call from down the hallway.

"Mom!" came the shout. It was Thomas.

Sarah's heart raced as she immediately crossed the room, tore open the door, and rushed down the hallway toward Thomas' room. It was only a couple of rooms away, but it seemed to take forever to get there. Sarah heard Mikhail pounding down the hallway behind her, but didn't look back. She rushed into Thomas' room and found him sitting up in bed, his covers a mess and tears streaming down his face. She sat beside him on the bed and pulled him into her arms, whispering to him to calm him down.

"Shh," she said. "It's okay. Mommy's here." How many times had she said that over the past eleven years? He was such a tall and mature boy, but he was still just a boy. That was sometimes so easy to forget, but then something like this would happen and she was reminded of just how young he really was.

"Is he okay?" Mikhail asked quietly from beside the bed. He didn't want to intrude, but he felt a connection with the boy already, and he wanted to help.

"He's fine," Sarah whispered as she stroked her son's back. "It was just a bad dream." She ran a hand through Thomas' short hair, curving her palm around the back of his head lovingly. "It's okay," she repeated. "Mommy's here."

Thomas continued crying for a few minutes, clinging to his mother's shoulders, his body rocking back and forth with hers.

Mikhail reached out and rubbed his hand down the back of the boy's head. "It's okay, buddy," he said softly.

Thomas pulled back from his mother at Mikhail's touch and looked up at him. "I was l-lost," he said, "and I couldn't find my mom. Everywhere I looked, there w-were only those Angels like the ones we saw when we went out last night. Nobody knew where my mom was and they w-wouldn't help me."

Mikhail stepped closer and placed his hand on Thomas' shoulder. "Your mother and I are never going to let anything happen to you, son," he said. "And, as for the Angels in Seraphim City…, they know you are under my protection. They would never harm you or allow any harm to come to you. If they did, they know they'd have to deal with me."

Thomas looked back at Sarah. He sniffled a couple of times and then said, "I think I'm okay now." He lay back down on his pillow, pulling his covers up to his chin.

Sarah leaned forward and placed a kiss on his brow, brushing his short bangs off his forehead, and said, "I'm just two doors down the hallway, if you need me."

Mikhail placed a hand on her back and she got up from the bed.

"'Night, mom," Thomas said. After a moment's pause, he added, "'Night, M'khail."

Mikhail smiled a lopsided smile over at the boy as he and Sarah walked toward the door. "Goodnight, son," he said softly.

Thomas turned over and sighed.

Mikhail and Sarah left the room, closing the door behind them. He took Sarah's hand as they walked back toward her room. Neither said a word as they entered her bedroom. Mikhail stopped in the middle of the room, his hand remaining firm on Sarah's, pulling her to a halt, too. He looked at her bed, then over to the open door leading to his room. He looked back at her just once, then turned and headed to his room, Sarah in tow.

There were only a couple of hours before sunrise and Mikhail was exhausted. But he wanted Sarah with him, and he felt that this was right. He didn't hesitate, but walked directly over to the bed. After shifting the pillows a little and pulling back the covers, he waited while Sarah climbed up onto his big bed and made herself comfortable. Mikhail carefully slid beneath the covers and aligned his body to the curve of the back of her body, his arms wrapped protectively around her, their knees and legs bent and pressed full-length against each other.

No words were necessary as Mikhail lowered the side of his head against her hair and her temple. He squeezed her just a little and kissed the rim of her ear. Sarah reached to rub the arm he had draped over her shoulder and then sighed. Soon, they were both sound asleep.

Chapter 7

Sarah felt when Mikhail awakened. It was like coming out of a dream that she couldn't remember, but she knew he was gaining consciousness, as sure as she knew anything. They were still cradled together, "spooning" she believed it was called. His big, strong arms were still wrapped around her, his entire front side pressed firmly up against her entire backside. She rubbed her hand along one of his muscled forearms, giving it a gentle squeeze.

"Mmm," he murmured, "that feels good." He pulled his arms more tightly around her. "Did you sleep well?" he asked.

Sarah breathed in deeply, then said, "Wonderfully." She straightened out in a long, full-bodied stretch, her arms reaching out as far as she could in front of herself. Mikhail didn't relinquish the hold he had on her with his arms. Eventually, she subsided back to her former position up against him. She dared to open her eyes and found there was rich sunlight streaming through the windows on the adjacent wall. She wondered what time it was. Thomas didn't normally get up particularly early, having just started puberty and everything, but Sarah still wouldn't want him to walk in on her sleeping with a man, even Mikhail. She wasn't ready for that.

She looked over at the nightstand next to the bed on her side and noticed Mikhail's watch lying there. She didn't even think about what she was doing. She felt a little tingle at the back of her head and the watch suddenly just seemed to hover and then float over toward her, the face of the watch in front of her so she could see what time it was.

Sarah bolted upright in the bed, going up onto her knees facing Mikhail and half-pulling Mikhail up before he allowed his arms to fall away from her. He was staring at her in stunned confusion. The watch dropped onto the mattress before her. Sarah looked at Mikhail, fear and confusion warring inside her mind.

"What's wrong?" Mikhail asked.

Sarah looked at him like he was insane. "Did you *see* that?" she shrieked hysterically.

Mikhail's brows narrowed in confusion and he gave her a sideways look of uncertainty as he maneuvered up onto an elbow to more fully face her. "See what?" he asked.

"The watch," Sarah said.

Mikhail looked down at the watch now lying on the bed close to the pillow they'd shared. His confusion seemed to double as he looked back up at her and he merely shook his head in response. He didn't understand what she was all upset about.

Sarah looked at the timepiece as if it might suddenly sprout spider legs and attack, like in some movie. "It moved, all by itself," she whispered.

Mikhail glanced back down at the watch, then back at her and simply said, "So?"

"So?" Sarah wailed. "So, that's…, that's…"

Mikhail slowly lowered his head, still looking her directly in the eyes, and then said, "Levitation?"

"Exactly!" she exclaimed, throwing her arms up and then letting them flop back down onto her thighs.

Mikhail slowly shook his head, hitched one eyebrow and said again, "So?"

Sarah plopped down Indian style on the bed and said, "So? So, it's levitation!" She didn't understand why he wasn't as blown away by this information as she was.

Again, Mikhail shrugged and shook his head, explaining, "So? We levitate things here all the time. So what?"

"So what?" Sarah asked incredulously, "I'm not an Angel. That's so what!"

Mikhail's eyes narrowed in confusion. He looked down at the watch, then back at her. "You... You mean humans don't levitate things?" he asked.

"Nope," she said matter-of-factly.

Mikhail looked at the watch again, his brows narrowing as he concentrated on his thoughts. After a moment, a determined look overtook his face and the watch suddenly whizzed back over to the table. Sarah sat stunned, her mouth hanging open at the sight of the timepiece moving all on its own. "Do it again," Mikhail said.

She whipped her gaze over to him. Could she do it again? She hadn't thought of what she was doing the first time. She'd just done it. To be honest, she didn't even know how she'd done it. She just knew there'd been a funny feeling at the back of her head and the watch had suddenly just moved to hover right before her eyes so that she could see what time it was.

As she was thinking of this, that same strange feeling at the back of her head came again and she watched in amazement as the watch once again rose from the nightstand and moved toward her. She held out her hand and the watch slowly alighted onto her palm. She felt the weight of the metal and leather piece settle onto her hand and she was amazed to realize she'd just done something that most people thought was impossible. She jerked her gaze back to Mikhail's face. Her eyes held traces of fear, confusion, and excitement.

"Hmmm," was all Mikhail said. Sarah was about to grill him on what he meant by that when he suddenly narrowed his gaze on her again, concentrating on her eyes. He reached a hand up to gently touch her temple.

"What?" Sarah asked. "What's wrong?" Fear lanced through her. What else could've happened to her overnight?

"Your eyes," Mikhail said confusedly. "I thought they were a hazel color."

Sarah scrambled off the bed, confirming, "They *are* hazel." She raced over to look in a mirror hanging on the far wall of the room. There, looking back at her, was the same reflection she'd expected to see, but with one great exception. The eyes regarding her were a stunning ice blue color and, as she watched, a brilliant swirl of white shot outward from her dilated pupils and she jumped, startled. Immediately afterward, her pupils became dark again, but with a slight swirling iridescence within them she'd never seen before. The color of each iris, however, was an amazing ice blue, almost an exact match to Mikhail's. There was not one hint of green or brown or any other color anywhere in them.

Sarah raised a hand to one side of her face. The reflection showed this, too. Again, the eyes regarding her flashed that brilliant white swirl of light in the pupils. Sarah started shaking. She swallowed a lump in her throat. She heard the rustle of bedclothes and then caught sight of Mikhail's reflection just behind her. She felt and saw his hands as he slowly rubbed her upper arms to calm her. She looked up at his face, clearly visible above the top of her head in their reflection and sucked in a shocked breath.

Mikhail's pupils flashed the same brilliant white swirl as hers had!

"It's okay," he said.

Sarah twisted in his grasp, turning to face him. She reached up and touched his temple, as he'd done with her. "What was that?" she asked breathlessly.

He narrowed his eyes in confusion. "What?" he asked.

"That flash, the swirl of light," she explained.

A look of total confusion overcame his face. "What flash?" he asked.

Sarah grabbed his chin and tilted it toward the mirror as she turned to regard his reflection there. His eyes flashed, as did hers, the brilliant white light swirled, then returned to the dark iridescent color she'd noticed a moment ago. Mikhail sucked in a surprised gasp of air. He, too, stepped closer to the mirror and touched his face with a hand. He pulled the skin on his right cheek a little to widen the orbit of his right eye, as if checking for foreign objects within it. There was another flashing swirl, then the same old ice blue tint he'd seen since he'd first discovered his own reflection, with the exception of a new iridescence slightly shining from within his pupils. He looked back at Sarah.

Sarah stared up at him, watching as every now and then the beautiful eyes of the man she loved would flash with the swirl. He seemed to widen his eyes each time they flashed. Sarah turned to look back into the mirror. Mikhail did, too. The next time their eyes flashed, they both realized they were flashing synchronously.

"What's happening?" Sarah quietly asked.

Mikhail shook his head and whispered, "I don't know." He turned back to face her and ran a hand gently down the side of her face. "I'll find out," he assured her. "You stay here with Thomas."

"You're *leaving*?" Sarah wailed incredulously.

Mikhail grabbed her hands in his and soothed her, saying, "It's okay. I'll be back. It's just that I have some work I need to attend to with the council and then I thought I would confer with my brothers to see if they could help me figure out what's going on with the two of us." He pulled one of her hands up to rub the back of her fingers along his lips.

"I won't be too long, I promise," he said, placing a small kiss on each knuckle of her hand.

Sarah dragged in a worried breath, her shoulders raising on the great gulp of air, then nodded her head. She didn't like the idea of him leaving her while she was going through goodness only knew what, but she knew he couldn't just give up his life completely just because she and Thomas had come to live with him.

"You stay here and rest," he instructed. "The sun's barely been up half an hour. Perhaps you could go back to bed?"

Sarah looked back at the bed and saw the watch lying there on the mattress. Her eyebrows narrowed. She didn't think she'd be going back to bed right now. She knew Thomas wouldn't be up for at least another couple of hours, if not more, since he was definitely *not* a morning person.

Suddenly, inspiration struck and she announced, "I think I'll go have a long, hot shower and then see about getting something to eat." Just to demonstrate her need for food, her stomach chose that moment to let out a long, low growl.

Mikhail smiled a lopsided smile and tapped his index finger on the tip of her nose. He then bent to place a quick kiss against her forehead, whispering, "That sounds good. I'll speak with one of the staff to make sure they have some breakfast waiting and ready for you when you're done bathing."

Sarah gave him a smile of thanks and then watched as he wandered over to an armoire to remove some clothing. He picked out what looked like an Ancient Greek chiton, which was just a knee-length rectangle of fabric that had been sewn up along the sides. There were no sleeves to it, but it looked good on Mikhail, Sarah decided, as he looped and tied a fabric belt around his waist. His shoulders were broad enough that the effect was stunning. He wrapped an arm around behind his head and pulled his long black hair from inside the top part of the garment.

He walked over to the bed and picked up his heavy watch from the mattress. After wrapping and fastening it around his wrist, he approached her and said, "The bathroom's through that door over there, unless you'd like to use the one in your room." He ran his hands up the length of her arms and continued, "I'll be back in a little while." He kissed her forehead once more and then moved out of the room, quietly closing the door behind him.

Sarah stood still for a moment, wondering what on earth she was doing. Everything here was different. Her life here was certainly different, what with people waiting on her and her living in utter opulence. She didn't have to be anywhere at any specific time. Thomas was safe just down the hallway. She could take her time in the shower! This was a very big thing for a single mom.

However, even her body had begun to change and Sarah didn't know if she liked that or not. The whole levitation deal had really scared her, but when she'd seen the new color of her eyes and then the flashing... well, she'd just about freaked out! It was a good thing that Mikhail's eyes had started with the whole flashing/swirling business, or Sarah knew she'd be wiggin' out big time already. Mikhail's eyes *were* flashing, though, the same as hers... even at the same time. So...

Sarah decided there wasn't anything she could do about any of the things going on until Mikhail learned more. With that decision made, she pivoted on the balls of her feet and headed for the bathroom connected to her bedroom, figuring that if Thomas awoke, he'd check there first for her.

The bathroom was just as huge and inviting as she'd found it to be from her quick tour of it last night. Sarah looked longingly at the tub, but knew she wouldn't feel comfortable enough yet to take a nice long bath. What if one of the staff walked in while she was lazing away the day in the giant tub? She knew she'd be mortified. Instead, she quickly used the toilet, then undressed and stepped into the shower. The minute she turned on the faucet, hot water shot out in great steaming streams.

Sarah adjusted the temperature of the water and then stepped into the heated pulses, turning and allowing them to massage her shoulders. She threw her head back to get the top part of her hair wet, then allowed her head to fall forward. She just stood there for a few moments, allowing herself to be completely warmed and comforted by the steaming water pounding her shoulders and back. Rivulets of hot water streamed down her front and her back and she closed her eyes, thinking of how much she wished those were Mikhail's hands moving down her petite form.

For some reason she couldn't fathom, Mikhail hadn't yet wanted to take things farther than just a few kisses. Sarah didn't understand his reluctance to engage in full-blown sex with her, and she *did* see it as some sort of reluctance on his part. Sarah, herself, was rarin' to go, she had to admit. She shook her head and opened her eyes to search for shampoo and soap.

Such thoughts were not good for her. She'd been alone for far too long to be thinking of anything beyond what they had done so far. She was in a strange land with strange people, if they could be called that, and she needed to keep her wits about her. Thomas was also here and she needed to make sure he remained safe. What she didn't need to do was to screw things up by rushing into a physical relationship with someone she barely even knew!

Sarah finished up washing and switched off the water. There were several shelves of clean towels folded and waiting in a cubby just next to the shower door and Sarah grabbed one and let it fall open. It reached all the way to the floor and was almost as big as the blankets she used on her bed back home. She pulled the full-length towel up to her front and hugged it to her body, sniffing its clean, fresh scent as she patted her chin and lips dry. She stepped out onto the ends of the towel and was still able to wrap her entire body, even her head, up in the cloth.

She quickly dried off, but then remembered she hadn't brought any clean clothes into the bathroom when she'd entered earlier. She was about to wrap the towel more securely around her body so that she could go into the bedroom, when she spotted a full-length oval mirror over in one corner of the bathroom. She tilted her head and wondered if Mikhail had chosen the mirror for this room. It seemed like something a woman would think of, not a man.

Sarah moved over to the mirror as she tucked the top part of the towel into a knot just above her bosom and looked at her reflection in it. Her hair hung down almost to her waist in long wet strands, most of it behind her, but a few tangled strands lay across her shoulders and down her front. Her breasts were full enough that the strands of hair in front had fallen over to the sides of the towel, by her arms. As Sarah stared at her reflection in the mirror, her eyes suddenly flashed and she quickly looked away. Her gaze, instead went to the knot in the towel she'd made just above her breasts, just at the top of the valley in between. She suddenly thought, "Slip the towel off."

Her gaze flashed back to the ice blue eyes staring back at her and she was shocked to discover she'd actually spoken aloud. She felt a strange pressure inside her head, though it only caused a little pain, so she paid it little heed. She looked back down at the towel's knot and found herself slowly sliding a hand up to undo it. With only a slight tug, the towel fell silently to land on the plush throw rug on which she stood. Sarah stared at her body, completely revealed now, in the reflection showing in the mirror. She'd never been one to look at herself in the nude. Firstly, she found it very embarrassing. Secondly, she'd been brought up to believe a true lady didn't do such things.

Yes, it was old-fashioned, but that was how she'd been raised.

Her gaze went to first one breast, then the other. "Cup them," she heard herself say. She jerked her gaze back up to her eyes, startled that she would say such a thing, feeling as if someone else was there telling her what to do. Her eyes flashed that bright white swirl of light once more and she found herself saying, "Don't look away from them. Concentrate."

She did a quick double take. Sarah didn't understand what was going on, but there was a strange feeling inside her body and she had watched her own mouth form the words she'd uttered without even fully knowing what it was she was about to say. Slowly, shyly, she raised both hands to cup her breasts. She gently massaged each one, lifting the full weight and then squeezing, just slightly.

"Squeeze the nipples harder," she heard her voice say and, after only a moment's hesitation, she did. On a moan, she closed her eyes and sucked in a deep breath. So enthralled with the tingling sensation of her fingers squeezing each nipple was she that she almost didn't hear herself admonishing, "Open your eyes and look!" Her voice had been so urgent, though, so she quickly obeyed and returned her gaze to the reflection in the mirror.

She was breathing a little heavy now as the command to squeeze just a little harder and to pull came from her throat. Sarah shifted her stance. She couldn't believe she was doing this. As she obeyed, her gaze slowly slid down to the dark patch of curls at the triangle between her legs.

"Move one hand down there," she heard her voice saying. Her eyes narrowed as she regarded her reflection. *How could she be saying and doing these things?* She wondered. She would be absolutely mortified if Thomas or

127

someone else were to walk in and find her standing before a mirror in the nude doing things like this. Her gaze slid back down to the dark patch and she said once more, "Move one hand down there."

Slowly, hesitantly, Sarah moved her right hand down to touch the damp, springy curls just between the tops of her legs. She still massaged her breast with the left hand, squeezing the nipple there, not so gently now and pulling it every now and then.

Her voice came again, a little hoarse now, instructing, "Spread your legs a bit and watch yourself pulling the lips apart."

Sarah wanted to protest, but didn't know to whom she could protest. She was the one giving herself these orders. She was the one creating the unbelievably erotic scene in the mirror. How could she protest something her mind obviously wanted?

She shifted her legs about shoulder-width apart and watched as her index finger and her middle finger slid down into the auburn curls and parted the lips there. Within it, the nub of her clitoris gleamed in plain view.

"Touch it," came the command. Sarah slid her index finger inside the wet warmth between the lips and lightly grazed the tiny nub. She nearly doubled over from the sensation, so turned on was she. She closed her eyes on a moan, but was quickly commanded to open them again. "Keep your eyes focused," her voice said. Sarah slid her gaze back down to where her right hand was working.

"Flick it," her voice said. Sarah did. "Faster," her voice commanded, and she moved her finger faster. Her hips were starting to gyrate on their own as a searing heat pervaded her groin. A tension was building inside her abdomen and Sarah wondered how much more she could withstand. She didn't really want to be doing this. She wanted, instead, for Mikhail to be here doing this to her. She wanted his mouth to be where her finger was, doing more than just flicking her overly-sensitive bud.

"Soon," she heard herself say. She looked back at her eyes in the reflection staring back at her. Another flash of white lighted up the image for just a split second, then was gone.

"Look back down," she told herself. Sarah complied. "Push your finger inside and use your thumb to rub," she instructed. Again, she complied. Her index finger pushed into the small, tight opening and upward. She rubbed the tiny nub of her clitoris with her thumb. She was half bent over doing this, still squeezing the nipple of first one breast and then another, pulling the tip as far away from her body as she could as she squeezed. Her breath was ragged and she didn't know how much longer she'd be able to remain standing there. The tension in her core was building at an alarming rate, now.

She let out a low moan and closed her eyes on the scene. It was too much to take.

"No," she said. "Look. Don't look away again. Keep watching."

Sarah reached out with her left hand and grabbed the edge of the mirror. She swiveled it so that it was facing the floor and she quickly collapsed onto her back, her legs falling apart at the knees. The angle of the mirror wasn't what she needed to be able to see her right hand, so she lifted a foot to press the mirror's edge, moving it so that it more fully revealed what she was doing on the throw rug.

She lay completely exposed, watching as her index finger plunged in and then retreated, in and out, in and out. All the while, her thumb circled and moved over her clitoris and her left hand massaged and pulled hard at the nipple of each breast. She was panting, her hips rising and falling with each plunge of her index finger.

"Put another finger inside," she instructed. Sarah complied immediately, uncaring of how embarrassing this scene would be, her hips rising completely off the floor as she did this. "Rub harder, faster," she said with a gasp. She did. In seconds, Sarah was beyond thinking. She was watching herself writhe on the floor of the bathroom like some possessed person and all she could think was that she didn't want it to stop. The tension built to a crescendo and Sarah suddenly arched her back, withdrawing both hands and squeezing her eyes shut as she shouted out a groan. The pleasure was intense. Her entire body was jerking uncontrollably.

Mikhail was doing his best to keep his breathing calm and unnoticeable. It was difficult with the image of Sarah's naked, wrenching form etched before his eyes and the memory of her thought of how she'd wished his mouth were doing to her what her own hand had been doing. He'd been sitting behind the privacy screen at his station within the council chamber when he'd suddenly caught an image of her standing before a mirror in a towel. The reflection in the mirror had been looking directly at him in his mind's eye. He'd still been aware of the council chamber and all those within it. He'd still been aware of his own body, of everything where he was, but he'd also been aware of everything going on with Sarah as she'd stood before that damned oval mirror. The commands he'd thought, she'd spoken aloud and he'd heard them in her voice, as if she'd been standing just beside him speaking the words.

The moment Mikhail had realized she was following his commands, he'd forgotten about his duties to the Great Sanhedrin. He'd concentrated instead on watching Sarah do whatever he wanted her to do to her delicious body. He'd given her commands that he knew went against what she was comfortable doing, but he'd been too caught up in the affair to stop. It had been the most erotic scene he'd ever witnessed. Even his own fantasies couldn't compare with what he witnessed her doing.

No one in the council chamber could notice what went on behind the privacy screen and all Mikhail had to do was to enter a vote whenever the signal came signifying that it was time to vote. Everything was done with the push of a button, so Mikhail hadn't needed to worry about being discovered.

Then, Sarah'd come.

Mikhail had sensed the wave of sensation building inside her by her body language and the flush of her skin and had been powerless to stop it. It had washed over her with such ferocity all of a sudden and he'd heard her cry of release. He'd witnessed it all and knew his chiton was soaked from where he'd spent his seed as he'd watched her come. It had been so erotic. He'd clapped a hand over his own mouth to keep from screaming out in his own release. Now, he needed to get out of the council chamber without encountering anyone.

Mikhail looked around at the dim faces he could detect through the privacy screen. None were focused on him that he could tell. He'd closed the screen before his station within the council chamber the moment he'd entered it in order to keep the sight of his flashing eyes from the council members. He wasn't ready for Seraphim City's society to learn of the changes he was going through, let alone its governing body.

Slowly, he gathered up the wet folds of his chiton and stood, quickly making his way around his chair so as not to make noise by moving it out of his way. He made his way to the private chamber located at the back of his station without incident and went through to the chamber's outside exit without stopping. He immediately threw up all six of his shields and took to the air, flying as fast as he could toward his home on the outskirts of Seraphim City. He didn't bother entering through the main doors. Instead, he rushed through the walls and just inside the closed entrance to the bathroom where Sarah's prone form still lay on the floor in front of the oval mirror. Mikhail noticed her body jerking in tiny spasms, much less noticeable than the ones she'd experienced upon her release.

He didn't know what demon possessed him to do so, but he reached down to untie the fabric belt he'd wrapped around his chiton earlier. Once it dropped heedlessly to the floor, Mikhail grabbed the wet folds of the shift below his waist and whipped it up and over his head, pulling the entire garment off and allowing it to fall to the floor forgotten. He quickly approached Sarah.

His breath escaped in a worshipful rasp. She was so beautiful and here she was, supine, all pink and wonderfully unhidden from his gaze.

Upon hearing his approach, Sarah turned her head to look up at him, her gaze taking in his stunning form, her eyes widening in shock at his engorged member protruding proudly from between his legs. Her embarrassed gaze quickly traveled the rest of the way up to meet his eyes. They flashed a brilliant swirl of white and he kneeled down onto one knee beside her. Sarah wondered how on earth she could explain what she was doing lying on the floor of the bathroom naked. What could she say?

Mikhail knew she was uneasy, but it was of no concern to him. He reached his hand out and gently ran his fingers up the inside of her thigh to the auburn patch of curls. It was slick with her juices and warm. Admittedly, it wasn't as warm as he was expecting, but its warmth was still exciting to him. He parted the lips there and inserted his own index finger inside her wet warmth, his thumb seeking out and finding the little pink bud of her clitoris.

He set to work repeating each and every step in the tutorial he'd given her earlier. He lay down beside her on his side so he could simply bend over slightly to pull the tip of her closest breast hungrily inside his mouth. He suckled her, first gently, then harder and harder, making sure to keep in rhythm with the hand between her legs.

Oh, how he wanted to take her! He wanted to devour her. He wanted to ram his full length into her as hard as he could.

"Yes!" he heard her urge him in a whispered shriek. "I want it, now!"

Her body was moving frantically against his hand and he pulled back slightly to insert another finger into her waiting warmth. His biceps flexed as he shoved his hand as far upward as he could, implanting his fingers deep inside her body. His thumb rubbed and circled, first one direction, then the other. He flicked and rubbed, rubbed and flicked. Watching her body moving and listening to her pants as he brought her closer and closer to the edge again nearly had him going insane. He lifted himself up on his elbow and moved over her to take the other breast into his mouth. He sucked her in, rolling his tongue around her areola. He sucked hard, scraped his teeth gently across the nipple, and then sucked hard again.

Sarah arched her back as he suckled her breast. She couldn't seem to get enough oxygen into her lungs. She was breathing so heavily, but he was pushing the air out of her each time he thrust his fingers deeper inside her. Her hips were rocking, trying to keep time with each thrust of his hand. Sarah reached a hand around to his back to get a better grip as her feet planted firmly on the floor. Her hand suddenly encountered something leathery, just at the middle of his upper back, between his shoulder blades. It seemed like some sort of flap and there was some sort of ridge or bump underneath it.

His hand was pounding into her now and she couldn't concentrate on anything else. She slid her hand up and gripped his neck, pulling her hips completely off the floor now to get him deeper inside her body. "Mikhail, please!" she implored.

Oh, how Mikhail wished he could take her. He *needed* to take her, but for the damned law!

Instead, he quickly pulled away from her, releasing his hold on her breast and pulling his fingers out of her opening. He immediately replaced them with his tongue. Sarah's hoarse cry of pleasure was all the encouragement he needed and he set to work administering every skill he'd developed over the millennia toward bringing a female to complete satisfaction. He felt pain from a sudden small pressure inside his head and didn't even realize he had moved his own body around and on top of her until he felt her lips closing around the tip of his shaft, her arms circling his thighs and pulling her head and shoulders closer to his body. She took him all the way back in her mouth, as far as she could without cutting off her air supply, her tongue circling and rasping against his sensitive flesh.

Mikhail was nearly insane with sensation. His entire body was aflame. He shoved his two large fingers back into her wet opening, then nuzzled his face between her wet lips and scraped his teeth lightly across her sensitive bud. He heard her sharp intake of air through her nose as she pulled her head back a little for air. She didn't release him from her mouth, though.

As soon as he backed off from her most sensitive spot, she sucked his member deeper into her mouth. Her tongue worked as a muscle to pull him in deeper and Mikhail couldn't control his hips anymore. He thrust forward, just a bit, and heard what sounded like a "pop." His scrotum covered her nose and she shook her head back and forth in quick, frantic jerks, desperate for air. Her hands gripped his thighs, pulling them apart, her hips starting to shake a bit frantically.

Mikhail pushed farther into her mouth, feeling himself going just that little bit deeper into the top of her throat. He was about to come, he knew, but the sensation was so unbelievable. Sarah's entire body was jerking in both her need for air and from the sensations she was experiencing. Mikhail ground his mouth against her wet apex, his fingers ramming into her deeper and harder, and he sucked her hard as he grazed his tongue cruelly across her clitoris, working that strong muscle as fast and hard against the growing sensitive bud as he could.

She was about to come. He was about to come. He wrapped his other strong arm under and around her bottom to bring her flesh even closer to his mouth and sucked harder than he ever had before at the same time he pulled his length completely out of her mouth. Sarah cried out in a loud, guttural shout of ecstasy, her head falling back onto the floor, her arms falling limply to the sides of his knees.

At her cry, Mikhail found his own release and he arched his head back on his own deep cry.

He fell over to the floor, lying on his side, one arm still stretched across her abdomen. He'd come all over her, he knew, but it didn't matter. He'd just experienced what had to be what humans called a religious experience. He'd never felt so much intensity before. He wanted to worship this precious jewel that had been given him. If there'd ever been any doubts in his mind that this creature, this beautiful, wonderful creature, had been created specifically for him, they were completely erased as of this moment.

Mikhail recovered first and maneuvered up onto an elbow to smile over at Sarah. "You okay?" he asked. His voice was a bit hoarse and he was exhausted, but he had to make sure she was all right first.

Sarah slowly lifted her eyelids and gave just the slightest nod. She then closed her eyes again and remained still.

Mikhail rolled over and stood in one fluid motion. He reached for the towel she'd earlier allowed to drop on the floor. He used it to clean his milky seed from her chest and neck. Then, he gently picked her up and, tucking her head securely up under his chin, he carried her from the bathroom to the big bed in his bedroom where he laid her down and covered her with the down comforter. He checked the doors to ensure they were locked, then climbed under the covers on the other side of the bed. He moved himself over to rest against her body, pulling her closer to his length, cradling her petite form and spooning against her backside.

Within minutes, they were both sound asleep.

Chapter 8

Azra'il made his way to his private chamber within the courthouse. He knew the members of the Great Sanhedrin were a bit piqued at his early exit, but he had more important matters over which to ruminate than what colors should be worn while working on the latest building under construction to celebrate the beloved Designers' return. He needed to figure out what was going on with Mikhail.

Azra'il had been in the council chamber earlier when Mikhail had been in attendance. He'd noticed immediately upon his brother's arrival that something wasn't quite right. Mikhail had not hesitated to pull the privacy shade on his station before he'd taken his seat behind it. The privacy shade had hidden his form from everyone's view... everyone's except for Azra'il, that is.

Azra'il had still seen Mikhail's aura. It had been unbelievably bright. There'd been such an intensity to it that at first Azra'il had thought Mikhail had been injured or incredibly angry about something. As the meeting had worn on, though, Azra'il had become aware of a different energy about Mikhail's form. There'd been some strange occasional flashing of bright light. Then, a pink haze had settled around Mikhail's own energy form.

Though he still didn't know what the flashing light had been, Azra'il believed he knew exactly what the pink haze had been – the human female, Sarah. She'd been with Mikhail psychically throughout the entire time he'd been in attendance at the council meeting. What was worse, Azra'il believed she'd caused such great energy fluctuations within Mikhail's own energy transmissions that he'd been forced to slip away from the meeting without alerting anyone, not even his own staff members on the council.

Somehow, Azra'il believed, this Sarah had caused a disruption in Mikhail's frequencies to the point that she had changed his normal bodily function. Azra'il had been sickened by what he'd witnessed and he was deeply concerned for his brother. He'd watched as Mikhail had valiantly managed to hold on as long as he could before he'd been forced to leave discreetly so that none would notice his loss of control. The privacy shade had not hidden anything from Azra'il's eyes other than Mikhail's facial expressions. Azra'il could only imagine the agony his brother had suffered.

Something would have to be done about this human female in their midst or she could end up bringing ruin to the entire city. Azra'il would have to think carefully on this issue before approaching his brothers. Mikhail and Gabriel had both already declared their desire to protect the girl from any harm, but Azra'il believed he could make them see reason. All it would take were the right words.

He poured himself a drink and took a seat behind his marble-topped desk. *Yes,* he thought, *the right words will make them come to see reason once more.*

The room was soft, if one could describe walls and a ceiling and floor as "soft". Looking down and all around, there was nothing but muted colors, grays, darker hues of whites and blues. The lighting in the room came from nowhere, it seemed. It just was. Traveling through the corridors revealed more and more of the same. There was no one in the hallways, no one anywhere. Continuing on down the corridors seemed the only thing to do. Looking back seemed no different than looking forward, except that part had already been seen.

Suddenly, there was a new room. It was much darker around the outside edges, but much, much brighter in the center. There was what looked like a giant glowing table there with a lighted dome directly in its center. Surrounding the table were ten tall figures in glowing white robes. The figures themselves glowed a brilliant white and, astonishingly, their eyes glowed even brighter than anything else in the room. They each had long, flowing white hair that seemed to be blowing softly in a breeze, though there was no detectable breeze within the room. It seemed as if there was no gravitational force holding the hair down. The figures, themselves, had long, gaunt faces with pale skin stretched tight over the facial bones. Their mouths were small, their lips almost undetectable. Their brighter than bright glowing white eyes seemed enormous in their otherwise unremarkable faces. They were standing around the table at various posts, but there were two posts that were unoccupied. This disturbed him. There was something wrong about those posts being unoccupied.

Shifting away from the table, he noticed the entire room appeared to be round with little computer components lighting up the walls through the darkness. Strange markings were etched into metal panels alongside the lighted controls. Those surrounding the glowing table in the middle of the room moved occasionally, but all still remained silent. Moving around the room afforded the same view as before. There appeared to be five females and five males within the group of glowing beings.

Upon closer examination of the round, glowing table, images appeared within the glowing domed center of it. It looked like videos of many different places and things. The glowing beings moved their arms, stretching out bony white fingers to touch the images showing on the lighted dome.

Images would appear larger or smaller, depending on what the beings were doing. Some images would disappear, all together. There seemed to be no rhyme or reason to what the beings were doing and no one spoke a word aloud.

Moving closer toward the glowing center of the room, the videos became clearer and certain places became recognizable. There was New York City, Sydney, Paris, and many other places that were foreign and unrecognizable. Moving even closer to search for other recognizable places or even people suddenly caught the attention of one of the female beings standing at the table. She stood directly next to one of the unoccupied posts and as she noticed him, she raised her head and a hand and pointed one of her bony fingers at him, her small slit of a mouth opening to emit a high-pitched sound unlike anything ever encountered by human ears.

The room faded as everything seemed to be going backward and movement was made in a flash from the round room, as if the entire dream were now being seen in reverse order, through corridor after corridor, and all the while the high-pitched wail of the female being could be heard.

Thomas woke with a start. He was lying on the bed in Mikhail's home. His chest heaved and he was audibly sucking air into lungs that just wouldn't seem to work. *What on earth?* he wondered. He raised his head and looked around the room. It was barely light out and Thomas didn't hear anything from anywhere else in the house. He looked over to a clock on the nightstand and confirmed it was still early. His mom wouldn't be expecting him to be up this early, he knew.

He was still shaken from the dream, but it hadn't been bad. He wasn't afraid, like he was after so many of his dreams. Usually, he awoke screaming for his mom after such a vivid experience. This time, though, he really just wanted to know where he had been and what had been about to happen in the dream before he'd awakened. Now that he thought about it, the dream had seemed so real, somehow. Those creatures, they had been something else, not human, not of this world. He was sure of it.

And the female... Thomas wondered about her. *What was she? Where had she come from? Was she real? If he quickly fell back to sleep, would he be able to continue with the dream?*

Thomas closed his eyes tight, took as deep a breath as he could, and tried to relax. He concentrated on relaxing each part of his body, all the muscle groups he knew about from the studying he'd had to do in health class at school. Before he realized it, he was asleep once more. This time, however, there were no dreams, merely a deep and peaceful sleep.

Sarah's eyes opened slowly, just as Mikhail's thumb began rubbing along her bicep in slow, lazy circles. She felt his entire body coming awake, though he didn't move anything other than his thumb across her arm. She knew he'd opened his eyes and that he was looking over at the far wall and not at her. She was looking over there, as well, though she wasn't seeing the wall.

What could she say to him? After what they'd done earlier in the bathroom, how on earth could she face him? She was embarrassed by her wantonness, but she couldn't bring herself to regret it. She'd needed to be touched like that, to be taken in such a primal manner. She knew he'd been satisfied as well. A surge of pride swelled within her momentarily. He'd wanted her, she knew it. He'd demanded of her and she'd met his demands with demands of her own. What they'd done had been something not acceptable by normal society, no, but it had also been something they'd both wanted and needed from each other. Sarah wouldn't cheapen the experience by apologizing for how she'd behaved.

The bigger problem she faced was that although she believed Mikhail wanted her, she knew he refused to make her his in the most basic of ways for some reason. She didn't get it. *Maybe it's an Angel thing*, she thought. She seemed to remember reading somewhere that Angels were supposedly androgynous. From what she'd felt earlier, however, Mikhail certainly was not! *Maybe he's waiting until we're married?* She didn't know what the reason was. She simply knew she didn't like it. She wanted him as her man. She wanted the rest of the world to know he was her man. It was plain and simple and if he thought she was going to just sit back allowing him to skirt around the issue, he had another think coming.

Mikhail lay holding her within his arms, searching for the words to express how he felt. He'd had the most amazingly earth-shattering experience of his long life and it had all been because of her. He knew beyond all doubts that she had been made for him and that he would only ever want her from this point onward throughout all time. If only he could think of a way to let her know how he felt.

Then again, how could he tie her down to him when he could never actually consummate their relationship fully? She was human and was therefore forbidden to him. His beloved Designers had made only that one law for their Seraphim. They had created all the lesser Angels to fulfill the needs of Seraphim. There had always been far more than enough lesser Angels ready and able to please the Seraphim, too. They each even had their own "followers" who had sworn their fealty to just one Seraph over the millennia. Mikhail himself had well over one hundred of these, though he tended to stick with all female Angels. It had been quite some years since Mikhail had taken one to his bed, however.

It was not unheard of for the lesser male Angels to devote themselves to one Seraph, even for intimate relationship purposes. Mikhail didn't know if any of his Seraphim brethren had ever actually taken another of the same sex into intimate relations, but he would not judge his brothers. Being a Seraph was not an easy task. He knew this better than any of his brothers. He took his duties very seriously and he would always. However, even he became lonely, even he experienced the occasional desire for something more. He saw this as a flaw in his design, which usually led to disturbing thoughts and feelings, for he didn't like to think his beloved Designers could make mistakes.

But, now there was Sarah.

She was completely different from the others in the human realm. He could feel her soul-energies, could detect the pure tones of her frequencies. They resonated throughout his being, pulling him in toward her, creating a yearning that would not be denied within his whole being. He wanted to touch her, wanted to feel her touching him at all times. He never wanted it to stop, never wanted to part from her. He wanted to join with her, to become one with her. There was no such thing as too close for him. He wanted to feel her within his own skin, wanted her inside him as he wanted to be inside her.

Mikhail suddenly whipped himself off of the bed, letting her go and jumping to his feet as if she'd burned him. He had to put some distance between her and himself. He felt as if he might do her some physical harm, just trying to get closer to her. His mind was filled with her. He couldn't tune out her frequencies. They were being carried along on massive action potentials from neuron to neuron within his brain. His cerebellum was tingling from the sweetness of the tones emitting from her.

He saw her sit up, watching him with a questioning look on her face. He was backing away from her. She was so innocent. She was so beautiful. Her very essence called to him and he, like a dog in heat, wanted, no, *needed* to go to her. He needed her more than he'd ever needed anything in his entire, long life.

He shook his head back and forth, doing anything to deny what his body wanted him to do. It was imploring him to cross back over to the bed to take her, to make her his. His tortured mind demanded that he follow the rules set in place by his beloved Designers. His back came up against the wall at the far side of the room and he slowly slid down it until he was sitting leaned up against the wall, knees bent, head bent. His hands covered his face and he felt as weak as a young child. His shoulders shook with the rage he felt at the warring thoughts within himself.

She was his. She'd been created for him. He was a Seraph and he must obey the one law. But, she'd been created specifically for him. She had to have been. There was no other explanation for everything that had happened since the day he'd first encountered her.

Suddenly, Mikhail's hands dropped and he looked up at her. Sarah tucked the top cover under her arms and sat up on her knees on the mattress, holding onto the poster at the end of the bed. She stared at him, concern etched on her lovely features. Her eyes flashed every now and then. Mikhail realized they were flashing a lot faster than they had been in the beginning. He could see his own reflection in the full-length mirror over on the wall close to the bed and he noticed that his own eyes were flashing at the same time as hers, just as quickly.

So much had changed since Sarah had come into his life. His reflection was proof enough of that, to be certain. He could now see a dim glow coming from within his own body. When he looked back at Sarah, he noticed a similar glow coming from within hers. This glow was different than just her soul-energy glow. There was something else going on within both their bodies and it seemed to be intensifying with each moment they spent together. Even his vision was changing, as he realized he saw color in things he'd never before seen color in. It was like seeing auras around everything, or like wearing night specs that detected heat.

Mikhail swallowed a lump in his throat as he watched her swing a bare leg off the bed to stand. She dragged the cover with her and came to stand just before him. She stretched the blanket out and covered him with it as she took a seat on the floor next to him. She didn't say anything. She put a hand onto one of his, but made no other contact with him. Her gaze focused on their reflections in the mirror on the far wall.

Mikhail swallowed another lump, then cleared his throat and tentatively said, "I-I'm sorry. I didn't mean to frighten you."

Sarah leaned back against the wall, but didn't say anything.

Mikhail continued slowly, explaining, "And I didn't mean to hurt you, earlier."

Sarah turned her head to look up at him.

"I lost control. I hope I wasn't too rough on you," he said.

She shook her head, but said nothing.

Mikhail looked back at their reflections in the mirror. In his mind, he was going over words and phrases he could use to explain his inner turmoil. How could a human be expected to understand... No! He would not think of her as a regular human. She was different, he was sure of it. He needed to explain things to her because he needed her to understand him through and through. He needed to know she understood him completely. It was important, more important than anything ever had been before.

Sarah suddenly whispered, "I've never been any good at relationships."

Mikhail stared at her reflection in the mirror, his eyes narrowing.

"Even with Thomas' dad," she continued, "I just couldn't seem to make it work." She shook her head, lost in thought. "There was just nothing ever there, no feeling. I mean, I was attracted to guys physically, but there was just always something missing."

Mikhail cocked an eyebrow and leaned over to bump shoulders with her, quirking through a half-smile, "I don't need the intimate details, you know?"

Sarah's attention re-focused on his reflection in the mirror and she ducked her head a little shyly, apologizing, "Sorry." She straightened back up against the wall. "I just wanted you to understand that I've never felt anything like this with anyone before," she continued.

Mikhail lowered his gaze momentarily. When he finally looked back up at their reflections in the mirror, he said quietly, "You're the first human I've ever touched intimately."

Sarah turned to face him, her eyes narrowed in confusion. Finally, she asked simply, "Why?"

Mikhail looked down at her. "Humans are forbidden to Seraphim for intimate relationships," he explained.

Sarah opened her mouth as if to interrupt, shaking her head.

Mikhail continued with his explanation, "The blessed Great Designers made Seraphim out of something completely different than the materials used to make humans. They explained to us that humans would be damaged if we became intimate with them."

"But, we..." she began.

"If we were to consummate fully with them," he explained.

Sarah stared at him in disbelief. "How... How did you survive all this time without... without...?" she asked, unable to complete her question, the very idea of it stymieing her beyond all comprehension.

"The lesser Angels were created for that purpose," he explained.

"Oh," was all she said. She looked back at their reflections in the mirror. Her face fell visibly on a wave of realization. *How could he ever want me more than one of those beautiful creatures?* She wondered. The Angels she'd seen each time she'd been out and about within Seraphim City, and even the staff within his household, had all seemed so beautiful and beyond comparison. They were all so tall and perfect-looking, much more than even the most beautiful humans she'd ever seen. How could someone like *her* ever compare?

Mikhail reached an arm over and behind her head, encircling her shoulders, and hugged her gently to his side. "You are more perfect to me than any Angel I've ever encountered," he whispered against her temple. He turned his head and leaned it against hers as he stared back into the mirror on the other side of the room.

"B-but, I'm human," she said. "You said you're not able to... um..., I mean..."

Mikhail hugged her a little more tightly against his side, his jaws clenching as he thought of ever losing her. "You're different," he rasped in a low, savage voice.

Sarah pulled back a little from him and looked back up at his face, their eyes locked onto each other. "So, you're going to risk becoming a fallen angel, or something, just because you think I'm different somehow?" she asked.

"What do you know of fallen angels?" he asked, a slight smile etching the corners of his mouth.

"I only know they're mentioned in the Bible," she said. She didn't continue, for she really didn't remember much more than that from the few Sunday school classes she'd had as a child.

Mikhail let loose a half-hearted chuckle and leaned his head back against the wall, his eyes sliding closed. "Your Bible doesn't tell the story the way it happened," he said. "We couldn't explain it sufficiently to the humans of that time, though they wanted to know. They just wouldn't have been able to understand it. So, we gave them the simplest explanation possible." He looked back down at her and said, "There was so much more to the story."

Sarah cocked a brow, silently encouraging him to go on.

Mikhail leaned his head back against the wall again, his gaze going to a far off time and place. He let out a long sigh, then started his story, saying, "Originally, there were six Seraphim, five brothers and one sister." His lips quirked at the corners, a half-smile almost managing to make it onto his face. "Suriyah – how we all doted on her," he said. "We all thought she was the most beautiful being on the planet." He laughed aloud at some memory, then said, "She knew it, too."

Then, his smile faded and he continued, "Our beloved Designers came then. Suriyah and I happened upon them one day while we were out observing the humans. We'd gotten into the habit of crossing over to the human realm to watch over them. They'd seemed so lost, even then. They were always fighting amongst themselves and Suriyah decided it was our duty to help them sort out their problems whenever and however we could.

"We felt them coming before their craft even came close enough to be seen in the heavens. Then, they came down from the heavens in great fiery clouds of smoke and heat. The humans were frightened and scattered as the ships landed. We stood our ground and watched. When our beloved Designers emerged from within the ships, we were enthralled by how different they looked. Some of them were tall, some short, some gray in skin color, some blue, some even seemed almost to be covered in a black leathery sort of skin. None of them looked quite like us, though. They came onto the land and declared they were the rulers of this world and that all living creatures here had been of their making and that we were to worship them.

"At first, none of us realized anything was wrong. I mean, we all accepted what we'd been told, for they certainly seemed far more advanced and knowledgeable of things than we. There was a great energy among us all as we decided to build Seraphim City in celebration of having finally become acquainted with our beloved Designers. Suriyah and Baphomet, our other brother, participated in the building process, too. They never said anything to any of us about any misgivings they were having.

"We brought our beloved Designers across the barrier between realms and showed them the wonderful city we'd created in their honor. We were so proud of our accomplishment and our beloved Designers praised us for our efforts. In the human realm, they'd been busy directing the humans in erecting huge cities filled with monuments to celebrate their return to this planet. Much of the technologies the humans have today came directly from the blessed Great Designers, you know?"

Sarah merely shook her head.

"We thought it was a little odd that our beloved Designers couldn't cross through the rift in the barrier between realms by themselves, seeing as how they'd created us to be in this realm. But, then they explained that we'd been created in the human realm, but that when the humans had been created we'd found our way over into this dimension on our own to be able to have a separate space from the ever-growing number of humans.

"That's when we learned we were supposed to watch over and control the humans. We were all okay with that, as we'd been doing what we could since we'd discovered humans in the first place." He paused in his story for a moment, his thoughts racing.

He frowned and said, "One day, there was a group of humans that decided they didn't need to do the work our beloved Designers had set out for them and they decided to rebel. They didn't want to mine the metals. They didn't want to build the cities for the newcomers anymore. There was a coup attempt at one of the palaces of one particular Designer. This one wasn't exactly well-liked by everyone, but he was one of the blessed Great Designers, so we all afforded him the respect he was due. But, the humans decided it was time for him to go.

"An attempt was made on his life. It was an ill-fated coup attempt, at best, for a human couldn't kill a Designer. After the attempt on his life, he declared that he would destroy the entire human race. Suriyah and Baphomet loved the humans more than any of us at that time and they were devastated by this news. They went to their most favored of our beloved Designers to plead for mercy on the humans. His name was Enki and he just happened to be the son of the blessed Great Designer who'd been angered by the humans.

"Enki reasoned with his father, for he loved his Seraphim, and he won the right for the humans to continue living. His father agreed that as long as Enki took on the responsibility for the operation of this planet, he would not harm the humans. The father left the planet, leaving everything in Enki's care. The problem was that there were still those humans who didn't think it was their responsibility to work for the blessed Great Designers.

"Enki ordered those humans to be expunged. He gave this order to his beloved Seraphim. None of us wanted to carry out the order, for we all enjoyed the humans of this world. Suriyah and Baphomet flat out refused to carry out Enki's order. None of us had ever killed any living creature up to that point. That's when Enki decided that Suriyah and Baphomet were not worthy enough to be Seraphim and they were to be banished from Seraphim City.

"The rest of us were devastated. Baphomet was one of the most loyal of Seraphim and Suriyah had always been the light of our lives. How could we live without them? Our brother and sister weren't going down without a fight, though. They both worked to convince the rest of us that the blessed Great Designers weren't really what they said they were. When Enki was confronted by one of the Seraph with this information, he said the rest of the Seraphim were no longer to associate with Baphomet or Suriyah and that all those loyal to them were to be banished from Seraphim City as well.

"In the end, it was put onto one Seraph to see to the task of banishing our sister and brother as well as to the destruction of the group of humans rebelling. The Great Sanhedrin was formed, with this one Seraph as the council's supreme authority, and the orders were carried out without delay. Our brother and sister were banished, along with their followers, to the Badlands, which is a lawless and wild section of our realm. The group of humans was assassinated. No mercy was shown, as per Enki's orders."

Mikhail went silent, his gaze on some far, distant place and time. The look on his face spoke volumes of the pain the memories were evoking.

"Wh-What happened to Suriyah and Baphomet?" Sarah asked shyly.

"I never allowed them back into the city," he said simply. "They and their followers became corrupt. Those who followed our sister became known as Jinn. Those who followed Baphomet became known as Shaitans, or Demons or other names, depending on the culture. There is no law in the Badlands and the Shaitans and Jinn became so twisted and evil that they even look different from those of us here in Seraphim City now, or so I've heard.

"I do not know what happened to our brother and sister. I know they were both declared King and Queen, respectively, of each of their groups, but I have not seen either of them since the day they were forced from Seraphim City. I hear of the exploits of the Shaitans and Jinn in the human realm on a regular basis. I've also had to clean up enough of the messes they've created there to know they've all become something wild, corrupted and evil and that they have found other rifts in the barrier crossing into the human dimension. They cannot be reasoned with anymore. They are lost to the Seraphim."

A wave of sadness washed over Sarah. She realized Mikhail had been the one who'd been assigned by this Enki to do the terrible deed of banishing his beloved brother and sister from Seraphim City. That also meant, she realized, that he'd been the one Seraph to report their treachery to Enki as well. She couldn't imagine the guilt and shame he must feel for having done such a thing. She reached over, suddenly, and placed her hand on his chest, just above his heart. "I'm sorry," she said, looking up at him.

Mikhail looked down into her eyes, searching for whatever it was that made her so precious to him. There was a light in her ice-blue eyes that warmed his heart and he bent slightly to place a soft kiss upon her lips. It was just a simple touch connecting the two of them, yet the moment their lips met they both went up in flames of desire for the other.

Mikhail quickly broke away from the kiss. He didn't want to think of touching her at this moment. It wasn't right, somehow. He disengaged his arm from around her shoulders and stood. After taking a few paces from her, he turned and regarded her, unconcerned with his lack of clothing. "You are not like the rest of the humans out there," he declared. "I know I've said that before, but it's the truth. I know it is. I can feel it."

Sarah grabbed the wall and maneuvered herself to her feet, keeping the cover wrapped securely around her body. "What makes me so different from them?" she asked.

He shook his head. "I don't know," he said honestly. "I just know I *feel* you, here in my heart." He pounded his fist onto the middle of his chest. His eyes narrowed and he continued, "You were made for me and I think I was made to be with you. Our being together has brought about changes in both of us that cannot be explained by any other reasoning of which I know. I mean, look at our eyes, how they flash and swirl, and the fact that I can hear and see everything you think and see."

Sarah nodded, her eyes wide. She, herself, had experienced things she couldn't explain. Each time Mikhail woke, she woke immediately and knew what he was doing. She'd sensed things in him during their escapade on the bathroom floor that she shouldn't have been able to sense. And, the color change of her eyes by itself should not have been possible.

"I will go to my brothers," Mikhail said. "Djibr..., I mean, Gabriel was the one who came up with the theory that you were not like normal humans. I believe he will support me and he and I will present our case to my other two brothers."

Sarah didn't know what to say. No one had ever done anything like this for her. She hadn't exaggerated when she'd told Mikhail she'd never been any good at relationships. She hadn't. The longest one she'd ever endured had lasted a mere four months and that only because of the physical distance between the guy and her. She just didn't know what to do when the whole physical part was over and done with.

Now, here was this incredible being offering to risk his reputation and status just to be with her. Sarah couldn't wrap her head around the idea of it.

She started toward him, drawn by the compassion and feeling of unwavering resolve within. She made it two steps before a blinding pain shot down her spine. She screamed as her muscles all went rock-solid rigid. She would have fallen to the floor had it not been for Mikhail's quick reflexes. One minute, he'd been two yards away from her and the next, he was crouched, holding her rigid form in his arms, her shoulders propped against a bent knee.

"Sarah!" he gasped. "What is it, love?"

Sarah's jaws were clenched shut. She could really only move her eyes, but the pain was so intense between her shoulder blades that she wasn't really even sure she could accomplish that much.

"Sarah!" he yelled.

"M-my b-ack," she finally managed in a weak whisper, her breath coming in halting, weak gasps.

Mikhail cautiously rotated her so he could see what was going on. If there was some injury, he should be able to heal it, as that was one of his gifts as a Seraph. There was blood everywhere, much of it still spilling from just between her shoulder blades at her spine. Mikhail reached to touch the wound, wondering what on earth could have caused her to suddenly just start bleeding. The moment his hand touched the spot, he understood, though it made no sense to him.

Between the spinal vertebrae known as T3 and T4, Mikhail felt the familiar spinal nodule found on all Seraphim. This spinal nodule allowed for the six shields of the Seraphim, what humans often mistook for wings. As he watched, the nodule closed itself off, halting the bleeding, and a slight fold of skin, which Seraphim called the cutapi, began forming over it. This should eventually hang loose over the spinal nodule in order to protect it but still allow for the shields to emerge without difficulty.

"Hold on," Mikhail soothed. He hoped he was right and that this really was a spinal nodule forming. That could only mean one thing: Sarah was *becoming* a Seraph. His heart raced as he maneuvered her gently back into a position where he could see her face. Her breathing was less labored now, he noticed, and her muscles were slowly relaxing. "You're going to be okay," he assured her.

"Wh-what's happening?" she asked.

He opened his mouth, then shut it and simply shook his head. How could he explain this to her? He didn't understand it, himself. If she was actually becoming a Seraph, that would clear the way for them to be together, wouldn't it? And, if that happened, then might they...?

"Mikhail?" Sarah interrupted his thoughts.

"It's okay, love," he whispered. He was too filled with nervous energy to say more. He *wanted* her to become a Seraph. He wanted it more than he'd ever wanted anything in his entire life.

Her body relaxed completely and he adjusted his hold on her, picking her up gently and taking her back to the bed. He laid her down on the mattress, uncaring of the stain that would be formed. Sarah relaxed back onto the mattress, her head resting on a soft pillow.

She was afraid to move, afraid something really was wrong with her and that if she moved too much she might end up paralyzed. She'd attended enough neuroscience classes this semester to know there were any number of issues that could cause permanent paralysis when it came to the spinal cord. The pain she'd experienced had most definitely involved her spinal cord, she knew, because she could still feel something back there out of whack.

Her breathing had become much easier, so she just laid back and tried to relax. Mikhail was here. He wouldn't let anything happen to her, she knew. All she had to do was to make it through whatever this was and everything would be okay. Mikhail would make sure of that. She closed her eyes. If she could count on him…

There was a knock at the door and Mikhail excused himself to go answer it. Sarah became a little nervous, thinking perhaps it might be Thomas. It turned out to be one of the staff.

"Is everything all right, my Lord?" the man asked.

"Everything's fine," Mikhail told him, barely opening the door to peer outside into the hallway. "Our guest was just frightened by a shadow, that's all," he explained to the man. Very soon after, he shut the door and returned to the bed to lie down on top of the covers next to Sarah.

"What's happening to me, Mikhail?" Sarah asked as best she could. Her face muscles and jaws seemed to be working again. At least, she wasn't all clenched up and taut the way she had been before. She was actually able to turn her head and look up at his face.

He reached over and brushed a strand of her long, auburn hair off her forehead, tucking it behind her ear, and said, "I'm not really sure what's going on. I think… I think you're experiencing some kind of physiological change."

She stared up at him for a moment before whispering, "That's impossible."

He looked down into her eyes. He smiled the half-smile she'd come to recognize as his usual and said, "Impossible or not, that's what seems to be happening to you." He sat up and turned so that she could see his upper back. "You see that flap of skin just at the middle of my back, between my shoulder blades?" he asked, reaching a hand up and behind to point to the spot.

Sarah remembered feeling that area when they'd been in the bathroom. She hadn't asked about it at the time. She'd been otherwise engaged and hadn't thought anymore about it since then. She hesitantly reached up a hand to touch the slight flap of skin she saw laying over what looked like a little bump on his spine, amazed that her arm was able to reach up like that, since it had been just a short time ago so stiff and painful that she hadn't thought she'd ever be able to use her arms or legs again. The flap of skin felt like some type of leather and she ran a finger under it lightly. She felt Mikhail shiver slightly and asked, "Does that hurt?"

He shook his head and whispered, "No." He didn't say anything more.

Sarah lifted the flap and was surprised to see an actual hole protruding slightly from the very center of his spine there. It, too had a little covering, but it was like a tube that had a cap on it. She asked, "What is it?"

Mikhail turned around and leaned once more on an elbow to better face her. "It's a nodule from which our shields extend when they're employed. All Seraphim have them. It's how we fly, protect ourselves, carry things... you know, we use them for all manner of things," he finished quietly.

Sarah thought back to when Gabriel had brought Thomas and her across the dimensions into this realm. She remembered the leathery-like covering she'd felt. It hadn't been exactly leathery, though. The flap above the tube-like opening was leathery feeling. She wondered how it worked.

"I can show you, if you'd like," Mikhail offered.

She'd forgotten he could read her mind. "This is weird," she said as she tried to move. She was shaky and stiff and her muscles didn't want to cooperate, but she finally managed to maneuver herself into a sitting position. She turned to arrange the pillow she'd been laying on into a more comfortable position behind her. That's when she finally noticed the blood.

She sucked in a sharp breath as a streak of fear lanced down her spine. Her eyes darted to Mikhail's.

"It's okay," he said, reaching a hand out to run down her arm. "I told you. You're just forming your spinal nodule." He reached around and ran his fingers under the cutapi, feeling the nodule there. "It's almost completely formed, it seems," he said as he withdrew his hand.

Sarah shivered from the feel of his fingers on the sensitive area of her spine and asked, "Well, isn't there someone we should call or have come look at it... like a doctor or something?" She could feel the hysteria rising within her, but she didn't know what else to do. There were still things going on in her spinal column. She could feel them.

"That's just the neurons growing. They'll have to grow much longer than any of the others in order to enervate your shields," Mikhail said.

Sarah suddenly grunted in frustration. "This is getting pretty annoying, you know?" she grumbled.

Mikhail shrugged. "What do you think it's like for me?" he countered. "I mean, here I've been alone for a million years, as far as I can tell, and now all of a sudden, I've got the thoughts of a human woman bouncing around in my brain." He stared intently at her. "Do you think that's an easy thing for me to adjust to?"

Sarah was quiet for a moment. She hadn't thought of matters in that light. All she'd known was that there was suddenly someone who was listening to each and every thought she had and now she was having to depend on said person to help her with a physical transformation. She looked over at him, wondering if he was listening to her now.

Mikhail reached up a hand and cupped one cheek, gazing deeply into her eyes. "Sometimes," he whispered, "the thoughts you have are so random and complex that I have difficulty keeping up with your thought processes. But, I like knowing this about you. I like being able to identify what you're thinking along with what you're feeling." He gently wrapped his arms around her and pulled her to rest on his chest.

Chapter 9

Thomas wandered around the house on the ground floor. His mom was still asleep, or so he assumed. He certainly hadn't seen her and Mikhail lurking anywhere downstairs. He was famished, though, and needed something to eat *now*.

The dream he'd had last night had wiped him out. He felt like he'd been put through the wringer. He'd tried desperately to rejoin the dream after he'd awakened that first time, but he'd been unable to. He wanted to know who those beings were. There was no way his mind could've come up with something like that on its own.

His mom had told him about the visions she'd been having. Now, it appeared Thomas was having some of his own. Either that, or he figured he'd better start looking for an agent because the stuff he was dreaming up was way beyond anything Hollywood had out at the moment. There'd been something about the dream, though, something he couldn't quite put his finger on. Somehow, those creatures had seemed almost familiar to him.

How that could be possible, he didn't know. But, he wasn't going to sit around and mope. If his mom had taught him anything, it was that you could never get anywhere by just sitting around moping and feeling sorry for yourself. You had to get out and about, do things to get your heart pumping. Thomas figured most people in the world who claimed they suffered from depression would not be suffering if they'd simply get up off their bums and get moving, do some exercise or something, on a regular basis.

Of course, he would never say anything like that aloud around other people. It was really weird how funny people got when it came to things like that. He'd found that talking around others was really tricky business. It was far better to keep quiet and just listen to what other people were saying. That way, when they asked something of you, you usually would know what was really going on. Of course, that always meant the school counselor had to get involved, calling your mom and telling her things like, "Thomas is just so quiet. We're concerned and believe you ought to take him to have him evaluated by a psychologist." That led to your mom coming home in tears crying about how she's such a bad mom and what could she do to make things better and so on and so on.

That wasn't always such a bad thing because Thomas sometimes ended up getting video games and such whenever his mom was feeling guilty. But, he knew he couldn't do that to her all the time. He didn't like seeing her cry. He knew she tried her best to give him everything. She hadn't gone out on a date in years, not since he'd been in grade school. He couldn't even remember the last time she'd gone out with her friends. She was always studying and working on getting her degree. Thomas figured he had to cut her a little slack now and then. It was hard, sometimes. He didn't like most of the kids at school, found them to be really stupid. They never thought about things. They just believed everything they were told to believe, never questioning anything.

Thomas, on the other hand, questioned everything. He figured we all had to really fight to be able to come to this plane, to be able to inhabit human bodies, so he thought it was his duty to figure out things as much as he could. He wanted to understand everything, to know as much as he could, to learn as much as he could in the time he had here.

For some reason, most other people didn't seem to think this same way.

Thomas had heard the religious people around his school touting about how they'd been put here by their god and how they couldn't wait until the day when they were retrieved by that god to go and live in some miraculous place called "Heaven." Thomas believed we all made our own heaven and hell. No one controlled his life, he figured. If they did, then Thomas had a few friggin' questions about some things!

His stomach growled and he was reminded of the reason why he was wandering aimlessly downstairs in the first place. Finally, as he opened yet another door, he found the kitchen. There were some of the staff milling about within, but they didn't seem to notice him. They were preparing huge meals, it appeared. Thomas wondered who would be eating all that food. There was already a buffet table over in the corner of the room that was heavily laden with all manner of entrees and desserts.

He inched his way over toward the table, looking around to make sure no one was watching him. Without turning to look at the table, Thomas snagged a couple of the hot rolls that were waiting there and stuffed them up under his shirt. After a short pause, he snagged a couple of bits of meat and stuffed them up under his shirt as well. No one took any notice of him as he moved on down the long table, stuffing this or that up under his shirt to add to his collection.

He was almost at the end of the table, almost to the dessert area, when one of the staff approached him. She was a kindly looking sort, with brown hair curled up into a bun at the back of her head. Her eyes were an inviting cool blue, the same as all the rest of the staff and people Thomas had seen since coming to this place, though Mikhail's were a much brighter shade! She approached without a word and held out a clean plate. Thomas looked down at the plate, then at the bulge his one hand was supporting in his shirt.

Reluctantly, he took the plate and, carefully unrolling the bundle from within his shirt, he allowed all the food he'd snatched to dump down onto the plate. With a red face, he looked back up at the woman. She merely smiled and motioned for him to take more from the table. Hesitantly, Thomas began piling more food onto his plate. He was so hungry he figured he could've eaten all of the food there, even the things he couldn't identify.

The woman handed him a huge cup full of some funny looking liquid, but Thomas wasn't about to complain. He balanced the plate as best he could onto one hand and took the huge mug into his other hand. It weighed a ton! How on earth the woman had carried it in just one hand by the handle, he didn't know. He was having difficulty carrying it with a hand and an arm. He nodded his thanks to the woman and made his way out of the kitchen. He didn't know if it was okay for him to eat things in his room or not, but he wasn't about to go looking for someone to ask. He was starving and he needed to eat now. He made his way up to his room and then made himself comfortable on the floor in front of the television.

This wasn't so bad, he decided. His mom was busy with Mikhail somewhere. He was left to his own devices. He didn't have his favorite games here, but he had some new ones Mikhail had bought him last night and there was television and the computer that Mikhail had had set up for him in his room after their shopping excursion. It beat having to go to school, too. Thomas was not about to complain.

The food was delicious and he really liked the drink, though he still couldn't tell exactly what it was. He gulped it down and was then surprised when there was a knock at the door and more food and drink was brought in for him. The same staff member who'd given him the plate in the kitchen was the one delivering the food. Thomas made sure to thank her before she left. She merely smiled and bowed to him before leaving.

Thomas was quite content here, to say the least. He could get used to this way of life, most definitely.

Mikhail watched Sarah as she slept. So much had happened in just a short time that his head was still spinning. Sarah had fully developed the spinal nodule and the cutapi now. They looked as if she'd always had them. He knew she would need training on how to use them, but he was still reeling from the fact that she'd developed them in the first place.

She was sleeping so soundly and looked so peaceful that Mikhail didn't want to move for fear that he would disturb her slumber. He watched her as if she might suddenly disappear. In such a short amount of time, she had become the most important thing in the world to him. When he thought of anyone ever trying to take her away from him, his blood practically boiled within his veins. He knew he would even fight his beloved Designers to the death were they to ever decide he could no longer be with Sarah.

He would fight any and all to the death to be with her.

Sarah's eyes slowly opened and she shifted to stare up at him. She lifted a hand up to cup his cheek. "I think I'm feeling better now," she whispered.

Mikhail smiled down at her. Her eyes were the usual ice blue of the Seraphim. She now had a spinal nodule for her six shields. He didn't even mind that she was so short. It made her seem as fragile as he believed her to be. He liked being the stronger of the two of them. He could look after her that way. He leaned down and kissed her forehead. Then, he moved down toward her mouth. Her breath smelled so sweet and her skin was so soft. He never wanted to stop touching her. He ran his tongue across her lips, coaxing them open to receive his muscle.

Sarah sighed and opened her mouth wide. His tongue slid in without hesitation. Sarah thought she could definitely get used to waking up like this. She slid an arm around his shoulders, pulling him more fully on top of her while running her other hand up his chest. Her hand slid around to the middle of his back, between his shoulder blades and she felt his spinal nodule. She suddenly shot straight up in the bed, her own hands going to touch and feel the new nodule there on her own back.

It was there. It didn't hurt. She lifted the leathery flap of skin there and felt the nodule itself. It was so strange, but it felt as if it had been there all along. Rubbing the tip of her index finger over the top of the opening of the nodule, Sarah felt something. The sensation was like something coming up from the very bottom of her spine. She could feel muscles working in her back she'd never known she'd had. The muscles flexed and something seemed to burst from within her nodule. Before she knew what had happened, Mikhail was flying through the air all the way over to the other side of the room, his body slamming into the wall there and dropping to the floor.

Sarah was off the bed in an instant. "Oh, my gosh," she gushed. "Are you okay?" She helped Mikhail to stand and he looked down at her, a huge grin on his face.

He immediately enfolded her in a big bear hug and squeezed, saying, "That's my girl." He was so proud of her, he was practically beaming. His woman was fully capable, obviously, of handling herself in a fight. He would be less worried about her should they ever get separated. Although Mikhail doubted he would let her out for the first couple of hundred years or so. He wanted to keep her heavy with their offspring before they went out onto the battlefield together.

That thought made him pause. Just because she'd developed a spinal nodule and cutapi and her eyes had changed, there was no certainty that she had actually changed into a Seraph. Would she now be immortal, as he was? There was no guarantee. He looked down at her, his face growing serious. She would always need his protection. She would always be vulnerable. To him, she was a precious ornament that would break easily if mishandled.

Mikhail now understood what made human men do the things they did. He would never stop trying to protect her. He would kill anyone or anything that ever tried to harm her. She was his and his alone. Mikhail knew that if the Great Sanhedrin decided she and he had no place together in this realm, he would move her and their son out to the Badlands. He could manage out there. If Suriyah and Baphomet had managed to make it out there in that wild, lawless land, then so could Mikhail and Sarah and Thomas.

Sarah stepped away from him. She wasn't sure how to feel. She was feeling all powerful and full of energy, yet she could feel something else. There was sadness, or a fear, deep inside her. She wasn't sure which it was or what it stemmed from, either. She could see that Mikhail was fine physically, but there was something in his eyes. It was some kind of warning she couldn't decipher. She could feel something coming from within him. As she studied him from beneath lowered lashes, she could tell he was struggling internally with some great emotion.

The thought that he might not feel comfortable enough with her yet to discuss it openly occurred to her then and she turned away from him. "I think I'll go have another shower," she said with a catch in her voice. She could feel the confusion and hurt inside him at her abrupt words, but she didn't know what to do. The sharing of emotions and some thoughts was getting very confusing for her and Sarah just wanted to escape it for a while.

She returned to her own room and, after turning on the water, picked out some clothes to put on after. Her stomach emitted an unusually loud growl as she stepped into the steaming shower and Sarah remembered she hadn't yet eaten today. That's when she finally remembered Thomas.

How on earth she had forgotten about Thomas being just down the hall, she didn't know. She had become so caught up in everything that was going on with Mikhail and her that she had completely forgotten about her own *son*! She had no idea if he was well or even if he was up. She believed he must surely be up by now, as it was almost noon. She had just determined that she would rush through the shower when she actually felt Mikhail's voice in her mind, assuring her, *I've just spoken with one of the kitchen staff. Thomas has eaten and is happily playing video games in his room.*

Sarah sighed in relief. It wasn't as if he'd spoken, she'd just felt his emotions..., his feelings on the subject, and she'd suddenly understood the message he was trying to convey.

Take your time in the shower, love, she understood, as Mikhail's voice rubbed softly against her mind.

Sarah heaved another sigh, this one deep and seeming to take with it all of her energy when she let it go. She leaned her head against the shower wall and merely allowed the pulsing jets of hot water to pound down over and around her. *It's too much*, she thought, though she wasn't sure if she had meant to direct her thoughts to Mikhail or not. He heard, of course.

It will become easier, love, he sent back to her. *Pull on your new energies*, his voice urged.

Sarah didn't know what he meant, but she suddenly felt a burst of energy radiating out from the full length of her spine. Her skin virtually danced with it, as if a shot of electricity had just passed throughout her entire body, and she very quickly felt completely rejuvenated.

She got out of the shower and toweled dry. As she approached the vanity where she had left her new change of clothes, she noticed her reflection in the mirror there. A shock jolted through her and she found herself mesmerized by the changes in her reflection. Her eyes were flashing much quicker now and their color was a much brighter shade of ice-blue than they had been before. Her hair seemed to be much longer and there were definite streaks of pure white strands dispersed throughout it. Her skin seemed to glow, as well, and she suddenly wondered how she was going to explain all this to Thomas. Fear crept back into her heart.

We'll do it together, sweetheart, came Mikhail's response in her mind.

Sarah sighed again and put a hand to her forehead. Her head was hurting, and no wonder – she had two people in there now! She finished dressing and went in search of Mikhail, whom she knew was finishing up with his own shower in his bathroom. It didn't seem fair that she couldn't read his mind as well as he could read hers, and yet she was the one who got the throbbing head.

"Believe me," he said as she entered his bathroom without even knocking, "my head is pounding just as much as yours."

Sarah studied him a moment, noting similar changes in his appearance to those she'd experienced, and then nodded just once, grunting, "Good!" Her stomach growled loudly again and she rubbed at her midriff with her hand.

"Come on, love, let's go get something to eat before we go talk with Thomas," Mikhail said. He grabbed her hand with his and led her toward the kitchen.

The talk with Thomas did not go as planned, though Sarah knew she should have expected as much. Thomas barely bothered to look away from the television screen to observe the changes Sarah and Mikhail discussed with him. A grunt was his only response when he finally did. They left the room when it was clear he had no interest in the subject.

As soon as the door closed behind the two glowing figures, Thomas paused his video game and just sat staring at the door. He hadn't known Mikhail long, but his mom had looked so different. He'd been shocked when she'd entered the room. Then, when she'd spoken and he'd looked and caught the strange flashing/swirling thingy in her eyes, and then in Mikhail's, Thomas had at first felt like freaking out and getting away from them. However, something inside him had cautioned him to remain calm.

Thomas had chosen instead to pretend an ambivalence he didn't actually feel.

He'd pulled off the performance well, apparently. The two had left, seeming content, if not a bit disgusted at Thomas' disregard for anything beyond the video game world, but comforted by his lack of adverse reaction to their physical changes. Now that they were gone, however, Thomas acknowledged, to himself at least, that he was freaked out a little by what he'd seen.

His mom didn't look anything like what she'd looked like before they'd come to this strange place. And, what was up with her eyes flashing like they'd done? Nobody's eyes flashed! This was like some kind of made-up thing he would see on a video game, not like real life. His mom and Mikhail reminded him of... of the figures he'd seen in his dream last night.

Thomas stared off into space, wondering if there could be some kind of a connection there. After all, he hadn't ever had any dreams like that before he'd come to stay at

Mikhail's place and it seemed like it would be just too coincidental for him to dream about certain attributes on a being and then for something like that to happen to his mom's appearance. Maybe it was kind of like a premonition and he'd just dreamed about the figures in the round room as a way to weave a story around the changes he foresaw in his mom and Mikhail? His mom had told him the brain sometimes created stories or pictures in order to help itself make sense of certain things.

That made as much sense as anything and Thomas shrugged, returning to playing his video game.

Sarah was deeply concerned as she and Mikhail made their way downstairs a scant five minutes after entering Thomas' room. Mikhail was silent, but Sarah could feel concern radiating from within him over this issue. She knew he was worried about taking on the role of Thomas' father. Sarah was worried about how things would go as well. She'd never delved into this realm before and it was all new territory for everyone concerned.

She squeezed the large hand holding hers and smiled up at Mikhail. "I'm sure everything will work out fine," she said.

Mikhail hesitated, then nodded once and continued leading her down the hallway. He entered his office and held a chair for her. Once she was seated, he rounded his desk and took his seat. "I guess we need to talk," he said. Sarah leaned back in the comfortable leather chair and faced him. "I, uh...," he continued, "think we need to discuss where we go from here."

A slight frown of confusion marred Sarah's face. "I told you," she finally said, "I'm no good at relationships." She shrugged and shook her head, saying honestly, "I really just don't know how to do it." It was a lame excuse, she knew, but she really had no clue as to how to start a friendship with a guy that wasn't based on sex. She never had done and, now that she and Mikhail had actually had physically intimate relations, she didn't know how she could stop things from heading down the same path all her other relationships with guys had taken. She knew she didn't want it to end. He was the most wonderful person in her whole world, other than Thomas of course, but she didn't know how to express that to him.

Mikhail leaned forward onto the desk, resting his elbows directly before him, and smiled at her, saying, "Sweetheart, you forget... I can basically hear everything you think. I feel that same connection with you. You became my entire world the moment I saw you and I don't want to let that go. I like what we've done so far, too, and I want it to continue." Here, he paused and looked away, frowning somewhat. When he finally returned his gaze to her, she saw a stony determination in his eyes and he declared, "I want us to be married."

Sarah was shocked!

At her startled look, Mikhail quickly held out a hand, saying, "Let me explain. I know I'm supposed to ask... and that there's no precedence for a union of two such as us, but I think it would help everyone concerned to accept the fact that you and Thomas are now to be a part of our society. I don't know if you've noticed or not, but there is definitely opposition to the two of you being here in Seraphim City."

Talk about your understatements of the year, Sarah thought. She had, of course, noticed the cool reception she and Thomas had received from many. Some had even seemed to go out of their way to avoid having to come anywhere near them, as if she and Thomas were in some way contagious and would give them some kind of disease or something if they came into contact with them. Yes, it was

171

pure, unadulterated racism. Sarah had grown up with it in the South and she recognized it well.

Heck, when she'd started first grade, her biological father had told her that black people had bugs on their skin and that if she ever touched one of them, the bugs would get on her skin and she'd never be able to get them off. That had scarred her for life. Even now, she still paused anytime she shook hands with someone of African American heritage. It didn't matter that she knew the truth. Her biological father's words had struck a chord of fear within her young mind that would be with her forever, unfortunately. If only she could remove that part of her amygdala, she'd be able to forget it. Of course, then she would never be able to feel pleasure again, either.

However, Sarah also knew what these people felt stemmed from simple ignorance and fear as well, just like in the human realm. She couldn't blame these people for looking on Thomas and her the way they did. After all, look how she'd reacted to Gabriel when she'd first encountered him.

If Mikhail and she were married, though... since he was the leader of all the Angels in Seraphim City, they'd have to accept it... right? She looked up at Mikhail and he nodded once.

"I think it would help Thomas accept me, too," he said quietly.

Sarah nodded, leaning forward and placing a hand on the desk. "I'm sure he'll adjust just fine," she assured him. She could feel his uncertainty and it hurt to know he felt such doubt. She sighed and relaxed back against the chair again, asking, "So, where do we go from here? I mean, do we have to ask someone's permission or something in order to arrange for a wedding?"

Mikhail rubbed at the back of his neck for a moment, thinking. Then he said, "This is where it gets tricky..." He stood and began pacing around the room, not really paying attention to anything in the room, just pacing. Sarah watched him for a few minutes, wondering about the confusion she felt coming from within his mind. Every now and then, she would catch an understanding of his thoughts so she understood that the marriage wasn't the only thing that would have to be approved by the leaders of Seraphim City. She had changed so much over the past twenty-four hours that Mikhail truly believed her to be a Seraph now. How he would be able to prove that to the council members and, more importantly, his brothers, was another issue.

Then, there was the issue of the two of them being allowed to have a fully physical relationship. Sarah felt Mikhail's thoughts turning to this issue again and again as he paced. Sarah would take him any way she could get him, she knew. If the council members and his brothers refused to allow them to have a fully physical relationship, she would do her best to be satisfied with whatever they could have.

At this thought, Mikhail stopped pacing and came to kneel before her. He took her hands in his and said, "That's not acceptable to me. You *are* now a Seraph and we should be allowed to mate, *fully* mate. I don't know about you, but I want to be able to be with you the way we were intended to be and if we're able to reproduce because of that… well," he shook his head and squeezed her hands tightly, "I would feel like the luckiest being on this planet."

Sarah blinked in surprise. She'd had no idea he would want something like that. After experiencing all his feelings of doubt as far as his ability to be a good father to Thomas, she had expected just the opposite from him. But now, she could feel the excitement welling within him and she knew this issue was extremely important to him.

She squeezed his fingers just as hard and nodded, saying, "Then, we'll do whatever it takes. Whatever we have to… I mean, if we can and if they'll accept us, right?"

Mikhail smiled and, cupping her cheek with one palm, he placed a kiss upon her brow, and said, "Yes." He leaned back on his haunches and smiled at her. "I'll go to my brothers and get their approval first. Then, my brothers and I will go before the council for their approval. Hopefully, this will all be taken care of within just a couple of days."

Sarah looked down at their clasped hands, then asked, "And if they don't approve?"

Mikhail leaned forward to kiss her once quickly on the mouth. "They will approve," he said matter-of-factly. "They'll have to once they've seen the changes in you." He stood and walked back around his desk again, continuing, "I should go as soon as possible to talk with my brothers. They're the ones who'll have to be convinced first." He arched a brow for a moment, deciding on just what approach he should use. "Azra'il will surely be the one to put up the most resistance to the idea of a union between us," he explained. "I don't think I should have too much trouble with Gabriel or Israfil, though." An image of Suriyah and Baphomet quickly flashed through his mind's eye and Mikhail frowned for a second. He knew Suriyah and Sarah would have gotten along great and that both Suriyah and Baphomet would have needed no convincing, were they still part of Seraphim society. They would have backed him without question in this instance.

Mikhail quickly shook off such thoughts. Why he'd been thinking of Suriyah and Baphomet so much lately he did not know. He had to get his mind back onto what was important. Suriyah and Baphomet had been banished a long time ago and had absolutely nothing to do with Mikhail's current situation with Sarah. He would just have to convince his other siblings and then the council all on his own.

"I'll go now to discuss this with my brothers," he said. "Will you and Thomas be okay while I am gone?"

Sarah nodded. There were plenty of lower Angels about in the house who were loyal to Mikhail, should they need anything, so Sarah knew it would be safe here. She was more concerned for Mikhail's safety, judging from the feelings she'd gotten from his mind over the past couple of minutes.

He chuckled on his way to the door and, looking back to give her a smile, said, "Don't worry, love. One look at you and my brothers will each be wondering where they can get their own Seraph beauty." With that, he exited the room.

Sarah stayed seated in the comfortable chair, her thoughts following him as he left the house. She could feel what he was feeling more and more, even when they were physically separated. She wasn't so good at reading his thoughts like he could hers, but she certainly had no difficulty feeling what he was feeling. She knew how he felt about her, his absolute certainty that she belonged to him, with him. She knew he believed she was now a real, live Seraph and that she had been transformed into such simply because she and he had been united. However, she also now understood how much he wanted to mate with her in hopes of reproducing.

Sarah didn't know if that was such a good idea or not, considering her age... and everything else, but she wouldn't deny him the chance. She wouldn't mind having a child, no matter what kind, human or Seraph, with Mikhail. There was no doubt whatsoever in her own heart. Mikhail and she belonged together. She'd been shown enough through her visions to know that.

She sighed and stood. She supposed she'd better go have, or at least attempt to have, another discussion with Thomas, this time about the possibility that Mikhail and she were going to be married soon.

Mikhail knocked quietly on the door. A muffled "Come" sounded from inside the room. Mikhail's nervousness spiked as he entered and he heard his own heartbeat as his blood pressure skyrocketed. He quietly closed the door and, taking a steadying breath, turned toward the desk at the other end of the room.

Azra'il was seated behind the desk and Gabriel sat in front of the desk and to the left. As they caught sight of Mikhail, they each jumped to their feet, their faces mirror images of complete shock.

"Brother!" Gabriel exclaimed in alarm as Mikhail advanced into the room. "Wh-what has happened to you?" he finally managed to ask.

Mikhail smiled beautifully and simply said, "Something wonderful." He took a seat in the other chair positioned to the right and in front of the desk, completely oblivious to the masks of incredulity adorning his brothers' faces.

Azra'il exchanged a nervous glance with Gabriel. They had just been discussing the possible negative effects of the human woman on their brother, and on their society as a whole, but neither of them had anticipated anything anywhere close to this.

After a moment's stunned silence, both Gabriel and Azra'il resumed their seats and stared mutely at Mikhail. As the silence stretched, Mikhail shifted uncomfortably and said, "My brothers, I assure you, I'm quite well." His eyes flashed excitedly.

Gabriel and Azra'il exchanged a dubious look and then Gabriel said, "Mikhail, surely you cannot be serious. I mean, anyone would be justifiably concerned by your physical appearance alone."

Mikhail held out a hand and assured them, "Rest easy, my brothers and fear not mere flashing eyes. I am in no way suffering any ill effects from time spent with my Sarah."

Azra'il half rose from his chair, arguing, "Mere flashing eyes? Have you looked in a mirror lately? I know you were not given the gift of being able to detect auras, Mikhail, or the ability to sense things as we, your brothers can, but surely even you have noticed the other very obvious physical changes you've undergone?"

Mikhail frowned in confusion. "What...," he started to ask, but was interrupted by Gabriel.

"We're just concerned for you, Mikhail," he said cautiously. "As Azra'il said, the eyes and the hair are not the only changes we've observed in you, my brother, and we're not sure you understand just what you've gotten yourself into."

Mikhail stood abruptly and began pacing back and forth before the desk. This meeting wasn't going quite as he'd envisioned it going. He had to get the upper hand here. He had to make them understand about Sarah.

"First of all," he began, "I don't know about any of the things you've noticed other than the flashing of my eyes, not that it matters anyway. And, after what has happened this morning, none of it matters." He paused before the desk and smiled, saying jubilantly, "My brothers, my Sarah has been transformed into a Seraph."

There was a momentary stunned silence from the other two as Mikhail grinned exultantly at them. To more fully emphasize the excitement of the moment, he explained, "I'm free now, you see... I'm free to mate with another in the hope of reproducing."

Azra'il immediately jumped to his feet, his chair flying through the air behind him only to hit the far wall and clatter to the tiled floor on its side as he shouted, "Sacrilege!"

Gabriel was standing now, too, gazing at Mikhail in utter stupefaction. There had to be some sort of mistake. Either that, or Mikhail had completely lost his mind. Even if Gabriel accepted the idea that Sarah had been created for

Mikhail by the blessed Great Designers, the very idea of her being transformed somehow into a Seraph, let alone the theory that Mikhail might mate with and conceive with her, was absolute insanity!

Mikhail quickly shook his head, explaining, "No, no, no. It's real. She's really changed and I think... I think this may just be the beginning. I think there's more to come and that maybe there will be one just such as she for each and every one of us. Don't ask me how, but I have a feeling this was how it was meant to be." He held his hands out toward his kinsmen, palms up, imploring, "Please, my brothers... please listen to what I'm saying. We're finally being given a chance at a life... one worth living."

Azra'il was clearly disgusted and angry by what Mikhail had said. He silently shook his head and backed away from Mikhail, his upper lip curling in his disgust. He turned away to stare out the floor-to-ceiling windows behind his desk.

Gabriel's face was a mask of sorrow. It was as if he was already grieving for Mikhail's demise. He clearly thought it was too late for his brother to be saved from outright annihilation from the blessed Great Designers upon their return. He shook his head, half turning away from Mikhail. "I'm sorry, brother," he choked, "I can't."

Mikhail took a step toward him, reaching out toward him, but he stopped short when Gabriel put up a halting hand.

"Don't... just don't," Gabriel pleaded.

Mikhail saw the glisten of tears in his brother's eyes and his heart ached. He had to convince at least one of them, though. He knew he would never be able to do this alone. Taking a deep breath for courage, he plowed onward, imploring once more, "All I ask is that you come see her. Come see for yourselves the transformation Sarah's experienced." An idea occurred to him and he turned toward

Azra'il. "Brother," he began, "You have the ability to see the tethers of humans' soul energies to that other dimension, correct? You've always told us about how they all have links to some other place where, you believe, they each must have more soul energy stored, right?"

Azra'il's only reaction was a slight glance down and toward Mikhail's general direction.

"Did you see such a tether on Sarah when she was here in this very room?" Mikhail demanded.

Azra'il crossed his arms and turned defiantly to face his brother. "Yes!" he stated emphatically. "She was tethered, just like every other human. She's just visiting this plane, just using that body as a conduit for her temporary existence on this earth... just like every single human being. She's human!"

Mikhail stepped up to Azra'il's desk and, placing his hands palms down onto its hard surface, he smiled a sinister smile, saying matter-of-factly through clenched teeth, "Well, she doesn't have a tether on her now."

Azra'il's face registered confusion, but only for a moment. It was quickly replaced by a look of disgusted disbelief and he said, "How would you know? You've never been able to see anything!"

Mikhail's eyes flashed and he nodded once. "You mentioned the changes you could detect in me," he said. Azra'il's eyes narrowed as he studied his brother in earnest for the first time since he'd entered the room. "Take a good look," Mikhail intoned. "My brothers, do you really believe the changes you see in me are only skin deep?"

Gabriel's mouth opened, then closed after only a moment. He could sense the soul energy coming from within Mikhail as usual. The only difficulty was that the frequency he normally detected from within his brother was different. The energy coming off him now was of such a higher degree at a much higher frequency, the tones of the energy coming at such strange and vibrant ones that Gabriel wondered at the fact that he hadn't noticed it when Mikhail had first entered the room. There was no resemblance in the Mikhail now before him to the brother he'd always known. This Mikhail was far superior to anything Gabriel had ever encountered before and he knew it. This Mikhail was far more superior to any Seraphim Gabriel had ever encountered, and a wave of something akin to fear shuddered through his entire being for a moment.

What if what Mikhail said was true? The thought slipped insidiously through Gabriel's mind. It took him so much by surprise that he stumbled backward a couple of steps, his face screwing into an expression of confused distress, and he quickly shook his head attempting to erase the traitorous thought from his mind. How could he even begin to think something so blasphemous, yet Mikhail was clearly changed. Gabriel looked over at his brother once more, his eyes narrowed.

Mikhail could feel the conflict within his brother and, while he sympathized with the struggle Gabriel was dealing with, he had to win this fight. He turned to him. "Come see for yourself," was all he said.

After only a slight hesitation, Gabriel nodded his head once and then turned and walked out of the room, closing the door quietly behind himself.

Mikhail watched his brother leave, a deep sense of relief filling him. It was quickly replaced by sorrow, however, as the anger and sense of betrayal he could feel coming in gushing waves from Azra'il struck him. He looked back over his shoulder at Azra'il and asked, "Is there nothing I can say to convince you to at least come and judge for yourself if what I've said is true?"

Azra'il's face was almost as red as his hair in his fury as he said disgustedly, "You may have fooled our brother, Mikhail, but you forget... I can see her presence surrounding you in this room, even now. I know the message you carry to me comes partially from her and that she is in everything you say and do. I saw what she did to you in the council chamber earlier."

Mikhail paled at this admission and Azra'il continued, saying, "That's right. I know exactly how much sway she now has over you and why." He shook his head. "You will fall, my brother. You will fall and there's nothing my brothers and I can do for you." He turned his back on Mikhail and after a moment, his shoulders slumped in defeat. "Go," he finally whispered. "Just go... and don't ever come back. You are lost to me now."

Mikhail felt as if he'd been punched in the stomach. Not since his dealing with Suriyah and Baphomet had he felt such a sense of loss, but now he could see that there would be no chance of reconciliation with Azra'il. The rift between them seemed wider than the universe itself. After a moment's hesitation, he silently turned and exited the room.

Chapter 10

Sarah knocked at the door before turning the knob and entering. Thomas still sat where he'd been earlier when she and Mikhail had come to talk with him. He wasn't playing his video game now, but was staring at the television screen, not even acknowledging her presence as she advanced farther into the room.

Oddly enough, she discovered he was watching a news program. Thomas never wanted to watch the news and would pitch a fit if he came into the living room at home and someone was watching the news when he wanted to watch something else. Sarah frowned and focused on the television to see what had drawn his interest. Pictures of her mom and dad immediately caught her attention and she stood riveted, suddenly very interested in what was being said.

Sarah watched the images on the television screen, shock and fear lancing through her in great waves as a reporter droned on informing the viewers of the situation with Sarah's parents. There was a legal contributor answering the reporter's questions regarding the case. It appeared the legal community was leaning toward the idea that her parents would soon be taken into custody, not just for questioning but for their own protection. Apparently, there were death threats piling up along with a crowd of protesters outside Sarah's parents' house and there was true concern over the aging couple's safety.

The reporter kept coming back to the question of whether or not the couple would be charged for not answering any questions regarding Sarah or Thomas. That was the only evidence Sarah had that Gabriel's influence over their minds was still working. She'd been worried it would have worn off by now, but apparently he'd done his job well. A video of an earlier attempt at an interview with Sarah's father was shown and whenever he was asked about Sarah and Thomas, he looked confused for a moment and then simply shrugged and said he didn't understand what the reporter was talking about.

"Mom," Thomas softly asked, "Are Gramps and Grams gonna be okay?"

Sarah focused her attention on her son, squatting down onto her haunches and hugging him with an arm. He felt so small, even though he was as tall as she. She felt a tremble race through him and she was suddenly filled with a steely resolve she'd never felt before. Looking back at the images still displayed on the television screen, an idea solidified in her mind. "They're both gonna be just fine," she assured him. She quickly stood and headed toward the door. Before leaving the room, her hand on the door knob, she turned back to Thomas and instructed, "Stay here until I get back, okay? And, if Mikhail gets back before me, tell him I've gone to get Grams and Gramps." Her eyes flashed quickly and Thomas nodded his acknowledgement. Sarah nodded once and turned and left the room, closing the door quietly behind her.

She had no idea what she was doing or even how she was going to do it, but she knew she had to go and get her parents before something bad happened to them. This whole thing was her fault, she knew. The news reports had been filled with excerpts from her vision blog, citing passages from within it that had apparently been used by religious groups in protests all over the human world. Now, her parents were becoming targets of these same fanatical, maniacal groups and, well... Sarah wasn't about to just stand idly by to watch that happen, not when she believed she could do something about it.

She had no idea how she was going to find the rift in the barrier between this dimension and the human dimension, but she knew she had to try. With her newly-developed abilities and shields, Sarah was confident she'd somehow be able to figure out a way to get to her folks and then to get them back to this dimension.

As she entered her bedroom, she felt the now-familiar pressure in her brain. *What's happening?* Mikhail's voice asked inside her mind. Sarah ignored his question as she concentrated on the task at hand, not thinking about it directly but allowing herself to open up to possibilities. Immediately, she felt the strange sensation of muscles working up and down the sides of her spinal column. She felt her cutapi lift at the long pull of her shields coming out of her spinal nodule and she let loose a long, slow sigh. It seemed to take longer than it had the one time they'd come out before and there was more material coming out this time.

Sarah didn't think about it, even when Mikhail's voice sounded again in her mind, demanding to know what was going on, his voice urgent and edged with more than a hint of fear. She raised her face upward as she felt the shields surrounding her, her eyes closed on the sensation. One word, *Go*, solidified in her mind and she felt herself lifting off. She could hear the rushing of wind and other sounds of outside and she slowly opened her eyes.

She was amazed to find that she was traveling at an incredible speed high in the sky over a darkened landscape. Occasional lights flashed below in zinging lines of light, like tracers. Sarah paid them little heed. She wondered for only a moment how she would find the rift in the barrier to the human dimension, but then decided not to even think about it. She would merely concentrate on the idea of crossing over and hope that would get her through, as it had with the whole flying thing.

No sooner had she conceived of this idea than she found herself experiencing the stinging jolts of electricity caused when one crossed the barrier. Amazingly, Sarah found herself hovering almost immediately high above a very well-lit Dallas. For a moment, she was completely disoriented. She hadn't passed through the same rift Gabriel had used when he'd taken Thomas and her through to his dimension. Instead, she must have accidentally found one of the other dimensional rifts Mikhail had spoken of that existed unbeknownst to all but those living in the place he'd called the Badlands.

A shiver of fear shot quickly through her form as the thought of the Shaitans or Jinn knowing of the existence of this particular rift occurred to her. How easy it would be for any of them to come into this dimension so close to where Sarah and her family had lived for so long.

Sarah quickly shook off that thought and steadied her concentration on reaching her parents' house. Almost immediately, she found herself moving at a dizzying speed toward the north of Dallas. Before she even had time to contemplate how she was going to manage to get into the house without being detected by anyone who might possibly still be gathered outside, she found her shields were already allowing her to pass through the bricks and other building materials that made up the house. The next thing she knew, she was standing in the darkened living room on the lower floor of the house.

The muscles along her spinal column flexed and Sarah felt her shields withdrawing back into their hiding place within the confines of her spine, her cutapi slipping closed after the last of the shields slipped into the spinal nodule.

Sarah walked toward the bedroom at the back of the house on the bottom floor. She could hear sounds from angry protesters still outside the house. There was another sound, though, coming from directly in front of her. Her mother's soft cries came to her through the darkness and then her father's soothing voice. Sarah found the two huddled together on their bed, holding each other. They immediately jerked in surprise as Sarah entered the room, the light from within her shining brightly enough to allow them to see her clearly without aid of any artificial light.

"Oh, my God!" her mom screamed. "Sarah's dead!"

Sarah's eyes widened in momentary shock and then she quickly stepped forward, reaching out to the couple on the bed, assuring them, "No. It's okay. It's me." They both held on tightly to each other, scooting as far away from Sarah's glowing form as they could without letting go of each other. "Mom, Dad, it's okay. I'm not dead. I'm okay," Sarah continued.

Sarah's father had reached the edge of the mattress and suddenly stood, pulling his wife to stand behind him. He narrowed his eyes as he looked at Sarah's glowing form. "Sarah?" he asked disbelievingly, fearfully.

Sarah closed her eyes for a moment and sighed in relief. "Yes," she said, opening her eyes to them. "I know I seem different," she said, "but you're just gonna have to trust that it's me." She hesitantly stepped closer to them, stopping when her dad took up a defensive stance to protect her mom. "Dad," Sarah explained again, "It's really just me." Her eyes were flashing, she knew, and the long white strands in her hair couldn't be doing anything to help in this situation, but she didn't know what else she could do to convince them she wasn't some ghost. Suddenly, however, she remembered what Gabriel had done when he'd taken Thomas and her. Sarah closed her eyes and concentrated on contacting her parents on a psychic level.

Amazingly, images of both of them appeared crystal clear in Sarah's mind and she felt an instant connection with their minds.

"Sarah?" she heard her mom suddenly ask aloud.

Sarah opened her eyes and looked at her. "Yes," she simply said.

"Oh, baby," her mom wailed as she quickly reached to hug her daughter. "Where have you been? We've been so worried about you and we didn't know where you had gone or if you were safe and then all these people started asking questions about you and talking about some blog or something they said you'd written on the internet." She stopped and hastily looked around the room. "Where's um... I mean, where's... uh...?" She stammered and looked confused.

Sarah took her hand. "Thomas is fine," she assured her, reminding her of his name.

"Oh yeah," her dad said looking around, suddenly seeming to remember he had a grandson and that he'd been missing as long as Sarah had been and still was. A flash of confusion passed over Sarah's parents' faces, but then their eyes seemed to clear when they both looked back at Sarah's countenance.

"Mom, Dad, I need you to listen to me," Sarah quietly said. "I only just found out about everything that's been going on." She turned and walked a little away from them, wondering how to explain everything to them. She didn't even know if what Gabriel had done to them could be undone or not. What if she went through all kinds of explanations and they didn't even really recognize her? What if he had to be there for them to be able to remember fully? They seemed to remember her, but they hadn't said anything more about Thomas and she really didn't know if they remembered him now or not.

Then there was the whole issue of the fact that she'd caused everything that was going on outside the house right now. How was she supposed to explain about the vision blog? Her mom was a Christian, always had been. Her dad, while he wasn't exactly a practicing Christian, had been raised as a Catholic, she knew. How was she supposed to explain to him that she'd been staying with a Seraph, or even that they were actually real and that she was now kind of one of them?

Sarah's head started hurting.

Then, a familiar pressure started in her brain and Sarah sighed in relief.

Mikhail had been on his way home from his unsuccessful visit with Azra'il when he'd first realized there was something wrong. Sarah's thoughts had been troubling and he'd seen clear images of two people, people he'd never met before but whom he'd immediately learned from her thoughts were her human parents. She was suddenly very afraid for them, for some reason, as her thoughts relayed to him. He tried reaching out to her, communicating, asking what was wrong, but she wasn't responding.

She'd never *not* responded!

Mikhail tried again, putting more force behind his thoughts to her, but still getting no response.

Something's wrong! his instincts screamed. He instantly pulled his shields out and around himself, taking to the air at break-neck speed. Mere seconds after taking off, however, he paused mid-air, confusion warring with the overwhelming sense of urgency that had lanced through him upon discovering something wrong with his woman.

Some instinct told him Sarah was no longer at the house on the outskirts of the city. Oddly enough, Mikhail could still sense Thomas' energies coming from there, but

Sarah's were nowhere near. Surprisingly, he could detect her tones coming faintly from an entirely different part of the city and he turned toward that direction. With only a thought, he was whizzing through the evening air.

There was light below and Mikhail didn't pay much attention, focusing instead on listening for Sarah's sweet tonal energies so he could track her. Eventually, however, he realized the light he could see below was actually traces of the track Sarah had taken to wherever she'd gone. He focused on the light, his thoughts moving him along it to a part of the countryside he'd never before visited until, suddenly, he found himself experiencing the stinging pricks against his skin from crossing through to the human dimension.

Mikhail was stunned! He hadn't even been aware there was a rift anywhere nearby. He'd been following along the path he was now sure Sarah had taken and then, unexpectedly, had discovered a new rift in the barrier to the human dimension.

He glanced below to the lights of a large city. The lights were very bright and Mikhail could detect much human soul-energy emitting from within the little buildings far below. Interspersed with the lights of the city's skyline, Mikhail could detect a different light, the one he'd been tracking from Seraphim City, and he knew it was what was left over from Sarah's flight above the city. He followed along the trail, wondering how on earth she'd managed to make such a journey without having had any formal training on how to use her new abilities.

A short time later, the trail of light came to an end in a large neighborhood a bit north of the city. There, in a large, two-storied brick home, Mikhail could clearly make out Sarah's energy source. She was there, inside the house. Mikhail headed down toward the building, but then paused suddenly. There were massive numbers of humans filling the streets surrounding the house. He pulled his shields more tightly around himself and looked around, wondering what was going on here.

There were what looked to be uniformed police surrounding the house and blocking anyone in the shouting crowds from getting to it. The crowds of people surrounding the house and filling the streets of the neighborhood held signs and shouted angrily in clashing chants. Mikhail could see fights breaking out between members of the crowds and it seemed all the officers could do just to keep people from getting to the house. It didn't look like a very good or even stable situation and Mikhail wondered how long the few uniformed individuals would be able to hold off the angry mob.

He quickly turned back toward the house, reaching out psychically toward Sarah to verify that she was unharmed as yet. He immediately felt her soothing presence in his own mind, reassuring him and letting him know how happy she was he was there. He smiled as he concentrated and then alighted next to her form in the room of the house where she stood facing the two humans he'd seen in her mind's eye before. He dropped his shields and, without even glancing at the two humans, he reached for Sarah, asking aloud, "Are you okay, love?"

She reached to hug him around his lower torso, snuggling her cheek against his chest as his arms encircled her. "I'm perfectly fine, now," she softly said.

Immediately, the two dogs in the room set up a staccato of barking that was loud enough to wake the dead. They lurched forward toward Mikhail's figure baring wicked teeth and snarling between barking bouts. Mikhail glanced at them and sent out a swift mental command along the frequencies canines normally utilized for psychic communication betwixt themselves. The two dogs hastily bowed their heads in submissive gestures and slowly approached Mikhail's feet. He reached to pat the head of each one before turning back to Sarah.

He rubbed a hand up her back into the hair above the nape of her neck, massaging the tense muscles there. His eyes slid closed as relief flooded his mind. He'd been so afraid he had somehow lost her. A shiver passed through him and he hugged her more tightly against himself, pressing a tender kiss to the crown of her head.

Sarah pulled back a little, looking up at him to offer a slight smile, saying in a teasing whisper, "You can't get rid of me *that* easily."

Mikhail chuckled softly and tapped an index finger against the tip of her nose before bending to place a quick kiss on her mouth.

Sarah pulled away and broke their embrace, saying, "Um, Mikhail, this is my mom and dad." She turned toward the two humans at the other end of the room and said, "Mom and Dad, this is Mikhail."

The two stared at Sarah and this newcomer who seemed so strange. Sarah, of course, seemed almost a stranger to them now, although she still resembled somewhat the daughter they'd known for so long. The changes in their daughter were a bit frightening, to say the least, and Sarah's mom squeezed her husband's hand tightly with both of her own, looking to him immediately for the support he'd always been ready to give in dire situations.

He didn't immediately respond, however. He was busy watching the creatures standing before his wife and himself, for that was all he could concentrate on. These things, he couldn't quite call them human. They were like nothing he'd ever before encountered and he wondered if what he was seeing was even real. His daughter wasn't as she'd been before. So much about her had changed but he couldn't for the life of him remember what she'd been like before. He just knew she was completely different.

The man standing to her right was just as impressive, reaction-wise. He had the same flashing eyes as Sarah, the same glowing... aura, the same streaks of white in his hair, though the man's hair was of a much darker color than Sarah's had ever been. There was a great energy emitting from the two creatures and Sarah's dad took a cautionary step backward, pulling his wife along with him. He wasn't entirely sure he and his wife were safe in the house with these two creatures. He could still hear the chants from the angry crowds outside the house, though, and knew it wouldn't be safe to go outside.

Mikhail caught the action out of the corner of his eye and he moved more protectively toward Sarah. She glanced up at him with a slight shake of her head, conveying mentally that everything was okay. *What's going on here?* he asked in her mind. Sarah caught the gist of his confused thoughts and looked back toward her parents.

How could she explain everything to both her parents and Mikhail? She didn't even fully understand what had happened, or even how it had happened. All she knew was that she'd been safe in the Seraphim realm when all of a sudden her parents had been shown on the television screen being interviewed about Sarah's whereabouts and being harassed by reporters and all manner of groups of angry people because of the things Sarah had written in her vision blog.

What is a vision blog? came Mikhail's voice in her mind again.

Sarah looked back up at him, allowing her thoughts to drift over some of the entries she'd been making in her vision blog for the past couple of years. After only a couple of minutes, Mikhail held up a hand and quickly shook his head, as if trying to dispel some errant thought or picture from within his mind. Sarah didn't know what to make of this, but she had more important matters to deal with right now other than finding a way to make Mikhail understand about the visions she'd been having for what seemed like forever to her.

She stepped forward toward her parents, although they each took another step backward away from her at her approach. She halted and took a deep breath. "I guess we need to talk, huh?" she offered.

Her father's eyes narrowed for a moment, then he stepped forward and, hesitantly putting a hand on her shoulder, asked, "Are you okay?"

Relief washed through her at his gesture. Sarah glanced thankfully up at him, a half-smile curling one side of her mouth upward, and nodded. She couldn't fool him, though, and it wasn't long before there were tears pooling in her eyes. Her father immediately stepped closer to her to enfold her in his arms.

"Shh," he whispered to her, his hand cradling the back of her head, pressing her face to his chest. He rubbed her back gently and assured her, "It's okay, sweetheart. Everything's gonna be all right."

Mikhail stood by watching the byplay between father and daughter, ashamed at himself for feeling jealous at the thought of the man touching his Sarah. The man had every right to touch his daughter in order to comfort her. Mikhail knew this intellectually, but the baser part of himself raged at the thought that she should need comforting from anyone other than Mikhail himself. He looked away from the couple and noticed the older woman standing across the room from him. She was staring at him, tears still running down her face unchecked. Mikhail caught strands of her thoughts and was a bit shocked to find anger and accusation toward him not so well-hidden within the depths of her mind.

The woman, whom Sarah had introduced as her mom, believed everything that was going on here, whatever it was, was a direct result of something Mikhail had done. She blamed him for the changes evident in Sarah's physical form and for the fact that there were angry mobs outside the house waiting to blast Sarah for some supposed malicious information the reporters had informed Sarah's mom Sarah had posted on the internet. Mikhail delved more deeply into the woman's mind to discover just what type of issue this was to the humans. He didn't like what he discovered.

Reporters had apparently gotten wind of Sarah's vision blog and the information contained within it. There had been some complaints sent in to the news stations and someone on one of their staffs had found a way to hack into the blog to discover the true identity of the blogger. That's when reporters had started showing up on the doorstep of Sarah's parents' house, constantly badgering her parents until the couple had gotten to the point of no longer being able to even leave their home.

The nature of the information in the blog was such that once the media started paying attention to it, there were the inevitable protesters who just had to follow. It seemed every religious group on the planet was represented within the angry crowds that had gathered outside the house over the past few days' time and they had all accosted Sarah's parents whenever they'd gotten the chance for things Sarah had written in her blog.

Mikhail knew there was no other way around this situation than to take Sarah's parents away from the danger. That meant he would have to house them at his place in Seraphim City along with Sarah and Thomas. He was okay with that, but he knew it would be just one more thing to upset those who were already not happy with the whole idea of having humans inhabiting the Angelic realm. He sighed and made up his mind. Sarah was his mate. He knew it with such certainty that to him there merely was no other reality. If keeping her safe meant he had to bring the entire human race over into the Seraphim realm, he would do it.

Sarah caught the drift of his thoughts and feelings and quickly looked back toward him, swallowing a huge lump in her throat. "You'd protect them, too?" she asked in a whisper. She hadn't known just how she was going to keep her parents safe with the angry mob outside and Thomas and her residing in the Seraphim realm. Now, here was Mikhail not even thinking about making them stay in the human realm.

Sarah's tears increased and she pulled away from her father, her arms wrapping around her middle as she stared at Mikhail. He was so unexpected in her life. She'd never encountered anyone who put her absolutely first. As a single mom, she'd never expected to find a knight in shining armor. She'd always had to be in control, always responsible for everything.

Whenever she'd failed to make rent or a car payment or something, it had been a pride-swallowing siege to have to go to her parents to beg for money from them, but Sarah had obligingly done whatever was necessary to get through the struggle. She'd never had anyone else's help, other than her parents'. Now, there was Mikhail. He stood before her like some ray of hope, literally shining through the dark morass of her life.

Mikhail mutely held a hand out to her, his beautiful flashing eyes locked onto hers.

Sarah took a deep, fortifying breath and placed her small hand in his large one. She turned to face her parents. Sarah's mom moved to stand beside her husband, both of them facing the two glowing beings standing in the middle of the bedroom.

"I...," Sarah began, but there she stopped. What could she say to them? Then, an idea came to her and she said, "I need you guys to look at something." She turned to look up into Mikhail's flashing eyes. "You, too," she said.

She moved over to a roll-top desk along the side wall of the bedroom where a laptop stood open and waiting. She pushed the tiny power button and it flared to life. After only a moment, she was able to log onto the internet and she pulled up her vision blog. She didn't log in, but merely visited the site. She noticed there were an unbelievable number of comments that had been made to it by now. She couldn't help that now, though. She turned to the trio behind her.

"I need you all to read this in its entirety so that you'll understand what's going on. It should answer any questions you have," she said. She turned toward the door, her mission clear in her mind.

"Where are you going?" her mom immediately demanded, fear clearly evident in her quivering voice.

Sarah turned once more to the trio. "I have one more entry to make to the blog before we go," she said. Her mom's face screwed into a mask of confusion, but Sarah didn't elaborate. She quietly left the room to head upstairs to the tiny office where she'd spent so many nights alone pouring her heart out to anyone who would listen, or read.

The three people remaining in the room turned and focused on the words on the shining screen before them.

Entry #715 – The Vision Blog – April 21 – 2:04 am

This will be my last entry to this blog. I have been away for a little while, as some of you may have figured out by my lack of submissions to this site. I didn't mean to just up and leave, believe me, but I couldn't exactly pass up the opportunity that was presented to me. Now, I'm glad I didn't because I found a whole lot of answers to the questions I had been struggling with over the past few months/years.

However, I never in my wildest dreams would have thought I would come back to what is going on right outside my parents' house! WTF!? What the hell is wrong with people? I mean, I may not agree with everything someone says, or even *any* of what someone says, but does that give me the right to go out and try to destroy that person's life or even their family's life simply because I happen to have an alternative idea of how things should be?

Get a floggin' life, people!

If I say I happen to think people who believe in any of the major religions of the world are all delusional, then that's my opinion and, as such, I'm entitled to it as a member of the human race, right? I'm not saying there aren't good things about just about each and every one of the accepted religions out there, but that doesn't mean I happen to espouse all of the things they teach. Who does? Even members of the same group don't believe the exact same things within their organization! No one even can. It's impossible. No two people can believe in the exact same idea in the exact same way because they are two separate people! Their lives have been different, even if they're freakin' identical twins.

And when I say I don't believe in those religions, I don't mean that I'm going to go around killing people because they believe differently than I do. I am *not* looking to be the instigator of another holy war on this planet, either in this dimension or another. I just wrote things that I was feeling and thinking. As an American, I have the right to express my opinion on any subject I choose. It's part of my Constitutional rights as an American citizen, whether I do it at a bar down the street or on a street corner or even over the internet. And those of you who don't like that can just *NOT VISIT MY BLASTED BLOG!!!*

Muslims – Get real about the whole treating women like dirt beneath males' feet! Who do you think you are? You think there are virgins waiting for you when you kick the bucket? Ha! Why would you want them? They're female! And this whole deal about blowing up your enemies, whether you have to blow up yourselves or not... how can you be so flippin' nuts that *that* actually makes sense to you?!

Jewish Folks – Can you be any more... *Jewish*? Actually, I don't have too much against the Jewish faith other than to say that they, like all other religions that have a deity/god they worship, need to get crackin' on some new way of expressing the important things in life because that whole god thing just doesn't really seem real anymore. And, if you believe something, don't let other people push you around! You believe it and that's it. If others don't like it, so what?! I don't agree with a lot of the things you believe, but who cares? You're you, I'm not you. Believe what you want, just don't bother me with it!

Christians – Have any of you actually *thought about* what is written in that Bible of yours?! That question applies to the Muslims and Jewish, as well, with their Koran and Talmud. I'm sorry for being so blunt about the whole thing, but I'm kind of fed up right now. The words written in those volumes were written by cultures from long-forgotten ages. Our world has changed so much since they existed that, in many instances, the things written there seem almost barbaric and would never be allowed to happen in our society. Then again, our society has become so very lost that some of the things written in those books *NEED* to be addressed again, need to be taught.

I would reiterate, I'm not trashing the entirety of any one religion. The things I believe are an amalgamation of teachings taken from all three of the above-listed religions and then some. The things I believe also came from people who had no formal religious education, people who had grown up living off the land, alone, with their thoughts as their only company. The common courtesies I've learned were quite often learned from them.

Now it seems even those aren't allowed. Everyone has to be politically correct and make sure to cover their own ass in order to keep from being blamed for offending anyone. I'm tired of not being able to say what I feel. I'm tired of being afraid of offending someone with the things I want to say.

The things I've written about in this blog have been things that were shown to me. I truly believe that now. I have been shown a great deal more since my last post and my life has changed in such wondrous ways, I almost feel sorry for the rest of you. You don't yet understand what's coming, but I do.

All of you are so caught up in all the issues affecting this turgid society that you've forgotten yourselves completely. There are so many clamoring to be heard that no one's voice can be singled out. Those of you who are unable to speak are pushed aside and those who are able either have to scream in order to get just a piece of the action or you have to get out of the way of those who are louder than you.

Look at what you've become.

I remember when I was a little girl, there was respect and honesty. People took responsibility for their own actions and they helped others who were in need without expecting anything in return. Those who had to take handouts felt bad about it and did whatever they could to get to a point where they could give back to the same society that helped them in their time of need. They didn't sit around asking what the government was going to do to make sure their entitlement checks continued coming or anything.

Pride was taken in everything done worth doing. You could count on things to be well-made, even if it didn't cost much, because the people making the thing believed it was their job to do a good job. They didn't believe it was merely their responsibility to show up and punch a clock and *who cared if they actually did what they were supposed to do while they were there?* They didn't believe it was okay to text and listen to music the whole shift or to show up drunk or high. They didn't believe management owed them anything other than the wages they actually earned.

Our whole society seems lately to be based solely on what the hell is in it for me. It's like everyone suddenly thinks it's okay to have someone else do everything for them, but no one is supposed to have to do without anything they might possibly see on television! They want. Don't ask anyone to do without because that just wouldn't be fair! Everybody's got to have the latest and greatest in gadgets and gizmos, even though part of the problem is that we've become so freakin' plugged in that we've forgotten how to even interact with one another on a face-to-face basis!

Look at what has been lost.

People used to sit around in groups, not drinking themselves into a stupor, but actually talking and relating with one another. People used to sit and hash out problems until they had acceptable solutions. Nowadays, even the political leaders, most of whom are millionaires and wouldn't be able to relate to the common man if one was to come up and smack them between the eyes, can't reach any type of agreement on even the most mundane subjects, let alone the life-changing issues that are daily being placed before them. It always leads to name-calling and black-balling anyone and everyone, from the opposition and sometimes even those from their own party.

People used to sit around and come up with grand ideas. People used to raise the kids as a whole village, not look at the youngsters as a way to make money or to entertain themselves with trash-talk about the youngsters' parents. Now, we have kids trying to get pregnant or get into trouble just so they can get the opportunity to appear on television in the hopes of becoming famous.

What is that?

And I hear Christians talking about how they'll be so happy when it's time for the Rapture! If there were a god, why would it ever want to have anything to do with such as this society? How messed up would that be? Look at the world. Everybody thinks they're the only good people or person on the planet and the rest are doomed whenever whatever messiah returns to take the "good ones" away to some wondrous place in the sky.

Have any of you ever even bothered to ask yourselves what the original purpose was?

Why are you here?

How did you get here?

What happens next?

My dear humans, I believe I know the answers to two of those questions. I also believe it won't be long before I discover the answer to the third.

You think I'm wrong for calling out your religious beliefs? You've come after me and my family because of something I wrote. My son is safe and my parents are about to be. I've been given a gift that has taken me far beyond anything you could ever even imagine, but if you dare, since I know once I post this you'll be doing your darnedest to figure out where I am so you can come make your convoluted and all-important point to me, I invite you to come after me. If any one of you has the ability to find me, you deserve to be given the answers to those three questions listed above, and then maybe you'll understand just what's going on and maybe, just maybe, you can help others to understand and change.

Don't get me wrong, I'm no prophet. I've been enmeshed in this society so deeply over the years that there have been many times when I've asked, "What's in it for me?" It's only been over the past couple of years that I've started seeing things in a much different light. Now, though, since I discovered the truth, I'm saddened when I look at the society in this realm.

You're destroying everything you used to hold sacred and you're giving nothing back. You have no sense of self-worth, yet you feel the need to have everything. You create nothing and destroy all. You refuse to change because you refuse to do without all but that which you absolutely need. Your children no longer respect the things they're given, or even you. They don't learn any type of self-worth, for how could they learn it from a society that doesn't teach it? They have no work ethic, no clue what life could be and most of them will never be able to make it on their own. Mommy and Daddy will have to go with them to the job interview and answer the questions for them so they can get a job that they'll quit after a couple of days because it's just too much bullshit and they'd rather be at home online or playing a video game with people they'll never meet face-to-face!

They have nothing but possessions for which to live. There is no spirituality out there. There's nothing being taught that makes sense to anyone anymore, so how could they? It's no longer applicable! These kids today couldn't conceive of a supreme being any more than they could conceive of a hot dog getting up on a screen at a drive-in theater and telling them to get out of their cars to go to the concession stand for popcorn and a soda before their movie. How are they ever going to make it?

Enough of my tirade. I certainly have no right to go off on anyone about how screwed up their life is. I've taken every wrong turn in the universe in my lifetime. I'm just lucky enough that now I've found my true path. It does sadden me, though, to look out onto this landscape only to see ruin. It used to have so much potential, so much energy. Now, the ground grows stale and toxic. The air itself seems to burn my lungs.

I'll be happy to go away again.

To those of you who are willing to work for a better tomorrow, I beg you, come find me. A better life awaits each and every one of you, if you'll just somehow manage to see past the walls you've built up around yourselves. I don't believe you will, though. I believe you'll bow your heads and do what you're told. You'll go to work tomorrow and the day after that and the day after that. You'll do what's expected of you and then you'll go out with your friends or you'll go home and drink and complain about how you're being screwed over by this group or that. You'll blame others for your misfortune. You won't take any responsibility. You will have learned absolutely nothing. Then, you will flow back to that place where we hover to await the time when you can come back to do it all again, only the world will be in even worse shape by then.

That is your destiny, I fear. So, go. Go on. Go back to that life you've chosen and congratulate yourselves on a job well done. You have exactly what you've asked for. You've gotten back exactly what you've given.

You will excuse me if I choose not to stay behind to watch your downward spiral? I hear my name echoing from that other place now, and so I must leave you. Those of you daring enough to make the leap of faith…, I'll be waiting just on the other side of the night, in that other realm. Come join me.

Sarah quickly logged onto her blog site, went back to the window she'd been writing in, selected everything written there and clicked on "Copy". She hesitated for a fraction of a second before right-clicking and pasting the whole thing as a new post. She saved the post and logged off.

The background on the screen was an animated scene of traveling through space and she sat back in the little office chair, staring at the screen where little specks of light came

The Vision Blogger

and went in a 3D image. The fake stars and planets passed by, like they would out the windshield of a car steadily traveling along an intergalactic highway. As she stared at the screen, Sarah could imagine herself slowly slipping away to some other place in her mind. However, she was suddenly pulled back to full awareness by a gentle pressure inside her brain and she knew Mikhail was pulling her back.

Sarah stood and, pushing the little button on the monitor to turn it off, she made her way on steady legs down the stairs and back to her parents' bedroom.

Chapter 11

There were wisps of clouds floating in from unseen avenues. He was back in the circular room again. Lights still flickered here or there on the control panels lining the walls of the room, however the monitoring station in the center of the room was now dark and abandoned. He felt again a strange sense that something was not quite right as he regarded the empty stations before him.

Where had they all gone, those strange beings with the glowing eyes and skin and long, white hair that defied gravity? As the thought solidified in his mind, he felt as if he was no longer alone in the room. He turned until he faced the room's newest occupant. She stood silently in one of the many exits from the room which radiated outward every few paces along the curved outer wall. Her eyes emitted only a faint glow.

He recognized her instantly.

She'd been the one who'd seen him during his last "dream-visit," if that's what one could call it. How he knew this, he wasn't sure, he just sensed that she'd been the one.

He narrowed his eyes in concentration as he studied her.

Her form moved not at all. There was only the slow, subtle burn of light radiating from her eyes, along with the much more subtle glow her entire body emitted. She had on the now-familiar long, colorless flowing robe he'd seen all of her kind in the last time and her long white hair fanned around her countenance unmoving, almost as if frozen in place. Amusement rippled through his mind at the sight, but quickly abated as a frown marred her beautiful face.

She was beautiful, he realized. Her skin, although porcelain white, was as smooth as new-fallen snow. Her form, at least that which he could see under the robe, was thin yet healthy. She was tall for a female, though he wasn't sure if that was normal for females of her kind or not. Looking at her, however, he felt a certain sense of kinship, as if the two of them were very well-acquainted. A shiver raced through him at this thought, for she was so very alien, foreign, different.

Brat. The word breezed through his mind on an annoyed feminine voice and his own face screwed itself into a shocked frown.

He didn't know if he could speak, or if she would be able to understand him, or even if either of them was actually in that room at all, or if this was just some crazy dream his brain had conjured up because of all the things that had happened over the past few days. But, in his mind he focused on the concept of the question, *Why?*

In the next instant, he felt like jumping out of his own skin, for the breezy feminine voice actually answered him!

You always acted so superior, the voice said in a whisper of annoyance that held no more substance than a mere afterthought.

He was floored! "What do you mean?" he asked, though he wanted to scream it.

His heart rate was so fast it felt as if someone was playing bongo drums within his chest.

The female's eyes suddenly flashed a brilliant white, so bright that he had to quickly look away. That's when he noticed he was moving backward again, away from the room like he'd done before at the end of his dream.

You're not ready, yet, the soft, feminine whisper sounded in his head once more, as he whooshed backward through corridor after corridor.

Thomas awoke in confusion at the scene before him. He found himself standing directly in front of the television mounted to the wall of his room in Mikhail's house in Seraphim City! On the screen, there was a picture of his mom and another of him. The newscaster was blabbering on and on about how he and his mom had gone missing, but that there had been some kind of update to something on the internet and that because of that there were now possible legal issues to be considered.

Thomas didn't understand what the reporter was talking about, so he tuned out the man's voice and concentrated instead on the fact that he hadn't been dreaming at all. He had thought he'd dreamed his visit in the strange round room with the alien-looking female. But how could that be? When he'd come to, he hadn't been, as he'd thought, in his bed asleep. Instead he was here, standing before the television.

He even remembered getting up from where he'd been sitting on the floor playing video games. He'd just stopped playing and had switched inputs to see if there was anything on television, when a video of his grandparents had flashed on the screen. He missed them both so very much, so he'd gone over to the television screen to get a better look at their images.

That's when he'd drifted away.

How had it happened, and why? His mom was the one always talking about visions and things she just somehow "knew," not him. He'd never experienced anything like that. He was just a kid! Kids didn't have visions – did they?

A shiver wracked his body and Thomas quickly scurried through the doorway to the hall, intent on finding someone, *anyone*, else in the house. His mom wasn't here and he knew Mikhail wasn't either, so Thomas headed downstairs. He felt so alone, abandoned almost.

As he reached the ground floor, he turned toward the back of the house. A door at the very back of the hallway silently swung open to reveal the darkened figure of the woman who'd been bringing him his meals and snacks all day. She stood there in the entryway with her hands on her hips, just looking at him. Thomas couldn't clearly make out her facial features, but he knew it was the same woman. Regardless, she was another person and Thomas didn't want to be alone.

He hurried toward her.

She turned aside at his approach, one arm moving to encircle his shoulders and the other holding open the door to the kitchen and motioning him into it. Thomas sighed in relief at the warmth radiating from her and happily preceded her into the giant room.

Sarah watched as Narayana led the new arrivals to the household, including the two strangely quiescent canines, off to their new quarters. Mikhail had assured her there was plenty of room for everyone, but Sarah still felt as if she and her family were over-burdening him and his staff. Upon their return to the house on the outskirts of Seraphim City, Mikhail had stayed only long enough to assure Sarah that his staff would take care of her family. Then he'd gone off in search of Gabriel to update him on this new development. Narayana had entered, taken one look at the assembled group and had then taken over, ordering other Angel staff members to prepare rooms and kennels for the newcomers. She hadn't even blinked at the fact that there were now more humans in the house.

Sarah felt even more guilt over causing the staff extra trouble as she headed off toward Thomas' room. She'd just taken off and left him with these people, as if Angels should be expected to babysit a kid! It didn't matter what *class* of Angel they were, they were still Angels, for cripe's sake!

Stop that, came Mikhail's voice in her mind.

I can't help it, she thought back to him. *I feel awful puttin' all of them through this... askin'em to help my family and me when most of the people in this realm obviously don't want us here.*

Sarah suddenly felt as if he was standing beside her and his arms were wrapping comfortingly around her right there on the stairs. He wasn't, of course, but she felt it all the same. She felt love, concern, hesitation, and..., anger. Yes, there was definite anger coming from him. Sarah wondered about this and, of course, he caught the drift of her thoughts.

We will discuss things when I return, his voice softly echoed in her mind. *Go see to Thomas for the now,* he said. Then, his presence surrounding her dissipated and Sarah felt an odd sense of loneliness within her own mind. She was growing accustomed to having him constantly there inside her thoughts. It was strange, but she could swear she'd actually felt his mind disconnect from her own. Each time his mind joined, or linked-up with hers, a certain pressure was felt inside her head. It didn't hurt, but Sarah now recognized that sensation as a clear indicator of his presence in her mind.

Upon reaching Thomas' room, Sarah knocked and then slowly opened the door. To her surprise, Thomas wasn't sitting before the television playing video games. Instead, he and a female Angel sat at a card table along an adjacent wall. There was some kind of board game set up on the table with game pieces Sarah did not recognize. Thomas was staring down at the board, contemplating his next move. He looked up at Sarah's entry into the room.

She immediately got the sense that she'd startled him somehow, though there was no physical sign that he'd been shocked upon catching sight of her. The Angel sitting across the table from him quietly excused herself and quickly left the room. Once the door was closed, Sarah walked over to lay a hand on Thomas' shoulder, needing physical contact with him like she always did.

"You doin' okay, kid?" she asked, glad to finally be back with him so she could see for herself that he was safe. It wasn't that she didn't trust the Angels to watch over him; again, they were *Angels*. Sarah had always been overly protective, never trusting anyone completely with Thomas' safety, not even her parents. Now, however, as she gave his slim shoulder a gentle squeeze, she felt a shudder tremble through him, though he still displayed no outward sign of unease.

"I'm fine," he said as he shrugged her hand off his shoulder and got up from his chair. Plopping down diagonally onto a comfortable love seat before the television, he asked distractedly, "Were you able to see Grams and Gramps?"

Sarah took a seat in a chair next to him and nodded. "Yeah," she said, then hesitated. After a second, she continued, "Actually, as I'm sure you saw on tv, things weren't going so great back at home, so I decided it would be best to bring them back here. So I did."

Thomas shot her a shocked look instantly. "You brought them here?" he asked. "To stay?"

Sarah nodded.

"What about the puppies?" he immediately demanded.

Sarah almost laughed aloud. Both dogs were almost taller than her when they stood up on their hind legs, but Thomas still thought of them as the little puppies they'd been when they'd first adopted them from the shelter. "I brought them, too, of course," she said with a grin.

Instantly, he was up and headed out the door.

Sarah leaned her head back and closed her eyes for a moment, letting go a sigh of relief. Everything back in the human realm had blown completely out of all proportion and she was glad those closest to Thomas and her were now safe in the Angelic realm and that everything was okay. *Isn't this about the time everything goes to hell?* The thought insidiously insinuated itself in her mind and Sarah jerked to attention. She was out of the chair and the room in just a couple of strides, heading for the stairs and wherever her family was. She knew she shouldn't obsess over protecting them, especially here in the Angelic realm, but Mikhail wasn't around and Sarah hadn't exactly explained things thoroughly to her family members, including Thomas, and so there was plenty of room for them to offend any of the Angels, inadvertently. Sarah couldn't let that happen, not after everything all of them had already done for her family and her. She hurried down the stairs.

Mikhail rapped twice on the door to Gabriel's office. He'd disliked leaving Sarah and her family just after getting them to the house, but there had been no getting around this. Sarah had changed too much for the other Seraphim to ignore her now, as had Mikhail himself. They were both experiencing changes that, if they continued, would soon lead some in this realm, like Azra'il, to have serious concerns. Mikhail had already noticed a serious streak of prejudice toward humans among his people. In all honesty, he truly couldn't blame them. Humans of this time were not exactly the greatest examples of their kind. Mikhail thought of his Sarah and sighed with relief that she was no longer human. By no stretch of anyone's imagination would she ever be able to be mistaken as such now.

Her son and parents, on the other hand...

"Come," Mikhail heard Gabriel say from inside the office and he went in, closing the door behind him.

Israfil and Gabriel sat at the desk on the far side of the cluttered room, with Gabriel behind it and Israfil in front. Upon catching a glimpse of Mikhail's countenance, Israfil audibly gasped in surprise but remained silent. "See what I mean?" Gabriel asked in an aside to him.

Israfil just nodded, never taking his eyes off Mikhail.

Mikhail advanced into the room, nodding to the duo once and saying, "Brothers," as his greeting. Each man nodded back, but remained silent. Mikhail was amazed to find he could pick up on about 30% of what Gabriel was thinking. He wasn't getting it all, but it was enough for him to know where he stood with him. Israfil's thoughts were completely hidden from him, though. He stared for a moment at Israfil, wondering at the significance of that fact. But as Israfil stared back, Mikhail quickly directed his gaze elsewhere, not wanting to cause a scene.

He eased into the other chair facing the desk, just beside Israfil.

Both pairs of eyes remained affixed to him.

Talk about a tough crowd, Mikhail thought. This wasn't going to be easy, but he'd never been one to back down or beat around the bush in the face of great odds. "My brothers, I've come to inform you that I'm hosting my Sarah's entire family at my home now and that I intend to continue doing so indefinitely."

"You *what*?!" Gabriel demanded, completely flabbergasted.

Israfil remained silent and still.

Mikhail continued. "I came here to enlist your aid," he calmly said, though he felt nothing even *close* to calm. "If both of you are behind us, perhaps Azra'il and the Sanhedrin will be more accepting of this whole business..."

"Mikhail," Gabriel interrupted, holding a hand up, palm facing outward, as if stopping his brother physically. "What exactly do you mean by her *'entire family'*?" he asked.

Without hesitation, Mikhail said, "In addition to her son, there are her parents... and two canines."

"Here?" Gabriel asked.

Mikhail nodded.

"*Now?*" Gabriel asked.

Mikhail nodded once more.

Gabriel slumped back in his chair, his hands covering his face, his fingers rubbing his eyes.

"Why would you do this?" came Israfil's quiet and steady voice for the first time.

Mikhail explained to them the whole situation, holding back not one single detail. Afterward, the group was silent while each gathered his thoughts. Finally, it was Israfil who broke the silence, saying, "I'd like to speak with Sarah."

A spark of hope sprang to life inside Mikhail's chest. If Israfil stood by them, then there was no way Gabriel would refuse them, for the two of them had always had a healthy respect of each other's opinions. "Whenever and wherever," Mikhail said.

Israfil stood immediately, saying, "No time like the present."

Mikhail and Gabriel also stood, but it was Mikhail who responded, suggesting, "Actually, I think it would be better if we wait until this evening. Her family has only just arrived from the human realm and needs time to settle in. I was thinking, or hoping really, that you would join us for dinner tonight?"

Each one looked at the other, then back at Mikhail, and nodded once, saying simultaneously, "Fine."

Mikhail named the time and, after a conservative "Good-bye," he left the main part of the city to return home. His mind immediately sought out Sarah's. He had intentionally shut off his link with her for his visit with his brothers for fear that she would pick up on some of their feelings of prejudice toward humans, but he felt the absence of her mind intensely. It was amazing how quickly he'd adapted to having his mind linked with hers. He wasn't even experiencing any headaches from it anymore. In fact, he almost felt as if he was missing an actual physical part of his body, like an arm or a leg, when he wasn't linked with her mind.

For a moment, he felt a bourgeoning panic welling inside. *Where is she?* he wondered, tension swelling within him. *Why can't I find her?* However, just as that thought flashed through his mind, he felt the now-familiar pressure inside his skull and he clearly heard her voice inside his mind.

Calm down, he heard her say. *I'm here at the house with everyone and everything's fine.*

Mikhail relaxed and completed the journey home without incident. He made his way through the house out to the beautifully-landscaped gardens at the back. There, sprawled on the meticulously trimmed lawn near the stone patio's edge, lay Thomas and the two dogs on their backs, one on each side of the boy.

It was a beautiful afternoon, without a cloud in the sky, and Sarah and her parents were sitting on the iron lawn furniture near where the boy and dogs lay, enjoying what appeared to be tall glasses of lemonade.

Mikhail headed straight to Sarah, who stood on his approach and slipped easily into his waiting arms, raising her face for a quick kiss. He felt as if he'd been away from her for years and just touching her again eased an ache he hadn't even been aware he'd been suffering from.

"I'm glad you're back," Sarah whispered in his ear as she gave him a gentle hug.

Mikhail sighed and turned. He kept one arm around Sarah, as she did with him, and moved to join the older couple of humans sitting nearby. "Hello, again," he said. "Sorry I had to run out earlier. I got back as quickly as I could."

"Oh, that's no problem," Sarah's father said. He held out his hand toward Mikhail and said, "I'm Tom Baker."

Mikhail shook hands with the man without breaking his hold on Sarah, saying, "Tom. It's good to formally meet you, at last. I'm Mikhail, as you already know."

"And this is my wife, Marian," Tom said, gesturing toward Sarah's mom as the woman rose to shake hands with Mikhail.

Mikhail gently shook hands with her, saying, "It's a pleasure to meet you, madam." She reminded him of how Sarah had looked when he'd seen her for the first time in Azra'il's office. He wondered if this was what Sarah would have looked like had she never encountered him. His hold tightened around Sarah slightly at the thought of her growing old and dying. The woman before him, he now knew, had only what he considered a small amount of time remaining on this plane before the body she inhabited ceased functioning. Of course, that was still a couple of human decades away, so Mikhail felt no need to worry on Sarah's part, for the moment. The idea of something like that happening to his Sarah, though – Mikhail simply couldn't fathom it.

Sarah's grip on his side tightened infinitesimally and he knew she'd picked up on the drift of his thoughts. The Designers willing, they'd never have to deal with the possibility of her body dying. It certainly had changed enough physically to indicate it should be different from human bodies. Hopefully, she had become immortal, like all Seraphim. And, judging from the amount of soul-energy Mikhail could detect emanating from within her current form along with the fact that she had developed a cutapi and even

215

used her shields, he believed her to be a complete Seraph now.

Another slight squeeze from Sarah brought Mikhail's attention back to the patio and he did his best to play the part of her man, just as he planned to be for the rest of all eternity.

An hour later, Sarah entered the bedroom she'd shared with Mikhail ahead of him, but turned to face him upon reaching the middle of the room. He'd just taken off immediately after her parents' arrival without explanation as to why he so urgently needed all of a sudden to go talk with Gabriel. Then, after he finally showed up back at the house, all he'd bothered to tell her was that they would be having a couple of guests over for dinner. To say she was pissed would be the understatement of the century.

"So…," she said, waiting for him to start.

Mikhail closed the door to the bedroom and locked it. Sarah loved the way he moved and how he looked at her, but she was angry with him for just rushing off like that and she wanted an explanation. Judging by the look in his eyes, though, he currently had no inclination toward explanations of any kind. He reached her and gently enfolded her in his arms. Sarah's arms crept up and around his neck of their own volition, though she tried to resist.

Mikhail lowered his face to take a gentle nip of her skin where her neck and shoulder met, releasing a deeply pleasured moan as he kissed the spot he'd nipped. Sarah told herself she would stop him in just a minute so they could talk.

"Mmm…," Mikhail softly said in an erotically deep voice. "No talking right now. Just touch and taste and feel." As he said this, his fingers went to work on the buttons on her button-fly jeans and he started backing her up toward the big bed in the center of the room.

"Mmm," Sarah moaned. "You feel so good." Her mind was warring with her body. She wanted more than anything to strip him down and spend the rest of the afternoon touching, tasting and feeling him. In the end, however, her mind won the battle. When her backside came up against the mattress, she broke their kiss and pushed him slightly away from her.

"No," he said, but then quickly relented. He took her hand in his and half-sat on the bed, with one knee bent horizontally on the bed and the other leg straight, its foot planted firmly on the floor. "Okay," he said with a sigh. "What's wrong?"

Sarah looked him directly in the eyes, his flashing simultaneously with hers. "Who's coming for dinner?" she asked.

After only a moment's hesitation, he told her, "Israfil and Djibr... I mean, Gabriel."

Sarah could feel an excitement within him at this news and she asked, "So that's really where you were earlier? Seeing them?"

Mikhail nodded as he reached a hand around the nape of her neck to pull her closer for a kiss. Sarah allowed the kiss, for she was starving for the taste of his lips. As the kiss deepened, however, she broke away once more, determined to get more answers.

"Why was it so urgent for you to go see them all of a sudden earlier?" she asked.

Mikhail sighed, dropping his head to rest against her shoulder. Sarah felt a whole range of emotions flitting through him, including that same anger she'd sensed earlier. It wasn't quite as strong now as it had been but she could still sense him struggling with it.

217

"I had to let them know what was going on," he said quietly. He raised his head to look at her. "I don't want anything to get in the way of us being together, but it's not as simple as it might sound," he said. "There are plenty of Angels who won't be happy about humans living here in the Angelic realm. You must have discovered how... upset some of them are that you and Thomas are here. And now, your parents are here, too." He dropped his head to her shoulder again as his hands began rubbing her arms and her back. "I'm sorry, but some of the Angels here will take some time to get used to the idea of humans living in our realm." He stopped and suddenly raised his head to look her straight in the eyes. "But I won't let them treat you like some human, nor Thomas, for that matter."

Sarah narrowed her brows in confusion. Thomas *was* human.

"He's *our* son, now. Not someone to be considered an outsider," Mikhail said, as if that would be explanation enough.

When Sarah went to speak again, he quickly cut her off with a long, slow kiss. Sarah could feel desire coursing through him and she let the kiss continue. Before long, they were both lying on the bed, each one half undressed, and both of them were panting for breath. It never took them long to get to this point, the point where they wanted to continue but were too aware of the rules of the realm.

Sarah pushed away from him, whispering in a raspy voice, "We should stop... before everything gets out of control."

"Shh," was all he said as he reached for her, dragging her up under his hard frame. He was finished with waiting. After what he'd witnessed in the human realm with her using her Seraph abilities like a pro, he knew in his heart she was fully-Seraph and he would wait not one minute more to take her. He gave her a scorching kiss and then moved down her soft neck, licking and nibbling along each inch of his downward path. Her shirt was already gone. Her bra soon joined it on the floor. Mikhail spent only a cursory amount of attention on her breasts, molding them with his fingers, then giving each a short tug and suckle with his hot mouth. Then, he resumed his downward trek across her flat abdomen to the open V of the fly to her jeans.

He sat up on his knees and grabbed the waistband of the jeans, half-picking her up off the bed to slide them off her buttocks and then down the length of her slender legs. The jeans joined the bra and shirt on the floor, followed closely by the pristine white cotton underwear she wore.

Sarah was panting for real, this time, not because she couldn't get enough breath, but because she was so nervous. What was he doing? He was the one who'd told her there was no way she and he could ever mate, yet here he was starting something that could only have one outcome. She looked up at his flashing eyes, fear and confusion marring the perfect vision of ecstasy he wanted to see when he looked back at her.

Mikhail returned to settle on top of her, his face directly above hers, and he whispered, "There's no stopping today. You are my life. I give you the gift of my energy... as protection and fulfillment. You shall become a part of me and I shall become a part of you." He framed her face with his hands then, and finally said, "We shall become one and damn the consequences."

A tremor of fear shook violently through Sarah's body, but she was the one who reached for him, bringing his face down to hers for a kiss so deep and emotional she never wanted to let go. Mikhail was so much a man that she worried she wouldn't measure up for him. His voice quickly sounded in her mind, assuring her she could never disappoint him in any way and Sarah, emboldened by his assurances, found herself taking the lead by pushing him off of her and onto his back.

She smiled down at him as she went to work on the button and zipper of his slacks, throwing another quick smile up at him as she encountered his boxer briefs. Her hand slipped under the waistband and she felt his thickened member throbbing there for her. It was as hard as anything possibly could be and the amount of heat pulsing from it nearly scorched the skin of her palm and fingers. She used her wrist to push the waistband of the boxers down to reveal the prize her hand held. Her eyes feasted on the physical evidence of his desire for her and she smiled, once more, as she bent her head to capture the tip of his staff with her mouth.

Mikhail's upper body came up off the bed as she sucked hard and then nibbled lightly with her tiny teeth, licking each section she nibbled immediately afterward. Then, she sucked hard on him again. He laid back onto the bed and, closing his eyes, let out deep breaths of agonizing pleasure. Each time she sucked, licked or nibbled, he thought he was going to go insane and he wanted her to stop, but he couldn't even think of her stopping. It felt so good just having her touch him this way, but he wanted more. He wanted to be inside her, ramming himself up into her to the hilt, showing her exactly how much better he was than any puny human ever could be.

"Enough!" he fairly shouted, as he grabbed her shoulders and forced her mouth from him. He pushed her off him and back onto her back, where he covered her quickly and settled between her legs. He used his own legs to widen hers and then reached down to position himself so the taking could be swift. "I'm sorry if I hurt you this first time, my love," he said.

Sarah would have smiled, had she not been so very desperate for him to enter into her to make her his. "I have a

220

son," she told him distractedly, her hands moving to touch him anywhere she could, pulling him back toward her in an attempt to urge him on.

"This won't be like any other time you've done this though, love... I promise you," he said. Then, without further ado, he grabbed hold of her shoulders with each hand and pushed nearly his full length up and into her in one fast jerk.

Sarah gasped at how much she felt. He completely filled her, it seemed, yet she sensed he needed to go deeper. How she would be able to accommodate him, she didn't know. But, when he pulled back slightly and then jerked up against her again, she felt more of him enter her, going a couple of inches at least farther into her waiting warmth. She wasn't anywhere near as warm as he was, though, and she felt as if she was going to spontaneously combust if it got any hotter in her lower innards.

"Gods, Sarah," Mikhail gasped. "I'm going to come! I'm sorry!"

Just as Mikhail made a last thrust, pushing himself over the edge to a place he'd never before achieved, Sarah suddenly set off into outer space without warning, rocketing through the cosmos on a journey she wished would never end. She'd never experienced anything like this before in her entire life... Hell, in any of her lives! She knew for the first time what it meant to completely know another soul and she never wanted to let him go.

Minutes later, or was it hours, as she slowly drifted back to where she and Mikhail lay entwined on the mattress, it didn't matter to her that this was the middle of the afternoon, or that what they had just done was completely against every rule known to Angel-kind, and probably mankind. What mattered was that she and Mikhail were now mated and he loved and knew her completely and she loved and knew him completely and nothing and no one would ever be able to come between them.

The ends of Sarah's lips curled upward slightly at the thought and she nuzzled her head more comfortably against his strong chest, feeling his big arms tighten about her petite frame. They fell asleep in just that pose, each replete and carefree for once in their entire existences.

Chapter 12

Sarah slowly came awake from a dreamless sleep. What had awakened her? She lay still and silent against Mikhail's chest. Her first thought was that Thomas had called her, but as she listened, she heard no sounds from outside the room. Only Mikhail's soft, rhythmic breathing broke the silence. Sarah supposed she was just being overly cautious now that she and Mikhail had finally taken the last step toward solidifying their relationship. She felt as if he was as much a part of her as Thomas was and she would do anything to protect him.

Just as she'd decided she'd been imagining things and was on the verge of falling asleep again, she heard a distinct whisper in a child's voice in her mind. Her eyes flew open and she jerked into a sitting position, her sudden movements fully awakening Mikhail immediately.

She was pale as a ghost and every muscle in her body radiated with tension as she struggled to drag oxygen into her lungs. "Sweetheart, what's wrong?" Mikhail urgently asked, concern gripping his chest. What they'd shared earlier had been beyond any earthly experience he'd ever had and afterward, Mikhail had fallen into an exhausted, dreamless sleep. His mind had caught onto Sarah's just before she'd moved, however, and he'd known upon opening his eyes that something was very wrong. In fact, he could almost swear he'd heard the soft whisper of a child's voice just before he'd awakened.

Sarah's breathing was not improving and Mikhail moved her onto his lap in a sideways position so he could see her face while still keeping an arm around her shoulders. That's when he saw it.

Sarah gasped again, struggling against some unseen force to pull enough oxygen into her lungs, but it just wasn't working. Mikhail had pulled her onto his lap and she held onto his shoulders for dear life, wondering if she was going to make it or not. *Was this a result of what we did earlier?* she wondered. After all, he'd said it was forbidden for Seraphim to mate with humans. Perhaps they were incompatible on some physiological level that wasn't blatantly obvious and, now that they'd mated, her body couldn't handle it and was dying? That still didn't explain why Sarah had heard a child's whisper in her mind, though.

Sarah suddenly realized Mikhail had stopped moving. He had stopped rubbing her back to comfort her and had even gone silent. As she sat there in his lap, gasping time and again for air, he sat staring downward, unmoving and silent. A frown deeply marred her face and she glanced down quickly to see what on earth could have captured his attention to the point that her inability to breathe was no longer of the greatest importance to him.

Just below her navel, in the center of her lower abdomen, a distinct dot of light could be seen radiating from within her.

Sarah sucked in what air she could on a terrified gasp, heaving desperately and grabbing at her lower abdomen, trying to get a better view of this new thing that was happening to her body. Mikhail immediately grabbed her hands and pulled them away, softly crooning, "Shh…, it's okay, Baby. It's okay."

Sarah jerked her terrified gaze up to his face, on the verge of asking if he was completely insane, when her breathing and everything else in the world suddenly seemed to stop. Mikhail's face shone with the brightest sense of joy and happiness Sarah had ever seen. He was still staring at the dot of light, neither his eyes nor any other part of him moving, but the mind behind his eyes was moving like lightning as thoughts raced through it. Sarah forgot the need for oxygen as her mind-link with his strengthened all of a sudden and she got caught up in the whirl of thoughts and emotions.

They had done it! They had conceived! Mikhail had lived on this planet for more than one million years and had never once been able to conceive with any of the Angels and, just when he and the other Seraphim had believed they'd discovered in humans the answer to their prayers regarding mating and conception, the blessed Great Designers had come along and denied them their prize, deeming it taboo.

But now, Mikhail and his Sarah had proven the Designers wrong. *What if this isn't the only thing they'd said that was wrong?* The traitorous thought flashed through Mikhail's mind and he suddenly caught Sarah's fading mental response.

Oh, you have no idea, my love…

His eyes dashed to her face and he realized from how blue her lips were that she was about to pass out from lack of air.

"Breathe, Baby! Breathe!" he shouted at her as he whacked her on the center of her back with the palm of his hand. Sarah coughed and gasped, then coughed more. He held her in his arms, making sure not to squeeze too tightly, but willing his strength into her, as her breathing began to stabilize.

Khamet waited in the antechamber off to the side of the council chamber of the Great Sanhedrin. He'd come as instructed to await orders as to when to proceed with the operation. Everyone was in place and Khamet knew, as did the one he'd come to see, that this might be their only opportunity for success. So much was riding on this operation and Khamet, for one, was betting everything on this one shot. He shuddered at the thought of what might come to pass if the operation failed to achieve its goal.

A door to his right suddenly opened and he straightened from where he'd been standing leaning against the wall. The one he'd come to meet walked into the room and quietly closed the door. Only then was Khamet acknowledged. "Go ahead," said the council member with a wave of dismissal.

Khamet nodded once and left the room, taking the same back stairs he'd used to get into the antechamber. He made his way swiftly through the mid-afternoon traffic within the city. With any luck, he and his team would be able to set the wheels in motion by this very evening. This thought spurred him on and he hurried with even greater haste toward his destination.

Sarah chuckled a little as Mikhail kissed her abdomen again, directly on top of the little dot of light showing through her skin there. He'd already kissed it about a thousand times since discovering it. He was laying face down between her legs, resting his head on her abdomen, listening. He'd been that way for the past thirty minutes. Every few minutes, he would raise his head and turn to kiss the little dot of light. Then, he'd lay his head back down onto the spot he'd just kissed and squeeze Sarah in his arms.

It was funny, really, this big brute behaving so. But Sarah loved it. She ran her fingers through his long black hair, gently massaging his scalp. He sighed and Sarah wished they didn't have company coming so they could drag this on and on. At that thought, her fingers stopped their ministrations and she said, "We have to tell everyone." The little dot of light was very bright and Sarah didn't think there was any way to hide it forever from others, if at all.

Mikhail suddenly lifted his head and looked at her, excitement making his eyes virtually dance in his head. "Oh, my gosh," he exclaimed, pulling himself up and off her. "I have to go tell my brothers!" He zipped around to the other side of the bed, grabbing his clothes from their various resting places around the room.

Sarah frowned, not ready for her wonderful time with him to be finished with yet. "They're coming to dinner this very evening," she said. "Why can't we just wait until then to tell them?"

Mikhail paused only a moment before pulling his slacks the rest of the way up and explaining, "You don't understand, love. They'll both want to get started searching for their own human counterparts once they hear about this. In fact, if it were me, I'd be angrier the longer it took one of my brothers to notify me." Whipping his shirt over his head, he pulled it down over his rippling abs. After he'd pulled on his socks, he turned toward her on the mattress and leaned over to give her a quick kiss. "I'm sorry," he said. "I just think they'd all want to know sooner rather than later."

"All of them?" Sarah asked. "Even Azra'il?"

He looked her directly in the eye. "Especially Azra'il," he said quietly.

Sarah lowered her gaze to the tiny dot of light. She allowed her fingers to lightly rub the spot of skin where it shone through. She'd only known of its existence for less than an hour's time, yet she already felt fiercely protective of it. Azra'il, she believed, would not be so quick to rejoice at the news of its existence.

Mikhail reached to cover her hand with one of his. "Everything will be all right, love," he assured her with a sly smile. "You'll see." He rose from the mattress and went in search of his discarded shoes. Once they were on, he returned to her, bending and placing a soft kiss on the now-favored patch of glowing skin. Then, he raised up to give Sarah a deep, heart-felt kiss, his emotions conveyed clearly to her through it. Finally, he pulled away, running a hand along the side of her cheek and under her jaw, and then he smiled and was gone.

Sarah lounged back against the pillows, her fingers absently rubbing the little patch of light as she thought about what Mikhail had said. She knew he was probably right about Gabriel and the other one, whose name she could never seem to remember. They both seemed very nice and Sarah had no doubt that after a million years of each having no chance of being able to experience having a family of their own, they would want to begin looking for their own "other halves", as it may be. But she couldn't for the life of her understand why Mikhail would believe someone so filled with anger, as she'd sensed Azra'il to be the one and only time she'd been in his presence, could ever accept that it was possible he might be able to find happiness within another's arms. People like that were usually so wrapped up in their own personal Hell that there was no room for anyone else in the equation. Sarah should know. She'd lived that way for more years than she cared to recall.

You're wrong, my love, Mikhail's soft voice sounded in her mind. *You just have to dig a little deeper beneath the surface with him to understand, that's all. Now, quit worrying about all this and get some rest for our child.*

Sarah felt his mind-link connection with her grow slack and she figured he must be nearing the government offices in the heart of the city. Mikhail had shared with her the details of his visit with Azra'il that last time, including the fact that she'd been detected almost immediately by the powerful Seraph. Because of this, she knew it would be more beneficial to their cause if she were nowhere around, either physically or telepathically, when Mikhail confronted his brothers.

Her fingers continued to absently rub over the glowing spot, but stopped when Sarah heard again the faint whisper of a child's voice. She couldn't actually understand the voice, but it gave her a great sense of elation each time she heard it. Mikhail had told her he could hear it through his mind-link with her. Sarah wondered if he could hear it now, without the link. The thought of him missing out on this angered her a bit and Sarah wished he hadn't cut the link. She would like to express to his brothers just how peeved she was with them, especially Azra'il.

The whispered child's voice sounded again in her mind. *Must be a girl,* Sarah thought, judging by how talkative she was already, and still only in the womb.

A knock on the door brought Sarah's attention back to the room and she suddenly realized she wasn't dressed at all. "Hold on a sec," she quickly called out. The last thing she needed was her mom and dad walking in to find her first, lying completely naked on top of Mikhail's bed, and second, showing a glowing dot of light from within her abdomen! She knew it would have to be dealt with somehow at some time, but she didn't want to have to be the one responsible for doing it – not alone, at any rate, and not now. It was just too soon.

So, she quickly pulled a nightgown out of the dresser, pulled it on and scooted beneath the sheet and thick down comforter on the mattress and then called, "Okay! You can come in, now!"

To her surprise, Narayana walked in carrying a tea tray laden with tea and finger sandwiches. There were also lemon cookies, she noticed as the faithful servant placed the tray over Sarah's lap. Her stomach growled and Sarah reached for one of the sandwiches. She heard again the child's whispering voice and suddenly found herself munching on one of the delightful lemon cookies instead. *Great!* Sarah thought. *Next thing you know, I'll be eating Cole Slaw and beets! Ugh!*

She detested both items.

Narayana bowed to her after pouring the tea and silently left the room, closing the door behind her. The tea was hot and soothing and Sarah drank the entire cup in just a few gulps. She hadn't realized how dehydrated she'd become.

Stifling a yawn, she set the empty cup back on the saucer on the tray and moved the tray over to the bedside table on her side of the bed. She smiled at the thought that she already considered this as her room, too, even though she'd really only known Mikhail for a short time. It seemed, even with all the issues that kept creeping up, the two of them were settling quite nicely into each other's life.

A barely audible child's whisper rushed suddenly through her mind and Sarah smiled and then yawned, pulling the covers up and tucking them under her chin. *Good night, Sweetheart,* she thought just before closing her eyes. *Mommy and Daddy love you.* Then, she was asleep.

"Mom!" Thomas yelled.

"Why won't she wake up?" Marian screamed. They'd been trying for what seemed like hours. Tom just shook his head in frustrated confusion. Marian looked around again for some clue as to where they were and how they'd gotten there. It looked like the sky might be getting lighter, but she still couldn't make out anything other than thick copses of trees. From where she sat, she believed it could be broad daylight and they wouldn't be able to tell because everything was so overgrown.

The smell was the worst part. The rotting vegetation made breathing unbearable and Marian almost envied Sarah's unconscious state. She looked back down at her daughter's still-sleeping form, though she didn't dare touch her.

Sarah's skin was deathly pale and there was a strange sort of glow coming from her entire body. It and an even stranger spot of light emanating from Sarah's midsection, just below her navel, was the only light allowing Marian and Tom and Thomas to see each other.

When she'd first awakened, she had immediately moved to wake Sarah. She was stopped, however, by Sarah's hair! Embedded within the usual head full of thick auburn hair were long, starch-white strands that... attacked, for lack of a better word, whenever Marian or Tom even got too close to Sarah's sleeping form.

Marian didn't know what to make of it! But, she had to keep trying, she figured. Otherwise, they were going to die. She just knew it. She didn't know how, but she believed it.

"Sarah!" she yelled again, motioning to her husband and grandson to join in. They gathered as close to Sarah's form as the hair would allow and shouted simultaneously, "Sarah!"

There was nothing. She just kept sleeping. No movement. Nothing. So, they yelled again, and again, and again.

Mikhail waited impatiently while Israfil went in search of an Angel he knew of who was an expert on Human *and* Angel anatomy and physiology. Mikhail had tried to explain to Israfil and Gabriel that Sarah was no longer human, but that she was now a Seraph, like they were. Of course, neither one had believed him. When he'd told them he had fully-mated with her and that she was now pregnant with Mikhail's offspring, well, he'd thought both of them were going to die of apoplectic fits, then and there!

Israfil had calmed first, coming to the sane and logical conclusion (Mikhail supposed, if he had to have one) that a physician had to be summoned for an official examination. That really would be the most objective and scientific way to prove everything Mikhail had been asking them to believe. Then, they'd have all the proof needed to convince Azra'il.

Mikhail felt a little twinge of guilt at not having asked Azra'il to attend this meeting to hear his good news. Maybe it was all Sarah's worrying earlier – he wasn't sure. He just knew when it had come down to the wire, he wasn't quite ready to deal with Azra'il yet. He would get whatever proof Gabriel and Israfil needed in order to be satisfied he hadn't finally flipped his lid after all these years and then he would go with them and the good physician to present everything to Azra'il. Only after Azra'il was sufficiently convinced would Mikhail allow his Sarah anywhere near his most powerful brother.

The thought of Sarah brought a smile to his lips. He felt the need to contact her as an overwhelming force and he was on the verge of doing so when Gabriel coughed. Honestly, it hadn't even been a real cough... more a clearing of his throat, really. Mikhail frowned. He caught about half of what was going on inside Gabriel's mind now and he was shocked to find it wasn't all pleasant.

Mikhail and all the other Seraphim had all seen and lived through a great deal more than any of them would care to mention, as is the price of immortality, and old prejudices did tend to fester and rot, sometimes to such a degree that when they did rear their ugly heads, they did so with a vengeance. The way Gabriel was currently thinking of Sarah would normally have sent Mikhail into such a rage that only a fight the size of a world-wide apocalypse would satisfy him. Today, however, Mikhail chose to wait.

He knew without a doubt that he was right about Sarah and, once the physician confirmed it, neither Azra'il nor Gabriel nor anyone else within the Angelic realm would ever be able to deny what was rightfully Sarah's and his. They would finally be able to live freely, in the open. And, they'd be safe to raise a family of their own.

No. Mikhail would not link with his Sarah, for the now. He would await the arrival of the physician, as planned, and then he and his brothers, along with the physician, would descend upon Sarah. But not without a quick telepathic warning from Mikhail. He wouldn't put her through that. He would warn her of what to expect. Then, once everything was confirmed, Mikhail, his brothers and the physician would stand before Azra'il and the Great Sanhedrin to present the evidence and to ask that, in addition to full asylum being granted to Thomas and his grandparents, Sarah and Mikhail be allowed to live as a mated couple along with their offspring.

Mikhail's lips turned up at the corners as he thought of his little fairy-light of a child. He'd heard it whispering through Sarah's mind on several occasions this afternoon and he wondered if it was still being so chatty as the day faded into evening.

He sighed in frustration. This was taking too long. He wanted to be back with his woman and their child.

Finally, he caught a good deal of thoughts from the physician accompanying Israfil. His name was Hantsushept. This dour Angel was very upset at having been pulled from his evening's plans to accompany Seraphim on a mission of such great secrecy and urgency he could be told absolutely nothing until their arrival. He didn't even know where he was being taken, just that it was of the utmost urgency to get him there.

All he knew for sure was that he very much disliked flying of any sort, and he'd been forced to endure the short flight from his home to the government seat in the center of Seraphim City. He most definitely was not feeling friendly toward anyone at the moment.

Mikhail figured now was as good a time as any to break the news to Sarah and he reached out to her telepathically to establish a mind-link. He stilled suddenly, frowning. He detected nothing of her presence. He tried again, this time blocking out everything else. If she'd gone somewhere again, he would be able to track her by the energy trail she'd leave behind when she flew. Israfil and the physician entered the room, but Mikhail took no notice. His mind was entirely focused on establishing a link with Sarah's mind.

Israfil frowned at how rude Mikhail was being to the physician, though Hantsushept didn't seem to notice. He was too enthralled with Mikhail's flashing eyes, his unusually bright glowing skin and the long strands of white hair that would occasionally float about, as if gravity could not hold them down.

"Fascinating," the physician declared as he approached Mikhail's unmoving form. Without warning, a strand of the long white hair whipped out, lashing across the physician's face, causing a thin but very deep gash across his cheek and the bridge of his nose. Everyone but Mikhail gasped in shock at what they'd just witnessed and each one of them took a healthy step back away from the distracted Seraph. "Did you *see* that?" Hantsushept asked, wide-eyed and bleeding.

He took a handkerchief from his pants pocket and held it to the wounds on his face, all the while cocking his head this way and that, moving left, then right, trying to get a better view without putting himself in harm's way. His eyes, though tearing up from the pain of his hair-inflicted wounds, were alight with voracious intrigue and even the thought of further physical damage wasn't enough to keep him away.

As soon as any one of the long white strands even looked like it would strike, Hantsushept backed off, only to go at his subject from a different angle. "Absolutely fascinating," he declared again.

Israfil silently admitted to himself that, if he wasn't so involved in this whole business, he would probably find it just as fascinating as the physician. Israfil had always been more of the level-headed, staid member of the Seraphim team. His family members were the ones who had been born with all the serious powers, but with them came really bad tempers.

Now, however, as he watched Mikhail, it seemed his brother wasn't even aware of their presence in the room. As far as Israfil knew, Mikhail had never displayed any signs of any telepathic abilities. His special power was that of healing ability and strength. It always had been. So, why did Israfil get the impression that Mikhail was currently utilizing some form of telepathy?

He cautiously approached his brother, saying, "Mikhail?"

There was no response.

Gabriel was watching this byplay with curiosity. After just a moment, he seemed to sense what Israfil had sensed and he, too, attempted to rouse Mikhail from whatever study in which he was involved.

"Brother," they both said in unison, approaching and circling Mikhail's still form.

That seemed to get through on some level because Mikhail's brows dipped just a little in a slight frown and he softly said, "I can't find her... it's like she just disappeared."

Gabriel and Israfil looked meaningfully at each other, astonishment, and perhaps even a bit of fear, creeping up inside them due to the fact that this situation quite possibly had just become much direr than they had previously believed.

"Oh, my God!" shouted Marian. "What's wrong with her? Tom, what's wrong with my baby?" Marian broke down, tears streaming down her face as she reached desperately for her husband.

Tom enveloped her in his arms, lending his strength to her in the only way he could. He was just as frustrated as she was and he didn't know what to do. They couldn't get close enough to touch Sarah to try to wake her and she wasn't responding to them yelling at her.

He threw his head back, as if the answer they needed would be somewhere in the dark canopy above them, his eyes searching for anything. All he saw was darkness. He looked back down at the glowing figure of his daughter. She looked so alien to him. The glowing skin, that strange dot of light emanating from her core, the deadly hair. *What the hell had happened to her to make her like this?* he wondered.

"Oh, God, it's hopeless," Marian sobbed. "She's gonna die and there's nothing we can do about it!"

"Shh," Tom soothed her. "We'll find a way to take care of her." He looked around for something to use, like a stick or tree branch or something. It was difficult to see in the pitch darkness of the area, but he thought he saw what looked like a palm frond nearby.

As he reached for it, Marian screamed, "Thomas, no!"

Tom whipped around in time to see the deadly white strands of hair enveloping Thomas' slight form, pulling him toward his mother's head while wrapping more and more securely around the boy. When Marian and Tom approached to try to disengage Thomas from the strands, other ones whipped out at them, lashing and zinging through the air.

"Do something!" Marian shouted at Tom, but Tom didn't know what on earth she expected him to do. He could get no closer than she without being ripped to shreds by the white strands of hair. With no options, he merely wrapped his wife in a protective embrace as they watched the scene playing out before them.

Thomas didn't seem to be being hurt by the white strands. They were just holding him in place, just next to Sarah's head.

"Son?" Tom asked cautiously. "Are you all right?"

Thomas didn't answer, didn't even show any signs he had heard his grandfather.

After a second, Tom squeezed Marian, but kept watching the boy. The only thought in his mind was: *How on earth are we going to get out of this?*

Thomas stared at his mom. His Grams was going crazy, squalling and carrying on like it was doomsday, or something. Maybe it was? Thomas certainly didn't know what to do. His mom was lying on the ground, glowing, like she had been since they'd started staying with Mikhail. She wasn't moving, though, and that scared Thomas. *Why won't she move?* he wondered.

They'd screamed and screamed at her, trying to wake her up, but she still didn't respond.

As he stood there looking at her, he thought about the white strands of hair and how they reminded him of that girl he kept seeing in the round room. If only she would appear and help them, they'd be able to wake his mom and get out of this mess. No sooner had this thought developed in his mind than he found himself standing once more in the round room, the strange girl standing immediately before him.

Focus, she said without any sound.

What do I do? he asked in his mind.

You must focus on reaching her, her voice said.

How? he mentally asked.

Concentrate. Get closer to her and concentrate only on reaching into her mind, linking with her.

But, the hair! I'll be... he shrieked mentally.

No. It won't hurt you, came her voice.

Thomas slowly approached his mom's prone figure, blocking out the sounds of his sobbing grandmother. The hair raised and whipped around, like it was getting ready to strike out at him.

Concentrate, came her voice again.

Thomas' vision narrowed, seeming to tunnel down until all he could see was his mom's face. He felt someone place a comforting warm blanket around him and he relaxed, his eyes fixed on his mom's face. He suddenly felt weightless and his vision blurred. He wanted to blink, to say something, to do... something, when he suddenly heard a little girl's voice. He couldn't make out what she was saying, but it seemed kind of slurred or like she was having difficulty talking.

All of a sudden, Thomas felt like he was being physically pushed aside inside his own mind, like somebody else was taking control of everything. It was a horrible feeling, extremely repulsive, and Thomas struggled fiercely against the intruder in his mind.

Mikhail suddenly tensed, his entire form tightening, and he urgently said, "Wait!" His eyes narrowed in concentration and then, after a tense moment, completely closed. His breathing became labored and he gritted his teeth, a white line forming around his taught lips, as if he was exerting a great deal of energy, though he made no other visible movement.

Chapter 13

Thomas railed against the intrusion into his mind, lashing out with weapons he'd forgotten he possessed. For a moment, it appeared the intruder was thwarted, but then Thomas felt him surge back en force. Thomas ended up merely hanging on for dear life.

Nera! he called in desperation. *Help me!*

Her soft voice came from what seemed a great distance. *I cannot help you.*

Nera! he shrieked mentally.

You must let him in, came her whispered voice.

Thomas panicked. Let him in? Was she *crazy*?

Then, a familiar and welcome voice sounded in his mind. *Thomas..., son..., calm your mind for me.*

M'khial? Thomas asked in his mind, relief washing over him.

Yes, my son. It's me. Where are you?

I-I don't know.

Is your mother with you, son?

Yeah, but she won't wake up, Thomas responded pitifully. *I don't know what's wrong with her.*

Mikhail pushed back the fear that threatened to overwhelm him at this news. *It's okay, son,* his voice soothed. *We just need to figure out where you are. Can you describe to me where you are?*

It's real dark here. I can't see anything.

Mikhail mentally sighed in frustration.

My grams and gramps are here, too, came Thomas' voice.

240

Are they okay?

Yeah, but my grams is real scared.

There was a long silence in Thomas' mind and he panicked when he suddenly heard the little girl's voice again.

Calm down, son, Mikhail's voice soothed again.

Who is *that?* Thomas demanded wildly.

I-It's your baby sister, came Mikhail's voice after a short pause.

Thomas thought about this and finally relaxed.

Son, I need you to relax a bit more, Mikhail's voice instructed.

Are you gonna come get us? Thomas asked.

Yes, my son, but I'm going to have to get my brother so we can find you, okay?

Thomas tensed for a moment, then thought, *Okay.* He felt a wash of relief coming from Mikhail's presence in his mind.

I need to leave you for a few minutes, came Mikhail's voice. *Do you think you can stay focused on your mom until I return?*

I... think so, Thomas responded.

Good. I'll return momentarily with my brother.

Thomas felt Mikhail's presence pull away from his mind and he concentrated on relaxing as much as he could.

Mikhail's eyes opened and he turned to Gabriel. "I need your help," he said, approaching him.

Gabriel quickly backed away from him, fearful of the deadly hair strands.

Mikhail stopped, frowning in confusion. Then, he caught thoughts from two of the three men around him and his gaze darted to the wounds clearly visible on the physician's face. After a moment's hesitation, Mikhail shook his head and grabbed his hair into a bundle, wrapping it around his hand and securing it in his fist.

"Right," he said, then turned back to Gabriel. "Now," he started, but then stopped again as he noticed the expression on his brother's face. "What?" he asked in exasperation.

"How long have you had this telepathic ability?" Gabriel asked angrily.

Mikhail sighed, closing his eyes in exhausted frustration. He didn't have time for this. He didn't know where Sarah was, if she was alive or dead, or anything, really. All he knew was that she was with Thomas and Thomas was in a semi-active mind-link with her. If Gabriel could use his innate tracking abilities to find them by linking with Thomas, then Mikhail could get to her.

He opened his eyes as a steely determination stole over him and he said matter-of-factly, "We can have this out now, or you can help me save Sarah and our daughter."

Gabriel paled.

Israfil gasped.

Hantsushept said, "Fascinating."

For a tense moment, no one moved or said anything. Then, Gabriel made up his mind. This was Mikhail, after all. It didn't matter what changes he'd gone through or even if he had been totally taken in by this human. He was still Mikhail.

Gabriel nodded once, sighed, and said decisively, "All right. What do you need from me?"

Mikhail's tensed shoulders relaxed and he said, "Okay. I was able to establish a mind-link with Thomas, the boy, and he has a weak mind-link with Sarah. However, according to Thomas, she's not awake and he can't seem to get any kind of response from her. Wherever they are, it's dark and the boy isn't able to see anything."

Gabriel thought over this information. He usually had a general idea of where his subject could be found when he used his abilities to find someone. Mikhail didn't seem to have the first clue where the humans were, though. "I don't know if I'm capable of scanning... everywhere," he said, frustrated.

Mikhail nodded.

"Are you able to mind-link with anyone?" Israfil suddenly asked.

Mikhail hesitated. "I... think so," he slowly said.

"Do you think you could mind-link with two people simultaneously?" Israfil asked.

"Yes," Gabriel said, excitement creeping into his voice as he caught onto the idea formed in Israfil's head. "If you could link with me and then the boy, or vice versa, while he's linked with Sarah, I might be able to latch onto her essence through him. Once I do that, I can find her."

Mikhail nodded once and said determinedly, "All right. Let's do it."

"Okay," Gabriel said. "So, um, how do we, ah...?"

Mikhail stepped forward, placing his unbound hand on Gabriel's shoulder. "I'll link with you, first," he explained. "Then, I'll link with my son. From there, assuming he's still linked with Sarah, you should be able to connect, or whatever..."

"Okay," Gabriel agreed. "What do you need me to do for the link with you?"

"Just calm your mind and try to relax," Mikhail said. "I'll do everything to get you to Thomas."

Mikhail closed his eyes.

Gabriel closed his eyes.

Israfil watched his two brothers, a frown marring his beautiful features. He wasn't sure this was such a great idea, but he could think of no other way to find the humans. And, if what Mikhail had said about the girl was true, it sounded like she might be hurt, or even dead, so time really was of the essence. Israfil glanced over at Hantsushept. As quirky as the

Angel was, Israfil was glad he was on hand, should his physician services become necessary.

Gabriel's breathing suddenly became labored. He gasped and then seemed to hyperventilate, falling. Israfil caught him before his head could hit and he lowered his brother's struggling form carefully to the floor. Gabriel's hands grabbed at his head, one on each side, and he continued gasping for air.

Hantsushept came to kneel on the opposite side from where Israfil knelt. He checked Gabriel's pulse, looked him up and down, then up again, and swallowed hard. "I, uh, haven't much experience with Seraph physiology," he stammered nervously. "None, really."

Israfil looked down at his struggling brother, then back toward the Angel, nodding once and saying, "Do whatever you can."

Hantsushept nodded and returned his attention to Gabriel's still-struggling form.

Israfil stood and turned to study Mikhail's unmoving form. One hand still held the lethal strands of hair, but the other now hung limply by his side. His eyes remained closed, but a steady light shone through his thin eyelids, no longer flashing as it had been before. His breathing was slow and steady.

Gabriel calmed suddenly and Israfil returned his attention to him. "What was the matter with him?" he asked Hantsushept.

The Angel shook his head. "I-I don't know," he reluctantly said.

"Well, how did you calm him?" Israfil asked.

"I didn't do anything," Hantsushept replied. "He just suddenly stopped struggling... I don't know why."

Israfil frowned.

Gabriel was nervous. He'd only ever mind-linked with one other Seraph, but that had been a very long time ago. Now, Mikhail was attempting to link with him and Gabriel was unsure of the wisdom of allowing such an intrusion into his mind. After all, what if...

All of a sudden, Mikhail's presence filled every corner of his mind. Gabriel felt as if he was being forced out of his own mind for lack of room. There was a tremendous force of energy vibrating at an extremely frightening tone throughout his mind and Gabriel cowered in the face of such power. His head felt as if it might explode and Gabriel could only stand by, waiting, hoping beyond all he held sacred that Mikhail knew what he was doing.

Then, as if someone had flipped a switch, all was calm. In his sudden confusion, Gabriel clearly heard Mikhail's voice chuckling, *I haven't quite lost my mind just yet, brother.*

Gabriel gave a mental shiver and thought, *Your energy is so... overwhelming.*

Mikhail pulled back a bit. *Sorry. I'm new at all this, you know? Just give me a moment to re-establish a link with my son.*

Gabriel took a mental break. Taking a step back, figuratively speaking, he re-examined all the changes he'd noticed in Mikhail since Sarah had come under his protection. His skin had a much brighter emanation of soul-energy light, his eyes did that flashing thing within their pupils, and his hair... well, what could anyone say about that? Now, it appeared Mikhail had gained some *major* telepathic abilities.

Gabriel didn't understand how a simple human could have caused such drastic and unheard-of changes in a Seraph. Because of the one law the Great Designers had declared for all Seraphim, there was no precedent in this case. He knew what the Sanhedrin's position would be on the matter, the same as Azra'il's. They'd go strictly by the law. If that happened, the humans would be returned to the human realm at the very least. Judging by the changes in Mikhail's physical appearance, though, it wouldn't surprise Gabriel if all four of them were ordered to be executed.

Mikhail was a different issue. The crazy things he'd been saying and his odd behavior were one thing. But, if Mikhail and the human truly had mated, no force on earth would keep Mikhail from being banished to the Badlands.

Did Gabriel believe in the possibility that Mikhail and the girl had conceived? Not for a moment. But he loved his brother and didn't want to see him punished so severely for something he did without full knowledge and control of his actions. The Sanhedrin wouldn't bother considering any lapse in mental judgment, though.

The only solution Gabriel could conceive of for this issue was to just go along with Mikhail until it could be discovered what the human had done to cause such drastic physiological changes within him. Then maybe Gabriel and Israfil could figure out some way of reversing the changes, especially that lethal hair.

Convincing Mikhail that he was delusional, however, was going to be the steepest mountain any of them had ever climbed, and Gabriel didn't *even* want to think about that until he absolutely had to.

Suddenly, the pressure inside Gabriel's head increased and he felt Mikhail's overwhelming presence surge forward once more. This time, however, Gabriel felt another, much more different kind of presence along with Mikhail's. Gabriel was surprised to discover this was the boy human. His confusion at the boy's curious presence was pushed aside, however, as Gabriel felt the underlying urgency edging the boy's thoughts.

Don't worry son, Mikhail mentally soothed the boy. *My brother is here to help us discover your location.*

Gabriel concentrated. As he instinctively adjusted to the boy's energy vibration patterns, he was quickly able to discover the foreign patterns hidden within them. It was odd. They were all over the place, covering a much broader spectrum than normal human energy patterns displayed. It was as if there were two separate patterns, in addition to the boy's, but the patterns were so strong it confused Gabriel. Humans never displayed patterns anywhere near this strength.

He felt a tremendous desire to take a mental step back and study this new paradox, but the underlying current of urgency demanded he set aside his own desires and concentrate on the reason for this mental endeavor. Gabriel concentrated on directing his efforts toward following the foreign energy patterns outward, but the boy's patterns kept interfering. He tried again.

After two more failed attempts, Gabriel gave a deep mental sigh of frustration and sent out a mental command to the boy. *Relax! I need you to calm down so I can get a fix on your location.*

Okay. I'll try, came the boy's voice.

Incredibly, all but the foreign patterns immediately abated. The boy's presence was now barely even detectable, as if his attention had been suddenly directed elsewhere, pulling the majority of his energies with it. This made things much simpler and Gabriel was easily able to detect two distinctly separate patterns. He wondered which one he should follow. After only a moment's hesitation, he picked one and followed it.

It only took one taste of her essence for Gabriel to latch onto her and, after he got over his initial confusion at how she tasted, his innate tracking ability immediately kicked into gear, snagging a fix on her location soon after. Once he had this, he wasted no time on any other curiosities and tracked his way back toward the boy's mind.

The boy was there, as was Mikhail, and Gabriel was sure to express his thoughts clearly to them. *She's weak, but she's alive. They're in the human realm, though, in the middle of nowhere. We'll have to get going quickly to get through the barrier and then make the rest of the journey to them, if we're going to make it to her anytime soon.*

You're coming to get us? came the boy's hopeful voice.

Hold on, son. We'll be there soon, Mikhail's voice soothed. *In the meantime, I need you to make sure your mom and your grandparents are okay and that they're ready to go when we arrive. Can you do that for me?*

Yes, sir, came the boy's now-excited voice.

Thank you, son, Mikhail sent out to him. *I must leave you, now, but I'll be there soon with my brothers to get you all.* With that, Mikhail pulled himself and Gabriel away from the mind-link with Thomas and back to Gabriel's office in the heart of Seraphim City.

Gabriel gasped as his eyes flew open. He was shocked to find he was lying on the floor of his office, Hantsushept kneeling beside him on his left and Israfil standing on his right looking down at him, concern clearly etched on his face. Gabriel reached a hand up to his brother and Israfil helped him to stand, Hantsushept climbing to his feet as well.

Gabriel looked around for Mikhail, only to find him already sitting on a chair at the other side of the room. His eyes were closed and he looked as if he was meditating. Gabriel turned back to Israfil and made a quick, jerking motion with his head, clearly requesting that he follow. Israfil cocked an inquisitive eyebrow at him, but nodded and followed behind him.

Gabriel led the way to his private water closet, closing the door quietly behind his brother after he'd entered the small room.

"Are you okay?" Israfil immediately asked.

Gabriel nodded, saying, "I'm shaken by the experience, but Mikhail took good care of me."

"Well?" Israfil asked, getting right to the business at hand.

Gabriel shook his head, explaining, "I don't know, Iz. I mean, he's as delusional as we feared, but he's also unbe*lievably* powerful. I thought my head was going to explode when he linked up with me."

Israfil frowned at this piece of news. "Mikhail shouldn't have been able to mind-link with anyone, Djibril, let alone two people at once," he said.

"I know," Gabriel agreed. "It's worse, though. This girl, Sarah, her energy patterns were off the *chart*. I've never seen anything like it. And there was some other pattern there, almost as if there was someone else there monitoring everything we were doing."

"Someone else?" Israfil asked.

Gabriel nodded.

"Did you recognize the pattern?" Israfil asked. It had been a long time, but he knew it was possible the only other telepathic Seraph in the world was involved in this debacle.

Gabriel shook his head. "I've never encountered anything like this," he said.

Israfil slowly shook his head and paced a few steps in the little room. After a moment, he turned and asked, "Do you think it could've been some kind of link the Designers incorporated into her genetic make-up so they could monitor her? I mean, if they can't reach us themselves, might they be monitoring her and using her to contact us or to communicate with us through her?"

"The Designers," Gabriel slowly said, realization dawning. "Of course."

Israfil smiled suddenly, clapping Gabriel on the shoulder and saying, "Looks like your original theory may very well have been correct, brother."

Gabriel notched an eyebrow up and said, "Try convincing Azra'il of that."

Israfil's smile faded and he nodded. "Well," he said, heaving a sigh, "I guess we'll just have to keep Mikhail and his little band of humans safely away from him until we've got enough proof to convince him."

"Right," Gabriel agreed. "Come on, then. Let's go rescue some humans."

"Oh," Israfil said, putting up a hand to keep his brother from opening the door just yet. "Something happened while the two of you were in the mind-link."

"What?"

"Mikhail's eyes stopped flashing and didn't resume when you were done."

Gabriel was astonished. "They're blue again?" he asked, a spark of hope springing to life within his chest.

It was quickly quashed, though. "No," Israfil said. "The light took over completely."

"Oh, my."

"Yeah."

There seemed nothing more to say, so Gabriel opened the door and he and his brother returned to the other room.

Mikhail had moved to the desk while they'd been in conference in the other room and he looked up from the computer monitor he'd been studying as the two entered the room. "Everything okay?" he asked them.

Both men merely nodded, each staring at the strangely glowing eyes of the brother they loved so much they were willing to risk everything in order to save him. Gabriel swallowed a lump in his throat as he watched those eyes. His heart bled for his poor brother.

A part of him wanted to go to the humans only to kill them, wipe them from the face of the planet. That's what they deserved after having done this to Mikhail. Another part of him just wanted to kneel down and hold his brother, telling him everything was going to be all right.

He looked away from Mikhail.

He could do neither of those things. He had to help his brother and, unfortunately, that meant he had to help the humans as well.

"I've pulled up a map on your computer," Mikhail said, turning his attention back to the screen before him, pushing aside the anger Gabriel's thoughts brought to life within him. "If you can show me where Sarah and the kids are located, I'll find us a new rift through the barrier, something near there, so we can get them back into the Angelic realm and to safety more quickly."

"Another rift?" Israfil demanded, stunned. "You can *do* that?"

"Yes," Mikhail absently nodded, still intent on the map showing on the screen.

Gabriel and Israfil exchanged a meaningful look. Then, Gabriel slowly walked over to the desk and, taking a quick look at the layout presented there, he pointed to a section of jungle in South America. "They're there," he said, his voice not much more than a whisper.

"Ah, excellent," Mikhail said. "Now, if you'll just give me a few minutes, I should be able to find us a rift near there." He walked back over to the chair he'd occupied earlier when he'd first attempted this trick and, after settling himself comfortably onto the chair, closed his eyes. He hadn't been sure if he'd be able to do what Sarah had done, but when he'd first tried it, it had easily just come to him. Now, his mind opened and he knew exactly what to look for and where and he was soon whizzing telepathically over field and stream toward exactly the place he needed.

Gabriel and Israfil merely watched in terrified silence. They had no idea what was happening to their brother, nor how to stop it. All they could do was watch and wait.

Hantsushept, who had been silent throughout this entire time, looked at Mikhail's still form and quietly said, "Fascinating."

Chapter 14

The area they'd been left in was thicker than any other in the vicinity. Mikhail followed Gabriel impatiently. He almost wanted to grab his brother and help him to fly faster, for Mikhail knew *he* could do it. But he was grateful his brothers were willing to come on this journey in the first place. He would do nothing to jeopardize losing his one link with Sarah, not now, not when they were so close to reaching her.

The trees and vines became too thick for flight and they touched down to walk the rest of the way. The Angel Hantsushept looked as if he might become physically ill himself, until Mikhail reached over to place a soothing hand on his shoulder. With only the slightest exertion of will, Mikhail was able to restore the Angel's usual good health, if not a good humor, and he immediately returned to his place behind Gabriel.

Only a couple of minutes later, they finally came to what looked like a clearing, except that the canopy of the trees was so thick in this part of the jungle that not even the weak morning light of the sun penetrated to the jungle floor. Sarah's dimly glowing form was clearly visible, though, and Mikhail's own body glow added plenty of light to the scene, though the humans couldn't detect it because of his shields.

The three Seraphim surveyed the scene before them before allowing their shields to drop so that the humans could detect their presence. There was no telling if those who'd brought the humans to the clearing had actually left, or if they were laying in wait to attack.

The two older humans sat nearby with their backs to them, their arms wrapped around each other as they watched the two younger humans in silence. The boy sat just behind where his mother laid, his body heavily wrapped in many long, white strands of hair from her head.

Gabriel stared in shock at the girl and wondered suddenly if those long, white strands of hair were as lethal as Mikhail's had proven to be. A strong shiver of fear raced through him and he silently swallowed a huge lump in his throat. Then his entire frame tensed and his eyes bulged wide open as he caught sight of what appeared to be an entire soul in the shape of a tiny dot, its energy light emanating from within the woman's lower abdomen clearly visible through the simple white nightgown she wore.

Gabriel didn't understand at first. He stood there, transfixed, grasping at every straw in the container to explain how this one human could be carrying an entire soul inside just that part of her body. That's when he realized he was wrong. This was no human woman. Mikhail had been right... about everything. Somehow, she *was* a Seraph and she and Mikhail *had* mated and they *had* conceived.

Gabriel turned to stare open-mouthed at Mikhail.

Israfil looked around the little clearing for anyone else. After all, someone had to have brought them here. Surely, they wouldn't have just left them here without making sure they were rescued, or something? He paced a little off to the right, deciding it would probably be best to check along the edges of the clearing, just beyond the tree line.

As he stepped into the thick undergrowth there, he almost stepped on a bloodied hand. It wasn't attached to a human, though, as he'd originally thought. It was an Angel lying there, face down on the jungle floor. He quickly bent to check her pulse. She was dead. Her body was completely covered in dried blood and Israfil could see what looked like long open cuts across nearly every part of her body.

He looked up and, out of the corner of his eye, caught sight of a young man sitting beside her, almost completely hidden by a thick, flowering vine. The boy couldn't have been more than thirteen years old, Israfil figured. He had dried tear tracks down each cheek. The rest of his face, along with his hair and clothing, was covered in thick cakes of dirt, as if he'd been camouflaged with the stuff.

"Hantsushept," he called. "Over here."

The Angel quickly and quietly made his way across the clearing to Israfil. Israfil needed only to show him the body for him to suddenly become fully occupied. Once done, Israfil stood and held a hand out to the young man. When the boy made no move to take his hand, Israfil used the power *he* had been blessed with and the boy stood soon after. Israfil wrapped the boy in his shields and led him back to the clearing to join up with Gabriel and Mikhail.

Upon his approach, Israfil noticed Gabriel's stunned expression and turned to see what had so captured his attention. He saw Mikhail, the two older humans, the boy and... then he understood. He, too, felt a sense of astonishment wash over his entire being. There lay all the proof any of them would ever need. Mikhail had been telling the truth all along and no one, not even Israfil, had believed him.

A pang of guilt flushed through Israfil and he wondered if Mikhail would ever be able to forgive him.

Mikhail stared at the scene before him, unmoving. He sensed the others moving about, but he just stood there. Thomas was there, wrapped in a cocoon of Sarah's beautiful new white hair as he maintained his one-sided mind-link with his mom. She looked so pale and weak.

What if she dies?

The thought cut a streak of pain through his entire soul as it screwed its way insidiously through his mind. Mikhail couldn't even conceive of losing her, not now, not ever.

Something inside him suddenly screamed, *Move!* and after only a moment's hesitation, he whipped into action.

He lowered his shields as he stepped into the clearing, crunching dried brush underfoot and alerting the humans to his presence.

"Oh, my God!" Marian exclaimed as she let go of her husband, stood, and raced over to him. "Mikhail! I'm so glad you've found us." She was crying and she threw her arms around him in a tight embrace.

Mikhail could feel her anguish and he wanted to help her. Truly, he did. But, he merely smiled down at her and politely disengaged himself from her so that he could get to Sarah's prone form nearby. Thomas looked up at his approach. He burst into tears and reached up, then the white strands of hair covering him merely fell in one coordinated whoosh from his body. Mikhail immediately took the boy in his arms, picking him up to hold him securely against his chest. Thomas wrapped his arms around Mikhail's neck and his legs around his waist, sobbing and holding on for dear life.

"It's okay, son," he said to the boy. "It's okay." He ran a hand up and down his son's back, whispering encouraging words to him while rocking him back and forth. He'd never felt this close to a child, much less a human child, but he realized he truly felt like Thomas was his own. This little boy had lived with no father in his life for such a long time, and now he was looking to Mikhail to fill that role. Mikhail decided then and there that he wouldn't let him down.

After another minute, though, he knew he needed to get to Sarah. He moved the arm he had been holding Thomas up with and let the boy slide down until he stood before him. Mikhail crouched down and looked up at him, explaining, "I'm here and I'm going to take care of you, but I need to check on your mom now. Okay?"

Thomas sniffled and looked at his mom, then turned back to Mikhail and nodded.

"I'll take care of him," Tom said, coming forward to take the boy's hand. He led him over to where he and Marian had been sitting. Mikhail nodded to him, then turned and took the couple of steps remaining toward Sarah's form, fear creeping with icy fingers up his spine with each step.

She lay supine on the jungle floor, displaying no signs of life other than just a slight rise and fall of her abdomen with each little breath she took in her unconscious state. Though it was clearly visible through her clothing, Mikhail quickly opened the buttons of the cotton nightgown she wore over the spot on her lower abdomen where the light from their daughter shone through. Once he had it uncovered, he bent down to place a kiss on it and then, turning his head to the side, he laid his head upon the spot, whispering, "It's okay, sweetheart. Daddy's here."

He heard no response and that reminded him they still needed to figure out what needed to be done to help Sarah. He moved up to take position just above Sarah's head. The long strands of white hair reached out to him the moment he came within range and wrapped around whatever part of him they could, pulling him closer to her.

Mikhail noticed his own hair struggled to break free of the leather bands in which he'd wrapped it prior to the start of the journey between realms.

He paid the hair no heed, though, and bent to his task. He allowed his innate healing ability to take over, reaching out with his senses to discover what injury or other issue had caused her to be and remain unconscious for such a long time. He heard Hantsushept approach them and he felt his body heat when the Angel knelt down next to them, but he didn't break his concentration. In just a couple of passes, he knew without a doubt she'd been poisoned. It was everywhere throughout her body, whatever it was, and Mikhail had no idea if he'd be able to fight it enough for her to break free of its hold on her.

He looked up at the physician and explained, "She's been poisoned. I don't know what it is, but we've got to do something, or it will kill both her and the baby." He heard the two older humans gasp, and he heard Thomas say something to them, but Mikhail didn't turn toward them for any explanations.

Hantsushept did a double take and stared open-mouthed at Mikhail for a moment, until Mikhail reached over and grabbed his shirt with both hands, shaking the Angel roughly and demanding, "Do something, man! It's killing them!"

The physician blinked and quickly nodded, returning his gaze to his new patient. At first glance, he'd thought she was human. After all, that's what the Seraphim had been calling her since he'd been brought on board this strange mission. But, now that he took a closer look at her, he saw she was not human. She looked almost like – but that couldn't be.

Hantsushept scooted back from his patient, studying her and thinking.

"What are you *doing*?" came Mikhail's enraged demand.

Hantsushept didn't cower away, this time. He merely held up a hand and shook his head. If this girl was a Seraph, she was unlike any Seraph he'd ever encountered, not that he'd encountered more than a handful, at best, his entire time on this planet. If she was a Seraph and it was truly just poison, her body might be able to heal itself without any outside assistance. The dark one had said she was with child, though, and the little light glowing from just below her navel indicated he was probably correct. That changed matters.

He sighed and looked up at Mikhail. "If it is poison, I can see if I can figure out what kind it is by tasting her blood," he said.

Mikhail frowned and looked at the man like he was demented.

Hantsushept merely shrugged, saying, "It's one of the gifts with which I was born. Don't ask me to explain the mechanics of it. I just use it to the best of my ability in order to help others." He looked back down at his patient. "However, even if I'm able to discover what type of poison was used, I can't do much for her because I don't know Seraph physiology well enough."

Mikhail's eyes darted this way and that as he frantically thought of some way to help Sarah. "Well, wouldn't there possibly be an antidote we could give her, once you figure out what kind of poison it is?" he asked.

"I don't have any antidotes with me and, honestly, I would be afraid to inject anything into her, not knowing her physiological systems. Whatever I give her might turn out to be even more poisonous than the poison itself," Hantsushept explained.

Mikhail gritted his teeth and let loose a frustrated growl, turning to pace away from the Angel. He turned right back around, however, and said, "Test it on me."

Hantsushept frowned up at him. "So you die, too?" he asked.

"If it will help find a cure for the two of them," Mikhail barked.

"Your death would not help them," Hantsushept stated logically.

"Mikhail," Israfil suddenly said, as he dropped his shields and entered the clearing, bringing with him a young Angel covered in what looked like dirt. Mikhail narrowed his eyes on the boy. "This is Samuel," Israfil continued. "He has some information that might be useful here."

The boy cautiously stepped forward toward Mikhail, looked up at him, then quickly looked back down at his feet and mumbled, "I-I know what type of poison m-my mom and Khamet used on them."

Mikhail immediately grabbed the boy's arms, shaking him and demanding, "Tell me!"

Samuel's eyes widened in fear of the glowing man with the strange, glowing eyes, and he quickly said, "It was C-Calisto R-Root tea. Khamet had her put Calisto R-Root in the tea and serve it to them all."

Hantsushept gasped. Mikhail shot an angry glance at the Angel and the physician said, "That's the deadliest poison in our realm, lethal to Angels. There is no antidote."

Mikhail turned back immediately and shook the boy again, hard, angrily demanding, "And what was your part in all of this, huh? Were you left behind to make sure they died? *Were you?*"

"Mikhail!" Israfil barked out, shaking his head. "Leave the boy be!"

Mikhail turned his ghastly glowing eyes on his brother, a sneer marring his perfect mouth, and viciously said, "I'll do no such thing!" He raised his hand in preparation to strike.

Suddenly, Hantsushept yelled out, "Wait!"

Mikhail stayed his hand, but didn't let go of the boy as he looked over his shoulder to see what was going on with the Angel. Then, he heard a soft choking sound and he saw a slight movement in Sarah's form.

In a flash, he'd released the boy and dashed across the clearing to Sarah. Kneeling beside her, he smoothed strands of white hair away from her face as she fought for breath through coughing fit after coughing fit. "Sarah?" he said. "You can do it, love. You can do it. Just keep fighting. That's the way."

He grabbed her hand and brought it up to his lips, gently rubbing the back of it and willing his strength into her. "Come on, love. You can beat this," he softly said, praying to all the Designers to make it so. She merely continued coughing and gasping for air.

Mikhail looked desperately to Hantsushept for help, but the Angel just looked back down at the coughing patient and waited.

Mikhail noticed Sarah's body glow seemed to be brightening and he hoped that was a good sign. Surely, it would fade with the approach of death, right? He hoped that made sense and continued encouraging her, keeping his gentle hold on her hand and cringing each time she made the terrible hacking cough noise.

After about ten minutes of this, she seemed to be getting better. The coughing fits were becoming fewer and farther between each other and her breathing had certainly improved. Her body glow was now almost as bright as it had been before and when she finally opened her eyes, Mikhail was stunned to find the pupil of each eye was completely filled with a bright, unwavering light. No longer were they flashing or swirling, and her irises had gone all white.

"Muh-Muhkh-Muh" she stammered suddenly.

"I'm here, love," he said, moving up right next to her ear, but not letting go of her hand. "It's okay. You're going to be just fine, love."

"Y-You?" she managed to ask.

"I'm fine," he said. "We're all fine. We just need you to relax and breathe."

"T-Tho-Thomas?" she asked, gasping between each fumbled attempt.

"Thomas is fine. Just *breathe*, Baby." Mikhail finally let go of her hand as he moved to lie down next to her, reaching an arm across her chest to caress her cheek on the opposite side of her face from him. "Please, Baby, just relax and breathe," he said.

Sarah seemed to understand him, finally, as she stopped talking and merely breathed in and out for a while, her muscles relaxing and her breathing becoming much easier. Mikhail rubbed his thumb across her cheek and back down again, over and over, whispering encouraging words to her and occasionally kissing the shell of her ear.

All of a sudden, she seized up again, gasping for breath and choking out, "I-I-I ca-I ca…"

"Calm down, Sweetheart," Mikhail begged her. "Please, just breathe, Baby."

She reached up and grabbed hold of his hand at her face, weakly squeezing it and wheezing, as she struggled with her words again. "I can't-I-I can't he-I ca-I can't… h-hear… her."

Mikhail's eyes squeezed tightly shut as a sharp stab of pain shot through his heart, but he carefully wrapped his arms around her weak form and whispered, "Shh, it's okay. She's fine. She's going to be just fine."

"But, I-I can't-I can't hear… her," she choked out, tears now streaming out of the sides of her eyes and across her temples only to pool in the shells of her little ears.

Although inside he was struggling with the very real possibility that they might lose their daughter, Mikhail continued to soothe her, saying again and again, "Shh, she's fine. She's going to be just fine. You have to believe me. She's all right."

"Mom?" Thomas said as he quietly approached the couple.

Mikhail looked up at the boy, whose eyes were rimmed with red, sore lids from earlier, and he reached over to pull him closer to his mom. "Look," he said. "Thomas is here."

Sarah's glowing eyes opened a bit and she looked up at Thomas, a slight smile fighting to gain some footing on her lips. "Sw-Swee-Sweet-heart," she stammered.

Though he'd looked a little hesitant when she'd opened her eyes to reveal their strange new glow, he reached to grab her hand and said, "You don't have to worry about Sheely. I helped her fight off the poison."

Mikhail went very still, as did Sarah. Even her breathing issue seemed to take a pause and she asked, "Wh-What did you say?"

"The poison," Thomas explained. "Sheely was crying because she thought it was gonna get to her like it did to you, but I helped her find a way to push it away from her. It took a lot of her energy and she got really tired, but she's gonna be just fine. She's just sleeping now."

Sarah weakly turned her head to look at Mikhail, her eyes widening at her first real glimpse of his eyes the way they were now. She reached up and touched his brow, searching his eyes, as if memorizing the way they looked now in his beautiful face. Then she said, "Sheely." After a short pause, she said, "I like that."

Mikhail smiled at her and said, "Me, too."

Sarah yawned and Mikhail reached over to rub her cheek once more and placed a quick kiss on her forehead, whispering, "Get some sleep, Baby.   When you wake up, you'll be back home in bed."

Sarah sighed and fell instantly asleep.

When next she woke, as promised, Sarah lay in the room she and Mikhail shared at his house on the edge of Seraphim City. She was nude, lying on her side and Mikhail's large frame, nude as well, was pressed up against her entire length behind her. Her head lay on his bicep, while his other arm was draped over her so that he could hold her right breast in his hand. Everywhere she looked, colors seemed much brighter and more vivid, as if her vision had improved a thousand-fold. As she realized this, Mikhail's thumb began rubbing on the nipple in his hand, and she sighed sleepily, "Mmm…"

Mikhail nuzzled his nose into her hair just behind her left ear and whispered, "Welcome back, sleepy-head."

Sarah could hear the smile in his voice and her own lips quirked upward. She lay there in silence, his thumb slowly rubbing back and forth, again and again, and she wished this would never end. Then, she heard the little girl's whispered voice in her mind and her eyes flew open as she gasped and tensed. Mikhail's thumb stilled instantly.

Sarah still couldn't understand anything that was said, but she now knew her daughter's name and it made her feel so good to hear her voice as she chattered on and on. Eventually, Mikhail chuckled behind her, whispering, "We're in trouble. Any female who talks this much in the womb has just got to be trouble."

Sarah smiled. She turned then and faced him. "Hi," she softly said, reaching up to touch his face. It seemed so strange seeing his eyes like they were now. She had just gotten used to them flashing all the time and now they were just all white with the bright light coming from the entire pupil area. If she looked closer, though, she could see that there was still vitreous liquid swirling around inside there, but that it was lit from what she guessed was the optic nerve. Either that, or the liquid inside the eyeball had somehow been infused with iridescent molecules of some sort.

"How are you feeling, love?" he quietly asked.

She took a deep breath and blinked a couple of times. Releasing the breath, she said, "I think I'm feeling okay…, pretty good, actually." Her advanced healing abilities had truly kicked into gear and healed her from the inside out, taking care of any after-effects of the poison. After a short pause, she asked, "Are my eyes glowing like yours?"

He smiled and nodded, reaching up a hand to caress her just at her temple. "They're beautifully brilliant," he said.

"What caused that to happen?" she asked, flushing a bit from his poetic compliment.

"I-I think it was a result of our mating, but I'm not really sure," he said hesitantly. "I've noticed I'm gaining abilities, things I've never been capable of before, and it seems to happen mostly after we've been intimate with each other." He ran his fingers into her hair to gently grasp her head and urge her toward him. He nuzzled her cheek, "Of course, I don't know if that's a requirement, but I don't mind if it is." He softly placed his lips upon hers, slowly rubbing back and forth, drinking in the smell and feel of her as if he hadn't touched her in eons.

Eventually, his body demanded more and he moved her beneath him, as he rolled to partially cover her, opening her lips with his and deepening the kiss. He didn't completely lay atop her form for fear of putting undue pressure on Sheely. At this thought, he reached down without breaking their kiss and rubbed the spot where Sheely lay, hoping it was comforting to the child.

Sarah moved her hand to rest on the juncture between his legs, rubbing and encircling him with her fingers and palm until he was rock hard and panting. Looking up at him, she threw a leg over his, inviting him into her warmth, urging him closer with her hand, pushing her pelvis closer to him and tensing the muscles in her leg to pull him closer.

Mikhail broke away from her, slightly pushing her away from him with a gentle hand on her shoulder. When she frowned and lifted a brow in inquiry, he whispered, "I don't want to hurt Sheely."

Sarah looked down and covered Sheely's spot on her lower abdomen with her hand in a protective gesture. Then, she looked back up at him, smiling, and said, "It's okay, at least until the last trimester. That's when we'll have to take it easier."

Mikhail frowned. "You're sure?" he asked.

Sarah nodded, assuring him, "That's what's regularly the rule, for humans, at least. I don't think it would be too different for us – do you?"

He reached down to cover her hand with his, frowning and thinking hard on the subject for a moment. Then, he looked back up at her as one side of his mouth lifted in a conspiratorial semi-smile, saying, "I think we could at least try, as long as you promise to tell me the very *second* you feel any discomfort."

Sarah smiled and nodded, reaching to pull him closer to her. "Oh, I promise," she said before she took his mouth with hers and poured all her longing into a kiss that completely ravished her lover's mouth, driving him crazy inside with longing and fulfillment.

An hour later, Mikhail walked into the study on the first floor of the house, surprising the two men sitting in the comfortable conversation area before the windows at the far back of the room. Israfil immediately inquired after Sarah and Mikhail said, "Oh, she's fine. No ill effects, apparently. She's sleeping now. I think she just needs a bit more rest and she'll be good as new."

Gabriel and Israfil exchanged a guilty look, then Gabriel said, "Brother, I-I'm sorry we didn't believe you."

Israfil nodded in agreement.

Mikhail nodded once, and after giving them a lopsided grin, he said, "It's okay. I was experiencing it, you weren't." He shrugged. "I think if the situation had been reversed, I would have thought you two were delusional as well."

The other two looked down immediately, swallowing thick lumps in their throats.

"Forget about it," Mikhail said as he took the one remaining seat in the area. "There are far more important matters for us to discuss than this."

"Yes," the two agreed in unison, nodding to Mikhail.

"We need to figure out who the ring-leader was in this plot to kill Sarah and my children and her parents," Mikhail said. "Then we need to take the evidence to the Sanhedrin to see that justice is served."

Both men nodded again.

"Then, there's the whole thing with getting approval for Sarah and the rest to be granted asylum in Seraphim City. It shouldn't be too difficult of an issue with Sarah herself, since she's no longer human, but the other family members might have a hard time being accepted."

Again, the other two men agreed.

"And, last, there's the issue with Sarah and me – and Sheely." Here, he paused.

He had been thinking a great deal on this subject, wondering if Sarah had been sent to him by the Great Designers, or if there was some other explanation for her existence at this time and in this place. For so many, many years, he and his fellow Seraphim had lived in solitude, never being allowed the luxury of mating with anyone other than the Angels they ruled, and never with any hope of having children of their own.

Now, he at least was being granted that ability, and it was all because Sarah had been born with the special ability of containing so much of her soul-energy within her human body. He didn't know if that was because she had some sort of mutant gene that just happened by some fluke of nature to occur upon her conception, or if it had been pre-ordained by the Great Designers, or for whatever reason. He just knew that she had been absolutely, perfectly created for him, and only him. There was no doubt in his mind, because of the particular changes they'd both experienced after coming together.

The issue here, however, was whether or not this *was* just a fluke of nature, or if there might possibly be other humans out there who were created specifically for all Seraphim. Mikhail suspected that might have been the subject he'd interrupted when he'd stepped into the office a few minutes ago, judging from the thoughts he'd picked up on from Gabriel as he'd entered. Neither of his brothers knew the extent of his telepathic abilities to this point and Mikhail intended to keep it that way, so he kept quiet about the things he'd heard.

"Well," Gabriel hesitantly said, "Israfil and I were thinking we should take some time to get to know Sarah so we can discover some things about how she came to be one of us..."

"Or, if maybe she knows of a way to contact the Great Designers," Israfil chimed in.

Mikhail quirked an eyebrow at the fact that they'd immediately started talking about what he'd been thinking about, but then he merely nodded and said, "You'll have to talk with Sarah on that score. It will be up to her how much involvement she wants to have in this." He didn't want to tell them she had no idea how to contact the Designers. They didn't need to know the details of how very close telepathically Sarah and he had become over the space of such a short time together... not yet, at least.

"I, uh...," Gabriel started again, "would like to discuss the changes both of you have experienced since she came to live here, if that would be okay?"

"I think we need to take care of getting them approval to be here, first," Israfil said. "Don't you?" After a short pause, during which he looked back and forth expectantly at each man, he explained, "I mean, we can take all the time in the world studying this situation and figuring out what it all means, but until we get approval for Sarah and her family to actually be here, there's always going to be the danger of something like what just happened happening again, right?"

After only a moment, both Mikhail and Gabriel nodded in agreement.

"Right," Israfil said. "So then, first things first. We'll have to go talk with Azra'il."

The three Seraphim nodded, stood, and left the room. As Mikhail, who was at the front of the small procession, opened the front door of the house to exit, he was stopped by an Angel standing on the other side of the door. The man's face was a show of surprise and his hand hung in the air, as if he'd been about to knock on the door. He quickly recovered, however, and immediately asked for "the Seraph, Mikhail".

Mikhail said curiously, "I am Mikhail."

The Angel silently handed him an envelope and turned and left. No explanation or anything.

Mikhail stood there watching the man leave. Then, he looked down at the envelope, ripped it open and unfolded the package of papers within. Gabriel and Israfil waited patiently behind him as he read. After only a second, he gasped and turned to look at them, saying, "I don't *believe* this!"

"What?" the two Seraphim asked in unison.

Mikhail shook his head and said, "Sarah's been accused of murder! This is an official warrant for her arrest from the Great Sanhedrin!"

Chapter 15

"What on *earth* could have possessed you?" Mikhail demanded.

Azra'il relaxed back in his chair, his elbows resting on the arms of the chair. "Yes, please do come in," he said sardonically, rolling his eyes.

Mikhail advanced up to the desk, where he slapped the arrest warrant down onto it. "You authorized this...*Why*?" he demanded.

Azra'il glanced down at the document, then back up at Mikhail's face, quirking an eyebrow, and explained, "I was shown a body of one of the citizens of this city and given enough information leading to a reasonable assumption of that *human's* guilt for said citizen's death." He shrugged. "So, I followed procedure and issued an arrest warrant."

Mikhail stared at Azra'il. He could hear most of what was going on in his brother's mind, same as with Gabriel, and he was heartbroken by the fact that Azra'il had taken his statement at their last meeting to heart. Azra'il considered Mikhail to be truly lost to him, all because of his love for Sarah. He didn't believe Mikhail could be right about Sarah belonging here in the Angelic realm with him. He would not even believe it if the entire world were to tell him it was true.

A great sadness enveloped Mikhail at this discovery. Then, as he thought about it more, he became almost angry. Why? Why wouldn't Azra'il believe his own brothers? Sure, he thought Mikhail had been duped or brainwashed by a human, but Gabriel and Israfil? Especially Israfil. They'd always been very close, so why would he not believe him? As he thought this over, though, Mikhail realized why. Azra'il was afraid to accept that this might actually be a possibility, that humans might actually be the answer to the age old issue of Seraphim being able to reproduce.

Instead, he chose to assign every evil trait ever encountered, and then some, to Sarah and all humans. If he didn't do this, it would mean their precious Designers had been wrong, and that would mean everything in which they'd believed for so many thousands of years had been lies, all lies, all corrupt and evil, told to Seraphim for evil purposes and not out of concern for Seraphim at all as they'd believed all this time.

No. Azra'il would not listen. He probably wouldn't even believe if Mikhail brought Sarah and their child before him for him to examine with his own eyes. He'd believe it to be some trick, or that Sarah was causing some sort of delusion in him. He simply wouldn't buy it.

Mikhail sat on one of the two chairs before the desk. "What information was given you and by whom?" he asked suddenly.

Azra'il shook his head. "That will be brought out in the human's trial. As head of the Great Sanhedrin, you will be able to discover and examine the evidence at that point, if it is your will to do so. However, I feel I must inform you that, due to your... *involvement* with this human, the question of your... suitability as the head of the order has been brought before the entire body. I believe there is to be a vote on the matter this afternoon."

"A vote?" Mikhail demanded, leaning forward in the chair.

"Yes, as to whether or not you are to be forced to involuntarily resign from the council," he said.

Mikhail sat back against the tall back of the chair, looking away from Azra'il. He was so disgusted and angry.

Someone in this city was behind this, and it sounded like it was someone either very close to the council or even *on* the council *itself*. He had to find out who was doing this, but he wasn't willing to let Sarah be tried for murder in order to do that.

Mikhail, came Sarah's voice in his mind. He sat stunned, doing his best not to alert Azra'il of the fact that Sarah had just mind-linked with him. She'd called to him out of the blue, without any kind of a warning or anything. He hadn't even felt the familiar pressure in his head.

Very carefully, he reached out to her. *Sarah?* he asked.

Yes.

How long have you been linked with me?

Since I woke up a couple o' minutes ago. She paused for a moment, then her voice came again. *So, I'm bein' accused of murder, huh?*

Mikhail's eyes slid shut. He'd wanted to delay informing her of that for as long as possible, if at all. He heard her chuckling and realized that plan was shot to hell.

You should know better than to try to keep things from the mother of your daughter, you silly Seraph.

Mikhail smiled and opened his eyes again. Azra'il still sat at his desk watching Mikhail, his eyes slightly narrowed as he studied him.

Don't judge him too harshly, Mikhail. He feels a tremendous anger, right now... kind of like what you were feelin' a moment ago.

Mikhail studied his brother's face. He could hear the thoughts going on there, but he couldn't feel any of the emotions. Sarah, apparently, could feel the emotions, but not hear the actual thoughts, though he guessed she could probably figure out what someone was thinking judging by their emotional state.

You're gittin' it, now.

He looked up, as if she were floating beside and above him. *Thanks. I'm slow, but I catch on eventually.* He heard her laughter again.

Do I need to worry about officials comin' here to take me to… jail?

His face hardened and he stood. *I'll never let that happen.* He stepped closer to the desk, picking up the bundle of papers comprising the official arrest warrant. "You can keep this. I'm afraid my Sarah is unavailable for trial… and you can take that directly to whoever is elected to take my place this afternoon!" he said as he threw the papers in Azra'il's face and turned to leave the room.

Azra'il's mouth dropped open, then he said angrily, "Mikhail, you walk away from this and you know what everyone will believe. I won't have any option but to condemn you both and you know that!"

Mikhail opened the door and looked back at his brother. He nodded and said, "I hope I see you again, someday, hopefully after you've come to your senses enough to listen to reason." With that, he walked out and closed the door behind him. Gabriel and Israfil were in the hallway waiting for him, as they'd agreed on upon reaching the office earlier. They'd been waiting in case Mikhail ended up needing help with convincing Azra'il of Sarah's innocence.

"Well, my brothers," Mikhail said to them now, as they all started walking toward Gabriel's office, "I'm afraid our list of issues has just become much longer and *much* more complicated than we ever could have imagined possible."

Israfil's eyes narrowed. Mikhail still couldn't catch any of his thoughts.

Gabriel's thoughts were coming through very clearly now, though, and Mikhail had no trouble catching everything he was thinking.

So this is how you've been spendin' all your time, huh, goin' around readin' everyone's thoughts?

Mikhail's face screwed into an annoyed frown. *How come I can't detect you linking with me, now?*

I don't know. I didn't even try to link with you. I just woke up and I was there with you. Hey, what's this list of issues you were talkin' 'bout with your brothers?

What the..., agh! Get out of my head, woman! He was so frustrated that she seemed to be having no difficulty catching onto whatever he was thinking, yet he wasn't picking up on anything from her except what she wanted him to. He wanted that stopped immediately. Then, he heard Sheely's tiny voice from somewhere in the background. *Wait! Is she okay?*

Yeah. She's just yappin', as usual. I still have no clue what she's sayin', but she sure is sayin' it!

He chuckled and his brothers looked at him in inquiry. He noticed them looking at him as they walked and just shook his head, waving a hand in dismissal. *Go see about your parents, or Thomas, or something. And, don't worry about anyone showing up to collect you. I'll be there as soon as I finish up with Gabriel and Israfil.*

Do you... need me to inform anyone we're movin'?

He was stunned. How had she...? He hadn't even finished that thought through to fruition earlier. How had she discovered it?

You felt it, remember?

He sighed. After a moment of hesitation, he nodded. *Yes. Go find Miriam and tell her everything. She'll know what to do.*

Okay..., Mikhail?

Yeah?

Are we gonna be okay?

He sighed again. *Yes, love. This is just a hiccup. We're going to be just fine. You'll see.* He poured all the confidence he felt into his statement for her benefit.

Okay. I love you.

Mikhail's breath caught in his chest and he felt as if a star had just exploded inside his entire being. He gasped at the exquisite feeling and swallowed a giant lump in his throat. *I love you so much, Baby.*

I know. I can feel it.

He laughed outright, this time, uncaring what his brothers thought. They merely glanced at each other and shrugged.

Go on, now. I need to talk with my brothers and make some arrangements.

'Kay. Bye.

Mikhail heard nothing more from her. He and his brothers reached Gabriel's office in the Western wing of the building and entered. Once inside, after everyone was situated, Mikhail informed them of the conversation he'd had with Azra'il, though he did some hefty editing to avoid letting on how much information he'd gleaned from Azra'il's thoughts. He still wasn't sure about Israfil's feelings on this matter, so he didn't know if it was safe to disclose the extent of his new abilities.

His brothers quietly considered for a while what they'd been told, each lost in his own thoughts, while Mikhail patiently waited. Israfil was the first to break the silence. "He wouldn't tell you who supplied the evidence to him?" he asked.

Mikhail shook his head. "No. He said it would all come out in the trial."

Israfil pursed his lips. "The boy, Samuel, said someone named Khamet and his mother had poisoned Sarah and her family, remember?" He looked over to Gabriel. "Your man's name is Khamet, isn't it Djibril?"

Gabriel's eyes narrowed and he said, "Y-Yes, but surely there's more than one Khamet in Seraphim City?"

Israfil nodded. "Of course. But, we should at least do what we can to ensure he's not the one, right? Say, if we were to show up unannounced at your home with Samuel, might that not give us enough of an indication of your man's innocence or guilt? I mean, if he's innocent, he should have no reaction to the sight of the boy, and if he's not..." He didn't finish the sentence as his brother reluctantly nodded.

Mikhail asked, "Where's the boy, now?"

Israfil said, "At your home, with the human child, Thomas. The child's guardian, Miriam, suggested the two might be a good match, so she installed him in a room next to the human."

Mikhail stood and paced for a moment. He returned to stop before his brothers and said, "I'd like you both to start thinking of Thomas as my son, if you would." He paused. He needed to explain the depth of his feeling for the child, but was unsure what words to use, for he had never before felt anything so tender toward a child. He didn't know if they had either, so whether or not they would even be able to understand such feeling was another issue. "I feel like I'm his father," he said. "I mean, when we found them in that stinking jungle, he looked for me to save him, and I felt that responsibility to the depths of my soul, as if it was meant to be." He stopped, confused by what he was saying, but feeling that it was right. "Does that make any kind of sense?" he asked.

Gabriel nodded, filled with awe and a bit of envy that his beloved brother could be so strong as to handle such emotion. He wasn't sure he would measure up, were he in Mikhail's place. Mikhail almost thanked him for such a kind sentiment, but stopped himself just in time.

Israfil merely nodded and continued, "Yes, well, Miriam thought *your son* and Samuel might get along quite well, if that's all right with you?"

Mikhail nodded. "Yes, anything to make the transition to life here would certainly be welcome," he said. "Anyway, I think this Khamet is only a pawn in all of this. From what Azra'il said, it seems as if there's someone much higher up involved, possibly even someone on the council, I'm thinking."

His brothers nodded in agreement.

"The difficulty," Mikhail continued, "is that we've got to move quickly on this, what with the charges already having been leveled against Sarah. I refuse to allow her to be taken into custody for this."

Both men turned serious faces toward him. They knew what he was going to say, but they just couldn't believe it, for it was unthinkable.

"We'll be leaving today," he said quietly, looking away from them.

Gabriel slowly shook his head. "Mikhail," he whispered, shock settling in like a cold stone at the bottom of his gut.

After a moment, Israfil stood and approached Mikhail, placing a hand upon is shoulder. "Well, then, we'd better not waste anymore time," he quietly said. Mikhail looked at him, seeing lines he'd never noticed before now etched along the sides of Israfil's mouth. It was as if his brother had suddenly aged a great deal. He still couldn't catch any kind of reading on him and it frustrated him to be so in the dark as to what Israfil was thinking.

Mikhail reached up and clasped Israfil's arm, saying, "Thank you."

Israfil just nodded, then turned and left the room. The other two silently followed.

Sarah sat back against the headboard, wondering if she should say something. He obviously didn't know she was still linked with him, but she honestly didn't know how to break the connection. She'd been trying since he'd asked her to, but to no avail. She'd awakened from her nap after he'd gone to discover she was linked with him, but she hadn't forged the link, herself, at least…, she didn't remember forging one. She guessed she could have done so in her sleep, but why would she not be able to break the link now?

She knew she had to get moving to alert this Miriam person about the move. Otherwise, it seemed she would be getting a free ride to and free lodging at the Seraphim City jail house, or whatever it was they had here. Since she had no real interest in adding *that* particular adventure to her bucket list, she decided she'd deal with this mind-link business later. If Mikhail didn't know she was still linked, then she wouldn't worry him with the issue, right now. They could deal with it later, when they were safely, well, at least just… *away*. From what she'd heard, this Badlands place wasn't exactly the most civilized place in the world. She didn't think too many Angels thought of it as a great place to go for a vacation or anything.

She hopped up from the bed and stretched. She was going to miss being in this house. It was so comfortable, she'd already started thinking of it as her home. But, wherever Mikhail was would be home to her. It didn't matter if it was in the wilds of the Angelic realm or in New York City, for all she cared. She and Thomas would follow that man to the ends of the earth.

As she sat on the toilet, her mind turned to this Miriam character Mikhail had told her to find. Israfil had said something about her being Thomas' guardian, that's what he'd called her. Did he mean it like she was Thomas' *Guardian Angel*, or something else? Sarah shook her head and finished up in the bathroom. All this was irrelevant. There was too much for her to be thinking about and taking care of right now for her to be concerned with trivial matters like this.

She went to pick out some clothes in the huge walk-in closet and suddenly felt a familiar pressure inside her head. *I like the cream dress there,* came Mikhail's voice in her mind.

Then, the cream dress it will be, she shot back at him. She smiled as she took the dress off the hanger.

Did you miss me?

Sarah hesitated, wondering how to deal with this. He was linked with her now. How was she supposed to keep from him the fact that she was still linked with him? She suddenly felt a tremendous sense of confusion laced with fear, but it wasn't coming from her. It came from Mikhail.

Sarah? Sarah?

I'm here.

Wh-Where did you go, love?

I didn't go anywhere.

She could feel the confusion he was feeling. She could see what he was seeing. She tried again to break her own link with him, but the connection just wouldn't break.

After a moment's pause, his voice came in her mind once more, though it was now filled with uncertainty. *My brothers and I are on the way to the house. We're almost there, so you need to hurry and get dressed.*

I'm on it… Don't worry so much.

She could feel him smiling and she relaxed. Everything would be okay. They'd get through this.

That's right, love. We will.

She smiled. *I love you.*

I love you, too. He broke his link with her. She felt it. It didn't matter. Hers with him was still strong as ever. It was curious, but she could see everything he saw and feel everything he felt. It didn't interfere with what she was doing. It was just like visions of things she would be thinking about normally while she was doing something else. Like picturing a scene in your mind while you're reading a book, or

280

something. It didn't stop you from being able to read the words on the page, but you had the picture of the place in your mind at the same time you were seeing and reading the words on the page.

The brain was a powerful machine, *indeed*.

Sarah finished dressing and left the bedroom, headed down the hallway to Thomas' room. Hopefully, she'd find this Miriam in there with the boys. She figured Miriam was probably that woman she kept finding with Thomas each time she went into his room. She'd seemed like a nice enough person the few times Sarah had met her. However, Narayana had seemed like a nice person, as well, and look how wonderfully *their* relationship had ended.

Sarah picked up the pace a little at this thought.

Chapter 16

Mikhail walked into Thomas' room to find Thomas and Samuel sitting on the floor playing a video game, while Sarah sat on the couch behind them watching. She looked up at him and smiled as he entered and closed the door behind him. Thomas and Samuel stopped playing and stood.

Mikhail walked over to Sarah, nodding to the two youngsters as he passed them, saying, "Boys." He took Sarah's hand and pulled her up to stand beside him, reaching down to place a hand on Sheely's spot. That's what Sarah had told him she was calling it now. It felt warm, much warmer than the rest of Sarah's body. "How is she?" he quietly asked Sarah.

"Yammerin' away, as usual," she said, smiling up at him.

He gave her his most handsome lopsided grin and then bent and captured her mouth in a quick kiss. Only the sounds of the boys still waiting behind him made him break it and he quickly stepped away, turning back to look at the two youngsters. They were looking anywhere but at the two adults in the room, completely embarrassed by what had just been going on.

Mikhail took pity on them and said, "Samuel, I wanted to talk with you."

To Mikhail's utter surprise, Samuel nodded and said, "I'm ready to go, sir."

Out of the corner of his eye, Mikhail saw Sarah's entire frame stiffen. A part of him wondered what had caused her to do that, but another part of him wanted to know how Samuel could have known Mikhail had come to take him somewhere. "Go?" he asked the boy.

"Yes, sir," Samuel replied. "Though, I must tell you, sir, it isn't necessary."

Mikhail's eyes narrowed, a frown forming between his brows as a serious suspicion took shape in his mind. "What isn't necessary, Samuel?" he quietly asked.

"Taking me over to visit Seraph Djibril's manservant, sir," the boy explained.

Mikhail's face cleared of all traces of emotion immediately. Sarah had a new ability. That was the only explanation as to how this child could have known.

Mikhail...

He turned to face her, his face completely devoid of emotion. He clamped down on any emotional feeling inside himself. *Later. We'll discuss this later.*

Sarah's mouth sagged open a bit and she stared dumbstruck at him. He was suddenly a blank slate to her. She got no reading, whatsoever, other than that which she could see.

Mikhail turned back to the boy. "Why is it not a necessity?" he calmly asked the boy.

"Because I can tell you it's him. That's the only Khamet I know, the one who works for Seraph Djibril."

Mikhail nodded, then said, "Okay. Come on downstairs and let's talk with my brothers. I need you to tell us everything you can remember, all right?"

Samuel nodded and then preceded him out of the room.

Mikhail did not look back at Sarah as he closed the door behind himself.

As soon as they were gone, Thomas plopped back down on the floor and started playing the video game again by himself. After a couple of minutes of just standing there wondering what on earth she was going to do about this situation with Mikhail, Sarah told her son, "I'm gonna go have a shower."

He grunted in acknowledgement. That was all she got, so she left the room, gently closing the door behind her.

Once she was gone, Thomas paused the game again, allowing the wireless controller to fall onto his lap. His mom and Mikhail were really starting to look a lot like Nera. He wondered if they were going to eventually look exactly like her and the others he'd seen in his visions. A part of him railed at this idea because it was his mom! Then, he wondered if Nera and her people had done this to his mom and Mikhail. If that was the case, Thomas wanted to know why. He wanted to demand that they either explain to him why his mom had to be changed into one of those white-haired, glowy-eyed things, or...

You really want to know? Nera's voice sounded in his mind.

Suddenly, he found himself standing in the round room again. This time, the others were there... all of them standing around the center part of the room again, staring at the images on the little virtual screens before each one of them at their stations. There were the two empty stations again, and Nera's. Again, it bugged him about the two empty stations, but he didn't have time for that.

He turned to her. "Did you do this to my mom?" he demanded.

One of her eyebrows shot up and she gave a slight shrug. "Many eons ago, perhaps," she said sibilantly.

Thomas shook his head, wildly demanding, "What on earth does *that* mean?"

"It means," Nera explained as she walked around him, observing his denim pants and wrinkled tee shirt, "your mother and her mate are doing as they are intended to do, but you, on the other hand..." She let the sentence hang,

284

looking him up and down, shaking her head and making a slight clicking sound. "Your mission is very soon coming to a dangerous point," she warned. "The time has come for you to put away these childish things you've been focusing on and get training."

What is she talking about? he wondered.

"They're going to need all the help they can get to get through this, you do realize?" she demanded. He merely frowned at her. "Oh, for goodness' sake!" she gritted, exasperated. "You just might have to get your feet dirty on this one, like you did before."

His frown deepened and he looked at her like she was crazy. What on earth was the woman talking about?

"This!" she screamed at him. As she said it, she shot her hands out toward him, close together with wrists facing each other and palms flat and outward facing, as if pushing him away from her. Though she was a good two or three yards away from him, a blast of energy shot from her hands and outward toward him. He saw it rippling through the air toward him, even though it was just energy.

He stood there marveling at the fact that he could see energy, while another part of his brain did something very unusual. It allowed him to construct a shield around himself so that when the blast of energy hit, it bounced off the shield and rippled away in waves that struck the walls of the round room and some of the others standing nearby. Those it struck were knocked down and there was a bit of grumbling coming from them immediately afterward. They didn't look too worse for wear, however, as they climbed back to their feet shortly after having been knocked down, so Thomas didn't pay too much attention to them.

Instead, he looked around at the damage the waves of energy had caused to the walls of the round room. There were deep dents in the metal coverings lining the walls and several fires had erupted when the electrical components embedded within the walls had overloaded. From hidden compartments near each of the fires, little tubes emerged to spray a fine mist of some retardant onto the fires, immediately smothering them before much damage could be incurred.

How had he done that?

"Do it to me," Nera instructed.

"What?" he asked.

"It is your turn to do it to me," she said.

He thought about the movements she had made, step-by-step, and, after swallowing a lump of embarrassment and fear that he was about to make a complete fool of himself in front of all those present, he mimicked her movements, thrusting his hands out toward her while taking a giant step forward.

Nothing happened.

"Is that it?" Nera asked, laughing at him.

An annoyed frown managed to dip one of his eyebrows down on his face and he stepped back to try again. After the third failed attempt, Thomas was getting angry because Nera's laughter was becoming louder and louder. It was almost a cackle now, and Thomas wanted to just shut her up! He tried again and this time she did fall to the floor, but she fell because she was laughing so hard she couldn't remain standing any longer.

"You can stop laughing any minute now," he snapped.

After a moment, she climbed back to her feet, still chuckling. "You have to let go of all emotion, genius," she told him. "Emotion only feeds on the energy. You only want to be a conduit, not the generator."

"I-I don't understand," he admitted reluctantly.

She bit her lip for a second, then sighed. Stepping up to him, she looked up and away, thinking aloud, saying, "Now, how did you put it when you taught me... Oh, yes. I remember now." She stepped over to stand by his side, facing the same direction as he, her hands hanging limply by her sides. "There's a lot of energy flowing around in the Universe," she said. "It's always there, everywhere you go. Some places contain more energy than others, but everywhere you go, there's energy. If you remain calm, you can see, feel, and sometimes even hear the energy around you. That will give you an indication of how much there is and what you've got to work with, understand?"

Thomas frowned for a moment, then nodded hesitantly.

"Okay," she continued. "So, if you concentrate on the energy around you, you can actually affect it with your own energy... with your brain waves. You can bend it, push it away from you, pull it closer to you, make it go in circles, if you want... pretty much anything. You can make it vibrate slower, meaning it is dulled and spread out on a much thinner wavelength. Or, you can make it vibrate faster, which makes it stronger, shorter, and more closely confined."

Thomas interrupted her, saying, "Like what I did when I threw up my shield?"

"No," she said, shaking her head. "Your shield came from inside your body. If you'd used the energy flowing out in the room here," and here she gestured around the room with her hand in a circling motion, "you would've been knocked out cold by the blast." She turned and placed one hand on his upper arm and the other hand on his chest. "Your energy is much stronger than *any* energy you will ever be able to gather from the Universe. Yours is much purer and, therefore, much more destructive." She let her hands drop and turned away from him. After a couple of paces away from him, she turned back to face him. "That's why you only want to be the conduit, not the generator itself. If you were the generator, you might end up doing much more damage than you really wanted to do."

She widened her stance. "Now, hit me with your best shot," she said.

She wasn't laughing now and Thomas took a deep breath and concentrated. He remembered seeing the energy before coming at him in waves and, after only a moment or two, he thought he saw something in the air move. He took another deep breath and closed his eyes. *Concentrate!* he silently told himself. When he opened his eyes, he almost gawked. There was energy... everywhere! He saw it flowing in waves, in straight lines, in curves and arcs. Some of it even seemed to have substance and color. He was so busy looking at the energy that he barely managed to get his own shield up in time to protect himself from Nera's surprise blast.

"Hey!" he said angrily.

"Well," she said. "You were taking your time, so I just thought I'd get you going." She widened her stance again, clearly waiting for him to fire upon her.

Without another word, Thomas pulled on the energy surrounding him, slammed his left foot forward, and powerfully thrust both hands forward as she'd done both times before. He watched as a great blast of energy shot outward from his hands toward her. Nera's shield went up just in time, but she was pushed backward a yard or two anyway from the sheer force of the blast.

Thomas stood up straight, a lopsided grin on his face. "Cool!" he said, excited now. "Let's do that *again*!"

Nera laughed. "Okay, but I want you to put some real power into the thrust, this time," she said, widening her stance in preparation once more.

Thomas took a deep breath and slowly exhaled, adjusting his eyes again so he could see the energy waves throughout the room. The majority of the bright waves seemed to be concentrated around where the other beings were in the center of the room and Thomas focused on pulling that energy toward him, bending it and, as he suddenly lurched forward with a giant step, he forced it forward in a heavy blast, thrusting his hands out in a lightning-quick motion.

Out of the corner of his eye, Thomas saw several of the others in the room go flying, and when the blast struck Nera's shield, she was knocked all the way back to the curved wall where she stopped. Luckily, her shield held, but the wall didn't fare as well. The entire thing went completely dark for a moment, then sparks flew from each and every component embedded within its surface and several explosions shot flames outward and then up the curving wall. Wires were hanging out everywhere and Nera's shield was covered in them.

Those who'd been knocked over by the blast were helped by the others to stand and Thomas got the distinct impression they were not as happy about this last successful attempt as he was. Several of them glared over at Nera, while the rest glared at Thomas. He could hear voices, but he didn't understand what any of them said. Nobody's mouth opened or even moved, however.

Nera finally managed to get herself disentangled from the wires hanging out of the wall and she walked over to join him, saying, "Listen, I think that's enough for today."

Thomas agreed and turned to walk with her toward one of the many exits from the room. He stopped suddenly and said, "Hey, wait. How could I have taught you something that you just had to teach me?" When Nera made no response, he then asked, "And, how did I know how to make a shield to protect myself?"

Nera looked away from him, chewing on her lower lip. When she looked back, after a moment's hesitation, she shook her head and said, "You have to go back now."

Like before, the minute she said this, he started whizzing backward through the dimly-lit corridors, passage after passage, until he found himself back in his room, alone, at Mikhail's place. He was angry with Nera. Why wouldn't she answer his questions? Why?

Then, a thought occurred to him and he quickly shot up from his position on the floor in front of the television. *Was that just a dream?* he wondered. After a moment of turning this over in his mind, he raced out of the room and down the stairs.

It was early afternoon by the time Mikhail finally finished up in his meeting with his two brothers. He was exhausted from having to keep all emotion out of everything he was doing. There had been several times during his discussion with Gabriel and Israfil when he'd felt as if he could have exploded with anger, but he hadn't allowed himself to feel one bit, not anything. Now he was paying the price for that control and the day was still so young and so much remained left to do in it.

He climbed the stairs to the second floor, wishing he could just go have a shower and then a long nap. But, he had to get everything packed up because there was no time left. The council had voted and Azra'il was now acting head of the Great Sanhedrin. Khamet had been pardoned of his role in the incident in which Narayana had ended up dead. The reason given for his pardon was that he could not have been expected to behave otherwise in a situation such as this. He'd seen Sarah and her family as a threat, so he and Narayana had devised a plan to rid this dimension of humans.

When Mikhail had learned of the council's judgment, he'd nearly lost his head with rage. But he knew Sarah would be able to renew her link with him somehow if that happened. He still hadn't figured out why she'd done what she'd done, but he couldn't allow her to do it again. He had to protect her, even if that meant protecting her from herself.

He knew, as acting head of the Great Sanhedrin, Azra'il would waste no time sending official guards to arrest Sarah and he needed to hurry and get her as far out of the city as he could as soon as possible. Gabriel and Israfil had gone into the city to do what they could to delay matters. If they were able to gain an audience with the Great Sanhedrin, or even just with Azra'il, they might be able to get this thing pushed off for a while – *if* they could gain an audience.

Opening the door to the room he shared with her, he was surprised to find her asleep on the bed. He quietly closed the door behind himself and locked it. Then, he walked over and gently took a position behind her, laying his entire front up against her entire back and cradling her close to his long frame. He was so tired, but he would only lie down with her for a few moments before waking her so they could finish getting ready to go.

Just a few moments...

Mikhail looked around the area. He recognized it, but it wasn't possible. This place had been swallowed by water many tens of thousands of years ago. Lemuria, it had been called.

"Yonaguni," Sarah said as she walked past him to stand a little off to his right in front of him a short way. She looked back over her shoulder at him. "The divers haven't been able to get too much information out to the public yet. It's all *classified*, you know?" she said sardonically. After a moment, she asked, "Why did you try to block me earlier?"

He didn't want to have this out with her here, not in this hallowed place where so many humans had died. He looked up at the giant structures and along the long, paved avenues. He remembered watching them, wishing there were something he could do to help more of them. He and

Suriyah and Baphomet had gotten as many as they could out of harm's way, but it still had only been a drop in the bucket.

"Tell me what happened," Sarah said.

"No," he said, shaking his head. He didn't want to talk about that day. He didn't want to be here. They needed to get going so they could get far enough from Seraphim City to be safe, at least for tonight.

She was staring at him as if reading his thoughts and he quickly made an effort to stop all emotion inside his mind. She laughed and then said, "You know, you can't block it out completely. Emotion is part of bein' a sentient being. It's in each and every part of you."

He merely watched her, not saying anything. If he didn't feel anything about anything, she wouldn't be able to guess what he was thinking.

She smiled a slow, Cheshire cat smile, then laughed at him outright. After a moment, she came back to him and pulled him into an embrace, her arms circling him just at the waist. She rubbed her cheek against his chest and he found he couldn't resist taking her in his arms. He bent his head down and slowly rubbed his own cheek against the top of her head. "We need to get going," he softly said.

Sarah looked up at him. "Not until we're done here," she said seriously.

"But, Azra'il and the council, they'll be coming," he said hesitantly.

She shook her head. "They can't reach us here."

He frowned. When he looked around, he wondered if they were actually *in* Lemuria or if this was some sort of dream they were sharing again.

"I don't know how to answer that question," she said absently, snuggling her face against his chest again. "You're too concerned with details, though. You need to loosen up."

He pushed her gently away from him. She'd done it again.

She sighed and said, "Tell me what happened here."

Mikhail couldn't help it. He couldn't hold his anger in check any longer. He turned and stalked a short distance away from her. Sarah stayed rooted to the spot where he'd left her, watching him intently. He didn't want to remember that day. He didn't want to think about it at all. It had nothing to do with anything anymore, so why should he rehash it?

"You're wrong," she whispered.

"Why?" he demanded, whipping around to face her.

She merely stood staring at him.

"Fine!" he shouted angrily, his voice cracking out like a lightning strike. "Let's just get this whole thing out in the open so you can experience it all! I won't hold anything back, either, just so you can see and hear and feel each and every bit of it, okay?"

She just stood there, stark still, silently staring at him.

"Suriyah and I had been here all day," he said. "She loved it here, loved all the little human kids. They were so intelligent and they loved her. She taught them things about nature and they taught us about architecture, for they had tremendous mathematicians within their numbers. Some of their design and building techniques have never been discovered by later generations of humans. It was so long ago, I'm sure they're even lost to my people, now.

"But they knew such infinitely advanced architectural methods that you could almost cut yourself on some of the corners on their structures. Mind you, this was all without the aid of lasers or any of the things humans use for such clarity today. They were just that good." He paused here, his eyes growing sad as a deep frown marred his beautiful face. "It didn't do them much good that day, though," he finally said, his voice almost a whisper.

In his mind, Sarah saw it all as he finally allowed all of it to play out before his mind's eye. He relived the entire memory without saying a word, but she didn't need the words. She saw the thing in the sky, she felt the wonder and then the fear as it was discovered what was happening. Sarah got caught up in the memory and she felt almost as if she was suddenly an active participant. Her heart beat faster and faster as the thing in the sky came closer. It was deafening and all the people were running willy-nilly in all directions, screaming in terror.

She looked to her left and saw a wall of water fifty meters high coming toward the city. To the right was a mountain, but it was much too far away for her to make it there safely before the wall of water hit. In front of her suddenly appeared the most beautiful young woman Sarah had ever seen. She was gathering the people together, ushering them toward a tall man farther away from Sarah and Sarah realized suddenly that it was Mikhail standing back there, calling the people toward him, then wrapping his shields around them and whisking them away and up the side of the mountain.

Sarah could see someone far off in the distance doing the same thing with the people there, though he was too far away for her to see anything other than a figure. She assumed this was the elusive Baphomet, which meant the young woman had to be Suriyah. Mikhail returned and gathered another group together to take up to the mountain. He was too far away for her to reach, though.

Sarah ran instead to Suriyah, holding on tightly to the tall woman as her Seraph shields wrapped the group in their leathery-feeling protection and they lifted off. It wasn't long before Sarah found herself standing on the side of the mountain, watching in fear and sadness and disbelief as the thousands more still in the city were hit by the crushing wall of water. Structures flew apart as if they were made of paper, not stone blocks.

The screams were the worst part, that and the crying children. Sarah looked around at the few hundred littering the mountainside. The majority of them were children. They all stood there watching as everyone they knew was beaten and crushed by the wall of water, then washed away. Bodies could be seen floating away on the tide as it drifted back out into the ocean.

The thing in the sky was much lower now on the horizon, but the survivors were no longer afraid of it doing any damage here. While it had been high in the sky, it had appeared that it might be coming here, to Lemuria. But now, it was far away. It didn't even look that big now. It finally disappeared over the horizon with the sun's rays.

Sarah stayed there with the children, as did Suriyah. She didn't know what had happened to Mikhail, but he was no longer there when she looked for him. For nine days, they stayed there, nine long, hot days during which many graves were dug and many more deaths occurred. Finally, toward the end of the ninth day, a vimana similar to those the Angels used in Seraphim City appeared above the ruined remains of the city and several strange creatures emerged from it when it landed.

Suriyah took as many children with her as she could into the thick woods, hiding them from the creatures. Sarah went with her immediately, for she could feel a great sense of menace from these strange new beings. As they hid, they watched the creatures taking the remaining children. Suriyah kept those with her quiet as she listened to the words the strange creatures spoke with each other. Sarah could feel fear and anger rising inside Suriyah and she took a moment to study her.

She came to understand that the children were being taken to be used as slaves and that Suriyah had learned from Baphomet that this was the intention of all of the creatures like these, even the ones the Seraphim had come to know as the blessed Great Designers. Suriyah listened to the creatures' conversations and through her understanding, Sarah came to know that Suriyah was a seer and that she had foretold of this happening, but that Mikhail and the others hadn't believed her. Only Baphomet had believed her.

One of the creatures struck a child who dared fight back against his oppressors and Suriyah finally had had enough. She broke free from her hiding place and approached the creature, where she whipped her arms through the air, causing all manner of debris to start telekinetically flying and crashing against the creatures outside the large vimana. Sarah was astounded by the moves and she could see that several of the creatures watching Suriyah from inside the vimana were stunned as well. Before long, all the alien things outside were dead, their beaten and bleeding bodies twisted into all manner of grotesque positions that were guaranteed to not support life.

That's when the vimana took off. It frightened the remaining children so that Suriyah had to rush to them to protect and soothe them. Otherwise, Sarah believed she would have gone after those inside it, as well. However, by the time the children calmed down, it was gone with all the children the creatures had collected.

Sarah pulled away from the scene at this point. She ended up in a room with Mikhail and Suriyah. They were arguing and Sarah was very quickly able to pick up on the gist of the argument. Suriyah was trying to convince Mikhail of what she had seen. He refused to believe the Designers could do such a thing to their own creation. When Suriyah admitted what she'd done to those outside the vimana, Mikhail sent her away.

Sarah stayed in the room with Mikhail, watching him. Eventually, he turned to her and said, "So, you see, Suriyah and Baphomet killed Designers. When the Designers in our part of the world learned what had happened, I was ordered to banish them from Seraphim City. I did what I had to do." The sadness and anger in his heart was almost her undoing. His love for his brother and sister was immeasurable, but his fealty to his gods and his people took precedence over all.

She wanted to tell him about what she'd witnessed, but this was not the time. His heart was breaking at having to relive what was one of the most painful times in his very long existence. Instead, she went to him, placing her hands on either side of his face to pull it down to hers and she kissed him. Into it, she poured all the love in her heart, in her being, in her very soul. He hesitated but a moment before dragging her roughly up against his big frame, his arms crushing her to his chest. He opened his mouth, his tongue demanding entry into her mouth, and she offered no resistance, only love.

He moved his mouth to her throat and Sarah thrust her head back to give him easier access. He bit her, causing welts on her sensitive skin, but she didn't care. He ripped her shirt and bra and roughly thrust her breast into his mouth, sucking deeply on the nipple and areola and squeezing painfully to press her more closely toward his hungry mouth. When he grazed her with his teeth there, Sarah cried out and he gentled a little, but the fight was not over yet.

Sarah wrapped her legs around him as he picked her up in his arms and started walking. She didn't know where he was taking her, but it didn't matter. When he laid her down onto a mattress, Sarah opened her eyes and was surprised to discover they were now in their bedroom back at his house on the outskirts of Seraphim City. They were still in whatever dream world or vision they'd been in throughout the entire encounter, though. Sarah could tell by how the walls of the room seemed to disappear and then reappear with irregularity when she concentrated on them.

Mikhail quickly removed his own clothing and then hers and then he joined her on the bed. He wasn't gentle as he had been their previous times together. Instead, he grabbed her hips and flipped her around so that she was facing away from him. He reached a hand over to pull her roughly back against his long frame, his thick erection piercing the space between her legs, protruding in front of the juncture between them, just below her pubic area.

He roughly reached to move her hair out of his way and then lowered his mouth to where her neck met her shoulder. He bit a little more softly now, but it was still a bite, as he rubbed himself back and forth between her legs. The hand across her hip reached down and grabbed himself in front of her, encircling the head of his penis and rubbing it as he continued pushing and pulling against her.

Sarah reached a hand behind herself to grab his hip and he quickly grabbed her hand to place it where his had been, showing her how he wanted her to rub and where. She used her thumb to circle the wet head of his penis as he pushed and pulled, again and again, his seed spilling out of the tiny opening there in small dribbles.

He was sucking on her neck now and his hand moved to part the lips between her legs, sliding and rolling, back and forth against her clitoris. Sarah arched at one point and he growled into her ear, "I want you so much, baby!" She felt and heard his anguish. For some reason, he was holding back, not allowing himself to go any farther than this.

Sarah wouldn't let him do this to himself. In a show of strength she hadn't known she possessed, she pushed his hand and arm back from her, turning and climbing up on top of him. His eyes were wide with shock as she quickly and forcefully slid his entire length up into her body in one fluid motion, bringing them together in a way they had never experienced before.

Sarah began to move, using her knees to push herself up, then lowered herself down, reaching back to brace her hands against his thighs. She arched her back, thrusting her breasts high in the air as she pushed herself up once again almost to the tip of his shaft, then slid back all the way down again. She felt a pressure building inside her body, deep down inside it, and she couldn't stop herself from doing what she did next, even if she'd wanted to.

In one swift move, she swung one leg over his arm, grabbed the arm and pulled, so that immediately, he was laying on top of her with one of her legs almost up to his shoulder, the other encircling his waist and back and he pounded into her with all his might. She grunted with each thrust. He started making a low, growling noise that grew in intensity with each thrust. Then, at the same time, on one last, deep thrust, they both experienced a supernova, each crying out in guttural voices they never could duplicate in any other way.

When they returned from their journey through the stars, they each heard the happy chattering of Sheely's voice. Covered in sweat and still unable to breathe properly, Sarah looked around at the room's walls. They were very solid now, the bright sunlight of late afternoon shining through the tree branches at the windows creating patterns on everything. They were back in the real world. Soon, guards would be coming to arrest her for Narayana's murder.

"No," Mikhail said. *I won't let that happen. We'll be gone before they can get to you.*

I'm sorry I've caused all of this. She turned and pushed her face up under his chest.

Mikhail reached to take her chin in his hand, pulling her face back where he could see it. *You have done nothing wrong, love. They don't understand. They can't.*

Sarah stared up into his eyes, her own narrowing in confusion. He hadn't established a mind-link with her, yet he was in her mind.

After a moment, he asked, "Is this what happened to you?"

She nodded. *Yes. I tried to break the link with you, but I couldn't. It just wouldn't go away.*

I'm sorry, love. He reached up to push a few errant strands of white hair from her cheek. They floated right back to where they had been as soon as his hand got out of the way.

Why are you apologizing now? She smiled slyly up at him.

Because I thought you'd kept the link going intentionally to find out what was going on.

She slowly shook her head back and forth, reaching to trace a finger down the side of his temple. *I love the way your eyes glow like this.*

He smiled and bent his head to kiss her.

That's when all hell broke loose.

Chapter 17

There was a loud bang and then shouting and screaming from seemingly every corner of the estate. Mikhail and Sarah both immediately jumped from the bed, racing to pull on clothing so they could get to the boys' room.

Mikhail was the first done and he was already in the hallway running for the door at the other end before Sarah could even get out of their bedroom. When she finally reached the room, it was utter chaos. Miriam was a mess, squalling and carrying on about not being able to find Thomas. Mikhail was helping Samuel get his shoes on and Sarah immediately turned and shot down the stairs, intent on finding her son.

At the bottom of the stairs stood three very tall, very *large* Angels in full guard uniform. They looked like something out of a Trojan War film and Sarah wanted to stop and laugh at them. But this was no laughing matter. The three immediately took up a defensive stance and Sarah was amazed to find she was suddenly overwhelmed by a sense of peace and calm.

The three studied their opponent. This seemed to be the one they had been sent to apprehend, but there were striking differences in her appearance from the likeness they'd been shown. First off, she didn't appear to be human. There was a glow radiating from within that was brighter by far from even any Seraphim in the realm. Then, there were her eyes. None of the three had ever seen anything like it, these glowing, brighter than bright orbs which seemed to fasten on each and every one of them all at the same time, noticing every single detail.

The most striking feature of the creature before them, however, was its hair.   Each man watched in stupefied wonder as white gleaming strands rose to frame the creature's head, hanging in the air as if suspended. It waved and wandered, bobbing up and down slowly, as if in anticipation of snagging anything that just happened to wander close enough to become ensnared in its trap.   The light coming from the giant stained glass window at the top of the stairs seemed to sparkle off the strands as they moved, giving the impression of razor sharpness to each strand.

Sarah's heartbeat was steady. She fairly floated down the remaining stairs, not even feeling them pass beneath her feet.   All emotion was dampened. She could hear the heartbeats of each Angel below, could feel the rush of blood through each one's veins. As she neared the bottom of the stairs, objects on the walls and sitting on tables and chests along the hallway and in the entryway began rattling and seeming to jump in place.

The one standing at the front of the little triangle of three pulled out a scroll, unrolled it, cleared his throat and said, "By order of the Seraph Azra'il, Acting Head of the Great Sanhedrin, Commander General of the Elite Sanhedrin Guard, and all lower Sanhedrin councils, er… you, Sarah Baker, of the er… human… realm, are hereby to be taken into legal custody of said Elite Guard for the murder of the Angel Narayana of Seraphim City until such time as your innocence or guilt can be determined and judged by the presiding council members of the Great Sanhedrin."

Throughout his speech, the Angel had become more and more conscious of the objects dancing and vibrating all around him.   The creature on the stairs before him had remained perfectly still, other than the constantly flowing movement of its hair and the slight swirls within the glow coming from within the pupil of each eye. It didn't even appear to be breathing, this thing with the flying hair. It made no response whatsoever to the declaration he'd read and so, with a slight signal to his men, the three moved forward.

At the first sign of aggression from the Angels, Sarah remembered the scene she'd witnessed in the dream world where Suriyah had defeated the creatures. Sarah quickly imitated the same movements Suriyah had made, causing any and every movable object available to go whizzing through the air to strike at and beat the Angels repeatedly. In seconds, the three were bruised and bleeding, with a couple sporting broken bones which protruded from the skin on arms or legs or fingers. Each one was lying on the floor merely trying to cover and protect their heads from damage.

This was the scene witnessed by the three at the top of the stairs.

Sarah! Mikhail's voice sounded like a whip cracking in her mind and she jerked to attention, whirling around to find him. Immediately, the debris flying through the air stopped where it was in flight and dropped to the ground. Several items crashed and broke into shards of glass or crystal to scatter all over the floor.

Mikhail stood there at the top of the stairs with Miriam and Samuel, all three pairs of eyes staring in utter stupefaction at the carnage below. Sarah remained completely untouched and unharmed. She wasn't even breathing hard, hadn't even broken a sweat, and Mikhail simply couldn't believe his eyes. The only person he'd ever witnessed perform the maneuver Sarah had been practicing with ease when he'd entered the stairwell was Suriyah.

A part of Mikhail suddenly wondered just what Sarah had seen when she'd stayed behind in the dream world during his recounting of what had happened that day at Lemuria. He'd left, but he knew she'd stayed behind with

Suriyah. Baphomet had followed him that day back to Seraphim City, but Suriyah had remained behind with the survivors.

More sounds of trouble came from the back of the house on the first floor and Mikhail broke free of his reverie and rushed down the remaining steps to Sarah, first making sure she was okay, then grabbing her limp arm and pulling her along with him toward the back of the house. They still didn't know where Thomas was, nor Sarah's parents, but there was obviously something going on at the back, so Mikhail figured that was their best bet.

Thomas was in the kitchen eating a sandwich when the door from the outside was suddenly kicked in. Five guards dressed in what looked like some kind of Roman Guard costumes entered. He stood there for a moment, gawking at the group of large men, wondering if they were there for a costume party or something. Then, the one closest to him made a move to grab Thomas' arm and that was all it took.

Earlier, after he'd returned to himself in his room from his vision with Nera, Thomas had gone outside to a place in the gardens that was secluded from all prying eyes. There, he'd practiced and practiced the maneuvers Nera had shown him. At some point during his workout, the old memories of different movements had returned naturally, as if they'd just been waiting for his body to make an effort so they could return.

He'd remembered things from a time, he knew not when, but his soul remembered and it translated the memories into movements for this body. He had accomplished things with energy manipulation the likes of which even his own imagination could never have engineered and now, as the closest fearsome guard reached for him, Thomas didn't even think, he just moved.

The man went flying into a wall on the other side of the room, hitting it with a loud crash. All the plates and other dishes in the cupboards lining the wall suddenly came tumbling down onto the floor with the guard's body, each splintering into little shards of broken china.

Another guard rushed at him and Thomas' shield came up, causing the man to literally bounce off it. The guard seemed stunned for a moment, then he tried again. This time, however, he was too late and the blast of energy Thomas shot out at him threw him against the wall on the opposite side of the room from where the first guard had crashed. This guard landed first on top of the giant stove, then bounced and finally hit the ground, where he remained motionless.

The next attack came from all three remaining guards simultaneously, each growling as they all charged at Thomas from different angles. They were so big and so fierce-looking that, for a moment, Thomas felt a slight twinge of fear. Then, as if someone had flipped a switch in his brain, everything became peaceful and calm. It was as if the men were barely even moving and Thomas studied even the tiniest details of each man, noticing chinks in this one's armor, or that this other one wore a brace on his knee from a recent injury, or that the third one had a knife tucked into the boot on his right foot.

In slow motion, as it seemed to Thomas, each man threw his punch. Thomas easily evaded each one, countering with his own, pulling on the energies surrounding himself and them and knocking each one of the three into countertops, doors, and even half-way through the window above the sink. Thomas wasted not one minute, but rushed immediately outside into the gardens. He had to get to his grandparents whom he knew to be taking a walk out there, as he'd passed them as they'd been on their way out the door when he'd entered the kitchen earlier. He quickly found them and led them off to a far corner of the lawn, back behind a gazebo he'd discovered earlier in the day. There, they waited.

Mikhail pushed through the swinging doorway to the kitchens and found a group of guards lying bent and broken all over the place, but there was no longer anyone else in the kitchen area. For a moment, all he could do was to stare at the scene before him. Then, he noticed that the door leading out to the back of the house stood wide open and he quickly pulled Sarah and Samuel through, with Miriam following closely behind them. Off in a corner of the gardens, Mikhail caught sight of Tom Baker, Sarah's dad, peeking over a hedge to see who was coming and Mikhail rushed off in that direction, dragging his two wards with him. Again, the faithful Miriam followed along.

Thomas, Marian, and Tom were all huddled together on the other side of a gazebo near a small pond at the back of the property. Marian was crying again, but she didn't seem to be hurt or incapable of walking. Thomas and Tom looked fine, though they seemed a bit confused as to what was going on. Sarah immediately went to put an arm around Thomas' shoulders. Several other house staff slowly started showing up, having run and hidden when things had gotten rough inside the house.

Mikhail surveyed his little group of forty or so and then, nodding once, said, "All right. We're going to the Badlands. Anyone not able or willing to go is welcome to remain here. I do not know that any of us will be returning, however, so you may end up having to pledge fealty to another Seraph. I will not hold that against any of you. You have always been my most trusted friends, my family, and I will respect your wishes. So, choose now, for we must be gone before more guards arrive."

Not one person moved or even made a noise.

Mikhail surveyed the lot, then nodded once more and said, "Very well. There are too many of us to carry, so we'll have to strike out on foot. We'll head in a Northwesterly direction, avoiding populated areas as much as possible, but keeping as close to the coast as we can. We need to get as far from Seraphim City tonight as we can before stopping to make camp." He paused, then said, "This is going to be a difficult journey. I suggest we get started."

A short while later, Thomas looked back. Seraphim City was only just visible now over the tree tops, the afternoon sun creating a haziness that made the building tops seem to shimmer in the distance.

He was glad to leave there. It hadn't been home to him. Miriam and Samuel had been his only true friends there and, as they had both chosen to remain loyal to Mikhail and accompany him to the Badlands, Thomas felt no sense of loss at leaving the city. He certainly wouldn't miss any of the others from Seraphim City. The way everyone else in the city had treated his mom, Mikhail, and Thomas made the idea of leaving more than welcome in his mind.

He turned his back on the city. His future was ahead, somewhere out there in the wilds of the area these strange creatures called the Badlands.

Gabriel and Israfil raced toward Mikhail's home, fear lending speed to their flight. Azra'il had kept them waiting on purpose. He'd known why they'd requested an audience with him, but he'd gone ahead and sent his elite Sanhedrin Guard to arrest Sarah, even while he'd kept his brothers waiting in the vast hallway just beyond the council chamber doors. As soon as one of the guards sent had returned, bloodied and battered, passing before the two waiting Seraphim, they'd known. Of course, they'd left immediately, but it seemed they were definitely late for the party.

Israfil was the first to arrive at the house and he was stunned by what he saw. There were two guards littering the entryway to the house and five more strewn about in the kitchen. No one else remained in the house, though, and Israfil wondered which way Mikhail had decided to take out to the Badlands. In their meeting earlier, they'd mapped out two separate possible routes to take, considering they would have humans and possibly some lower Angels accompanying them on this trip, but Israfil needed to figure out which route they'd taken. He was sure that was where they were headed. Mikhail never did anything without a plan.

Gabriel finally showed up and was just as shocked by the carnage in the house as Israfil had been. "Where's everyone else?" he asked.

Israfil shook his head. "My guess is they're already on their way to the Badlands, as Mikhail had planned. Do you think he would've chosen Sargon Pass?" he asked, already at work trying puzzle pieces to see if they fit.

"I don't think so, not with the older humans and with Sarah being with child," Gabriel said. "I think that one was to be taken as a last resort."

It was a good bet Azra'il was already arranging a search party, so time was definitely of the essence here. They both knew it, and so they decided to try the route Mikhail had said would be the easiest on everyone in the group. Getting there took a little time, since they had to make sure no one saw them leaving the estate. It would be *just the thing* to go and lead the elite Sanhedrin Guard directly to its quarry! They kept all six of their shields up the entire time, hoping beyond hope that Azra'il wasn't with the search party.

After about thirty minutes of searching, they finally spotted the group. It looked like all of Mikhail's people had chosen to accompany him! Neither one of the brothers was surprised by this, though. Mikhail had always been generous to his people, always treated them well. Earlier, when they'd been planning out this day, Mikhail had asked Gabriel if he would take in as his own any of those who chose not to accompany Mikhail and his new family out to the Badlands. Gabriel had been honored to have been asked, but had informed his brother he didn't believe any of them would ever want another Seraph leader other than Mikhail. Mikhail hadn't been so sure, though, so Gabriel had agreed. Now, as he and Israfil set down not far in front of the group and dropped their shields, he smiled to himself in congratulations, for he'd been right.

Mikhail saw his brothers as they dropped their shields and waited for the group. He was never so relieved to see anyone in his life. He'd been afraid they wouldn't be able to get in to see anyone at the council hall. He thought this was a good time for a break and he led Sarah, who had been completely silent this whole time, physically and psychically, over to a huge boulder so she could sit down to rest. Thomas immediately sat next to her. It struck Mikhail that his son hadn't said anything either since they'd left the estate. He looked them over and the both seemed to be fine, so he merely shook his head and turned back toward his brothers. He approached them with hope in his heart. "What news, brothers?" he asked.

Israfil sighed heavily and the hope inside Mikhail faded.

"We never even got in to see anyone, neither Azra'il nor the council," Gabriel explained. "Azra'il sent the elite, as

I'm sure you're aware, while we waited... I guess he wanted to separate us, somehow, to keep us out of this." He shrugged.

"How did you know he sent the elite?" Mikhail asked.

"When we saw one of the ones you'd nearly killed return to report to the council, we suspected something was up, so, we went to your place first, then came here."

Mikhail didn't bother correcting them on the issue of who had beaten the guards... Not that he actually *knew* who had done it in the kitchen. He didn't have time for that at the moment, however. "Well," he said, "we've got to make Battle Rock before stopping to make camp, I figure. At least, if we can get that far, maybe they won't be able to find us."

Israfil shook his head. "You're going to need to dig in now," he said adamantly.

When both Gabriel and Mikhail turned confused gazes his way, he explained, "I figure Azra'il will be leading the search party directly to wherever he picks up the soul-strings... Remember? He can see them?"

Both of his brothers realized their mistake as Israfil spoke and they both simultaneously came to the realization that there was about to be one *heck* of a battle. Mikhail took only a second of thought before he said, "All right. He wants a fight? Well, we'll give him one." He walked over to where Sarah and Thomas were sitting. He knew Sarah would want to be wherever her human family members were during the battle, but he really needed her to be hidden. He didn't think he could handle this if he was constantly worrying that either she or Sheely were about to be hurt, or worse.

Mikhail had trained the elite. He knew their maneuvers, the way they strategized, everything. He wasn't afraid for himself at all. It was Sarah and Sheely and Thomas who mattered to him. He took Sarah's arm and pulled her up to stand, contacting her psychically, *Are you okay?*

She looked at him, her expression completely blank.

"Sarah?" he asked aloud.

I will not sit this out like some helpless little lamb you must protect. I will remain with my family and I will protect them. You know I can do it. You saw...

After a moment's hesitation, he merely swallowed, nodded, and turned to go organize the rest of his people. There were plenty of hiding places in this area and Mikhail took up station about ten yards across from where Sarah and her human family had hidden. He had a clear view of their hiding place and he'd instructed Israfil and Gabriel to keep watch on it for any sign of attack. He knew Azra'il would have the elite head straight for that spot, for that was what Azra'il would be seeing, only that.

Just before crouching down to a fully-hidden pose, Mikhail contacted Sarah once more. *You're sure you're okay?*

After a short pause, he heard her voice in his mind. *I don't know what's happening, but I feel like... I know I can protect them from these weak beings. So, don't worry about us. Just keep as many of your people safe as you can. I'll take care of my family and Sheely and we'll deal with whatever this is after all's said and done.*

Mikhail frowned and almost got back up to go take position next to her. He didn't like what she'd said at all. What had she meant when she'd said 'whatever this is'?

Relax, came her voice in his mind again. *Everything will be just fine... I love you, Mikhail, and we're going to have Sheely..., and then, Thomas and Sheely and you and I will be a family.*

Mikhail's heart swelled at those words and he squeezed his eyes shut. *Thank you, sweetheart. I can't wait for that day. I love you, too.*

It was twenty minutes later when the first group of elite came on the scene. They were in vimana and were gunning fast for the spot where Sarah and her family hid. Israfil had been correct in assuming Azra'il would target the very location where the humans were. The slight whining hiss of the vimana engines was the only indication they got that the elite were about to attack and Mikhail had difficulty fixing the location from which they were coming. Vimana didn't make much noise at all when they flew, but if one knew what to listen for, it at least could give you a short amount of warning time.

As the first appeared over a hilltop, Mikhail lunged into the air, his shields going up full force to protect him from the round machine and he careened into it as hard as he could. It didn't do much other than to divert its trajectory and the guard piloting it simply veered off to the left to circle about and try again. Another appeared over the hilltop and another, and then another. When all was said and done, there were seven vimana circling the area, each one fighting for an opening, each one being blocked by either Mikhail, Gabriel, or Israfil, for the pilots couldn't see Seraphim in full shields. Mikhail and his brothers could block them, but they couldn't seem to stop them from coming back.

"This isn't working!" Mikhail shouted to his brothers. That's when the elite's ground reserve made its move.

Mikhail looked down to see at least fifty guards storming the hillside where Sarah and all the rest were hidden. He swiftly swooped down to where she was hiding, intent on protecting her and the kids at whatever cost. He didn't even think about his shields as he reached to take her hand in his. *Hold on, baby. We're going to defeat these bastards here and now!* The moment his hand touched hers, however, a peculiar sensation overtook his entire being.

Mikhail had always been a soldier, a fighter. Each and every time he had entered battle, the old familiar feel of the rush of adrenaline would take over and he would ride a wave of energy to the finish line, victorious and invincible. However, as he gripped her hand in his, a sensation of utter peace assailed him and he found himself merely standing there with Sarah, waiting.

The vimanas circled and tried one spot, then circled and tried another. There were too many for just Israfil and Gabriel to hold back and eventually, one got past their defensive line. By that time, however, Mikhail and Sarah were confronting the first of the ground troops. The small squad rushed at them, pinpointing the area where Thomas and his grandparents hid. They couldn't see Seraphim in full shield mode, either, so it was a shock to them when Sarah suddenly dropped her shields just as they were upon her. Mikhail didn't understand why she had done this, but he went ahead and dropped his own as well, confusing and even frightening the elite before them for a moment.

The Angels stared at the two creatures standing before them. They had been told what to expect from the Seraph Angel, Mikhail, but, they hadn't been told how he looked now, and here was another creature that looked very similar to him, even though it was a female. As the Angels gazed upon the two, their eyes bulged and their mouths dropped open in terrified amazement as the hair on each one of the creatures suddenly changed and became only white while each one of them rose into the air, as if floating, about half a meter off the ground. The eyes of the creatures glowed so brightly some of the guards had to turn slightly away and shield their own eyes. The hair on the creatures was suddenly going wild all on its own, rising and writhing, like razor sharp white snakes waiting to strike.

Thomas had had enough! These damned Angels, or whatever they were, had caused him and his family enough grief! He was going to end this and end it now. Disregarding his crying grandmother, Thomas stood and walked a few paces away from where his grandparents hid. He concentrated on pulling all the energy he could from his surroundings. He closed his eyes and prayed this would work, concentrating on his breathing. After only a second or two, he began to feel the hum of energy collecting around his body. He opened his eyes and he could actually see the waves of energy twisting and curling about him like water. Focusing more intensely, he pulled all the energy together and, in one blinding show of force, he slapped his hands together and then quickly spread his arms wide, emitting an arc of pure energy whose blast radius encompassed a wide range, barring the area his grandparents still occupied.

Soldiers were knocked backward several yards, and then came the vimanas, dropping like dead flies from the sky. Thomas fell to his knees, panting for breath. He hadn't known he was capable of such a show of force and he hoped no one had noticed him performing the little feat. As soon as he could manage it, he climbed to his feet and returned to the place behind the rocks where his grandparents still hid. Thomas believed his mom and Mikhail should be able to handle things from this point forward – at least, he hoped so. He didn't think he had another shot like that in him yet. He crouched down next to his elders and hugged them.

The Angelic soldiers moved in for the kill. Then, from somewhere behind the two floating creatures, there came a sound like none any of the guards had ever heard before. It was almost like a sonic boom, but there'd been no warning sound leading up to it. All had just become eerily still and then... boom! There was a blast of hot wind that knocked almost everyone down in his tracks. The two glowing creatures remained where they were, floating above the ground. The only indication they'd been affected at all by whatever had just happened was the flapping of their clothing and hair, as the hot blast of wind forced them forward. As soon as the gust was past, however, their clothes settled back into place and their hair resumed its wild dance around each ones head.

Then, like dead flies, vimana dropped soundlessly from the sky, only to crash here or there onto the ground. Pilots were pushing open the canopies and making their way out, yelling that all the electrical components had suddenly just stopped working. Amid all this, the creatures remained where they were, floating there before the lead ground troops, waiting.

Failure was not an option for an elite guard. Mikhail had pounded that into them to such a degree that it wasn't even something they thought about. It just was. Either you did what you had been ordered to do, or you failed to do it. And failure was not an option. So, each and every pilot and ground guard returned to the original goal of taking down the small group of humans. If this duo of *uber*Seraphim meant to stop them, then they must be annihilated by the elite.

They were still being attacked by more invisible Seraphim and there was something about one of the invisible ones that seemed to confuse anyone who got near it. Quite a few were being lost due to this. Those who could manage it gathered as well as they could around the two floating creatures. They surrounded all but the rear flank of the creatures, which they couldn't get to because of the terrain, and then they attacked simultaneously.

Suddenly, everything was slow motion. Mikhail could pierce the thoughts of each and every one of the guards and he knew exactly what move each man intended, when and in which direction. There was no sound. All but he and Sarah moved at a snail's pace in a soundless, heavy world. Sarah and Mikhail merely watched. It was comical, seeing these big, strong men moving at such a pace, their facial expressions taking forever to form and then change.

One of them reached a hand out toward Sarah, a wicked-looking knife held in it jutting toward her form. Mikhail's immediate reaction was to annihilate the Guardsman and he went into full attack mode. He threw out a blast of energy toward the Angel without even realizing what he had done and then swiped the guard with the backside of his first shield in a move he'd never taught any elite Guardsman. The Guard was hit full-on by the blast and shield and went careening off twelve yards away from Sarah's form only to crash hard against a nearby tree, the sound of his breaking bones echoing throughout the previously soundless environment.

Sarah frowned and directed a pleading glance toward Mikhail as another Guard took the place of the first one. Once Mikhail heard her mental plea, he cocked his head at an angle, waiting for an explanation. Sarah took a deep breath and then she reached out and lightly touched the next Angel's forehead with her index finger for just a second. His slow-moving figure immediately closed its eyes and began a leisurely descent to the ground. Mikhail watched this byplay with amazement. He realized she had sent the Angel into a deep, restful sleep. In a flash, he'd learned from her that by shooting a dart of electricity into the man's brain, to a place she knew of called the Reticular Formation, or the brain's sleep center, no harm would come to the Guardsmen and they would sleep until she allowed them to awaken.

Still holding her hand, he tilted his head at a different curious angle facing the oncoming Guardsmen. He reached forward to the guard closest to him and touched that Angel on the forehead with an index finger, concentrating on affecting the same area of that man's brain and watching in amusement as the same thing happened to this one. Angel after Angel approached, and Angel after Angel went down, until the entire area was littered with sleeping Angels, utterly unaware of where they lay or of the continuing battle raging around them.

As the last elite ground troop fell, Mikhail finally released Sarah's hand. Immediately, everything returned to real time and both of them fell from their floating positions to stand on the ground once more. The glow from their eyes dimmed to about half what it had been throughout the encounter and their hair gently floated back down to rest in long white masses around each of their bodies.

They stood there staring at one another for a few minutes. It was so odd to see the changes each of them had endured, yet neither one seemed to mind. Mikhail saw what he looked like through the image in her mind. Sarah saw what she looked like through the image in Mikhail's mind. They both compared themselves to one another, finding they liked the almost translucent skin which seemed to be lit from within, the brightly glowing orbs where their normal eyes had once been, and the hair...

It was so very long and so very white and it would float up every now and then of its own accord. At one point, Mikhail reached out a hand toward Sarah's hair and it sought out his hand, rubbing against the skin of his palm, nudging his hand upward, closer to her face. Mikhail smiled and stepped closer to her again, cupping her cheek and bending in to place a soft kiss upon her lips.

Gabriel and Israfil picked their way through the sea of elite Guard bodies, making sure not to touch any of them for fear of waking them. When they got close enough to their brother, they gasped to see how much he and Sarah had transformed during the battle. However, Israfil got down to business immediately, for he knew his most beloved brother, Azra'il, would not be defeated so easily.

"How long will they sleep?" he asked Mikhail and Sarah.

In unison, the two turned their glowing eyes upon him and said in one ominously sibilant voice, "These creatures will awaken when we allow them to do so."

A shiver raced down both Israfil's and Gabriel's backs. What had happened here? Just this morning, Mikhail had been discussing the Angels of Seraphim City and how his one desire was to protect both his family and them. Now, he and Sarah spoke of them as if they were some sort of sub-class of beings. Israfil wasn't sure if things had just gotten better or worse and he swallowed a lump of fear before nodding to the two and suggesting, "Then perhaps we should get moving so that we can make some headway before you have to allow them to awaken."

The two glowing creatures before him slowly blinked, but said nothing.

A sound from behind the two caused everyone to look and Thomas, Marian and Tom appeared from out behind a massive tree trunk, all three of them immediately wide-eyed and open-mouthed at the sight before them. When Thomas caught sight of Mikhail and his mom, his heart rate increased and a corner of his mouth lifted in anticipation. They now looked very similar to Nera and her kind.

Thomas could still see a few differences, like their skin wasn't quite as bright as hers and they didn't appear to be just gaunt figures. Their hair wasn't quite as active as hers, either, but he could see it rising up every now and then, so he knew it was capable of becoming active like hers. The point, however, was that they were well on their way to becoming like Nera and that meant that Thomas himself was going to become like her, he reasoned. At this thought, he was very pleased.

Marian and Tom were a different matter. They gawked at the couple before them, unable to believe that the translucent female being before them had once been their daughter. Their daughter had been blessed with the most beautiful Auburn hair any child had ever had, but the creature before them had all white hair, and it was alive, floating around every now and then with a life of its own! And that wasn't even the worst part. The creature's skin glowed like there was a light bulb inside it, and the eyes... Marian couldn't bear to look at them.

She turned to bury her head against Tom's chest, a fresh bout of tears starting. She'd been through so much in such a short time. Now, she just felt tired and afraid. She needed to be held and told everything was going to be all right. And, that's just what Tom did.

The two creatures standing before them merely gazed upon the human couple, their facial expressions unchanging, no sign of compassion evident on their stony faces. Only their iridescent eyes changed with the swirling of the vitreous fluid inside the white orbs.

Gabriel stepped forward and called out, "This battle is over, my friends, but the war has only just begun. We must be ready at any moment for the next attack. However, for the now, we must move quickly, for we need to make as much headway toward the Northern Coastal region as possible before these guards awaken." Each and every Angel around them nodded and gathered their few belongings in preparation for continuing the journey.

Israfil took a step closer to Mikhail and Sarah and said, "Your people still need your guidance. If you wish them to return to Seraphim City, we will take them, but we cannot protect the humans." The two beings stared at him. It seemed to Israfil as if Mikhail and Sarah were now part of a whole and that this whole deemed all other beings as separate creatures from itself. Did that mean the two of them had actually transformed into some other kind of biological entity that existed in two separate physical bodies? He did not know.

What he believed, however, was that Mikhail and Sarah would never be able to be thought of as separate and that, because of this, they would never be able to be as concerned with others as they had been before. Sarah didn't even seem concerned with the fact that her parents were upset about her physical transformation. She'd just stared as her own mother had cried. There'd been no reaction there.

Still, Israfil was willing to help in any way he could. He didn't blame anyone in this case. He believed what had happened to Mikhail and Sarah, and indeed continued to happen as a developing and evolving thing, was part of nature, part of the natural way things were supposed to develop. They hadn't chosen this path, it had just happened. Israfil was glad of one thing, however. It seemed Mikhail could not mind-link with him.

Just as this thought slid through his mind, however, what sounded like Sarah's voice lilted through his mind, saying, *Your secret is safe with me, my friend.* His gaze darted to her face and his muscles tensed. Then, he heard her lilting voice say, *You're wrong about us no longer caring. Yes, we have each other, but we care so very much for all of you. Trust me when I tell you you are all precious to both of us and we will protect you with every fiber of our being. And…, I will never tell anyone.*

After a moment, Israfil nodded once to her and then looked back at Gabriel and said, "We need to get moving." The entire entourage quickly returned to the task of moving everyone as far from Seraphim City as possible, but at a much harsher pace this time. They knew they had to reach a safe enough distance before looking for a place to stay for the evening.

After four days and nights of traveling at a break-neck pace, the group came to a large river that ran a short distance more to the west before emptying into the nearby ocean. Mikhail and Sarah were by now thoroughly strained from keeping up their hold on the still-sleeping elite Sanhedrin Guard. Mikhail, Israfil, and Gabriel all agreed this spot would do as a good place to build a new home and the entire group of refugees began the tedious process of building temporary shelters to be used until permanent structures could be erected.

"There has to be some way to make him see reason," Gabriel said. He and Israfil were discussing their options for the future. Israfil wanted to return to Seraphim City, if for no other reason than to see to his people and his estate. But he also wanted to be with his brother.

Of all his siblings, Azra'il was the only one who knew of Israfil's ability, and of his loneliness. Israfil and Azra'il had been together for as long as either one of them could remember and they both shared a bond much stronger than their relationships with their other siblings. That was why Israfil knew there would be no persuading Azra'il to the fact that Sarah was no longer human. Israfil knew they could take Sara, Mikhail, and a whole slew of Angelic physicians before Azra'il, and still he wouldn't be convinced. He would claim it was an illusion of some sort or that someone had altered his perception to make Sarah appear to not be human.

Azra'il certainly believed the rest of them suffered from just such a delusion, and for a moment, Israfil wondered if perhaps it could be true. He quickly dismissed the thought. Israfil had seen far too much that could be explained no other way than to be that Sarah and Mikhail had changed. Sarah was no longer human. Mikhail was no longer Seraph. Both of them had just spontaneously... *evolved* into some other life form.

Israfil shivered. It was a bit awe-inspiring to gaze upon the two of them, Israfil had to admit. They seemed almost to exist in some separate realm, as if they were merely visiting this one by inhabiting these new bodies, changing them to suit their needs. How it had all happened, though, and why, were questions that remained unanswered. Hantsushept, the Angelic physician who'd helped when Sarah and her human family had been drugged and kidnapped, had chosen to pledge his fealty to Mikhail after that incident and he and his family had come along to live in the Badlands with Mikhail when everything had happened. Hantsushept was busy studying as much as he could about what had caused Sarah's and Mikhail's transformations. It was a difficult task, since they were still very much alive and Hantsushept couldn't exactly run many tests on them or take many samples.

Again, Israfil shivered at the thought of the changes he'd witnessed in Sarah and Mikhail. His thoughts were brought back to the present, however, when Gabriel said, "Iz, we've got to find a way to get through to him!"

Israfil shook his head and sighed. "I think it would be a complete waste of time, brother," he said. "Azra'il didn't watch the gradual change, as we did. To be honest, if I hadn't seen things happening as they did, I wouldn't believe it, either."

"But, if all four of us go to see him – You, Mikhail, Sarah, and I – don't you think he might listen? I mean, just the sight of them should be enough to convince anyone in *my* opinion," Gabriel said.

Israfil merely shook his head, saying, "Djibril, I know you mean well, but I know our brother, and you are way off base with this train of thought."

"What if we bring Azra'il here to see them?" Gabriel asked hopefully.

"And show him exactly where they are so he can send more elite Sanhedrin Guards after them? Yes, that would be wise, would it not?"

"I'm surprised he hasn't already sent more, or forced those who failed initially to return until they succeed," admitted Gabriel.

Israfil had been wondering about that, himself, and he made a mental note to ask Mikhail about the soldiers he and Sarah had rendered unconscious on the hillside. It didn't make sense that Azra'il hadn't yet sent more troops. That would have been the logical thing to do.

Israfil shook his head again and said, "I don't know. I think we need to talk with Mikhail on this before we do anything."

Gabriel agreed and the two of them went off in search of their newly-transformed brother.

Mikhail, Israfil, Gabriel, and Sarah all met in the main shelter to discuss their plans. It was then Israfil and Gabriel learned the elite Guard who'd attacked their group before was still under whatever thrall Mikhail and Sarah had placed them in.

"Is there any sign Azra'il is following?" Israfil asked.

Mikhail and Sarah merely stared at him, their glowing eyes seeming to change every now and then with the swirling vitreous liquid inside their pupils. When finally they spoke, it was as one. "There is nothing but confusion and fear felt from Azra'il," they said in unison. "None has yet found those who slumber in the forest and no one follows from Seraphim City."

"We have to go back and explain what happened," Gabriel said.

"We have to get those elite Guardsmen back to Seraphim City," Israfil stated. After a moment's hesitation, he asked, "Can you keep them asleep until we can get them back to the city?"

"How are we to transport that many men?" Gabriel immediately demanded.

"Well," Israfil floundered, "then we'll have to take someone out to them or at least let them know where to find them."

"Are the two of you okay with that?" Gabriel asked.

Both white heads nodded solemnly.

Gabriel nodded once back at them. "Right," he said, rising to his feet. "Then, I'll go get ready to leave for the city. Hopefully, we'll be able to convince someone, either Azra'il or someone on the council, that they're all mistaken."

Sarah silently arose and walked with Gabriel to the shelter's entrance. Israfil's eyes narrowed as he watched her move out of the shelter alongside Gabriel's retreating form. Looking back at Mikhail, he realized the creature sitting before him hadn't moved at all, not even in response to Sarah's departure. *Interesting*, Israfil thought.

Chapter 18

"So, what's the deal with you and Mikhail?" Tom asked her. He never had been one to beat around the bush. Sarah had always liked that about him.

"Mikhail and I...," she floundered. After a moment's hesitation, she simply said, "He and I are one and the same." There really was no other way for her to describe her relationship with the man who constituted the other part of her own self. Whatever was inside her was inside him and vice versa. They were only separate physically. In all other respects, they were as one. Of course, each could still have his or her own thoughts and feelings, but they were instantly known by the other, as if the other had heard the thought from the first or felt the first experiencing the feeling. If one had never experienced this strange new way of living, how could anyone explain it to someone else? It would be like trying to explain the concept of a snowflake to some tribesman who had lived his entire life in a year-round hot zone.

"Well," Tom finally said after she failed to elaborate further, "as long as you and Thomas are happy, I guess you have my blessings." Tom looked around at the breathtaking views of the valley laid out before them and confessed, "I don't even mind that he's having a house built for your mother and me in such a miserable location."

"I know," Sarah said. "I'm afraid this was all that was available in the neighborhood, though, so you'll just have to do your best to live with it, I guess."

The two smiled at each other and Tom gave her a hug.

Mikhail stood by the sawhorse, assisting a couple of his people with the section of rafters they were constructing for the main house. He smiled as he caught the images and thoughts from Sarah's mind of her time with Tom. A part of him was glad she hadn't gone into further detail with Tom about how closely-linked she and Mikhail were. All of this was new to Mikhail, having someone who didn't necessarily need him for what he was, per se, but who wanted him for who he was.

Sarah felt something for him that far transcended love, as he did for her, and Mikhail knew that the two of them were linked in such a way that he would simply cease to exist if she died. Mikhail had always been, he figured, since he'd been on the planet far longer than any other to his knowledge. But Sarah, she had only been here for a very short amount of time, though Mikhail suspected she may have been here many times before in many lifetimes. Azra'il had once described to Mikhail his reasoning behind believing humans returned again and again to their dimension and, judging by what Sarah had shown him of her "blog", he believed she had lived in the human realm many times.

He didn't know if she was now immortal or not, though. If she were to die now, would she be able to come back? He just didn't know, and that scared him to the depths of his very soul.

Be calm, my love, came Sarah's voice in his mind. He immediately relaxed. They'd been through so much already. Mikhail just wanted to make the rest of their time together as wonderful as possible. He looked over the part of the main house they'd managed to build so far, envisioning how it would look when it was completed. He had included enough rooms in the plans for several more kids. Sarah had been a bit shocked by this when he'd first shown her the drawings, but then she'd smiled and placed a hand on Sheely's spot, as if assuring their daughter that Daddy was making sure to have a room built for her, too. Mikhail could hear Sheely's little whispered voice chattering away in the background of Sarah's mind and he smiled. One of the greatest advantages of being constantly linked with his Sarah was that he always got to hear his daughter's voice whenever she spoke, which was a lot!

If you don't concentrate, Sarah's voice sounded in his mind again, *you're gonna mess up and the whole house is gonna fall down even before we get to finish moving in!*

Mikhail laughed aloud at that, causing several of the Angels working with him to turn to see what was so funny. Mikhail just shook his head and continued working.

"I just need a small sample," Hantsushept said in frustration. Sarah glanced at the floating white strands of razor-sharp hair as they waved about her head, ready to strike out at the physician if he got any closer to her than was acceptable. Sarah wasn't sure, but she believed she was probably able to control the hair strands on some sub-conscious level, but she knew she had no desire to have any of the strands cut or damaged in any way, even for the sake of scientific advancement! She shook her head and said, I'm sorry, but you'll just have to find some other way to get the information you desire. My hair and I are off limits."

"What about Sheely?" he instantly asked. Since the incident in the jungle in the human realm, all those loyal to Mikhail had been calling the unborn child by this name. Hantsushept still wondered about how the young human child had managed to discover the baby's name, but the creature before him had forbidden Hantsushept to even so much as interview the boy regarding the incident.

"What about Sheely?" Sarah asked, slightly annoyed now.

"Well, do you know if you're doing everything you should to help her? I mean, humans require extra vitamins and nutrients when they're pregnant, right?"

I'm on my way right now, love, came Mikhail's voice in Sarah's mind. *If he needs to run any tests, he can take samples from me. Perhaps that will give him enough.*

Sarah relaxed a bit. She didn't exactly enjoy the thought of Mikhail enduring pain for the sake of scientific research either, but she knew *she* wasn't going to do it.

No, you're not, was Mikhail's thought on the subject. *And, don't worry about me enduring pain... If he hurts me, I'll simply do unspeakable harm to him.*

Sarah laughed aloud, shocking Hantsushept. Mikhail appeared just then, dropping his shields and coming to place a kiss on Sarah's forehead, along with a hand on Sheely's spot. Hantsushept kept his distance as both beings' lethal strands of hair began writhing in protest of his close proximity.

"Forgive me for taking so long," Mikhail said. He turned to Hantsushept and asked, "Now, what was it you needed?"

A slight shiver raced through Hantsushept, but logic won out over fear. "I need hair samples, urine samples, and blood samples, to begin with," he stated matter-of-factly. Without waiting for his new patients to respond, he said, "Then, I'll need to do complete work-ups on both of you, especially you, m'dear," and he pointed at Sarah.

"Why her?" Mikhail immediately demanded, stepping between Sarah and the Angel.

"We have to do everything we can to ensure proper prenatal care for Sheely."

Mikhail's heart leapt into his throat at the mere thought of anything going wrong with Sarah's pregnancy and Sarah instantly knew of his distress. She stepped forward and placed a comforting hand on Mikhail's arm, assuring him, "It's okay. I'll do whatever I have to for Sheely's sake."

He could feel her nervousness, but he was in a quandary as to what else could be done. He didn't know what issues needed to be considered as far as Sheely's development went, and he certainly wasn't willing to put Sarah's precious life at risk on what could turn out to be a difficult, if not dangerous, pregnancy. He reached to cup her cheek. *You're certain?* He silently asked, gazing intently into the swirling mists of her eyes. Sarah smiled and nodded and he bent to touch his forehead to hers, closing his eyes. *I could not bear to lose you, love,* he silently whispered in her mind.

"Okay," Hantsushept said, rolling up his sleeves. "Let's get started, shall we?"

After one long, meaningful look into Sarah's eyes, Mikhail turned and nodded to the physician, asking, "What do you need me to do?"

"Well, first off," Hantsushept said, pulling on tight-fitting non-latex gloves as he attempted to approach Mikhail, "get your hair under control so I can take a sample."

Mikhail concentrated on his hair, willing the writhing white strands to rest easy. Each time the Angel approached, however, the hair flew into action, darting in this direction or that to keep Hantsushept away from Mikhail. From a military strategist point of view, it really was an excellent method of protection. However, Mikhail needed it to settle down and he just couldn't seem to get it to cooperate. Again and again, Hantsushept approached while Mikhail concentrated, and again and again, the razor-sharp white strands of hair whipped around, threatening to slice off digits or limbs or anything else to which it could lay purchase.

Finally, Sarah stepped forward, again placing a comforting hand on Mikhail's arm, saying, "Let me help." She reached up with her other hand to gently grab the back of Mikhail's neck and looked deeply into his eyes. Hantsushept watched in amazement as both pairs of eyes before him suddenly blazed with intensity and, miraculously, the deadly strands of hair on each head immediately calmed.

Hantsushept wasn't about to waste this opportunity. While the two creatures concentrated on whatever they were concentrating on, he stepped in close. Carefully, he took a strand from each creature and placed about five centimeters' worth of length onto his palm, holding the length steady between his index and middle fingers. The strands still moved, but only in minute little quivers. He positioned a tiny scissors at the ready and snipped. The creatures' hair moved and Hantsushept leapt back in fear of its deadly strike. However, Sarah's eyes blazed again and then Mikhail's gave an answering blaze of its own and the hair on their heads settled once more.

Hantsushept quickly contained and labeled the hair samples, then went to work drawing blood from each of them. When he was done, he stepped back far enough to be safe and cleared his throat. When the two merely continued staring at each other, Hantsushept cleared his throat again, but much more loudly this time.

The pair suddenly became aware of their surroundings and their eyes dulled a bit and broke contact.

"Are we finished?" Sarah asked.

Hantsushept made a harsh, guttural sound of ridicule. "You've only just begun, m'dear," he said. "Now, we need to get complete physicals for both of you, along with urine samples." He rummaged in his supply kit, which was apparently the Angelic physician's version of a doctor's black bag, and eventually pulled out two handy hermetically sealed plastic cups with lids, just like human physicians used.

Mikhail and Sarah looked at the cups, at each other, and then said in unison, "You've got to be kidding."

Hantsushept considered the cups, then said, "On second thought, why don't you just get these to me as soon as you can." He handed them the cups, then took out a hand-held device and approached Sarah.

Her hair immediately lifted, readying to strike, and she quickly said, "Sorry." She tried to gather it together to bind it, but it seemed to know what she was about and it swung wildly all over the place to avoid capture. Sarah suddenly heard Sheely's voice urgently whispering to her, almost frantic.

"What's wrong?" Mikhail asked, immediately covering Sheely's spot again with his hand.

"I don't know," Sarah said, shaking her head. She could hear Sheely's voice quite well, now. Sheely still used that other language, though, so Sarah had no idea what had upset her baby so. "We need Thomas," Sarah said. Thomas had been the only other person to hear Sheely; in fact, he'd even seemed to understand her judging from the fact that he'd been the one to tell them her name.

Mikhail looked at Hantsushept, then back at Sarah. He didn't want to leave her if something was wrong, but he knew Sarah was right about them needing Thomas for this.

"Mind-link with him," Sarah said.

"From this distance?" he asked. "I mean, I know I did it when he was mind-linked with you, it's just that..."

"Just try," she said, smiling up at him, though he could feel the worry inside her.

Mikhail took a deep breath, closed his eyes and concentrated. Within seconds, he found himself standing in a clearing all by himself, his hands and feet moving in practiced patterns of defensive and offensive strikes. Mikhail, who was *the* person to call on in times of war, did not recognize these routines. He'd never seen moves like these, nor did he understand what type of wounds these strikes intended, until he suddenly saw a rush of energy erupt from the hands he was pushing out before himself. When Mikhail looked around himself, he found he could see rivers of energy flowing around him, above him, below him, and even through him! He was amazed by the techniques the young body he was in utilized and he paid close attention to each maneuver, noting how stiff the muscles in this part of the body were, how lax they were in other parts, how much power the boy put into each thrust.

All of a sudden, Sheely's urgent voice sounded again and the boy immediately stopped.

Sheely? Mikhail heard Thomas' voice ask in his mind. Sheely's voice suddenly became much more than an urgent whisper as she frantically launched into a desperate diatribe with her half-brother. Mikhail knew immediately what she'd said, even though he still couldn't understand the language she spoke, himself. The fact that Thomas understood made it possible for Mikhail to understand. Mikhail reached out immediately and jerked Hantsushept away from Sarah, though she'd already let loose the hair strands she'd been holding.

"What on earth?" the Angelic physician demanded in an annoyed tone.

"The radiation from that device... Sheely says that's bad for her," Mikhail explained.

"Sheely says...?" Hantsushept echoed. Then, his face became utterly enraptured and he asked, "You can talk with the child? Understand her?"

"Thomas can," Sarah smiled proudly. "Mikhail can mind-link with Thomas, which allows us to understand her quite clearly."

Hantsushept's eyes widened as she said this and she realized he'd suddenly come to the realization that she and Mikhail were linked. A certain fear crept into her and Mikhail slowly grabbed her hand and gave it a gentle squeeze, silently saying in her mind, *Easy, love. He's a friend.*

Sarah swallowed the lump of fear in her throat and nodded slightly, though she didn't look at him. *I'm sorry,* she silently whispered to him. *I'm just nervous from dealing with all this.*

Mikhail quickly enfolded her body in his arms, holding her close to his chest. He felt a slight tremor dance through her limbs and he said, "You're exhausted, love. Go back to the shelter so you and Sheely can rest."

"But, the physicals," Hantsushept immediately complained.

"We're done for today," Mikhail stated, his tone brooking no arguments.

Sarah looked up at him. *Are you coming with us?*

Not right now, love. I need to go talk with Thomas.

A frown line appeared between her brows, but she nodded her understanding. Mikhail bent and kissed the frown line, then straightened and watched her walk away. He then nodded to Hantsushept and took off in the opposite direction.

Thomas was still in the clearing by himself when Mikhail arrived. He sat on a fallen tree trunk... waiting. Mikhail decided the best thing was to just be honest with the boy. He took a seat next to Thomas and was silent for a moment.

"Sheely okay?" Thomas finally asked.

Mikhail nodded, saying, "Thanks to you, yes." He looked around at the trees and rocks ringing the clearing.

Thomas was silent for a few moments. Mikhail let the silence stretch. He felt an odd energy coming off the boy. It vibrated in strange waves, its patterns unlike anything Mikhail

had thus far experienced with his newly-developed abilities. Eventually, Thomas asked, "Does my mom know?"

Mikhail nodded. "She saw."

Again, Thomas was quiet.

Mikhail leaned forward to rest his elbows on his knees. After a moment, he looked back over his shoulder at the boy. "You were the one who helped out in the battle, weren't you?"

Thomas tensed for a moment, but then figured he'd best get the whole thing out in the open here and now and nodded and said, "I remembered suddenly how to take down the vimanas."

Mikhail considered this for a moment, his eyes narrowed as he studied the young man beside him. He realized that even though Thomas looked like a boy, he most likely was something quite different, and he quietly and cautiously asked in a low voice, "You mind if I ask who you are?"

Thomas didn't immediately answer. Most of today, he'd been wondering that very same question. He'd been able to do some pretty incredible things over the past few days, like shooting out the EMP to bring down the vimanas, and they were all things he somehow already knew how to do, as if he'd learned them long, long ago. How could that be? He was just a kid. He hesitated before saying, "I-I'm... your son... Past that," he shrugged, "I... don't really know."

After a moment, Mikhail asked, "How much do you remember from before?"

Another hesitation, then, "Bits and pieces, mostly just pictures and feelings, though."

After another moment's hesitation, Mikhail looked back at the boy and offered, "Maybe we could work together, you and I, to figure out things? I mean, if you'd like to do that with me."

Thomas swallowed nervously, but after only a short hesitation, he nodded and said, "I'd like that, Mikhail..., er, Dad."

Mikhail quickly turned away from the boy to hide the tears forming in his eyes. "I'd like that, too, son," he said in as normal a voice as he was able to perform. He felt like dancing or flying or... *something* in celebration.

As he watched Mikhail walk away, Thomas felt a sadness settle over him. His mom and Mikhail were obviously changing into the same type of beings as Nera and those like her. They were confused and unsure of everything that was going on, he could tell. Thomas wanted to help, but he didn't know what to tell them. And now, on top of everything, Mikhail wanted to know who Thomas was? It seemed Mikhail, and through him Thomas' mom, had been able to get into Thomas' head without his knowledge and so they now knew he wasn't... normal.

Thomas couldn't remember. No one else seemed to know either, other than Nera, and she wasn't telling. Thomas didn't even know how to contact her.

All you need do is to think of contacting me, came Nera's voice in his mind.

Thomas suddenly found himself standing once more in the round room. The virtual monitors were powered down and dark. Nera and he were the only two in the room.

Thomas frowned at her. He wasn't happy with her. Too much had been going on and she'd simply abandoned him during it all.

"I did not abandon you, brat!" Nera scoffed. "I prepared you as best I could before you were forced into battle."

"But you didn't tell me anything about my mom and Mikhail changing into one of *your* kind!" Thomas nearly shouted, his anger with her a palpable thing.

Nera merely shrugged a shoulder. "As I said before," she explained breezily, "they're doing as they're supposed to be doing. Nothing more, nothing less." She moved over to peer at the darkened control panel on the round monitoring station. Then, she said in a low voice of warning, "Time grows short, though."

"What does *that* mean?" Thomas barked, frustration making him testy.

At that moment, another of her kind stepped into the room, just inside the passageway, and stood still for a moment staring at Nera. After a slight pause, Nera said, "Excuse me for a moment, please." She turned back to the monitoring station and touched a few places on the screen. After studying the scene on the screen before her, she turned and left without explanation. The screen remained active and Thomas approached it, curiosity winning out over anger.

He recalled the movements the others of Nera's kind had made when they'd been at their stations before and he copied them, finding he was able to switch between different places and individuals with just a wave of his hand in the correct place.

He didn't understand the writing or what looked like mathematical equations denoted on the virtual screen each time an image displayed, but it was something to do. He waved his hand and caught a glimpse of an old woman in a small house situated by a calm blue sea. He waved again and saw a young man in a sharp-looking business suit sitting behind a desk doing some sort of work on a computer. He waved again and everything suddenly went black.

He freaked out!

He waved again. Nothing. He waved again. Nothing. He waved yet again. Finally, a light appeared on the corner of the screen. It looked like some sort of spacecraft. Thomas wondered if this was a broadcast the monitor was somehow picking up or something. The image on the screen suddenly shifted and Thomas saw some kind of creature he had never seen before.

Nera chose that moment to return. She immediately noticed the image on the screen and quickly approached the station. Without asking, she stepped in front of Thomas, slightly shoving him to the side and taking control of the monitor. She waved her hands and pushed virtual buttons here and there causing the images on the screen to flash from one image to another and another. They were flying by so fast Thomas couldn't keep track of things. It all became one endless blur.

Finally, she switched off the monitor and turned to face him. Her face wore a deep frown... well, it was deep for her, at least.

"I'm still waiting for you to answer my questions, Nera," Thomas said.

"I shall answer all the questions I am allowed to answer," she cryptically said.

"Allowed?" he asked. "So, like... there are rules?"

Nera laughed, the sound healthy and full of joy. "Of course, there are rules," she said. "There are rules to everything in existence. The trick is to figure out what those rules are and just how rigid they are. Some of them can be broken under the right circumstances. Some can be by-passed all together. It just depends on the rule and the circumstances."

"So, what are the rules regarding the questions I have about who and what I am... and what's happening to my mom and Mikhail?" Thomas asked, annoyed once again.

"You should know," Nera intoned, a sly smile playing about her lips. "You created those rules yourself."

Thomas sucked in a shocked breath. He stood there looking around himself. Everything seemed so familiar to him. He felt as if he knew what everything here was, what its purpose was and how to use it, though for the life of him he couldn't think of any specifics. Everything was just... familiar beyond what it should have been.

Nera turned slowly to regard him, her face now a mask of ominous warning in and of itself. "You must remember, and soon, however," she said, her voice trembling. "If you haven't remembered by the time of their gathering, all will be lost."

He frowned, at a complete loss as to what she meant.

Nera approached and placed both hands on his cheeks. "Remember, my love... remember!"

Thomas immediately jerked awake from the vision. He stood in the clearing, birds chirping, bugs buzzing around in the air, the sound of the river nearby as it gurgled and rushed over the rocks in the rapids.

How had that happened? He'd never before entered or left the visions as quickly as he had this time. There'd been no warning, nothing. He'd simply gone from one reality to another in a flash. Whose *gathering* had she spoken of and why had she called him her *love*? Yuck! She'd called him brat on several occasions. That he could deal with. Her getting all mushy on him? No way! He might think she was beautiful and all, but... no way!

Thomas' stomach growled and he decided he'd deal with all of this later. He headed off in the direction of the main shelter. Miriam should be helping with afternoon tea about now, so he knew he would be able to sneak some of those delicious cookies she always made about this time of day, and maybe some of that juice he liked so much, too!

Hantsushept looked a bit nervous. "Well, I've completed my initial investigation into some of the issues you've been experiencing," he said. "I must remind you that, although I've studied human and Angelic anatomy and physiology for ages, I still have only a cursory understanding of *your* make-up. Although you appear to be similarly built to us, I'm afraid it will take a great deal more time and research to obtain a clearer understanding of the functions allowing for your... ah, particular oddities." He paused, as if waiting for them to comment on his diatribe.

Mikhail and Sarah merely stared unblinking at him.

"Yes, well...," he cleared his throat. "On the subject of your anatomy, m'dear," he said, motioning toward Sarah. "You definitely have Seraph characteristics; at least, for all intents and purposes, you appear to be Seraph-like."

No change showed on the faces of the creatures before him.

Hantsushept cleared his throat again. "Yes, well. After my initial examination of the hair follicle samples we took, and of the blood samples, my assistants and I have been able to map your DNA down to, um, its base pairs." Here, he paused.

Still, the two before him remained silent and still.

"Um, humans have around three billion base pairs and Angels around the same, maybe a little less." When no response was forthcoming still, Hantsushept continued, "Well, um, it appears the two of you have about the same as this."

The pair's eyes narrowed slightly, but that was the only sign of reaction displayed.

"Yes, so, as I was saying, it appears the two of you have around three billion base pairs. As one would expect, this makes your genetic make-up fairly easy to map since it's apparently so similar to ours, though one has to consider many other factors as well, of course."

"How does this pertain to Sheely?" the pair asked simultaneously.

Hantsushept shook his head. "I'll have to have a sample of amniotic fluid in order to tell you much of anything useful about Sheely, I'm afraid. I was able to confirm the pregnancy from the levels of HCG in the blood samples, but anything more would require a sample of the amniotic fluid."

The pair was silent.

"It's a common enough practice in the human and Angelic realms, drawing samples of amniotic fluid," Hantsushept said defensively.

After a moment, Sarah nodded and asked, "Where do I need to go to change?"

Hantsushept rose to show her into a makeshift examination room off of his temporary office. Mikhail remained seated before the desk. He couldn't bear the thought of Hantsushept touching any part of Sarah's body, much less the idea of him inserting a very long needle into her, so he decided to stay put.

Sarah continued assuring him in her mind that everything was fine. She changed into an exam gown and laid on the exam table. She wasn't the best patient at the best of times, let alone when she was afraid something might be wrong, but she knew she had to be brave, if not for Sheely's sake, then for Mikhail's.

You are brave, love, Mikhail's voice reassured her silently.

Hantsushept slowly inserted the long needle into Sarah's abdomen, careful of the placement so as not to damage Sheely's tiny form. As he withdrew fluid from within the sac, he gasped slightly. The liquid inside the syringe glowed with a bright iridescence, rather like that which appeared to fill the orbs within Sarah's and Mikhail's eye sockets.

Sarah and Mikhail heard a fair amount of protest from Sheely at the intrusion into her perfect little world, but the tone suggested mere annoyance rather than panic, so they both just whispered soothingly to their unborn daughter. She quieted as soon as Hantsushept's needle was removed and Sarah quickly dressed and returned to Mikhail's side. He placed a hand on Sheely's spot, whispering to her and Sarah in soothing tones in his mind the whole time.

When Hantsushept had handed off the glowing fluid to one of his Angelic assistants, he resumed his seat behind his desk.

"So, you have evidence proving Sarah is a Seraph, you said?" Mikhail asked.

Hantsushept quickly corrected him. "No, no. I said she has Seraph characteristics and that she appears to be Seraph-like," he explained. "I was able to obtain some blood and tissue and hair samples from your Seraphim brethren, Djibril and Israfil and, when I compared both of your samples with both of theirs, I discovered something a bit… disturbing."

When he merely sat back in his chair to stare at them without further elaboration, Mikhail looked at Sarah, who raised her brows and shrugged, then he looked expectantly back at the Angelic physician.

Hantsushept ran a hand through his hair in frustration and finally said, "From what we've been able to see so far, you both appear to be something else… and, you both seem to have… to have some new form… of… cancer."

Fear shot through Sarah immediately at the mention of this word. Every human in the modern world who knew anything about cancer feared that word. Sarah's own mother was a breast cancer survivor, so Sarah knew how difficult a thing it was to beat.

Mikhail felt Sarah's fear and so a part of him reacted to it, even though he, himself, feared no mortal illness or disease. He wasn't sure about Sarah's and Sheely's constitutions, though. Were they, like he, immune to such things?

"Wait," Sarah said. "You said we *both* appear to have it?"

Hantsushept nodded.

"You mean Sheely and me?"

"No, I mean you and Mikhail."

Sarah and Mikhail looked at each other in confusion. "How can Mikhail have...?"

"How can he no longer be a Seraph?" Hantsushept interrupted to ask, shrugging. "I don't know the answers to these questions. All I know is that a good many of the cells in your body seem to be stuck in cell division mode, which is what all cancers basically do, so that the cells cannot perform their otherwise intended functions. So, either you both have some new form of cancer, or..." He stopped and stared at them expectantly again.

"Or what?" Mikhail demanded.

"Or...," he shook his head, "you're not done yet?" He stared at them once more, as if waiting for them to give him the answer, his gaze darting back and forth between the two.

"Done what?" Mikhail asked impatiently.

Hantsushept shrugged, "Forming? Evolving...? Your guess is as good as mine."

Can we go now? Sarah silently asked of Mikhail. *I don't like this.*

Mikhail reached to take her hand. "I think we need to think about things a bit, Hantsushept," Mikhail said, rising to shake hands with the Angel.

Hantsushept nodded and shook Mikhail's hand. "We'll keep studying these samples," he said. "Hopefully, we'll find some good news for you soon."

As the two walked back toward their temporary shelter, they could hear Sheely's happy chatter. Sarah rubbed Sheely's spot lightly. Her hand was always over Sheely and she quite often rubbed absently on the spot.

Mikhail gently held Sarah to his side with an arm around her shoulder. He could feel her disquiet and he silently assured her, *I don't believe we have anything to worry about, love.*

I know, she thought back to him, reaching up to give a squeeze to the hand on her shoulder. *But, if we don't have some here-to-for unheard of disease, then what is happening to us?*

Mikhail frowned as he pondered her question.

Do you think it'll affect my human family as well? Sarah silently asked.

Mikhail hugged her, then thought, *We'll just have to keep an eye on them. Humans, I can heal. I-I don't think there's anything technically wrong with* us *simply because I cannot detect any disturbances in our energy flow. That's normally how I'm able to detect illness or injury in others.*

Sarah squeezed his hand again and smiled reassuringly up at him.

Sheely's chatter continued on.

Chapter 19

"I told you he'd never go for it," Israfil said matter-of-factly as he stared at his brother across the desk before him. He and Gabriel were seated in Gabriel's office at the statehouse discussing the failed attempts they'd made at even just gaining an audience with both Azra'il and the Sanhedrin, both Great and Lesser. No one wanted to talk with them. Not one Angel in the entire city who hadn't already pledged fealty to one or the other of them. Israfil wasn't so sure all of those would be willing to talk with either of them at the moment, judging from the reactions they'd gotten so far since they'd returned.

No one had actually come out and said anything disrespectful to either of them. They *were* Seraphim, after all. It would be unthinkable. The only one who might do something that drastic would be Azra'il, and he was suddenly nowhere to be found. Even the elite Sanhedrin Guard had no clue as to his whereabouts. Israfil worried about this fact. Azra'il was not one to back down from a fight, so the fact that he was missing in action meant something was up.

"So what are we supposed to do, then?" Gabriel asked. "I don't even feel comfortable in my own home anymore." He sighed in frustration. This whole mess was becoming far more tedious as the day wore on and Gabriel was nearing the point where all he wanted was to wash his hands of it and move out to the Badlands with Mikhail and Sarah. At least there he was accepted, not looked down upon and avoided by all and sundry.

He definitely felt like a third wheel here. His man, Khamet, who had been involved in the poisoning incident with Sarah and her human family, had suddenly disappeared and Gabriel was finding it difficult getting along in his own home. He didn't know where anything was and no one there seemed to want to have anything to do with him. He'd escaped to his office this morning just so he wouldn't feel like he was intruding on everyone else's territory. As he looked across his desk at his brother, Gabriel figured Israfil had probably come to the statehouse for the same reason. He hadn't said so, but he'd been just kind of hanging out for the past hour or so, not really having a purpose, but not seeming in a hurry to leave.

Israfil suddenly focused his attention on a non-existent speck of dust on his perfectly-pressed slacks, reaching out to pluck it from his pants leg and saying softly, "What if what Mikhail suggested is true?"

Gabriel didn't need any explanation as to which thing Israfil was referring to. Ever since Mikhail had suggested that there might be the possibility of more humans being out there who were designed specifically to be Seraphim mates, Gabriel had wondered about it. He could not recall a time when he hadn't dreamed of having his own family, a true mate of his own with whom he could reproduce.

He, too, avoided eye contact with his brother as he swallowed a lump in his throat and said, "I think we'd best deal with one issue at a time, don't you?" It wasn't that he didn't want to discuss the possibility that there was a mate for each of them out there just waiting to be found by their Seraph opposite. It was just that... until everything in Seraphim City was settled on the whole human issue, there was going to be no peace. That wouldn't bode well for bringing more humans into this realm.

"Honestly," Israfil said, "I think we may be better off just moving out to the Badlands with Mikhail and Sarah."

After a second, Gabriel nodded and said, "I think you're right. Things here are not going to change for some time, it seems. Going there might just be the best until it calms down here."

Israfil nodded and said, "It would also give us the opportunity we need to get to know more about Sarah – and Mikhail, for that matter."

Gabriel's eyebrows shot up and he nodded. They definitely needed to understand more about what was going on with their brother and his woman before they even entertained the notion of the possibility of going out and discovering their own human counterparts.

Just then, a knock sounded on the door and Gabriel called, "Come."

A liveried messenger of the Great Sanhedrin entered carrying a sheaf of papers. The Angel approached the desk without greeting the two Seraphim. Then, he read from the top page of the stack of papers he held, announcing, "By order of the High Commander of the Great Sanhedrin, Seraph Djibril and Seraph Israfil are hereby to be placed under arrest pending further investigation into the murders of three elite Sanhedrin Guardsmen and one Khamet, Angel third class, of the House of Djibril. Said Seraphim are to submit willingly to their interment in order to immediately be transported to the Great Council Chamber where the Great Sanhedrin has convened to hear testimony regarding the case. Any resistance to such interment will be deemed a formal admission of guilt and will result in immediate expulsion from the boundaries of Seraphim City for all time."

Both Gabriel and Israfil sat in stunned silence. The messenger looked from one to the other of them. Then, again without a word, he retraced his steps to the door and opened it to allow an assemblage of about twenty elite Sanhedrin Guardsmen to enter into the room, each one coming to a halt in a defensive position, as if already anticipating a fight from the two Seraphim still seated at the desk before them.

Israfil was the first to recover from the astonishingly outlandish announcement, as he turned to his brother and said, "Well, at least we now know where Azra'il is." He stood and turned to the elite Guards awaiting them. Without another word, he held out both of his hands and was immediately bound with one of the binding tapes the blessed Great Designers had given the Seraphim millennia ago. The tapes blocked energy flow to the degree that they actually caused a very unpleasant sensation throughout ones entire nervous system. This rendered a Seraph powerless, unable to employ his shields for even the simplest endeavor.

Azra'il wasn't taking any chances.

Israfil offered no resistance and the elite Guards whisked him out the door and down the hallway toward the Great Council Chamber. Gabriel swallowed a great lump in his throat and slowly rose to step out from behind his desk. He, too, offered his hands up in immediate surrender, remaining silent and compliant. He knew this might be the only opportunity he and Israfil would get to plead their case on behalf of the humans and he didn't want to cause any chance for reprisal for anything he might inadvertently say while in captivity.

Azra'il had to be made to understand the bigger picture here. Gabriel just hoped it wasn't already too late, as Israfil suspected. He gasped as the binding tapes were slapped onto his wrists, the pain shooting immediately up through the neurons in his arms to his spinal cord, making it almost impossible for him to even breathe. The elite Guards roughly shoved him through the doorway out into the hall. Rows of Angels, sometimes three and four deep, lined the hallway from his office to the Great Council Chamber and Gabriel wondered if this was as big a spectacle as it appeared to him to be.

What did he do, sell tickets? Gabriel thought to himself. He said not a word, though, and was soon being shoved roughly through the doorway of the Great Council Chamber which, as the messenger had stated, was in full attendance for the hearing. He was led over to a side demi-enclosure where Israfil was already seated. Without a word, the elite Guard to his right rudely pushed a chair up behind Gabriel's knees, knocking him backward onto the hard seat, then walked away, closing the gate to the enclosure and taking up position just outside it.

Azra'il moved to the center of the room. He turned a full 360 degrees, looking at the members of the Great Sanhedrin assembled within the council chamber. Inside, he felt empty. He'd lost everything. He stood before this council of Angels as their last hope... all because of some ignorant creatures from another dimension.

As he thought of humans, he cringed, his teeth grinding together in his anger. It was because of humans he'd lost his beloved brothers. It was because of humans his own people no longer felt safe in their own homes. It was because of humans Angels had recently died in this dimension. There'd been no reason for their deaths. Angels were not, by their very nature, violent creatures. Humans, on the other hand, were born that way. They knew no other way to be. No matter how many visitations Azra'il's kind made with them, the humans simply could not grasp the concept of living peaceably with one another.

And now, there was the report that Djibril's man, Khamet, was dead. What a waste. Khamet had been Djibril's loyal manservant for millennia... now, he was dust. Azra'il wasn't sure if Angels were like humans in getting to return after death. He'd never seen an Angel with a soul-string and they were supposedly immortal. However, lately they'd all seen just how mythological *that* particular notion was.

"My fellow council members," he began. "I stand before you today to present evidence of the most heinous crimes ever committed within our dimension. Crimes that have resulted in the deaths of four of our own elite Sanhedrin Guardsmen, one maid and one loyal manservant who did nothing more than to protect their masters to the best of their ability.

"Of course, all of the evidence presented today could be classified as hearsay or circumstantial, at best. The eyewitness accounts are of things lower-class Angels could never be able to actually see, but multiple Angels witnessing the same things all at the same time should be proof enough for this council to gain a clear understanding of the events that unfolded in such a horrific manner as to result in the deaths of the four elite Sanhedrin Guardsmen and the two loyal servants.

"Said eyewitness accounts will show beyond a shadow of a doubt that the Seraphim you see sitting in this very room, if they were not the actual perpetrators of these crimes themselves, then were willing accomplices to and supporters of those who committed such heinous acts within our realm.

"Ladies and gentlemen of this great council, I am not proud to stand before you as a Seraph. I have lived my entire existence within the Angelic realm, protecting those who live here, forging agreements with each and every one of you to make sure this realm remains a safe and peaceful place for you all to raise your families.

"My brethren, when they are allowed to speak on their own behalf, will try to convince you that your future here is dependent upon humans being allowed into this realm. They will extol the virtues of humanity and plead for your sympathies toward those less fortunate creatures. My brethren will also speak of a coming change that will only occur if Angels and humans work together.

"I stand before you today to implore you to avoid the trap they set, for they are delusional. They have been duped by humans into believing Angel society is outdated and unable to continue functioning as it has done for millennia. My brothers will attempt to persuade you to believe you are no better than humans and that those hate-filled, warring creatures are your only salvation until the blessed Great Designers return. Indeed, I would not be surprised to hear them attempt to convince you that this was all planned by the blessed Great Designers themselves.

"Allowing humans into this realm was never planned by our beloved Designers and my brothers well know it!" Azra'il walked over to face his brothers, leaning on the wood railing surrounding the enclosure where they were housed. His eyes looked tired, but they were filled with absolute resolution when he looked into the eyes of each of his brothers seated there and the two knew immediately there was no hope of convincing him of anything having to do with the humans, nor with Mikhail and Sarah.

"Ladies and gentlemen," Azra'il said in his final turn, "I ask only that you judge my brothers fairly. You have elected me to the position of High Commander of this great council, even after what my brother, our former High Commander, did and I respectfully and humbly accepted the position. In doing so, I understood the absolute necessity of putting my own feelings aside for the greater good.

"My brothers and I are much heartier creatures than you yourselves will ever be. We've understood for all time what it means to be the caretakers of those weaker than ourselves and we've always stood for what is right and just. I never believed there would come a day when any Seraph would put his own desires before the safety and livelihood of the people.

"Until a human was brought into this realm, none of the four of us would ever have even thought of such a thing as being a possibility. However, that human was brought into this realm and one of our kind did put his own desires before his duties to his people and we see now the destructive power such actions can wield. One human caused this simply by the destructive tendencies inherent in her entire race.

"Some might say she ought to be granted clemency due to the fact that she did not choose to be destructive, that it was merely a by-product of her genetic pre-disposition. I tell you, my brothers knew of these inherent destructive tendencies in humans, yet they continued to consort with her until and even after Angelic deaths occurred. Indeed, they may have even caused Angelic deaths themselves, either by their own hands or by omission of action.

"Therefore, I cannot ask you to be lenient with these two, my brothers. I ask again only that you judge them fairly and in good faith. For their crimes, I am without doubt the blessed Great Designers shall inflict suitable punishment upon their return. How my beloved brothers will manage to live with themselves, knowing of their crimes against all Angel kind, until such time I cannot imagine." His opening speech given, Azra'il returned to his seat high above the council to preside over the hearing, though he did not look again in the direction of the enclosure housing his two brothers.

The higher council members called forth witness after witness, which was really just a practice in interviewing one elite Guardsman after another to find out what had happened when they had been sent to arrest Sarah Baker for the murder of the Angel Narayana. Afterward, the elite Guards from the battle in the Badlands were each brought up for interrogation, all fifty plus of them. Most of them didn't remember much since they'd only just awakened from their unnatural slumber in the forest a day ago, but the vimana pilots from the battle recalled enough to astonish the council members and gasps of shock and fear were heard throughout the assemblage.

Gabriel's manservant, the Angel Khamet, had been found by an Angelic cook last night in a back alleyway of Seraphim City with his throat sliced nearly all the way through. Gabriel and Israfil had been back for nearly two days now. This clearly indicated they had something to do with the murder, never mind the fact that neither one of them had even seen the Angel since they'd returned. Throughout the entire testimony period, Azra'il remained stone still on his chair, never once glancing toward his brothers. Gabriel and Israfil merely stared forward, unblinking, awaiting the end of the hearing so they could get on with their plan of moving permanently out to the Badlands with Mikhail and Sarah.

When it finally came time for Israfil and Gabriel to speak on their own behalf, they'd been sitting for nearly twelve hours without a break. They were hungry, tired, and they desperately needed to use the restroom. However, Israfil dutifully rose and approached the railing of the enclosure to say his peace. He did not address the council, however. Instead, he turned and looked up at Azra'il.

"My brother, I am a simple Seraph," he said. "I was not born with such grand abilities as you and my other brothers, as you well know. I was not made to see soul-strings or energy fluctuations, nor was I created possessing telepathic abilities or foresight as to what may yet be, nor was I put on this planet to fight unbeatable odds without fear of losing. I am just what I am. However, I have seen with my own humble eyes that which you refuse to look upon and I have discovered a thing which was not known to me all my life. I have discovered hope... Hope for myself, for my brothers, for all Angel kind and for all Humans. This hope does not depend on our beloved Designers, but I believe it was part of their plan for all of us, as you mentioned earlier in your speech. So, yes, I do believe humans and Angels are fated to be together."

Several snickers were heard around the room, but Azra'il's expression remained the same.

"I ask only that when you finally do come to your senses and open your eyes to the possibility... *just the possibility* that there could be something more out there waiting for you... you don't fear it. I want you to be willing to at least take a chance that it *is* real, that something else *does* exist, and I want you to reach for it with all your might because it could just turn out to be the most miraculous thing you've ever found... because I love you enough to still want that for you, even though you now send me and my brother away from you because of your fear of this thing. That is all I have to say."

Israfil moved back to his seat and sat, heaving a sigh of relief that he'd done all he could to get through to his most beloved brother. He doubted Azra'il would heed his advice on this day. However, there was always the possibility that his words would someday reach beyond Azra'il's stubbornness. That was all Israfil could hope for, and so he kept that little amount of hope inside, holding onto it for later. He watched as Gabriel stood and approached the railing and then a funny thing happened. As he sat there silently awaiting judgment, he suddenly heard a soft voice in his mind.

Gabriel stood and approached the railing, never once glancing upward, and simply said, "You're all wrong. We have done nothing but protect those in need of protection and now you're telling us that is unacceptable. Well, as far as that goes, I don't wish to live somewhere where one is not deemed worthy of protection merely because of their species. I am not better than any creature on this planet and I will do what I must to protect all in need of such protection, even when it means I must give up my life as I have known it for millennia and my home.

"Condemn me to the Badlands and I shall willingly go, for this is no longer the homeland in which I learned and dreamed and discovered so much. I shall proudly be banished to the outer reaches of our realm in order to start a new life with those willing to sacrifice, to stand up for what is right and just for all." After a slight pause, he said finally, "That is all I have to say to any of you." He returned to his chair and sat. He noticed Israfil's face and he became a little uneasy. His brother looked as if he was in some sort of trance.

The council immediately erupted in loud shouts and angry retorts and Gabriel turned his attention back to what was going on around them. Azra'il remained still on his seat, as did his other brother. The council would argue out what judgment was to be passed down and then they'd vote. All three Seraphim knew this process could take hours, if not days, and Gabriel was on the verge of asking for a restroom break when astonishingly the highest council member next to Azra'il called for the vote.

The house calmed amazingly quickly as each member bent to cast his or her vote. Within minutes, the thing was done. A liveried attendee was handed the final results of the vote in a sealed envelope, which he took immediately up for Azra'il's inspection. After he'd looked at the results and returned them to the envelope, Azra'il nodded and gave the envelope back to the attendee, who then proceeded back to the floor of the council room for the official reading of the decision.

"On this day, before the assemblage of the Great Sanhedrin in its entirety, along with its High Commander, it is ruled that Seraph Djibril and Seraph Israfil have been found guilty of aiding and abetting those responsible for the murders of four elite Seraphim Guardsmen and the Angel Narayana. It is also deemed that said Seraphim are guilty and fully responsible for the murder of the Angel Khamet.

"Punishment for the afore-mentioned crimes has been ruled upon and found to be that of death by Starcor."

Amid shocked gasps and loud shouts of denial, Gabriel sat in stunned silence, his mouth hanging wide open, eyes wide with disbelief. Starcor was a device the blessed Great Designers had given the Seraphim to utilize in only a worst-case scenario. It reversed ATP synthesis within the body, causing a complete breakdown of all systems instantaneously by robbing the body of all energy. Even though Seraphim were immortal, their bodies still required ATP to keep cells energized and without it, they would cease to function, essentially killing the Seraph as well.

Mikhail had once gone so far as to give humans instructions on the architecture of the device a while ago so that it could be used to win a war. It worked very effectively, but it had to be kept hidden now for fear of one of the human governments obtaining it and using it for their own ends. It was hidden deep within the walls of the Vatican to this day, though most others believed it to be housed in some secret location in Jerusalem or somewhere else in Africa.

Suddenly, without warning, everyone in the council chamber seemed to go mad. Angels were babbling incoherently, walking around in circles, bumping into each other, confusion painfully etched on each one's face. There was a flash of brilliance from the center of the room and then suddenly, Mikhail was standing there, his shields having dropped completely to fully expose his presence.

He turned his brilliant eyes on Gabriel and said, "Help our brother." Gabriel's gaze darted immediately to Israfil and he noted that his brother was still in whatever trance condition he'd been in earlier. He stood and took the couple of steps between Israfil and himself until he could grab hold of Israfil's arm with both hands, though they were still bound by the painful tapes. He pulled up on Israfil and was finally able to get him into a standing position. Israfil's gaze remained fixed on some point in space and he seemed completely unaware of anything going on in the room around him.

"What's happening?" Gabriel demanded of Mikhail as he led Israfil's stiff, uncooperative body through the gate of the enclosure and then over to Mikhail's form in the middle of the room. He could hear Azra'il's voice screaming out in damning denial, though it didn't seem as if Azra'il was actually aware of what was going on with Israfil and Gabriel and Mikhail.

"We must go," was all Mikhail said and he immediately wrapped his two brothers in his own shields and took off. The wailing gibberish coming from the confused Angels crowding the council chamber room disappeared and Israfil finally released a gust of air and lost consciousness.

Gabriel merely held onto his unconscious brother for dear life, wondering what on earth had just happened, but too thankful to have been rescued to voice any further questions regarding the past few minutes. After just a moment of flight, he closed his eyes tightly in order to keep from becoming sick. They were whisking through the sky at such an incredible speed that all he saw below and around them were streaks of light. He squeezed his eyes shut and prayed to his beloved Designers that they would all make it out of this in one piece.

Within minutes, they were touching down in a clearing by the river near their settlement. Several Angels looked at them as Mikhail's shields dropped, but none bothered to approach the Seraph. Gabriel lifted his still-unconscious brother's form and carried him immediately in the direction of Hantsushept's temporary offices, the painful binding tapes on his wrists forgotten for the moment as concern for his brother took precedence.

Mikhail followed along silently, the vitreous liquid in the pupils of his glowing eyes ever swirling.

As the brothers entered the office, Hantsushept and one of his assistants were already there waiting for them, along with Sarah who walked smoothly over to sidle up next to Mikhail. Their two pairs of glowing eyes turned to watch as the Angelic physician and his assistant went to work on the unconscious Seraph.

After only a moment, Hantsushept assured them all Israfil merely slumbered in a deep sleep state and that he would be fine after he'd replenished some energy through his natural processes. Gabriel looked unsure, even though he was exhausted himself. After only a moment's hesitation, Mikhail stepped forward and placed a hand on his brother's shoulder, assuring him, "I will stay with our brother for the evening. You go and rest now."

The bindings on Gabriel's hands miraculously became unclasped and fell to the ground. Gabriel stared stupefied at the now defunct bindings and then thankfully nodded to Mikhail and turned and left the office.

Sarah took care of the bindings still trapping Israfil's arms and hands and then approached Mikhail's side once more. After wrapping an arm around his hips, she thought to him, *He didn't like havin' me inside his mind like that. He might not be so happy when he wakes up.*

Mikhail squeezed her hand. He hadn't even known about the ability Sarah had just hijacked from Israfil, but she'd used it through Israfil and it had worked to perfection. There'd been no difficulty retrieving his brothers from the angry mob within the Council Chamber. Even Azra'il had been affected by Israfil's hidden talent.

Mikhail decided he would deal with the issue of how Sarah had found out about Israfil's here-to-fore hidden talent later and he responded mentally to her, saying, *It'll be fine, love. You and Sheely go rest, for the now. Israfil and I will be just fine here.* He leaned down to place a soft kiss on her forehead and then on her lips. He immediately wanted to whisk her off her feet and out of the office to some secluded area where they could spend the rest of the night making love. However, his feelings for his brother were strong and he knew Israfil would have questions when he awakened. So, he watched silently as Sarah and Sheely left the office.

Hantsushept re-entered the room and took readings from the patient, marking them on a chart and then leaving the room again. His bedside manner was not quite what some would like. *He gets the job done, though,* Mikhail thought.

After a few more minutes of just standing there watching his brother breathing in and out and in and out, Mikhail became bored. He walked over to the bedside and reached out a hand to touch his brother's arm. Immediately, Mikhail's natural healing abilities kicked into gear and he found he was able to pool enough energy to sufficiently replenish Israfil's reserves to the point that he no longer needed to remain asleep. Mikhail stepped back a bit, breaking his contact with his brother as Israfil gained full consciousness.

Israfil looked around the room, noticing Mikhail first, then the fact that he was no longer in the council chamber, but some other place. "Where...?" he asked, his voice groggy.

"You're in my temporary offices," Hantsushept answered him as he once again entered the room. He shot an annoyed look at the other creature in the room. He'd only been gone a couple of minutes and yet the creature had taken it upon himself to go and wake up the patient! "*If* you don't mind," he said to the glowing creature, Mikhail, "I need to examine the patient. So, if you'd just wait outside...?" He held a hand out toward the door to the little room, waiting expectantly for Mikhail to exit before he started his examination.

Mikhail looked from one to the other of them and then nodded once and left.

Turning back to his patient, Hantsushept said, "Now, let's get you sitting up so I can make sure you're functioning properly all over, shall we?"

Israfil assisted the Angelic physician in getting himself into an upright sitting position on the bed, though he mostly relied on Hantsushept, since his strength seemed a bit low at the moment. "What happened to me?" he asked the Angel.

Hantsushept paused to look at Israfil and then continued with his examination, saying, "I should think you would be the best one to answer that question. Now, take a deep breath."

Israfil breathed in, holding it until the physician instructed him to release it. After a couple more deep breaths, Hantsushept moved on. Israfil looked over to the closed door Mikhail had used to leave the room and asked simply, "What's going on with my brother?"

Hantsushept regarded the Seraph, noticed the direction he was looking and even looked himself before returning his attention to his work, saying, "I believe your brother and his mate have been undergoing a new evolution."

Israfil frowned in confusion, so Hantsushept explained, saying, "They seem to be evolving into a more advanced version of Seraphim. They may even have completed their evolution, though one can never tell with these things, you know."

There wasn't much Israfil knew about all this scientific jargon, so he remained quiet for the remainder of the examination. After a few minutes, Hantsushept announced, "Well, you seem to be fit as a fiddle, except for the fact that you still need some rest. I think it would be best to keep you here for the next few hours for observation, but other than that you should be okay to go in the morning. I'll go see about getting you moved to a more comfortable bed."

Israfil nodded and laid back down on the cushioned table as the Angelic physician left the room. Mikhail entered as soon as Hantsushept was gone and took a stance over by the far wall on the other side of the room from Israfil, leaning against it for support.

Israfil regarded his brother in wonder. Since coming to live in the Badlands, Mikhail and Sarah had become so much more different than anything Israfil had ever encountered. He could sense a calmness in the energies Mikhail emitted, though they were the purest tones he had ever felt. Israfil had long ago discovered he had the ability to sense and ultimately control the energy flow in others. He didn't often choose to employ the use of his gift because he believed it was too tempting a way to take away the free will of others.

Now, however, Israfil was faced with a new energy pattern, one that displayed only small, uncontrolled tremors, not the regular wild fluctuations like what he was used to when he was around others. Most people, Angelic and human alike, displayed pulses of wildly-fluctuating energy patterns as their brains took care of the everyday running of their bodies' regulatory systems. This was their autonomic nervous system. People didn't have to think about the things it took care of, such as breathing in and out, making one's heart continue beating, digesting food, etc. Their bodies just automatically ensured the smooth and continued functioning of all those systems without their hosts having to be aware of such work. But the smooth pulses coming from Mikhail suggested he was very much aware of, and in conscious control of, each and every energy wave he emitted... or at least as close to it as one could be.

As he thought this, Israfil realized the glowing eyes before him were trained directly on him. After a slight hesitation, he asked, "Are... Are you able to read my thoughts?"

Mikhail's brilliant eyes continued their study without waver, the liquid inside swirling in its iridescence. "We can enter one's conscious mind without difficulty now, though it does not please us to do so without one's permission," Mikhail finally said, his voice soft and low.

Israfil shivered slightly. He realized Hantsushept's theory that Mikhail and Sarah had evolved into higher beings than Seraphim might not be far off the mark. "We?" he asked. When Mikhail failed to answer, Israfil asked, "Are you mind-linked with another right now?"

"We are always linked," Mikhail said. "There is no separation... other than the physical forms we occupy."

Again, Israfil shivered and he blinked a few times, his mind having difficulty wrapping around the idea of never being alone in one's own mind. How was that even possible?

The glowing, swirling gaze merely stared at him.

Israfil imagined he could hear the pulsing of a slow heartbeat from somewhere. As the silence stretched, he not only heard it, but he began to feel it, as well! He swallowed a huge lump in his throat and was never so glad to see Hantsushept as he was when the grouchy Angelic physician suddenly entered the room to get Israfil moved to a more comfortable bed. After just one look at his patient, Hantsushept ordered Mikhail away from the office, assuring him he would be notified if there was any change in Israfil's condition.

As Mikhail left, so too did the sound and feel of the foreign heartbeat and Israfil slumped back onto the bed he was on in relief. After he'd been transferred to his new bed in another wing of the office, Israfil lay awake for the remainder of the night thinking about the changes he'd noticed in Mikhail and Sarah. Underneath it all, however, Israfil's mind kept circling back around to the two questions he absolutely needed answers to: Was there another out there in the human realm that had been designed specifically for him? If so, did that mean he would evolve as well should he and the human somehow manage to come together with each other?

Chapter 20

Gabriel knocked once on the door to the main chamber suite of the house. The door opened almost immediately, as if his visit had been anticipated. The Angel who'd opened the door silently motioned for Gabriel to follow him into the inner sanctum of the suite of rooms. Gabriel did so without comment.

Once the double doors to the next room were opened, Gabriel stepped through and then stopped in his tracks. They looked so different. There was almost no resemblance now to the pair he'd known before. Their eyes were steadily glowing, their hair was all white, the glow coming off their skin was so bright. Neither one of the two creatures before him spoke or even moved. They just sat there in their chairs, side by side, each holding the other's hand and staring unwaveringly at their guest.

The Angel who'd shown Gabriel into the sitting room quietly left, closing the double doors behind him. Gabriel didn't even notice. Instead, he approached the two creatures seated before him and only stopped when he was but a yard away from them. He felt awkward, as if he ought to bow down before the pair or something, though he refrained from doing so. Hesitantly, he spoke. "I-I'd like to know what happened yesterday," he said.

The two creatures made no move, still staring unwaveringly at him.

Gabriel cleared his throat and said, "I mean, I'm very grateful you rescued Israfil and me, but I would like to know

363

what happened... how you managed it." When no response was forthcoming, he tried a different tack. "Why was Israfil affected the way he was during the rescue?"

Mikhail's head turned and he looked at the double doors to the room just as they opened to admit Israfil. The newly-arrived Seraph approached the center of the room where Gabriel stood as the Angel who'd shown him into the room left again, quietly closing the double doors once more. The two Seraphim stood waiting for some explanation as to how the two creatures before them had pulled off their rescue the day before.

Sarah disengaged her hand from Mikhail's and stood. "My brothers," she whispered.

Israfil and Gabriel each gasped as they heard her voice not only from the words she'd spoken physically, but at the multiple layers of sound and information coming from her both physically and psychically, all at the same time.

Gabriel heard the spoken set of information. "You will return to Seraphim City with Hantsushept to collect as many supplies as possible so that we may continue on here," she said softly. "See to your people. Make sure they are safe. Bring with you any and all who feel the desire to return with you. All of Angel kind is welcome here, should anyone feel the need."

In his mind, however, Gabriel heard her voice as it said, *You will understand all that has transpired soon enough, my brother. All I ask of you now is that you bear with us as certain events unfold.*

Gabriel nodded hesitantly and bowed slightly. He couldn't help it. The frequencies coming off her were unbelievable and he felt as if he was in the presence of some sort of higher being, so he bowed.

Go, now, her voice echoed throughout the recesses of his mind. *Be safe and return soon to us, beloved brother.*

Gabriel turned immediately and exited the room to go in search of the Angelic physician.

Throughout her exchange with Gabriel, Israfil had been listening to a separate set of instructions through thoughts. As Gabriel left, Israfil stared in new-found appreciation at Sarah as he came to understand that she was communicating on a level he had never before even imagined. She'd assured him Mikhail was still innocent of the information she had learned about Israfil, other than his ability to control other people's minds which, she'd explained, had been necessary to inform Mikhail of in order to save Israfil and Gabriel from the angry mob in the council chamber yesterday.

Her voice whispered as an afterthought through the corridors of his mind, asking that he accompany Gabriel and Hantsushept on a journey back into Seraphim City. She wanted him to keep watch over the two of them and anyone else who chose to return with them to the new Badlands Complex to live.

Israfil doubted seriously that anyone currently residing within the walls of Seraphim City would wish to cohabitate with humans in any way, shape, or form after what had transpired at the trial yesterday and he silently informed her so. Sarah nodded slightly.

Israfil asked silently, *Are you linked with Mikhail, now?*

Sarah replied much the same way Mikhail had the night before, silently saying, *He and I are permanently linked now. We cannot break the connection. However, unbeknownst to my mate, I am able to keep certain things from him, such as the conversation you and I are currently enjoying. However, I believe we should end this silent rendezvous soon or risk raising his suspicions, wouldn't you agree?*

Israfil darted a quick look at his alien-looking brother and then bowed to the two creatures before him. Before he raised himself from his bow, he sent out to her one final silent message: *Thank you for not divulging my secret, my sister.* With that, he rose and turned, leaving the room as quietly as he'd entered.

What was all that about? Mikhail's voice asked in Sarah's mind as she resumed her seat next to him and replaced her small hand inside his much larger one.

Sarah turned and smiled up at her handsome mate. Sheely's voice chattered happily within both of their minds and Sarah leaned a bit toward Mikhail, her voice soothing his mind as she silently said, *They were both worried about us, wondering about the changes in us, our abilities, and the things to come. I thought it would do them good to go with Hantsushept into the city to secure supplies. That way, they'll have the opportunity to check on the Angels loyal to them at least, don't you agree?*

Mikhail could sense there had been more, but he didn't want to think she would deliberately hide things from him, not after all they'd been through. He closed off the part of himself that was quickly becoming eclipsed by the fear of just such a thing happening and, after bringing her hand quickly up to his face, he placed a soft kiss on her knuckles and then leaned over to rest his forehead against hers. *You know you can trust me with anything, love,* he silently conveyed to her, hoping she wouldn't pick up on the underlying emotion within that statement.

He was having enough to deal with because of the fact that Israfil hadn't told him about his ability to control the minds of others. How long had he had this ability? Since birth? Mikhail just didn't understand why Israfil had never told him about it. The fact that Sarah seemed to have developed the ability to withhold information from him on a mental level was just one more thing he'd have to deal with, and Mikhail just didn't have the emotional fortitude at the moment to do it.

Everything was too new and there'd been so much happening recently that he just wanted to block it all out and enjoy what time he could with his new family. He didn't want to let anything else bad develop that would take one second of time from him being able to spend with Sarah and Sheely, and Thomas, for that matter.

Sarah felt his emotions, all of them, even those he was trying to keep from her, and she loved him all the more for his attempts at deception. She wanted to share her knowledge with him. She desperately wanted to, it was just that she'd promised Israfil. How could she betray him when he was so very afraid of revealing his secret to anyone?

Sarah herself felt an overwhelming sadness at the thought of what she'd discovered about Israfil's past and she wished someone else knew so that she'd be able to discuss possible ways to help him. An idea suddenly occurred to her and she leaned away from Mikhail to look him in the eyes. After a moment, a smile slowly crept across his face and he nodded slightly, indicating he was more than willing to help her with the task she'd just thought of. To help his brothers find their own human counterparts would be a pleasure and Mikhail squeezed her hand more tightly as the two of them stood and made their way toward their bedroom.

Meditation always seemed much simpler of a task when one was comfortably lying down on one's own bed. However, after settling down, Mikhail found the allure of his mate's body held more fascination for him than the idea of looking for some other in the human realm and very soon he had no time or inclination for thoughts of others. As he touched and tasted, he was pleased to see that Sarah's mind quickly lost its interest in finding some beings out in the human realm, choosing instead to focus on her mate and his needs.

Thomas sat in the clearing, watching and waiting. He'd done this for the past two days, hoping Nera would grace him with her presence so he could apologize to her for his behavior before. She had kept silent since he'd gotten all upset with her, but he thought he could sense her, as if she was just on the outside of his periphery, just waiting to be welcomed back into his life.

Suddenly, Thomas found himself in the darkened round room. The only other occupant was a sullen-looking Nera. Her eyes, though they still glowed brightly, were rimmed in red, as if she'd been crying. Thomas couldn't stand the thought that he might have been the one to make her cry. His mom had always taught him to treat girls very gently and he knew that if she ever got wind that he'd made some girl cry, she'd be madder than a disrupted hornet's nest.

Thomas shivered a little at that thought, considering the changes he'd witnessed within his mom and Mikhail. He didn't *even* want to know how badly she could punish him, now, what with all the powers he believed she had acquired with her transformation.

Nera cleared her throat and Thomas returned his attention back to her. "I'm sorry," he quietly said.

Nera looked away from him, but then she nodded and said, "I'm sorry, too." Taking a quick, cautious look at him, she stepped forward and reached for his hand with both of hers. Thomas noticed she wasn't as tall as he'd thought her to be when he'd first encountered her and he wondered if he'd been wrong about her height or if he'd actually just grown so much over the past few weeks that perhaps he was catching up with her. Nera looked up at him and smiled. "You're going to be experiencing many changes over the next couple of months," she said, still holding his hand in both of hers.

Thomas frowned and then asked, "Does that mean *I'm* going to change like my mom and Mikhail?"

Nera looked down at the hand she held within her own and shrugged, saying, "I think that depends on how much practicing you go through. The more routines you can remember and practice, the more energies you subject your physical self to, that means more changes."

Thomas thought he understood and he nodded. After a moment, however, he reached out and tugged on a strand or two of her white hair. The strands slowly rose to rub softly at his skin and he asked, "And will you be around during that time to help me, or do I have to endure it all by myself?"

Nera looked at him, her bright eyes seeming to dim a little, as if she was pulling away from him mentally, afraid of getting too close. "I will never leave you, you know that," she whispered.

Thomas looked down at the hair softly rubbing along his wrist and forearm. He wanted to shout at her that he didn't know, that he didn't understand any of what was going on in his life. He wanted to make her understand that he was afraid, afraid for his mom, afraid for Mikhail, and afraid for himself. He wanted to demand that she tell him everything she knew about what was going on and what was going to happen, but he knew she couldn't. Somehow, he knew she wasn't allowed to tell him anything more and that, more than likely, it was because of rules he'd set in place that she wasn't able to tell him these things.

Over the past couple of days, he'd come to realize that he was not like other humans. He wasn't like the Angels here in the Angelic realm, either. He was something different, something no one had ever heard of and he needed to figure this thing out on his own. However, he wasn't about to discard Nera, the one person who knew him better than anyone else. He felt connected to her in a way that defied everything he'd ever been taught in his life and he knew somehow she was destined to play a major role in his future.

He stepped back from her, pulling his hand from within her clasp and walked a short distance away. After a moment, he turned back to her and said, "I'll keep practicing. I like the way it makes me feel. I also think it's helping me to grow stronger."

"Yes," was all Nera said as she watched him pacing before her.

"I think Samuel really likes the practices, too," he said.

Nera was silent. She just stood there, watching him.

Finally, Thomas stopped his pacing and turned to face her. After a moment, he quietly asked, "So, what are we to each other?"

Nera looked away. Thomas felt a rush of shame as he caught sight of tears in her eyes. He hadn't meant to hurt her by asking, but the whole deal where she'd called him her "love" a few days ago had kind of freaked him out and he didn't know what to think about it. He was only eleven years old, for cripe's sake. He wasn't supposed to like girls yet!

When Nera finally turned back toward him, she had gotten herself under control and she said, "We'll talk about that some other time, okay? For now, you just need to concentrate on learning the moves you've forgotten and growing stronger. Can you do that for me?"

Thomas looked her up and down for a moment, then nodded his head.

Nera nodded and then sighed, saying, "Okay. Well, I guess you should be getting back, then."

"Wait," Thomas quickly said, stepping forward toward her. He didn't know what he was doing, but something inside him guided him to stand just in front of her. He took one of her hands in his and brought it up to his lips, just the way he'd seen Mikhail do to his mom. He placed a soft kiss across her knuckles and looked into her eyes. There was a mask of shock that covered her face and, as he stared into her eyes, Thomas could have sworn he saw an actual glimmer of hope spring to life within their glowing depths. He smiled a shy lop-sided smile at her, the same way he'd seen Mikhail do, and said, "I'll see ya." In an instant, he was sitting back in the clearing.

He got to his feet and went in search of Samuel. If he was going to do this thing, he might as well do it right. He would devote himself to training as much as he could. He knew things always went better when one had a partner to train with, so Samuel was just going to have to do without television and video games for the foreseeable future, Thomas figured.

Azra'il sat in his chamber office, tapping the non-writing end of a pen on the sheaf of papers stacked on the desk before him. It was an order allowing anyone found in the Badlands to be killed on sight. The Great Sanhedrin had completed the paperwork and delivered it to his office just this afternoon. Azra'il knew they expected him to sign the order immediately, but there was something holding him back.

What had happened the other day in the Council Chamber had been unthinkable. Azra'il knew Israfil hadn't accomplished the feat alone, which meant that, either Gabriel was suddenly accumulating abilities and using them at will on an expert level, or someone else had assisted with their escape. Unfortunately, Azra'il, along with every other person in the Council Chamber, had been completely under the thrall of the energy Israfil had sent out, so he had no recollection of what had actually transpired.

Azra'il had seen the effects of Israfil's ability before, back when he and his brother had still been on good terms, before Israfil had been taken in by the human woman. It had always shaken Azra'il to see what control one Seraph could have over another being whenever he'd seen Israfil using it. Now he shivered as he recalled how very confused and disoriented Israfil had been able to make him. It had been Israfil's energies affecting Azra'il, of that Azra'il was summarily certain. He knew his own brother's energies well enough to know that for sure.

However, there had been so many people in the chamber that he knew there was no way Israfil could have enthralled them all. Israfil was strong, Azra'il admitted, but he wasn't *that* strong. So, who had it been helping Israfil – Mikhail?

Azra'il shivered at this thought.

The last time he'd caught sight of his former leader, Azra'il had barely recognized him. The majority of Mikhail's hair had grown long and white, his eyes had glowed, and there had been a brilliant radiance coming off him like none Azra'il had ever seen before. Azra'il had also felt power coming off his brother as well, and it had done nothing to ease Azra'il's mind regarding the situation with his brother. The female human had obviously brought about these changes within Mikhail, and Azra'il, for one, was frightened for all three of his brothers.

He looked back down at the sheaf of papers condemning all those outside of Seraphim City and then he suddenly pushed the packet away. This was not the will of the blessed Great Designers. Azra'il would not condemn his brothers, nor any misguided Angels, to death sentences merely because they'd been affected by a human. It wasn't their fault. That would be tantamount to condemning drug addicts to death sentences simply because they'd become addicted. Azra'il knew enough about physiology to know a good majority of that issue was on the physical level and that one actually needed medical assistance normally to combat addiction.

Of course, there were those out there who could manage to recover without assistance. However, a good majority of the populace, Azra'il knew, needed someone to fight for them, to help them get through the withdrawals and depression.

Azra'il had no love of those in the human realm, but he wasn't about to condemn his brethren or their followers simply because they'd fallen victim to a human. Seraphim had been put on this planet to safeguard everyone within the Angelic realm *and* the human realm. Azra'il, as acting head of the Great Sanhedrin, would now take this duty very seriously.

Before, all he'd been responsible for was the one role to which he'd been assigned by their beloved Designers. However, now that Mikhail had gone off and become a victim of the human woman, Sarah Baker, Azra'il would assume Mikhail's duties and would do his utmost to preserve the integrity of the office he now held by making sure all those within each realm remained as safe as possible. To his way of thinking, that meant Azra'il would have to find a way to recapture his brothers, all of his brothers. He'd have to bring them and the Angels who'd followed them back to Seraphim City and see what kind of rehabilitation program could be set up to help them all through this.

As for the human woman, Azra'il would not offer one bit of assistance. All he could find within himself to offer her would be a swift and painless death. He'd had reports that there was more than just her son with her in this realm as well. Well, Azra'il would decide what to do with any extra humans whenever and if ever that became an issue.

No, he would not sign the order condemning anyone today. Instead, he would call a special session to order and he would work with his council to devise a plan to first locate and then attack in such a manner that the bare minimum would be harmed, if any. With his mind made up, Azra'il reached over to call for his assistant. He'd best get going with his plan before his council began to question his ability to effectively govern the council body... a role Azra'il had once wished he could have, but one which he was now coming to dread with each passing day.

We'll find them, he thought to himself. As his assistant entered the room, Azra'il stood and sighed. *We have to...*

Epilogue

A few weeks after having moved to the Badlands, Sarah sat in the dimly-lit garden at the back of the house. She could hear the sounds of Mikhail and Thomas building with the others who had accompanied them from Seraphim City to come and live in this part of the Badlands. There were so many Angels who'd decided to follow Mikhail out into the Badlands that Sarah didn't know how they'd ever accommodate them. Mikhail had assured her there would be plenty of room, though, and she could sense the knowledge of how he planned to accomplish it waiting within his mind. She could have delved a little into the memory banks they both now shared to assure herself. However, she was still getting used to having all this new knowledge and memory inside her own brain and she was leery of utilizing it too much.

A little flutter skittered across her abdomen and she quickly reached to cover Sheely's spot. She rubbed softly at the spot and then relaxed as the fluttering stopped. Sheely was always there to bring her back to her normal rhythms whenever she began to panic about all the newness in her life. Sarah wondered how much she actually understood of what was going on in her mother's mind, if any. It seemed Sheely knew when Sarah was experiencing anything other than calmness, but did she understand what was going on? Was there some psychic link between Sheely and Sarah? Mikhail had assured her everything would be all right, but Sarah worried that there might be things she needed to be doing in order to make sure Sheely was healthy and well-

375

cared for… things humans didn't even know about that would mean life or death for a Seraph child.

Oddly enough, there were plenty of Angels who had followed Mikhail out into the Badlands who had medical experience and training. This eased Sarah's mind somewhat about the fact that she was going to have to give birth in someplace other than a hospital, but she still worried. None of them had ever dealt with anything like this. No Seraph had ever reproduced and Sarah knew from experience that this pregnancy was different than a normal pregnancy. She'd experienced that with her son, Thomas. This, this was something truly different.

She rubbed Sheely's spot again and sighed. She was only showing a little bit with a slight bump on her lower abdomen, and of course Sheely's glow from within that same area. Sarah wondered if it would take a shorter amount of time for gestation, since Sheely wasn't human. For that matter, Sarah wasn't human, either.

She rubbed at Sheely's spot again. At least she wasn't in a great deal of pain… yet. Mikhail was so big that she feared she certainly would be toward the end of the pregnancy.

Why are you worrying yourself with these things, love? came Mikhail's voice in her mind.

Sarah closed her eyes and leaned back against the wooden swing, allowing it to drift forward and back on its own. *I'm just tryin' to make sure I've thought of everything,* she thought back to him.

The link between Mikhail and Sarah was never severed. It couldn't be, it seemed. Neither of them had much control over what the other heard, though Sarah was occasionally able to block certain things from Mikhail's powerful mind. However, the link between them seemed to grow stronger each and every day. The more time they spent together, the stronger it became.

One good thing, at least in Sarah's opinion, was that Mikhail had announced last evening that he could now sense any physical pain or elation Sarah experienced within her own physical body. They'd been making love when he'd announced this. He'd been stunned by the depth of her feelings for him and then, when he'd brought her near to climax, he'd almost doubled over at the amount of physical elation he'd sensed within her with each thrust he made inside her body.

Sarah smiled as she thought of how rough that bout of lovemaking had gotten at that point.

Hmmm..., so you liked that, huh? Mikhail's thought came to her. *We could certainly try that again tonight, if you'd like.*

Sarah chuckled aloud as the swing continued back and forth. She slowly swung her feet back and forth to keep it moving. *You know,* she responded, *you might not think this whole deal of you being able to feel everything I can feel is so great once I go into labor.*

There was an immediate sense of puffing out one's chest within Sarah's mind. She knew Mikhail was letting her know he believed he could handle anything she could handle.

Okay, she thought back to him, *you just remember this day when you're feeling like you've got some sort of alien being ripping out from within your stomach and don't blame me.* Sarah heard and felt his amusement simultaneously. She smiled again and gently laid her head back to rest against the back of the wooden swing, giving a great yawn and closing her eyes for a quick nap.

There were insects buzzing about within this area that Mikhail had given her as her own personal garden and a nice breeze kept the air from being too warm. It was August and the days had become extremely hot during the daylight hours, leaving the nights none too cool, either. Sarah had thought to sit out in the garden for only a short time for some peace and quiet from the incessant hubbub within the house where the construction seemed to be never ending. However, she felt quite comfortable with the soft breeze that was blowing and she was contented enough to stay where she was for the now.

Her breathing relaxed and she allowed her thoughts to drift off where they chose. A laziness entered her mind and she turned her head to a more comfortable position against the swing. No thoughts. There was nothing. All was peaceful. Even the sounds of the construction within the house drifted away from her. There was simply nothing anymore, as if even she didn't exist.

Who are you? a voice she didn't recognize suddenly came in her mind. Sarah was so lulled by the lack of feeling that had settled within her, both mind and body, that she didn't immediately think anything of the intrusion. It was just something new to examine.

Who are you? came the voice again, this time a little more insistent. Sarah's eyelids slowly slid open to a slight slit. There, about two yards in front of the swing, was a pair of brilliant ice-blue eyes peering out at her from within the shrubbery and trees planted at this end of the garden. It was now quite dark within the confines of this section of the garden and Sarah could barely make out anything other than the fact that this appeared to be a very tall man, similar in height to Mikhail.

Sarah, she heard herself thinking back to the man. She felt only curiosity. Mikhail was less than a heartbeat away inside the confines of her mind, so he would undoubtedly already be alerted to this man's intrusion. Sarah believed he'd already be on his way out to see who this new person was and what he was doing here with her. He was so over-protective of her she feared he would someday lock her away from the rest of the world, both Seraphim and human alike.

Mikhail's woman, the man thought to her. *Interesting...*

Sarah pulled her head forward to concentrate more fully on the stranger. She wanted to see his face. As if reading her thoughts, he stepped forward onto the stone pathway. Sarah sucked in a quick gasp of breath. She'd never seen anyone as beautiful as the man standing before her. Mikhail was gorgeous to her mind, but the creature standing before her could make Angels weep.

A lop-sided grin slid across his face and he spoke aloud for the first time, saying softly, "As they often do in my presence." The voice she'd heard in her head had done nothing to prepare her for the real thing. The sound of his voice carried on the night air like liquid elation.

Sarah looked him up and down, wondering at the back of her mind why Mikhail hadn't yet shown up to defend her from this new stranger.

The man, who had long blond hair that hung loose in a smooth, sleek sweep down his back and who was rake thin, but beautifully dressed in the finest black slacks and black silk shirt she'd ever seen, smoothly approached and alit onto the unoccupied portion of the swing, all without causing any interruption in the back and forth motion of it at all. Sarah could feel heat coming from the man like he was a furnace and she wondered how he could emit so much heat without sweating. His clothing appeared perfectly dry, though.

Those ice-blue eyes, almost as bright as her own irises had once been, but without the flashing pupils, stared back at her with not the slightest hint of care that she knew he was staring at her. Sarah looked right back, making her own inspection of him. There was still no fear within her. Mikhail, for some reason, had chosen not to come to her at the moment. That was fine by Sarah. She wanted to know more about this stranger.

Seraph? came the silent question in her mind.

Sarah shook her head. "I once was Seraph," Sarah softly said, "but now I'm something else."

His brows narrowed and he looked her over once more, as if he'd missed something upon his initial inspection. "What do you mean?" he suddenly demanded. He gripped her upper arm to turn her more fully toward him on the swing.

Sarah? came Mikhail's voice in her mind. When she didn't immediately respond, he demanded, *What's going on? Is there someone out there with you?*

The stranger jerked away from Sarah as if he'd been burned. In a flash he was off the swing and disappearing into the shrubbery across the path from which he'd originated. Just as quickly, Mikhail appeared on the path, rushing toward her as fast as his long legs would carry him. When he found her sitting alone on the swing staring off into the brush, a frown appeared on his face and he quickly looked around as if expecting someone else to be lurking nearby in the garden.

When he found no evidence of an intruder, he quickly approached the swing and, sitting next to her, took Sarah's hands in his and pulled her toward him. Sarah allowed this happily and she snuggled up to his side, loving the feel of his arms around her.

"I could swear I sensed someone else out here with you," Mikhail said. His chin rested on the top of her head and he hugged her closer.

Sarah reached her arms around his midriff and simply said, "You did."

Mikhail immediately set her away from him, his face a mask of confusion and concern and anger, all at once, as he demanded, "Who was out here?"

Sarah's brows arched and she shrugged. "I don't know who he was," she confessed honestly.

Mikhail delved intensely into her mind, but there was something there blocking him from reaching anything from the past few minutes. It was like the experience he'd had when he'd been inside the house. He'd been just fine, working with Thomas and Sarah's dad and a few of the Angels who'd been working on the inside of the house, when he'd suddenly been unable to sense anything from Sarah's mind. He didn't know how long he'd been unable to sense her, but once he'd realized she was no longer transmitting to him, he'd immediately called out to her. That's when he'd felt some other presence near her, almost coming through her to him. He hadn't taken the time to analyze the information coming through her. He'd just immediately made his way out to her in the garden. Now, he couldn't access anything more in her mind than he'd been able to earlier.

Mikhail jumped to his feet and turned toward the dense foliage on the other side of the path from the swing. His eyes scanned the area intently for any sign of movement. His mind scanned the area for anything out of the ordinary... anything at all. For just a second, he thought he could feel something coming from within the darkness on the other side of the path. He narrowed his eyes and took a step closer. He caught what he thought were bits and pieces of soft laughter, almost as if he was hearing an afterthought of a memory of someone laughing. Then, it was just gone.

After a moment more of studying the darkness before him, Mikhail turned on his heel and strode back to the swing. He took a seat again and pulled Sarah back into his arms. "You okay?" he asked, kissing the top of her head and gently hugging her closer.

Sarah nodded silently, slipping her arms around his waist again and giving back his hug. She snuggled in closer to him, rubbing her cheek against his chest. Mikhail sighed and returned his gaze to the dark side of the garden. He ran a hand down the length of her arm and gently set the swing in motion again. He believed she didn't know who the intruder had been, but that was the problem. There were so many unruly Angels in the Badlands. He knew it could've been anyone, Shaitan or Jinn. He was just going to have to make sure she wasn't left alone ever again.

"Come *on*," Sarah said disgustedly, pushing herself up off his chest and slightly away from him. "You can't protect me like that."

Mikhail sighed. Compromise was not something he was used to and the fact that she could "hear" each and every thought he had through his emotions was sometimes very annoying.

Sarah made a face at him and stood. "How do you think *I* feel?" she asked.

Mikhail stood and looked down into her upturned face. After a second, he grinned. He knew what she felt for him and it had nothing to do with annoyance. She loved their connection, both mental and physical. He bent to place a quick kiss on her lips, which were upturned now in a small smile as well. He placed his hand over Sheely's spot and softly rubbed. Sarah's eyes closed and Mikhail felt a flutter from within, both on the hand he had on the outside of her abdomen and from the senses he'd recently acquired of what went on in Sarah's body.

He wrapped an arm around her shoulders and turned to lead her into the house. He would deal with finding someone suitable to accompany her when she wasn't in his company later. For now, however, he wanted to see to her safety all on his own up in their bedroom.

From within the dense foliage, brilliant ice-blue eyes watched undetected as the two creatures disappeared into the nearby structure. It had been years since there'd been any type of structures built in this region of the Badlands. He should know, since he'd been one of the first to traverse the wasteland. And now, it appeared, the very one who had banished his people to the Badlands was moving in... and with some new type of cross-bred Seraph, no less. *Well*, thought the man, *that just won't do.* He turned on his heel and, letting loose his shields, he rose into the air and returned home.

The Vision Blogger is just the beginning of this tale... find out who the mysterious stranger in the Badlands is in **Infinite G**, book two of the **Seraphim Calls** series. Take a sneak peek at this intriguing new addition to the series on the next page.

Seraphim Calls... can you hear them?

Infinite G

The moment Lisa exited the library and turned onto the walkway out front, she froze. She could *feel* him. A chill stole down her spine and she shrank down into a crouch. It was stupid, since there was nothing she could hide behind, but it made her feel just a fraction safer. Her eyes quickly scanned the area, darting to the left, then the right. She slowly turned her head and looked behind her. About twenty feet away, she thought she caught sight of a light. She couldn't be certain, but it looked almost like someone or some... thing was coming with a light just around the corner of the building to her left.

The light grew brighter and Lisa turned more fully toward its direction as quietly as she could, her tennis shoes making a slight scraping noise on some small pieces of broken glass that were strewn all over the dark street. The light got brighter. Lisa swallowed a lump in her throat and half-rose, her heart racing. She'd been feeling so good after the two young men had performed their ritual earlier. But now, she felt as if she was about to have a heart attack, she was so scared. This thing, or person, or whatever it was, she could *feel* it approaching her. Goosebumps ran all over her body and she jerked up and around just as a large hand landed on her shoulder from behind.

Lisa screamed and immediately took off running in the opposite direction from the light. Before she could take more than five steps, however, she suddenly found herself trapped inside a warm, leathery-feeling bubble that immediately surrounded her entire body and then conformed to her shape, like shrink wrap, pressing against her form until she was tightly cocooned within the leathery wrapping from head to toe. She couldn't move her head more than an inch or two and discovered it was pressed against a hot chest that seemed as hard as stone, though it was covered in some type of fabric. A silk shirt? It didn't matter! What was she thinking?

She struggled to break free, pulling on this arm, pushing with that foot.

Rest easy, baby, a strong male voice said in her mind.

Lisa froze. Was she going insane? It was that same voice she'd heard the other day in her flat, all chocolaty and smooth.

Chocolaty? Seriously? the voice asked in her mind and she thought she heard a deep, rumbling laughter from somewhere. Now he was making fun of her? Great! Lisa struggled against the leathery shrink wrap again, and again the voice came to her in her mind, saying, *Ow! Stop that!* Lisa stilled again, afraid she'd hurt him now. Again, she caught the sound of his laughter. *Go to sleep now, baby,* he seemed to whisper from some faraway place as Lisa suddenly felt more exhausted than she'd ever felt in her life. *Crossing the barrier isn't something I want you to remember from our first moments together,* she thought she heard. Then, there was complete silent darkness.